Sydney Watson

Life's Look Out

An autobiography

Sydney Watson

Life's Look Out
An autobiography

ISBN/EAN: 9783337011260

Printed in Europe, USA, Canada, Australia, Japan

Cover: Foto ©Raphael Reischuk / pixelio.de

More available books at **www.hansebooks.com**

LIFE'S LOOK-OUT

AN AUTOBIOGRAPHY OF
SYDNEY WATSON

LONDON

HODDER AND STOUGHTON

27 PATERNOSTER ROW

1897

Dedication

To my faithful friend and constant adviser, who first incited me to the prosecution of this work—F. W. PITT, Esq., of Wandsworth ; and to the three men who have had most influence on my life—viz. : WM. CHESHIRE, Esq., of Sutton, who, from my earliest sailor days, sought to win me to God, and whose daily life taught me first what life's stern duties meant ; to Rev. J. MARSHALL MATHER (author of "At the Sign of the Wooden Shoon"), who, in one frank, outspoken letter to a co-editor with himself (which was never meant for my eye), gave me the greatest *literary* help I ever received ; and to Rev. C. A. Fox (Eaton Square), whose exquisite poems first fully opened my dimmed eyes to Nature's lovely pleading glance—to this quartette of friendly folk, I humbly dedicate this book.

Preface

THE fact that very much which I have written, in story form, during the past ten years, has had its basis in personal history and adventure, has made it almost imperative now that something like a clear, full autobiography should appear; and this, in addition to the requests from many of my readers in many lands, for such a book, seems *raison d'être* sufficient to demand the publication of the present volume.

Besides this, since "praise is comely" (by which I suppose the Psalmist meant that it becomes the recipient of blessing to praise), then, surely, the chief reason for placing this life story before the public should be a desire to glorify the Grace which has saved me, and blessed me with all spiritual blessings in Christ Jesus.

I trust that the frank statement of the facts of follies here given may be a help to any lads into whose hands this book may fall, by opening their eyes to the pitfalls into which, during my unguided years, I fell—pitfalls which remain to-day, all about us, to trap the youthful, unwary feet.

To the many thousands of my regular readers (and it impresses me often with an overpowering sense of responsibility when I remember that they now number over a million a week); to the hundreds of my correspondents in every clime, I would say, " Thank you," for all your loving words of cheer sent to me from time to time ; and if often, especially during the last six years, my replies to these my correspondents have been brief, and often only in pencil, I would say, please forgive your oft-time *invalid* friend and well-wisher,—

SYDNEY WATSON.

THE FIRS,
VERNHAM DENE,
NEAR HUNGERFORD, BERKS.
1897.

Contents

CHAPTER IX

CHAPTER X

CHAPTER XI

CHAPTER XII

CHAPTER XIII

CHAPTER XIV

CHAPTER XV

CHAPTER XVI

CHAPTER XVII

CHAPTER XVIII

CHAPTER XIX

CHAPTER XX

CHAPTER XXI

CHAPTER XXII

CHAPTER XXIII

CHAPTER XXIV

CHAPTER XXV

CHAPTER XXVI

CHAPTER XXVII

CHAPTER XXVIII

CHAPTER XXIX

CHAPTER XXX

CHAPTER XXXI

CHAPTER XXXII

CHAPTER XXXIII

CHAPTER XXXIV

CHAPTER XXXV

CHAPTER XXXVI

Chapter I

PARENTAGE

" Feast now thine eyes on this surpassing view
  Of mountain, shore, and sea ;
Drink deep the woodland air, elysian blue,
  For days that are to be.

Paint on the inner chambers of thy brain
  The winged and glittering bay ;
Learn the near ocean's slumberous refrain,
  Calling ' Away ! Away ! '

Not for this day alone of Nature's cup
  Hast thou in transport quaffed ;
Far hence thy spirit shall be lifted up
  By this one perfect draught.
        *   *   *   *

For this is Nature's largess : colour, tone,
  Splendour of land or sea,
All that she once reveals, becomes thine own
  For days that are to be."

"YE'LL no forget my words, Willie, when ye're far, far awa' frae yer auld mither, and when ye find the world is caulder than ye thocht, and that men dinna mak' siller in piles, as easy as mayhap ye think. I'll miss ye sairly, and dootless I'll greet awhile when ye're gane, and——"

Here the poor mother's heart failed her, and her voice was choked with sobs for a few moments. Willie, as she had called him, rose from his seat, and with an impulse and tenderness that did credit to his heart and his nineteen years, took his mother in his arms. Kissing away her tears, he said, in a voice almost as shaky as her own,—

"Dinna greet sae sair, mither; I'll bide at hame awhile langer, if ye think I wadna be doin' the vera best thing for you, as weel as for mysel', by gaein' awa'; for I'm no expecting to find ony place like my ain hame, or onybody like my ain mither."

With a look of mingled pride and affection, the old Scotch woman, Janet Watson, set her son off the length of her two arms, while she kept her hands on his shoulders, and, looking at him steadily for a moment, drew him again silently to her breast. Printing one long, deep kiss upon his face, she said in a voice steady, but strained,—

"Willie, my ain laddie, dinna think I wad keep ye here anither day. I ken weel that ye hae chosen wisely, and that ye hae chosen as much for yer mither's guid as yer ain."

Other words passed between mother and son that morning, then finally the lad silently buckled a rough, well-filled, canvas haversack across his shoulders, took a stout staff in his hand, and, turning to his mother, said, "God bless ye, mither! Good-bye!"

"Good-bye, Willie, lad! Mind yer mither's words, remember yer puir father, and never touch whisky or ony kind o' strong drink. Ye'll no find mony o' that way o' thinkin', maybe; but be ye a mon o' yer word, and when ye say No! let it be No, *for my sake*, for yer ain sake, and for the sake o' this puir sin-soddened world we live in. Stick to yer Bible, yer kirk, and yer mither's God. The Lord bless ye, and keep ye, laddie! Good-bye!"

' Thus parted this mother and son, she standing at the door of the cottage watching till he should finally disappear over the brow of the hill, he sturdily trudging away till he came to the highest point, at which he turned, stood still for a moment, and looked all round.

His eye paused at the cottage, its open door showing that dear mother standing with her white handkerchief ready to wave a last farewell. She could not hear his whispered word, but she saw him wave his bonnet, and she signalled back with her handkerchief. In another moment each was out of sight of the other.

Janet Watson had been a widow many years, and had found it a hard struggle, at first, to battle through life with her three sons. But when the eldest, Thomas, emigrated to America, and " fell on his feet " from the first, so that he was soon able to send his mother some substantial monthly remittances, the strain upon her became considerably lessened.

Willie, the second son, whose home-leaving we are looking upon this morning, had early developed a natural talent for designing and painting ; and at the pressing suggestion of a schoolmaster in the neighbourhood, it had been decided that the lad should go to London and seek his fortune with pencil and brush.

When the departing lad had taken the last glimpse of home, and mother, from the brow of that hill, he strode on manfully, once or twice brushing away a tear with the corner of his plaid, yet every moment feeling stronger and brighter.

The morning was so gloriously exhilarating that his step became lighter and freer, for he had a soul full of poetry which answered to the music and rhythm of all he saw and heard around him. As one of his own countrymen has written, so Willie Watson could say,—

> "Sae weel I lo'ed a' things of earth ! —
> The trees, the buds, the flowers,
> The sun, the moon, the lochs and glens,
> The spring's an' simmer's hours !
> A withered woodland twig would bring
> The tears into my eye—
> Laugh on ! but there are souls of love
> In laddies herding kye !"

He was so absorbed with his surroundings, and with the thoughts of his journey, and of his recent parting, that he did not notice an old shepherd, who, leaning on his staff, watched him as with light step he tripped from point to point down the rocky road.

His reverie was suddenly broken in upon by the old man's voice,—

" Weel, Willie, lad, so ye'll be gaein' sooth the noo ; but ye'll no forget the auld hame, I'll be bun'! Be a good laddie, and stick to yer mither's way aboot the whisky. I'll no say I dinna tak' a sma' drap noo and then, but ye'll aye be safe if ye no touch the like at a'."

Having assured old Donald of his determination to remain firm to the principle of his early training, the lad held out his hand. The old man took it, and for a moment held it fast, as he said in a reverent tone,—

" Willie, laddie, may a' that's guid be yours ; but dinna forget the best—dinna leave God out o' yer life."

A few more words, a grip of hands, and Willie Watson was once more well afoot towards the distant town, where it had been arranged he should meet his younger brother, who had found employment there, and with whom he would stay the night before finally starting for the great city of his dreams —London.

The bond of affection between Willie and the

brother whom he expected to meet in the neighbouring town was a very strong one. It was not merely the Scottish characteristic of clan or family, but one of those deep-rooted brotherly affinities, alas! too rarely met with. In their home-life there had never been one disturbing element between them, and in their rambles or games amid the gloriously wild scenery in which their cottage home was placed, they were inseparable.

But it is not enough to have companionship in life, even when such companionship is free from all strife and bickerings. The human heart desires, feels after, and can only be satisfied with affinity of thought and spirit as the basis of friendship. In this matter the two brothers were singularly blessed and fortunate; and when they climbed together those grand old hills, though they understood not the fulness of meaning in God's book of grace, yet they at least realized a hidden, all-prevailing power as they read the book of Nature together.

In both there was a depth of true poetic feeling, and amid the beauties of their lovely land their hearts were drawn closer to each other. Their community of taste and thought would seldom find expression save in some such simple utterance as this,—" Eh, but yon is a grand picture!" yet each was fully conscious of the other's appreciation.

To the dull, unimaginative mind, the mountain water-brooks might be only noisy streams; but to these two brothers they were things of life and speech. Gazing upward, they sought to trace them where they sprang from

> "———— the heights afar,
> From lonely lands of cloud and star."

They watched them as

> "With gathering murmurs on they came,—
> O'er beds of boulders now rudely tost,
> In groves of bracken a moment lost,
> Then a liquid flash ! and the echoing host,
> Through many a rent and rift of gloom,
> Fissure and gully, they come, they come !
> Bright, bursting, bounding to their doom,—
> Over the chasms and over the rocks,
> And the black abyss of the thunder blocks,
>   From steep to steep,
>   As the angels leap,
> Till white with rocky war and strife,
> Their breathless tidings, life, life, life,
> Resound afar ! They heard them all,
> The passion and the perilous fall,
> The mirth, the music, and the call ! "

Every flower that sprang out of the sod upon those hills, or hid shyly amid the heather of the wide moors, was to these Scotch laddies a friend whom they gladly greeted upon life's travel.

All unconsciously, Willie, with his artist soul, was catching upon the imperishable lens of his mind's eye pictured beauties which should in future years be worth more to him than hosts of other men's pencilled thoughts of nature.

To him an autumn bramble with its

> " —— Crimson leaf,—a leaf all blood and gold,
> With its long purple stem of bramble thorns
> Trailing in arméd wreath——"

was food for thought, and subject for a lengthened pause amid some evening ramble.

All seasons of the year were alike to him, and supplied each its quota of ever-new beauty. The

> " Cowslips of spring !
>   From their fairy May-poles juicy and pale,
>   And tassels of yellow bells scenting the gale,"

waved a greeting to his eye, and while he plucked them and tenderly handled them as though, like himself, they had tender feelings, he revelled in their marvellous construction.

He trod the sward where the daisies grew almost reverently, for he feared to crush down the " small flower with its snowy frill and centre of coined gold." But he failed to catch the meaning of the daisy's birth, which is so beautifully expressed in the poet's lines,—

> " Lest man, grown dazzled straining at the sun,
>   Should find Him not, and doubt what He had done,
>   God, stooping, wrote upon the ground in daisies,
>   That all who hear not should behold His praises !
>   This common flower men's feet tread down
>   His fingers wrought who wears heaven's crown ;
>   And so the Flower of God was given
>   To be man's stepping-stone to heaven."

No ! The two youths admired the objects which surrounded them, yet neither of them had caught their inner teaching.

Willie had missed his brother very much during these last days of his sojourn at home; but this morning, as with sturdy limb he strides along, the prospect of their meeting again helped to lighten the sadness of his heart. Yet he knew that next morning he must part from that brother again. It is human, however, to live only in the present ; so, with an ever-increasing buoyancy of heart, Willie drew nearer and nearer to the town.

Had a stranger watched the meeting of the brothers

that evening, he would have seen little to mark the strong affection that existed between them. But things are not always what they seem, and to the heart of each of the young men the electrical thrill that passed through them, as their hands were clasped in a mighty grip, meant more than a torrent of words.

They talked far into the night, and made many new resolves and mutual promises. Then, having slept through the few hours that were left before daylight, they rose, and dressed almost in silence.

An hour later, beyond the town, the pair parted, hoping to meet again, amid life's hurly-burly, before many years should pass.

How little either of the lads dreamed how different the future of both would really be, or that it could be possible that each would make early shipwreck of life!

In due course the young Scotchman entered London, and began his search for employment. Unlike many others who have entered the mighty city of mightier possibilities, only to drift to lowest depth, to despair, and oft to swift, untimely death, William Watson almost immediately found excellent work, at unexpectedly good wages, the firm of decorators who employed him discerning his gifts from the first.

I could fill a volume with the story of this young Scotchman's triumphs—*and his fall*; but as this is not a biography of my dear father, but an autobiography of myself, I can do no more than indicate my father's career.

He was successful from the outset, passing from one stage to another, until he succeeded—as I have learned from some notes in my dear mother's handwriting—in getting one of his pictures hung on the walls of the Academy.

But before this, while engaged on some frescoes for the Duke of —— (his wealthy patron treating him as his guest and friend), he learned, at that ducal table, the taste of intoxicating drink, and forthwith fell under its snare.

When I was but a little, little lad, with one brother two years younger than myself, my dear mother was suddenly widowed, and we, her boys, were made orphans, by the death of my father, who took his own life in a fit of temporary delirium, while under the power of strong drink.

*   *   *   *   *

A very strong strain of Scotch blood runs in my veins, since, until my father's marriage to my mother the Watsons are said never to have married any but their own race.

My mother, on her father's side, belonged to an old Midland family—Worcestershire, I believe—her grandfather (between sixty and seventy years ago) being a well-known and wealthy cloth-weaver, named Cornelius Lench.

Chapter II

"ARE WE POOR, MOTHER?"

FROM a baby I was an exceedingly weakly child, neither the doctors nor my parents believing I should ever live.

Two incidents of these earliest days always amuse me when I recall them. The first I have no *personal* recollection of, the second I do remember.

When little more than a year old, and when I was so thin that a skin of softest chamois leather was made for me, to prevent my bones rubbing through the skin, the doctor ordered me to be carried about in the neighbourhood of large sheep-folds in the very earliest morning, that I might breathe the breath of the folds.

It was midsummer, and my father took lodgings for my mother in the country, somewhere near St. Albans, where a number of sheep were kept. At four in the morning, as I have heard my mother tell, she would take me out, lying on a pillow upon a low, sled-like carriage, and, until six or seven o'clock, she would draw me about through the lanes, that I might breathe the prescribed air. Weary work for my mother!

> " But a mother's love and God's love
> Are unchanging evermore."

The second incident of my earliest childhood, that

which I distinctly remember myself, was when, as a weakly boy of four, only about the size of an ordinary two-year-old child, I sat upon the stairs, with my little Scotch luggy in one hand, and my horn spoon, with a whistle at the end, in the other, and suddenly discovering that all my porridge was gone, I gave a blast upon my whistle that fetched Margy, a good Scotch nurse lassie, to my side, who was loud in her expressions of surprise that I had finished my meal so soon. For I must explain, that up to this time I had had the invariable habit of sucking all my food slowly, so that my breakfast of porridge and milk, under this slow process of consumption, often occupied me until noon, and was a real itinerant meal, since, luggy in hand, I would wander about the house and garden at my own free will.

Even in these early years, many of my days had to be passed in the semi-darkness of a blind-drawn room, owing to the excruciating headaches which have been my lot through all my life.

For many years past much of my time has had to be passed in a darkened room, with closed or bandaged eyes; and hundreds of times I have pursued my literary work with my right hand, while my left has been employed in gripping my throbbing brow, and I have reeled and rocked to and fro in my chair, like a sailor aloft, or a drunken man on the knife-board of an omnibus. In my boyhood's days I could not bear the weight of an ordinary cap upon my head, but had to have peaked caps (of the shape worn in those days) made of the lightest black material— silk, fine jean, etc. I mention these facts here, as many things which will occur later will be thus more easily understood.

My only brother, William Stuart Watson, was from the first a marvel of strength, and by the time he was twenty, though short and slight, he was a surprise to all who knew him, on account of the unusual strength and endurance he ever displayed.

I seem to remember nothing of my later childhood's days, until the awful event which made me an orphan and my mother a widow. The shock to my dear mother (it was she who found father's body) was so great that she has never since really recovered, and though still living when I pen these lines, she is, and has been for years, a bedridden invalid, but she is full of God, and the grace of love and of patience.

After my father's death she was prostrated with shock and weakness for a very long time. All the events of this period seem to have been blotted completely out of my memory, save one striking little episode, which has never faded from my mind.

How long after my father's death this item occurred I have no idea. But I had been away with friends — the shock of my father's suicide having seriously affected my health. I remember, so well, the night I returned home—a new home, a very, very poor one. My mother, looking very ill and worn, sat by the fire, too weak to rise from her chair to meet me, but holding out her arms to welcome me. My quick young eyes took in everything at a glance, I think, for I see it all to-day as plainly as I saw it then, more than forty-three years ago. The contrast between the beauty of the old home and the bareness and poverty of the new, struck a chill into my little soul.

But that which pained me most was to see a small, plaid, three-cornered shawl across my mother's shoulders ; for, in some way, such a shawl had become associated, in my mind, with extreme poverty.

Perhaps I had seen such a wrap worn by a very poor person, some beggar who called at the house, or some charwoman who had been to assist the servants in cleaning. I cannot say how the association had been formed ; I only know that it was so, and that in a youthful horror of surprise, I said,—

" Mother, are we poor now ? "

I remember how her dear eyes streamed with tears, as she held me tight to her breast. I can feel the hot drops fall on my face even now, and feel my own throat fill with sobs, and my own eyes flood with tears, as they did on that long-ago day, when she sobbed out her reply to my question :—

" Yes, dear boy, we are as poor as poor can be, short of being homeless."

Child as I was, there entered into my heart at that moment the determination that somehow, as soon as it was possible, I must find some way of earning money to re-instate my mother into her old life, and thus banish for ever that hideous badge of poverty (as I supposed the woollen shawl to be).

In spite of her tears and her sorrow, I made her smile as I uttered my childish vow, to make haste and grow up, when, as I declared, " I would buy her a house with a nice flower garden, like the one we lived in at Brixton, a silk dress, and a little chaise with a cream pony, like those which Cooke, at Astley's Theatre, had."

Many years afterwards it became a standing joke between mother and I, that among all the other things I had given her, I had never given her the cream pony and the other items of my boyish programme.

Speaking of the cream pony, and the celebrated circus people of Astley's—the Cookes—reminds me that, but for God's wondrous over-ruling, I should probably have been apprenticed to the great equestrians, and have been trained for a rider or acrobat.

I spent, as a little fellow, much of my time in the stables, and in the circus during rehearsals, and though I cannot remember how the connection came about, I know that my people were intimately associated with the Cooke family, and that one of them, a very famous contortionist,—*Dan* Cooke, I think, was his name,—was nursed, as a friend, by my dear mother, and died in her arms.

It has often occurred to me of late years, what a racy story the incidents of that man's life, as I remember them, would make, with all the romance of his marriage with a lovely French girl, who ran away from a French boarding-school with him. A beautiful woman she was; her face lives in my memory still.

I have no data to refer to, and I have no clear memory of events of the years that followed, until I found myself in my first place of work as errand boy at Ebbutt's, furniture dealers, at Croydon, where I received half a crown a week and my tea, and something which I remember more than the wages or the meals,—a great deal of kindness.

How, when, why I left there, I cannot remember, but my next essay in life was with a printer, named Jonathan Fullilove, of Croydon, whom, if I remember rightly, failed in business, and thus threw me once more out of employment. Through all my after life the colour of those printing days remained with me, for I believe I liked the work, and I distinctly recall the pride I felt, when, being left alone in the little works one day, I took an order for fifty raffle cards ; then, fired with a desire to please the master, and to see what I could do, I set up the dozen or twenty words, found a frame to fit them, locked up the type in the frame, and pulled off a couple of proofs before Jonathan Fullilove came in. Was that my first impulse towards literature, I wonder?

How, and when we came to live again in London, I cannot remember, though I distinctly recall the street, the house in Walworth Road where we lived, and which was but a few doors from a small brass-smith's, or something of that type, kept by a good man named Tinworth ; and, from the little I have learned of the life of Tinworth, that marvellous artist in terra-cotta, I cannot help thinking that in those early days he and I lived as boys together in that street, only a few yards apart.

This portion of my life must necessarily be very fragmentary in its record, from the fact that my memory will not recall even the most shadowy continuity of facts, a certain few events only standing out clear enough for mention.

Through all this time, my childish resolve to somehow relieve my mother of all expense on my account, and to win some kind of wealth that should some day make her independent, never left me ; and many were the strange thoughts I had of how to fulfil my desire, before the strangest of all notions, which launched me upon a sea of strange adventure, appealed to me in an irresistible manner. The story must occupy a separate chapter.

Chapter III

"WOPS, THE WAIF"

HUNDREDS of people, since the publication of "Wops, the Waif," have written me, or personally asked me the question, " Is ' Wops ' really the story of your life ? "

This present volume on which I am engaged must answer all such inquiries far more fully than I have been able to answer them individually.

The full history of how the " Wops " stories came to be written will find a place in these pages later on, but a few words are necessary by way of introduction to the incidents told in this volume.

Soon after the publication of the first few of my twenty-thousand-word stories, my dear old friend, W. B. Horner (publisher), begged me to lay hold of the chief events of my strange career, and fashion them into Gospel stories for his series. For a very long time I withstood his appeal, but finally consented, writing story after story, until the whole set was completed, some of those first written being by that time in print.

The kindly, persuasive old man framed a paragraph, which he much desired that I should consent to have attached to the stories, stating that the original of " Wops " " was still living, and, with his wife, was constantly employed, by lip and pen, in spreading the story of the Cross."

For a long time I stood out against this request, partly for the sake of the feelings of personal relatives, and partly because, had I begun to write “Wops” with the thought that my own identity was to be attached to the pages, I should have written the books in a very different style, and from a different standpoint.

I have had no need to regret writing the books, *as far as others are concerned*, since God has blessed them to the known conversion and blessing of hundreds of souls; but, as I say, I should have *written* them differently had I known, and should in that case have prefaced them with a note of explanation.

Now for the real history of “Wops, the Waif.”

The previous chapter will have, in itself, explained that I was not born, or brought up, in the street Arab class, so let me explain at once how it became possible for me to be the original of Wops.

I must have been, as nearly as I can find out, about thirteen and a half, when some one gave or lent me a book, called (as far as I can remember), “A London Merchant’s Clerk.” I read this book, and, like a flash, there came to me a hint of how to accomplish my great purpose of being no longer a drag upon my mother, and of becoming rich for her sake. The plot of the book was simply this :—

A little crossing-sweeper is noticed by a wealthy London merchant, who, becoming interested in the little waif, takes him into his office as an errand boy. Delighted with the lad’s efforts to please, finding him sharp and willing to learn, the merchant has him taught at a night school, advances him, in due time, to a stool in his office, and when at last, years after, the lad has become his confidential clerk, he takes him into partnership, and gives him his only daughter in marriage, the young couple having long loved each other.

Barely, baldly, this was the story. It fascinated me ; I thought of it day and night, till at last I determined to "go and do likewise," feeling assured that, if I but had the chance, I could please any philanthropic merchant, who would give me the chance of becoming his partner and marrying his daughter.

Every detail of the circumstances of my leaving home has faded utterly from my mind ; but from a mental negative plate of that time, the picture of my passing down Petticoat Lane, bent upon getting a costume sufficiently appropriate for entering upon the *rôle* of a crossing-sweeper, is vividly reflected before me to-day.

I was wearing a strong serviceable suit of boy's tweed, with warm woollen underclothing, and good serviceable boots. As I passed shop after shop (what dingy dens they were!) through those strange thorough-fares, of that strangest of all English Jewish colonies, I was accosted by one after another of the occupants of the shops. I think I was a little afraid of these alert business Hebrews, and to all their addresses and requests I held my peace, until I had gone in and out, up and down, most of the streets of the " Lane."

Then I began to return by the same route I had come, and one old Jew, who, on my previous passing, had been very importunate as to my needs, now again leant out of the deep doorway of his shop, and whispered, " Vats you vant? Vats you look for, shonny ? Come inside, I vill do goot pisiness vid you ! "

He drew back invitingly as he spoke, and I

followed him into the dingy, ill-smelling shop. To his eager question, “Vat you vant, to puy or to shell?” I blurted out what I wanted.

“I am poor now,” I said; “and I'm going to try to get my living by sweeping a crossing, and these clothes are too good; I want you to exchange my suit for a very old suit.”

The eyes of the old man gleamed cunningly, avariciously, as I told my story. “Vat you gif me pesides t' clo'es, ef I gif you old suit?” he asked.

I was staggered at the question. I had built a fairy castle of possible capital of cash, out of the fancied shillings he would give me, in consideration of extra value received by him, and now his greedy little black eyes were fixed upon me waiting my reply to his impudent request.

I was little more than a child, and tried to pump up a bit of bounce. “Me give you something?” I cried; “it's you that'll have to give me five shillings besides an old suit, because it don't matter how old the clothes are, the older the better.”

Years after that day, in Ceylon, I remember watch-ing a small, beautiful-plumaged bird, whose strange motions had attracted my attention, and whose every moment seemed influenced by some fascinating force outside itself, some force or some object upon which its eyes were ever fixed. The better to ascertain what this fascination might be, I silently passed round the bush, on one of the boughs of which the bird was perched. The mesmeric seance was then quite plain. A snake, with beady, glittering eyes, upraised head, and darting tongue, that never ceased its rapid move-ments, had fixed the bird with its mesmeric glance, and each moment the lovely, little, helpless victim was being drawn on to its destruction. Seizing a stone I hurled it at the head of the snake, and whether I hit it or not, I at least broke the spell upon the bird, which, with a fluttering scream, flew away.

The eyes of that Hebrew Shylock, in that dark den of a shop in Petticoat Lane, affected me, as the eyes, or the power, or whatever else it might be, of that snake affected the bird. I was as clay in the hands of a potter. He threatened to send for the police and give me in charge for trying to disguise myself, after having committed some crime.

Fearful of the very name of the police, trembling under the awful power of my persecutor's eye, I managed to stammer out, "Give me sixpence to buy my broom, and you shall have my clothes."

He gave me the sixpence, then rummaging about in a hole under the stairs, he selected a coat, trousers, shirt, and cap—no waistcoat—and bade me follow him into a room behind the shop.

There were two women, Jewesses, in this room, seated near the fire, talking rapidly together. They paused in their talk as the Jew entered. He spoke a few words to them in a language I did not understand. They looked me up and down, glanced at the bundle of rags he held in his hands, then with a laugh turned their faces once more to the fire, and gabbled away in the strange tongue in which they had before been conversing.

The old Jew began to hurry me to take off my clothes, but with a frightened glance at the two women, I said, " Please, I can't undress here."

Busy as the pair at the fireplace seemed with their gossip, my protest reached their ears, and both turned their faces to me, and laughingly said, " Never yous mind ush, shonny ! "

They turned their shoulders, as well as their faces, a little further round towards the fire, and resumed their talk, and I—— Well, the old man was worrying me, and I was full of fear and shame ; and as swiftly as I could I got out of my clothes, every inch of my poor little body hot with a blush, that I can recall shudderingly to this day.

Garment by garment, as I divested myself of them, the old man seized greedily ; then when I crouched down, nakedly divested of my last garment, he tossed me the thin, old, blue check cotton shirt, and the other rags he had routed out for exchange for my good tweed suit and warm under-clothing.

How damp and clinging that rag of a shirt was! But I was glad enough, in my shame, to jump into it as quickly as I could, and to follow suit with the other garments, until, clothed (save the mark!) I scuttled out of the room without a glance towards the women by the fire.

A minute later I was in the street. I shivered now, and from the burning heat of my recent blush of shame, I went chill with the misery of my new position, and the dampness and fusty smell of the rags in which I was clothed.

When presently I found myself turning into Bishopsgate Street, I looked about for a shop front, where I might see myself. I soon found my looking-glass, and not even my own mother would have known me.

My trousers must have been made for a very thin but tall man, and had taken upon themselves, as they tried to adapt themselves to my shorter legs, a myriad of crinkly folds, like the bends in the bellows of a concertina. My coat had extravagant long tails, which I found were actually dragging the pavement, like those of the proverbial Irishman of Donnybrook Fair. But as I had no wish for any one " to tread on the tail o' my coat," and certainly did not feel a bit like the pugnacious Pat of Donnybrook, I proceeded to tie each tail separately into an overhand knot. If I had had a knife I should certainly have cut them off, which would have proved an unutterable loss, for that very night I found those same tails (when un-tied) a valuable sleeping adjunct, since they formed a wrapping for my cold toes.

My Jew sweater had given me no waistcoat, but fortunately there were three buttons on the coat, and, by fastening these, the deficiency of waistcoat was covered. The cap that had been given me was a jockey-like thing of dirty, dark-blue velvet, a mere rag, with a hole, as big as a five-shilling piece, where the velvet button in the crown had once been. Through this hole a tuft of my much-rumpled hair, which was, for me, unusually long, stuck up like a wisp of stubble in a reaped field.

At that moment—it was such a long way from the merchant's wealth, and wedded daughter—I felt utterly miserable, and but for the memory of my *purpose* in doing what I had done, I could fain have gone back home. But remembering my resolve, I gave one more look at my transformed self, and moved on eastwards.

By four o'clock that afternoon, I had spent three-pence-halfpenny in a very poor birch broom, and began my new career with the twopence-halfpenny change out of the Jew's sixpence, plus a few pence of pocket-money I had when I left home.

I had wandered as far as The London Apprentice

public house, Shoreditch, and here, broom in hand, I paused and took stock of the land. Rapidly deciding that, angle-wise, from The London Apprentice to the public-house opposite, would make a good place for a crossing, I gave my attention to my concertina-crinkled trouser legs ; and drawing down the creases, I gathered up the waste cloth into a double wide fold that reached to my knees, and left my feet and ankles free.

I am afraid my wielding of the birch was more like the splashings of an inebriate whitewasher than the careful strokes of an R.A., but I managed my first bit of crossing work at last ; then I began to train my eyes to watch the faces of the passers-by.

I never attempted the professional whine, but am certainly conscious, after the lapse of nearly forty years, that a careful study of the faces of the pedestrians formed a useful trading capital in the sweeper's profession.

By nine o'clock that night I had made tenpence, then feeling dead-beat tired, and being very hungry, I gave up business for the day, and retired to a cheap cook-shop in the neighbourhood to supper.

There were no menu cards, but I remember that meal, and I give the items :—A pennyworth of baked potatoes (they had been baked under a leg of pork, and the gravy given with them was flavoured with sage and onions) ; a pennyworth of pease pudding—likewise gravied ; and, by way of pastry, a large penny square of baked plum-pudding.

That night I slept in a twopenny lodging-house, and awoke next morning shivering and ill, with a feverish cold, the result, doubtless, of the loss of my flannels, of the dampness of the rags I had got from

the Jew, and of the sudden change from stockinged
and booted, to bare feet.

I thought of mother, and cried a little, as I lay
shivering in that lodging, then set my little teeth
together, and declared I must be brave for *her* sake,
and go through with my purpose, and make haste
and grow rich. One thing came home sharply to me,
namely, that I must send her a comforting word by
post ; and before the day was out I had sent a poor,
little, rough scrawl, framed very ambiguously, to say
I had started off to make my fortune, that she was
not to fret, but that I should get on, and come back
and buy her the cream pony, and all else I had
promised her so long ago.

Like Saul, in his persecution of the Church, I *felt*
I was doing right and doing good service. And here
let me say a thing which has forced itself upon my
mind during later years, for I have made children one
of my special studies. I am convinced that *many*
of the escapades, and acts for which children are
reproved, whipped, or otherwise put into disgrace,
are not the outcome of *evil* intent, but often of *good*
intent, only, that the adult, the father, the mother,
the guardian or teacher, judges the act from the
standpoint of *their* thoughts, and not from the standpoint of that of the boy or girl who has transgressed.
We need, in dealing with young folk, to take the
trouble to find out the groove in which they *think*
and *plan*, and by what standard they judge the
rightness, wrongness, and fitness, or otherwise, of their
acts.

There *may* be no shadow of truth in the details of
the story of the *economical* child, but there is truth in
the principle underlying it, viz., that a child of ten

reasons from an utterly different standpoint to that of the parent.

The story goes, that a poor widow, who, like the historic personage "who lived in a shoe," and "had so many children she didn't know what to do," allowed one of her girls to be adopted by an aunt. The aunt died, and the child came back to her mother. The evening of her arrival was made a gala time, and, as far as her means would permit, the poor mother marked the occasion with a special spread for tea. The newly-returned child was the heroine of the hour, and each of the other children watched her and hung upon her every word with delight. Hungry with her journey, the child ate very heartily; but presently, the mother, noting how thickly she spread jam upon bread-and-*butter*, re-marked, "that that might pass for once, but she was not like the aunt had been, rich enough to afford jam on butter, that she was poor, and had *to study economy*."

In an utter amaze, the child replied, "Oh, mother, I thought *that* was economy, to make one piece of bread do for *two* things."

Only a story, very likely, but the principle fits the thought that is in my mind as I write, that children reason from different standpoints to those of older growth; and we need to understand a child before we hastily condemn it—or punish it—for some act, that may have been committed in all good faith.

Do we not get a hint of this principle in the old word of our God's, when He says, "Train up a child in the way *he* should go"? For years I have felt that the emphasis in this verse should be placed upon the personal pronouns, and that if every parent and guardian could or would take the trouble to study, and deal with the *individuality* of every child, the proportion of children who would not depart from the good old way would be infinitely greater. The two pronouns of the text go together, "the way *he* should go," has for its sequel, "*he* will not depart from it."

To return to my story. Ill as I felt, I shouldered my broom, went off to my "pitch," by The London Apprentice, and began once more to make my pathway through the light, greasy mud of the busy street.

I had just finished, when the landlady of the above house came to the door and beckoned me. She asked me a question or two, and seemed pleased to think that I had patronised her house front for one end of my crossing, but suggested that instead of taking a line across to the door of the opposite public-house (of course no lady, especially a publican, would be guilty of *trade* jealousy, so please do not suppose and infer such a thing), that I should strike my line of swept path from her door still, at one end, but let the other end cross to the corner, in the other direction, and right away from the rival pub.

"You do that, sonny, an' it'll be all the better fur you!" she added; then seizing my broom, as bail for my return, she sent me on a message, a few yards away, and told me she would give me a breakfast on my return.

She was as good as her word, and gave me about a pint and a half of coffee, four thick slices of bread and butter, and a bit of haddock; and from that day on, often trusted me on errands, and often gave me a hearty meal.

How I got through that day I can never think. By night I was so giddy and ill with the feverish cold upon me, that I could hardly crawl to my twopenny lodging. For days I was ill, but little by little I recovered, and became, in some measure, inured to the exposure of the new life.

One of my first investments, out of my limited savings, were two men's second-hand woollen undervests, and these having sleeves, served me for shirts, and helped to keep me from taking cold.

Chapter IV

TINY TICKLE

WHAT of Tickle? people often say; was *he* a real character? Yes, he was, but no pen of mine could ever faithfully depict him. I will not try to improve upon the few descriptive strokes with which I introduced him to readers years ago.

"Tickle, like his friend Wops, was poorly clad, but his clothes were somewhat better fitting. He was a little fellow, as often called 'Tiny' as 'Tickle,' and sometimes by both names together—'Tiny Tickle.'

"He was deformed, having a queer twist in his right side, with broad, high shoulders, into which his head was set, and without any neck apparently. His limbs were exceedingly small, and his face pale and elfin-like."

He was the shrewdest, sharpest little fellow I ever met, yet with a singularly delicate sense of other's feelings; as loyal in his friendship as any man or woman who ever lived. He could say the keenest things, that cut like a knife, or, anon, he could melt you to tears with the tenderness of his speech, and the gentleness of his voice.

The manner of our meeting helped to cement our friendship. He sold "lights"—not the modern vesta, but the old-fashioned fusee, whose remembered scent recalled memories of these early days, when years after, in Eastern lands, I once more sniffed the same odour when joss-stick was burned, or when, in Burmah and India, I smelt the burning smoke-stick that lay in the ash-pans where smokers sat.

I had never seen Tickle before the day when I spied a boy—a podgy, jowl-cheeked, pudding-headed boy—clouting him with the leather end of a sucker. I felt forced to champion the cause of the little blue-eyed fellow, and though I got a terrible black eye over the business, I managed to beat off the foe ; and Tickle, after begging a sliver of raw steak from a neighbouring butcher to lay upon my swollen eye, swore an eternal friendship and allegiance to me. I loved that boy like a brother.

We believed in, and practised socialism—at least as far as a community of goods between our *two* selves was concerned—for we had all things in common.

Tickle knew *his* London, which comprised the districts lying within the Kingsland, Dalston, Hackney, Shoreditch, and Whitechapel radius, and many a strange, almost unknown quarter did he show me, when on Sundays (as we often did) we took a day off from business.

His knowledge of that part of London led to our fixing up a strange sleeping spot, a description of which is necessary here, that some after-events may be understood.

It was a day or two after our meeting that he came to me, his face full of excitement, as he said, "Wops ! " (He had dubbed me by this name, because of my frequent use of the strange ejaculation, " Gollywops ! ") " Wops, I knows a stunning crib where we could doss (sleep) wi'out iver spendin' a brown on a lodgin'-house bunk."

Later in the day I went with him to view our proposed domicile. We went down a blind alleyway, at
the end of which was a broken-down shed. Passing
through the shed, we squeezed through a hole in the
wall beyond, and emerged upon a wretched, tumble-
down row of empty houses, that, as far as I can remember, were built in by a high, rough stone wall.

Against a part of this wall, in bygone days, there
had stood a narrow, covered, shed-like structure open
to the court, towards which its roof had sloped. Now
all that had disappeared, except just at the farther
end, where, in the angle formed by the two walls, a
corner piece of the roof about five feet wide was left—a
shaky, leaky, dilapidated bit of ruin, just supported at
the inner corner by a rugged post.

The top of the end wall, which was nearly eighteen
inches wide, had suggested itself to the mind and eye
of Tickle as a capital place for a bundle of straw to
be strewn, to form one bed. Swinging by two thick
rope handles (hammock fashion) to two of the slate
battens of the roof of this bit of ruin, and close to the
wide, tempting-looking ledge of wall, was an old egg-
chest.

It was an ideal sleeping-place for two such waifs as
Tickle and I, and that very night we entered upon
possession, having, by surreptitiously conducted expe-
ditions, carried two large bags of straw—begged from
a furniture packer in Curtain Road—to our eyrie.

From the first, Tickle occupied the egg-chest, and
I the straw-strewn ledge of wall.

What a life we lived! How happy we were in
those days! So happy, that I am afraid I was content with the old doctrine, " Eat, drink, and be merry,
for to-morrow we die"; and too often, I fear, I forgot

my high purpose of making money, for mother's redemption from poverty, though I used to salve my conscience by saying to myself, with the carelessness of boyhood, "At least, she is relieved from keeping me."

Ah, what a life we lived! On days when we "were in luck," we feasted, on other days we lived sparely, and retired early to our strange sleeping berth.

On the "lucky" days, we usually spent the evening at some "penny gaff," or the threepenny gallery of some cheap theatre. There were many such places in those days in London ; some of them I can easily recall. The Rotunda, in Blackfriars Road — this house, after a variety of changing fortunes, strangely enough became a centre of Christian work.

Then there was "The Panorama," Shoreditch ; "The Old Effingham," and several other houses in Whitechapel.

Oh the poison that came, through eye and ear, to the soul, in these dens! There have been moments since my conversion, when some injected memory of these days has burst in upon my soul, so that I would have given my right hand, my right eye, to be delivered from the smirch of these remembered things.

One of these nights I specially remember, because I believe it was there that I got the first notion of going to sea. Years ago I wrote my memory of that night, and cannot perhaps do better than let the bygone description come in here, intact :—

"AMONG THE GODS.

"'Chick-urr-er! Tal-lal-lie-tea-lie-a-tea! cruk-rrukk-uk-whack-err-ur!" The sounds are described

as accurately as our pen can syllable and write
them, but they must be really heard to understand
the shrill, penetrating, bewildering style of them.
To-night is a benefit night at the 'Old Effie,' otherwise known as the Effingham Theatre. The house
is filled with such an audience as only the East End
of London could supply. The boxes are crowded by
their own class of attendants, who might be judged,
by the uninitiated, as of the *lowest* class, though a
tour through the house would soon prove how many
strata there were between them and the *lowest*. But
it is only when we have paid our 'tuppence,' and
ascended to the gallery just under the roof, known as
'among the gods,' that we begin to understand what
is meant by the lowest classes, the 'great unwashed.'

"It is among these chiefly that the yells, and
howls, and strange, Indian-like cries heading this
chapter are perpetrated. The whistling, caterwauling,
and yelling continue, till a voice is heard shouting
from the centre of the front of the gallery, 'Who-ay,
Cullies, here's Hoppy with the rozin.' The reference
is to a short, lame man, who emerges from some den
beneath the stage, with a violin under his arm, sug-
gesting the identity with the 'rozin' announced. He
is followed by several others, with various instruments,
and an overture, of a style peculiar to the East End
theatre, is soon being performed.

" In a prominent position on the front seat of that
gallery, Wops and Tickle are joining in all the coarse
fun and wild horseplay, and are evidently regular
attendants, from the fact that they comment very
freely, and with an evident knowledge, on all the
players and surroundings.

" The special attraction to-night is announced as a

'grand spectacular nautical drama.' The play is of that coarse, sensational, inflammatory type that stains and stabs with deadly force all who witness it. The allusions and some of the situations are gross, if not obscene, yet it is painfully evident that the audience is only too well pleased at the very grossest parts of the play.

"There was tremendous enthusiasm this evening. Every scene was uproariously applauded, and at the climax the whole 'house' rose and cheered and encored with tumultuous feeling.

"Once outside the theatre, and having purchased their supper of a man at the edge of the pavement, who had announced his bill of fare as ' B'ked 'taters hall 'ot,' the two boys walked rapidly to their shelter—home they had none—talking and eating as they walked.

"' I say, Wops, I tell yer what it is. If ever——' Here sundry gasps for breath and strange gurgling noises in the throat of Tickle make known the fact before he himself announces it, ' Oh, crikee, worn't that 'ot!' Then remembering where he broke off, he continued, ' If ever I gets big enuff to jine, I'll go in fur the Navy. Fancy 'avin' sich a swag o' rhino to spend as that cove wot played " Jack Marlinespike " to-night had ! '

"Wops seemed unusually silent, so Tickle inquired, ' Wot purfession would yer like to be, Wops ? '

"Having disposed of his last piece of ' 'tater, skin an' all,' Wops, in the absence of a serviette, drew the sleeve of his ragged coat across his mouth, and replied, thoughtfully and slowly, ' That's what I've often thought about, an' it seems to me, 'cause I can't be the *first* thing I'd like, I'll have to be the second, that's if I can be took on fur it.'

"' Wat's yer fust, Wops ? '

"' A gennelman, Tickle.'

"' My eye, Wops ! but don't you haim 'igh,' said Tickle, his voice full of the surprise he felt.   Then he added, ' But why can't yer be a gennelman, culley ? '

"' Because it costs such a lot to get into that profession, little 'un, an' a jolly sight more to keep it up, when yer are in it.   So, as I can't be that, why, I've made up my mind to-night that I'll be a sailor, a man-o'-war's man.' "

And the determination expressed to Tickle that night never wholly left me ; it became the seed within me which was destined to bring forth a strange crop of fruit.

Chapter V

A FIASCO

ONE day, while standing at the head of my crossing, I saw Tickle approaching, accompanied by a smart, alert, gentlemanly young fellow, of three or four and twenty. Wondering at this strange companionship, I walked to meet the pair.

"This is Wops, sir," said Tickle ; then, in his own eager, impulsive way, he began to tell me that "this gennelman here a sort o' took a fancy to us sort o' chaps, an' wants us to go to a blow-out, a tea-fight affair, an'——"

Tickle gave his version, the gentleman smiling all the time. Then, when the eager boy had finished his speech, the doctor (for such I afterwards found him to be) gave me his invitation to a boys' tea, which, he said, he and some friends were arranging.

"We shall give you all as much tea, bread-and-butter and cake as you can eat, then we will have some singing, and—well, for the rest, we shall see what we shall see, when the time comes."

Of course, Tickle and I accepted the invitation ; and equally, of course, we were at the place appointed in good time.

Every item of that night lives in memory to-day as fresh as though it had all happened but yesterday. The howls, the yells, the whistlings, the horseplay and jokings, the hustling, and crowding, and struggling around that door, before we were finally admitted.

At last the door is opened. Thirty tickets have been issued; but quite sixty boys sweep in. The friend at the door is unable to withstand the rush, as, whooping and yelling, they clamber over the seats, and no one attempts to show a ticket. We said no one. This is hardly correct, for one waggish little urchin flings a large card advertisement at the ticket collector as he cries, " For me and my pals," and then he is swept on by the rush behind.

The scene when the door was finally shut beggars description. The initiators of the meeting were utter novices, and had never essayed any service of this kind before. The ladies sat helplessly horrified at the scene that ensued, while one or two men, of the humbler order of life, rushed frantically about, pulling, or trying to pull, the boys down in the seats, and hissing out all the time, " Hush, please ; hush, hush ! "

One of these men, who quickly lost his temper, was seized by the hair of his head, and by his shoulders, and hauled bodily, by a score of delighted boys, into their midst, and was tickled and pinched until he fairly shrieked.

The doctor, who had given Tickle and I the invitation, and who had been standing beside the ladies on the platform, evidently trying to reassure them, advanced to the edge of the platform, and tried, amid his own hearty laughter, to quell the din. Failing in his efforts, he hit upon a little ruse.

Remembering that he had his stethoscope in his breast pocket, he drew it forth, put the small end to his lips, and with puffed-out cheeks, and fingers moving rapidly over the supposed keys, he appeared to be playing on some musical instrument.

Above the din, the voice of one of the boys was heard in a shrill call, evidently understood by all, and when silence was obtained, he cried, "D'yer, stow yer patter! here's the gennelman a-trying to play the Varsovihannah on a wooden trumpet."

Taking the stethoscope from his mouth, and waiting till the laugh which followed this sally had quieted, the doctor said, "If you are quite ready, boys, and will keep quiet, we will serve out the tea."

Then noticing that the boy who had spoken appeared a sort of leader among them, he said, "I think, if I am captain to-night, you must be my lieutenant. What's your name?"

With eyes twinkling with delight and mirth, the boy gave his name.

"Very well, lieutenant, suppose you come out here by my side, and help to direct operations."

"Right yer are, guv'nor," shouted the irrepressible youngster; "I'm good at a hoperation, I can tell yer, when it's on spot and scalder" (which, being interpreted, meant cake and tea). Then, suiting the action to the word, with a yell of triumph he leapt over the intervening seats, landing on the platform, where, snatching up a huge piece of cake, and filling his mouth, he shouted, as best he could with a mouth so full, "Go on, Captain, with the hoperations."

The next few minutes, during the distribution of the provisions, was like Bedlam let loose. But by-and-by every one was filled, if not satisfied. Then came the more difficult problem, how to hold a meeting, and what kind of a meeting it should be?

A small harmonium had been brought. The few

friends gathered round the instrument with open books, and then the doctor said, " I will read the first verse, and then we will sing this hymn *to you*."

Clearing his voice, he commenced—

" There is a happy land, far, far away."

Then, thinking to interest the boys, and perhaps to elicit an answer that would show what their general idea of heaven was, if they had any, he asked, " Where is that happy land that is far, far away ? "

In a moment his lieutenant was on his feet, his laughter-loving nature all on fire as he commenced to sing, in stately style, a song that was then very popular—

" To the West ! to the West ! to the land of the free,
Where the mighty Missouri rolls down to the sea.
To the West ! to the West——"

The doctor tried to stop the torrent of song, but it was useless. The boys, one and all, joined in, and sang it through, then started another, and so it went on for a quarter of an hour ; then, suddenly seizing the lieutenant by the arm, with a grip that made the boy feel some sense of the authority and power that lay in that grip, he bawled into his ear, " Look here, boy, if you don't get them quiet I will have the police sent for, and we will never give you another tea."

Once more the lieutenant obtained silence, and said, in a tone of mock authority, " 'Pon my word, yer ought ter be 'shamed of yersels, a-making that row. The captain here says if yer don't 'old yer jaw, and let him do a bit of patter, he'll fetch the peelers, and besides that, he won't invite yer to another blow-out o' spot and scalder."

Once again the friends tried. They commenced to

sing, then were interrupted by the lieutenant, who suddenly said, as he noted the restlessness of the gathered boys, "Look yere, sir, tain't in their line, and you'll hev a bust-up again in a minit. Can't yer sing 'em 'Tippertiwitchet,' or summat like that?"

"'Tippertiwitchet'? Whatever is that?" asked the doctor, aghast.

"Lor bless yer heart, sir, fancy a gennelman like you not knowing 'Tippertiwitchet'! Why, the clown allus sings it in the pantomime. The chorus is good—like this," and off went the boy singing—

"Ri, ti, tiddy, iddy, ol, ti."

The boys caught it, and then all the previous scenes were surpassed by that which followed.

The meeting had proved a fiasco, in every sense of the word, and the room was cleared of the boys.

There will be many Christian workers to whom this bit of real life, as depicted above, will appeal in some measure. They will recall certain experiences of first efforts among wild boys equally as disheartening as were the efforts of the friends who gathered Tickle and Wops and the others into that room nearly forty years ago. Though, it is true, there has been an immense advance made since those days, advance in knowledge how to deal with the masses; and I am sure there has been a certain small change for the better, among even wild lads, since there is some *outward* observance of law and order when they are gathered together for their good.

And of workers who have suffered disappointment such as that recorded above of the doctor and his friends, some have said with a sigh—a sigh that has often had in it a bit of relief—"Ah, well, it is evident that *I* am not called to *work* for Christ; it will be enough for me if I just go quietly on *and let my light shine.* Such friends will rarely suffer much probing as to what *light-shining* really means.

Then there are other workers who have experienced disappointments, such as those I have described, who have gone honestly alone with God and have cried, " Lord, show me why, and where I have failed ! "

And He, tender, teaching, compassionate, has met the cry with soul-explanation; and many an one, who has thus failed and cried to God for help, has learned one of the most fruitful sources of failure in service, viz., the fact that such service has too often been the outcome of the flesh. They have done *something* ; but because it was conceived, thought out, and (too often) carried out in the flesh, it has failed. Then when failure has been followed by communing with God over the matter, and He has shown the humbled soul where the error has been, there has come the cry, " Lord, *what* wilt Thou have me to do? *where* wilt Thou have me to go? " Then guidance and blessing have followed. Not that there has always been *seen* the actual fruit of the labour in the measure expected by the soul of the worker, but there will have been, there always is, when there is this intimate communion with God, over service, the blessed, restful sense that one is doing *what* and *where* and *how* " my Lord the King appoints ! "

Over and over again my own soul has been blessed, in this connection, by keeping the thought of Mrs. Pennefather's wondrous lines before me. They say so much more than I can possibly express in so small a compass, that I cannot do better than quote them :—

'I said, 'Let me walk in the fields.'
He said, 'No, walk in the town.'
I said, 'There are no flowers there.'
He said, 'No flowers, but a crown.'
I said, 'The skies are black,
There is nothing but noise and din.'
And He wept as He sent me back,
'There is more,' He said, 'there is sin.
I said, 'But the air is thick,
And fogs are veiling the sun.'
He answered, 'Yet souls are sick,
And souls in the dark undone.'
I said, 'I shall miss the light,
And friends will miss me, they say.'
He answered, 'Choose to-night
If *I* am to miss you, or they.'
I pleaded for time to be given.
He said, 'Is it hard to decide?
It will not seem hard in heaven
To have followed the steps of your Guide.'

Chapter VI

"OVER THE RIVER—THE PEACEFUL RIVER"

AMONG the humbler workers who had shared in the disappointment of that uproarious lads' meeting was a delicate-looking man, about thirty-five years of age, a devoted, self-sacrificing worker for Christ. He was a shoemaker; and at his work, after that noisy and apparently useless meeting, he thought much of these boys.

He had never worked amongst this class before, but now a deep interest was stirred in his heart, and, after much prayer for guidance, he resolved to commence a small evening class for some of them, to be held in his own little home.

He could not do, in his tiny space, with more than a dozen boys, and these, having been mentally selected, he afterwards personally invited. Tickle and I were among the invited ones, and, from the very first, Tickle's little heart began to receive good, and he never missed an opportunity of attending a meeting. I soon noticed a change in my little pal, and though the one or two of the meetings to which I went made no impression upon me, Tickle's words and manner often made me serious, and were sufficient to sober me when I was rollicky and flighty.

Tickle was really ill at this time, only I did not

understand it or realize it, contenting myself by saying, " It's only a cough, and it will soon be better."

I remember the night when it first dawned upon me how thin and white my little pal was growing. It was one of the nights when the shoemaker's class had *not* met. It had met the night before, and the memory of the meeting lurked in the blue eyes of Tickle, and echoed back in his thin, reedy voice, as he stood leaning against the lamp-post softly singing,—

> " 'Tis eternal life to know Him —
>> Oh, how He loves !
> Think—oh, think how much we owe Him—
>> Oh, how He loves !
> With His precious blood He bought us,
> In the wilderness He sought us,
> To His fold He safely brought us —
>> Oh, how He loves !"

He caught my eyes fixed upon him, and smiled— I never saw a boy smile so sweetly as Tickle could— as he said, " Pretty, ain't it, Wops ? Little Katie sung it last night. I learnt that verse, an' I'm going to learn all t' others afore I'm done, an'——"

He looked me full in the face as he said, " I ain't goin' ter be satisfied till I've got right an' good, like Katie an' her father. 'Cos, look here, Wops, as *he* said last night, it ain't jonnick to let Jesus do all as He've a-done fur us, a-dyin' on the cross an' all that, an' we never to say ' Thank you, Lord Jesus,' or try to live square an' true to Him."

Tickle talked on, and told me all about the meeting of overnight, for I had not been there. I had not been for several weeks ; for, though I was not wilfully vicious, I was yet so full of wild pranks and fun, and had so little control over my irrepressible flow of animal spirits, that the "teacher" could not easily control me.

I felt all this, and after a time, with a sort of respect for the teacher, a respect which I could not have attempted to explain, I was frequently absent, making a variety of excuses for that absence. No thought of God seemed to strike me. It was different with Tickle. There seemed given to him a quick insight into divine things, and his little uninstructed soul yearned and hungered for something that seemed almost within his reach.

Twice or three times during the next week my little pal found his way to the house of the earnest-souled shoemaker, and there, one night, child as he was, he accepted Christ.

His cough was getting serious now, and his weakness was daily increasing. I usually went round to the meeting-house in time to go home with him, and I remember how, this night, I noticed how frail he looked as he came out, and when the other boys had trooped away on their various roads, I said,—

"Now, then, Tickle, yer jist got to stand on that there ledge, and let me guv yer a flying angel, and we'll be home in a jiffy; and you shall be tucked up jist about snug, and I'll git yer a penn'orth of soup, and that'll warm yer down ter yer toes."

Glad of the lift, Tickle stood on the edge of a broad ledge at the side of the pavement, into which some iron railings were set, and turning my face inwards, I popped my head between the little fellow's legs, and hoisted him rapidly but gently upon my shoulders. Thus linked, we darted in and out all the short cuts, till soon we arrived at our entry, and sighted the corner ruin with its wall edge and egg-chest.

He was full of the meeting that night, and told me, as he lay swinging in his egg-chest, how the blessing of Trust had come in his soul, and how, in the language of the hymn he had learned to love so much, " In His arms he was safely folded."

He had learned the whole of the hymn by this time, and lay in his swinging bed singing softly :—

> " We have found a friend in Jesus—
> > Oh, how He loves !
> 'Tis His great delight to bless us :
> > Oh, how He loves !
> How our hearts delight to hear Him
> Bid us dwell in safety near Him !
> Why should we distrust or fear Him ?
> > Oh, how He loves !
>
> " Through His name we are forgiven—
> > Oh, how He loves !
> Backward shall our foes be driven—
> > Oh, how He loves !
> Best of blessings He'll provide us,
> Nought but good shall e'er betide us ;
> Safe to glory He will guide us—
> > Oh, how He loves ! "

But that cruel, hacking cough came on, and he could neither speak nor sing for a time, so I made my way to a cook-shop close by, where both Tickle and I were well-known.

Stating my case, and telling the kindly-hearted woman how bad my little pal was, I asked her to lend me a jug, and fill it with good soup.

The journey back to our entry was certainly like " running the gauntlet," and more than once, when surrounded by troops of hungry boys of our own type, who threatened by their numbers to overwhelm me, I had to appeal to their honour. Wild, rough, wicked, untutored as they were, my password was always effectual, as I cried, " D'yer, it's for poor little Tickle, and he's bad."

How strange it is that, when we look back over the past years of life, that all the way, whether gladsome or toilsome, seems largely to be a blank, with only here and there some desert patch of trouble and despair, or anon some glad, fertile oasis showing up, while all the intermediate spaces are simply dull, forgotten blanks.

There are a myriad things of my past which I forget, but here and there some very striking little scene or episode stands out strong, clear, unforgetable. The events of that night, when I raced back with that jug of soup, are among these remembered bits. Every item of the setting of that night-scene remains with me.

The moon was full, but the sky had been so overcast with heavy, stormy-looking clouds that very little of its light had been seen as it slowly mounted. But now occasionally, as a hurrying cloud swept aside, the moonbeams flashed out and lit up the surrounding darkness. It was a subject for an artist, surely—the row of wretched houses ; the buildings lying back in shadow, as if in sympathy with the lives of the people of that neighbourhood ; the line of shadow running right through the ill-paved courtway ; the fantastic shapes of the old ruin in the corner standing out plain against the momentary brilliant moonlight, while under the bit of ruined roof that light struggled, revealing the top of the wall, with its straw and rag bed ; the swinging egg-case, in which, sitting up, was the thin, wasted form of little Tickle.

I see it all as I saw it then, and hear again the last murmured words of my sick chum before he finally dozed off to sleep, after taking his soup :—

> " With His precious blood He bought us,
> In the wilderness He sought us,
> To His fold He safely brought us—
>> Oh, how He loves !"

I could not sleep that night ; I heard the church clocks boom out their notices of one, two, three o'clock. My mind was full of the story of Christ's love, as told me by Tickle.

Suddenly—perhaps I was dozing—a crash, and a cry of "Oh, Wops !" startled me, and I leaped off my wall-bed, almost falling upon the body of my little pal.

I grasped the situation at a glance. Either one of the rope handles of the chest had parted, or else one of the rotten old slate battens, to which it had been fastened, had snapped ; for there, upon the old brick paving, lay poor little Tickle, with a terrible wound in his head, while the empty egg-case, swinging by one rope-handle, played pendulum over his prostrate form.

He was silent and insensible, and I knew I must get assistance at once, and raced, as if for my life, through the entry, and out into the thoroughfare beyond. My excitement found vent in a yell of " Tal-lal-lic-e-tee," which was immediately stopped by the weight of a heavy hand upon my shoulder, and the voice of a policeman, who suddenly stepped out of a deep doorway, demanded what I meant by yelling like that, where I was going, and what my " little game was ? "

I soon gave him my story, and the next minute,

re-inforced by two others of the force who appeared upon the scene, he was following my lead to our sleeping quarters, from whence they eventually bore poor, insensible little Tickle away to the hospital.

I followed, but, to my unutterable grief, I was not allowed to enter the building.

The next day was as long as an ordinary month to me, and as soon as I left my work I hurried away to the hospital, but only to be told that I could not see my little chum.

I felt I could not return to my quarters until I had tried every chance of seeing Tickle. I knew that the police and soldiers on duty were relieved at certain hours. I *thought* these reliefs were at midnight, and I determined to present myself once more at the hospital at midnight, hoping to see a new custodian of the door.

It was a bitter cold night, and when I returned to the hospital, I began "marking time" with my bare feet upon the steps, until I should be able to muster up courage to make my next appeal.

I heard no sound save the dull, low roar that, even at midnight, ever rises from the great city, and the scuff of my own bare toes upon the cold stones. Then suddenly a voice close behind me spoke my nick-name, and looking up, I found the doctor who had invited Tickle and I to the tea standing by my side.

He was on duty at the hospital. He had heard that the injured boy's chum had been imploring to come in to see his friend ; and hearing from Tickle who this friend was, he had come out in search of me, the list slippers he wore deadening the sound of his approach in my ears.

After a few moments' talk between the doctor and myself, I was led to a large ward upstairs; for Tickle was dying, and the screen was around his bed.

He was conscious, and gave me a feeble, but rapturous greeting. His happy soul was so full, that I verily believe he had lost the sense of pain.

"I'm *in* all right, Wops," he said; "I'm in that fold o' His, an' I don't feel a bit tired now."

For a moment or two I wondered of what he was speaking. He saw the puzzle in my face, doubtless, for he continued, "Don't yer know what I means, Wops?

    "'In the wilderness He sought me.'

"That's Jesus, you know.

    "'In His fold He've safely brought me,—
        Oh, how He loves!'"

His speech was but whispers, broken by pauses and panting breaths.

"You remember all I've told you, Wops, 'bout Jesus, an' I wants yer to ax Him to take yer into His fold too, then you'll be kept from doin' anythink wicked. Comin' home from the meetin' last night, I thought I'd maybe be able to help yer to be good, but it's all up wi' that now. But Jesus 'll help yer!"

My boyish soul was broken up under the stress of the pain at my heart, and the tender, yearning love of my dying pal, and I buried my face in the bed clothes and wept aloud.

The worldling, the mere philosopher, the man to whom no breath of the spiritual is tolerated, may smile at the joyful assurance of a dying street Arab; but that does not alter the fact that for the believer in Christ, whether gentle or simple, learned or illiterate, old or young, there *is* a real sense of assurance, of a living rest in God. If we take a *blind* man to the Thames embankment and say, "There, below there, *is* the river Thames," it does not alter the fact that the great stream *is* there, flowing on towards the sea, because the man's sightless eyes cannot see its flowing waters. And God's Word says, "To you therefore who believe He (Christ) *is* precious," and the *is* of the flow of peace and assurance to the believing heart, is as emphatic and undeniable a fact, as is the *is* of "There *is* the Thames." The physically blind cannot see London's river because they are blind, the spiritually blind cannot see Jesus, who is our peace, because they too are blind, for spiritual things can only be spiritually discerned.

The moments sped swiftly by at the dying bed of that little street Arab. He lay with my hand clasped in his, his little face beaming with joy, and his eyes wide open with a glad, far-away look in them. Through his parted lips there stole broken words of holy rapture, and sometimes a faint, rippling laugh of intensest delight.

By-and-by I felt his little hand quiver in mine; it was like the soft flutter of a captive sparrow seeking its liberty. "He's shiverin', doctor," I said, looking upward.

The nurse was silently weeping, and even the doctor's eyes were filled with tears.

The shiver of Tickle's slender frame ceased, and he was very still. The doctor lifted his two little thin hands and folded them across the silent breast, as he gently explained that my little pal was dead.

My grief took no noisy form, for the shock had stunned me. The doctor spoke to me. I scarce heard him, until, laying his hand upon me, to draw me away from the bedside, his "Come, Wops," pierced my dulled sense, and I gazed alternately at the little dead form and the sympathetic face of the doctor.

"Let me kiss him, doctor," I said; "I never have kissed him before, but I'll never see him again."

I bowed my head and kissed the little dead lips, my scalding tears falling upon the still face. Then, as my eyes fell upon the blood-stained bandage that covered the wound in the head of my dear dead chum, an impulse seized me, and lifting a heavy lock of his hair, I laid it tenderly over the bandage, covering the blood-stain.

He had told me of his mother, whom he just dimly remembered, and in my boyish ignorance I felt that I would not like his mother, in that other world, to see the traces of that hideous wound when the angels bore him thence.

Broken-hearted, I suffered the doctor to lead me away. Downstairs in the hall he talked with me, pleaded with me, tried to get me to promise that I would let him send me to a home for street boys, which some friends of his were establishing. But I would not, I *could* not, listen to him then. A kind of fierce, unreasonable anger with every one and everything filled my bereaved heart. I felt that I wanted to be alone, and I left the hospital, giving a conditional promise, that if ever I got to the end of all my resources I would seek out the doctor, and let him legislate for my future.

Out in the keen night air I walked, taking my barely conscious way towards London Bridge,—the nearest river point I knew. For a river, whether by night or day, has always had a singular fascination for me, filling me with ever-changing thought of the wonder of life—of which, surely, a river is, in more senses than one, a wondrous emblem.

Standing on London Bridge that night, and gazing upon the moonlit waters, listening to the hoarse voices of the bargees, the grind of their sweeps as they swept their craft onward, the splash of the waters, and with my tear-filled eyes seeing mistily the lights along the river's bank (there was no embankment then), the gaunt, grim wharfside warehouses, the black, ricketty piers and quays—standing watching all this, I think some faint idea of the eternity of things dawned upon my young, untutored mind, as I mused on the ever-flowing tide, and wondered, vaguely, what unseen force led those dark, deep waters ever onward towards the distant sea.

To-day, when I am older grown, my soul runs in line with the singer's thoughts :—

> "And I sit and think, when the sunset's gold
>   Is flushing river and hill and shore,
> I shall one day stand by the waters cold,
>   And list for the sound of the boatman's oar ;
> I shall watch for a gleam of the flapping sail,
>   I shall hear the boat as it gains the strand,
> I shall pass from sight with the boatman pale
>   To the better shore of the spirit land.
> I shall know the loved who have gone before,
>   And joyfully sweet will the meeting be,
> When over the river—the peaceful river—
>   The Angel of Death shall carry me."

Chapter VII

THINGS LOOK DARK

FOR three or four nights after Tickle's death I kept away from our old camping place ; why, I could hardly have said. Then at last, one evening, I returned, intending to take up my old quarters.

I stood in the open square in front of our ruin, and turned my eyes up to our sleeping corner. The old egg-chest hung by one handle, just as it had done on that fateful night, when my poor little pal had been hurled out upon the pavement below. The straw that had been his bed, the piece of tarpaulin that had been his coverlet, littered the ground. The straw from my bunk-like ledge, scrabbled down by my hurried descent, clung to the rough wall, and was scattered all about.

I shivered as I looked at all this, and a slow creep moved up the spine of my neck, so that I shuddered again. "It's no use," I murmured, "I can't sleep here again, I must try somewhere else."

I thought of "The Kitchen" (I think that was its name, it was the name by which I knew it), and I decided to go there. I had been once before, long ago, and knew all about the place. (The Kitchen was situated in a bye-street leading out of Spitalfields, and was frequented by all shades of the lowest classes for a night's lodging. The prices ranged from twopence to fourpence, and the occupiers were crowded and herded together in such a frightfully shameless way that every idea of decency was outraged. Men and women, regardless of age, sex, or condition, slept in the same rooms).

With a shuddering sense of horror, I turned from the place so full of saddest associations of my dead chum, muttering, " I'll never look on this place again, if I can help it, as long as I live."

Then, as the mystery of death once more assailed me, I looked up to where the moon sailed amid the light clouds, and asked the unseen God where Tickle was.

Could there have been granted me, then, some *visible* presence from that other world, I hardly think I should have been afraid, but, filled as I was with longing to know the mystery of death and the future, I should have poured out my yearning, untutored heart in a hundred questions, and should, I verily believe, have begun the quest for Divine things there and then.

But there was no open vision, and I turned my back upon the place, and moved eastwards to Spital-fields.

"The Kitchen" was fairly filled, quite a half hundred people, if not more. The huge fireplace was piled high with a glowing fire of coke and cinders, a fire before which a sheep or a calf could have been well-nigh roasted whole.

The place reeked with steaming clothes, and tobacco, for many of the women smoked, as well as the men. The odours were many and various, and most of them very pungent, as may be imagined from an enumeration of a *few* of the viands that were in process of cooking—sprats, red herrings, bacon rashers, steak and onions, Welsh rabbit, etc., were among the *cuisine* items.

The company was as varied as could, by any chance, be found gathered in any one spot in London. Wooden-legged sailors, who had never seen the sea, and whose lost limbs were suddenly *en evidence*, when they crossed the threshold of the kitchen, having been previously carefully strapped up to their seat, and hidden by a cleverly padded trouser. Ballad sellers—male and female. Begging-letter writers; beggars of every type, drawn from every class of life, high and low. Itinerant practisers of sleight-of-hand ; wandering musicians ; a man who, having converted the long spout of a tall tin coffee-pot into a whistle, made creditable music on the same, winning many shillings a day from the admirers of his skill. There was—— But why continue ? As the picture rises before me I feel I could write a whole book on so fertile a subject as " The Kitchen."

The sudden change from the dark court from which I had come, with all its unpleasant associations, to the light and busy life of the Kitchen, acted swiftly upon my spirits.

There was music and dancing. A fiddler sat close to the fire, playing an Irish jig, while the mad, reck-less revelry and dancing by the motley company made an animated scene.

When fiddler and dancers were fairly spent, some one called out, " Now, then, Bogie, guv us a song !" and a tall, gaunt man, dressed in a suit of shabby black, stepped forth and commenced to sing, in dolorous tones, " The Sailor's Grave." He was

almost immediately interrupted by a chorus of
voices. " There, stow that patter, and guv us some-
think comic ! "   Once again, with many a grimace,
and an affected solemnity of manner, he sang,—

> " ' My father was a grim old gruffin,
>   Who never liked no fun nor nuffin,
>   Nor never made the least endeavour
>   To make a joke or what-some-dever.' "

Here followed a quaint chorus, quickly caught and
heartily sung by this strange company ; and thus, till
midnight, the revel continued.

On leaving the Kitchen, next morning, I wandered
about the " Fields " in an aimless, restless fashion.

Once, for a good spell, I paused to watch a sight I
had never seen before—a silk weaver, at work.   In
those days there were hundreds of silk weavers in
Spitalfields.

How the sure, deft, accurate movements of that
keen-faced, intellectual, superior-looking man fascinated me !   Through the high window before which
his frame was placed, a broad shaft of tempered
golden light fell upon his work, himself, and that
wonderful flying thing, his shuttle.

When, years after, in one of my pastorates, I was
seeking guidance as to a subject for a sermon for the
last Sunday morning of a year, my mind was suddenly filled with the words in Job, " My days are
swifter than a weaver's shuttle," and that scene in
Spitalfields, of long ago, came back to me —" the
Spirit bringing all things to remembrance "—and I
saw light for a sermon in the last days of a year,
light and teaching which first came to my own heart
with searching and power, and which, at certain times

of each year since, have returned to me, to quicken my soul, and give food for self-searching, and consequent humiliation before God.

Will these thoughts help some other worker, some other Christian who may read this little volume? They may.

The flying shuttle of the weaver carries with it two distinct thoughts, the first, the primary thought of the text in Job vii. 6—that of the *swiftness* of Time's flight. But people appear to be' more readily impressed, at certain points of the year, or of their lives, with the *rapidity* of Time's flight, than by that deeper thought, "*How* have I spent my time? what kind of work has the shuttle of my life been weaving?" And it was this second thought that the long-forgotten picture of the Spitalfields weaver suggested to me, and which has been most convincingly, humiliatingly present with me many times since.

Night and day, to and fro, in sun and shadow, the shuttle of Time flies, every moment, every flight, weaving some thread, some colour, some pattern in the life, and whether the flight of Time be lengthened or shortened, seems of small account beside the greater thought, what kind of weaving is being made.

There is a pattern in all our lives, none are absolutely plain. Some prefer to weave erratic patterns of their own mad, foolish design—or rather, we should say, *want* of design. Others sketch out a rigid, sharp-cut design for their lives, or follow some equally sharply defined design supplied by another Life-weaver, yet, in both cases, man-made, and therefore *useless.* Others—and thank God there are more of these than the great world at large supposes—there are who have been brought to that place of repentant faith and lowly dependence, where, realising that they have no power of designing a safe life-pattern for themselves, have just turned all their case, pattern, weaving, and use of the woven fabric, all over to the Great Designer and Worker, and sing as they work :—

> " His goodness stands approved,
> Unchanged from day to day :
> I'll *drop my burden* at His feet,
> *And bear a song away.*"

There is a fabric-weaving that has a plain, solid foundation upon which the pattern is worked, and of this type of thing is Life. God has given a foundation upon which man's life shall be worked, and " other foundation can no man lay than is laid, which is Jesus Christ." (That is, there is no other possible *safe* foundation upon which to build, or weave the life.)

We have seen worked slippers of most exquisite pattern and working, which have not stood the strain of one evening's wear, because the *foundation* on which they had been worked *was rotten.* And the question for my heart, for the hearts of all who seek to please God, and who hope finally to go to dwell eternally with Him, is, Am I building, weaving my life on the *one only sure* foundation ; am I in Christ Jesus ?

Once assured by the Witness of the Spirit that we are born of God, that,—

> " Our hope is built on nothing less
> Than Jesu's Blood and Righteousness,"

then we can safely begin to study the pattern of life in The Word and in the Person of Jesus.

I have read of an old-time tapestry weaving, where the pattern was suspended high up above the weaver, and it often happened that the strain upon the eyes was so great that, giddy and sick, the weaver was obliged to give up his task. Did God think of *us* in this matter, in grace, that when man, dazzled by the Divine pattern, could not so much as lift up his eyes, He, the All-Wise, should have prepared a body for His Son, that we might see God in the face of Jesus Christ? Did God thus think of us? Surely He did!

There is a wondrous story illustrative of this truth, told by Alexander Dickenson. The interior of the dome of a celebrated church on the continent is a wonderful painting that took the great artist seven years to complete. But when it was finally finished, and the scaffolding on which the artist had worked was taken down, it was found that the great height precluded the eye of the visitor on the church floor below from seeing ought but a confused blur of colour.

For years the artist's work was unseen, then an old man, a caretaker, jealous of the house he loved so much, and desirous that all the beauty of this great dome work should be seen, suggested that by a certain arrangement of light and mirrors, with a large mirror set in the floor of the church, the painting should be brought *down* to the sight of the people.

His arrangement was carried out, and the gathered peoples gazing into the great lake-like mirror in the floor of the church, saw the reflected picture of the dome.

And when God said " Be ye holy, for I am holy," and the pattern was high, so that we could not attain unto it, He sent His own Son in the likeness of sinful flesh, to live the God-life on earth, and show us the

Father, and how to live the life which the Father would have us live,—in short, how to weave life's pattern.

Like the tapestry weaver we do not see the full pattern of *our* weaving, for we, like him, see only the wrong side (the *earth* side of our work. We see the knots, the bights, the tangles; but He, our tender Foreman, our great Designer, will put all things to rights, and show us the real finished work, of what sort it is, at the judgment seat of Christ (1 Cor. iii.).

What *colours* are we weaving with our life's shuttle? As we look back on our weaving are we not conscious that too often our colours have been too *neutral*, that there has been no definite *Christlike motive* in our work? Have we never even found *soiled* threads in our weaving—*impure motives*? or dark, black threads of doubt of others, threads of judging and misjudging? Have *you* found these things, you who read this old sailor's ramblings? *He* has often, and often, and often again, and the sight has sent him shuddering on his face before Him, who is faithful and just to forgive sin, and cleanse from unrighteousness, who delighteth in mercy, and who has said, " Where sin abounded grace doth much more abound."

Then the *texture* of our weaving? How *weak*, how uneven it has often been. The new year, or the shock of a friend's death, or some other event in life has quickened our resolve to live as never before, to live to serve God more fully, and to seek to win souls for Jesus. Then—ah, the pity of it all !—then self, in one of its thousand forms has crept insidiously upon us, and, Thug-like, has strangled our resolutions and our renewed efforts. Until some other quickening has come to us, and in a very agony of shame at our failure, (in the language of Wesley) our souls have cried :—

> " I want an *even strong* desire,
>   I want a calmly fervent zeal,
> To save poor souls out of the fire,
>   To snatch them from the verge of hell,
> And turn them to a pardoning God,
> And quench the brands in Jesus' blood."

Then, in our life's weaving, how many *broken* threads there have been—breaks of utter failure. In weaving, there is a special knot used for uniting broken threads; it is called a "weaver's hitch," and is peculiar to the trade—to the weaver it is simple enough, but not so to the general run of men. And our Great Weaver has His own way of uniting the broken threads of our poor weaving, when in the language of Hosea xiv. we take with us words of confession and turn to Him.

Will any one read this chapter, who has a seemingly fair life before the world, but who is knowingly out of gear, out of harmony with God, who has never cared to deal with God as to the great foundation truths of sin, ruin, and redemption? God help you friend! Look at Job viii. 14, and see what God calls your life. There is, and has been, it is true, some weaving, but it is that frail, hopeless, useless thing— the spider's web.

I see that shaft of sunlight, that wide high window in that old-fashioned room in Spitalfields, the foreign type of face that bent over the frame, the flying shuttle; I see it all, still, as I saw it that morning nearly forty years ago, and crowds of spiritual thoughts flock to the windows of my soul. But I remember I have a story to tell, as well as a homily to offer, and I hurry on with the story.

It was eleven o'clock that morning before I reached the place of my profession with the birch brush, and to my horror and amazement, I found that a big, low-looking bully of a lad had installed himself at my crossing. He had swept a broad, clean pathway, and now stood in a watchful, professional attitude, leaning on his broom.

I gazed at my burly supplanter, speechless for the moment. He turned his head, saw me, probably noted the puzzled, disconsolate look upon my face, and with a jerk of his bull-dog head in my direction, he roared out, "Well, ugly, wot's yer starin' at? Aint yer never seen a gennelman at business afore?"

"A wot?" I yelled, half crying with rage and disappointment; "a gennelman? Well, it's the fust time I ever knew a gentleman sneak a poor boy's crossing. I've been here ever since there was a crossing, I made it myself, and I've a good mind to ask the peelers (police) to shift you, so there!"

With a terrific lunge at me, with his broom, he poured out a volley of fearful abuse and threats, and I was glad to move sorrowfully, reluctantly away.

I might, if I had thought of it, gone into "The London Apprentice," stated my case to the landlady, and to the potman, and have got the latter to settle with the pirate sweeper. But I was too unnerved to think of that course, and made my way, slowly, out into the main road by Shoreditch Church, as sad a boy as was then upon the face of the earth.

Chapter VIII

"THERE'S NA' LUCK ABOOT THE HOOSE"

AN hour or two later, I sat upon one of the stone seats on London Bridge, my heart as cold as the stone I sat upon, and feeling as hopeless and lonely as though I had been a derelict on mid-ocean, or a castaway on some unknown, uninhabited islet in some distant sea.

The great tide of human and vehicular traffic poured its continuous stream, back and forth, past me; the great waterway below me was thronged with its own life and bustle, its kedges, wherries, steamers, and—east of the bridge—ships of largest size; everything around me was full of life, and I, a boy of fourteen, felt hopeless and dead.

"My luck is out, that's certain," I muttered to myself. "Dead out, it looks to me. I've lost my pal—he's dead; I've lost my doss (leastways, I can't stand to it now, after Tickle's dying, that way); and now I've lost my pitch (my crossing)."

I was not penniless, I knew, and taking out all I possessed, I counted it over, enumerating the coins as I did so, after the style I had picked up upon the streets. "A bob," I muttered, dropping the shilling from the counting fingers of the right hand, into the open pool of the left palm—"a tanner" (I passed a sixpence into the pool), " a joey, and a brown " (and a threepenny piece and a halfpenny joined the other coins). " One and ninepence halfpenny," I said, totalling up my financial possessions.

" No," I continued ; " I'm not dead-broke as far as 'chips' are concerned, but it looks as though my luck was out in other ways.

" Sweeping ain't all bread-and-honey, but it ain't the worst way in the world of getting a living, 'cepts when you gets bullied out of your pitch. Sometimes you're up, sometimes you're down, and sometimes—well you're betwixt and betweens."

That last side of my reflection was very true. The business of a crossing-sweeper was as full of fluctuations as the pocket of a spendthrift pensioner, who to-day will have a month's allowance, and to-morrow will wonder how he shall live out the current week.

Some days I was passing rich on *fourpence* for the day's takings, another day, I would be rolling in the unheard-of wealth of as many shillings.

A fourpenny day would mean very spare living, a fourshilling day would mean faring sumptuously— *without the fine linen*. A poor day meant crawling away at night to my wretched bed of straw, tired, and perhaps drenched to the skin, to lie down and shiver, or steam (according to the temperature) in my wet clothes, and to wish I'd never left my mother to embark upon such an unsatisfactory enterprise.

A wealthier day would mean high spirits, a good supper, a night at the theatre, where amid the warmth, the light, the music, the play, all thought save that of the delight of the moment would be forgotten.

Sitting on that stone seat on London Bridge, musing on my misery, thoughts of my mother crowded into my mind. I was not more than four miles from her, and again I was tempted to return, like a wandering prodigal. Then, as my old purpose of sparing her the work of maintaining me rose again strong within me, and dimly—more dimly now than it once had been—I saw that philanthropic merchant coming to lift me off the streets on to one of his office stools; as all this came over me again, I decided to do as I was still doing, send my mother an occasional ambiguous scrawl of cheer and assurance, and wait for *my fortune* before I returned.

I was suddenly aroused from my musings by the voice of a policeman, uttering his war cry, " Move on, here ! "

I was off like a shot, towards the Surrey side of the river. At London Bridge Station I picked up a job of porterage, which took me almost to the Black-friars Road. One or two other jobs turned up on that side of the river, and evening found me " among the gods " at one of the theatres in that quarter.

It was a play after my own heart on that evening, —a nautical drama,—and while the performers held the stage, I had neither eyes nor ears for anything or any one around me.

Suddenly there rang through the house the cry of " Fire ! "

As the fearful cry rang out through the building, though nothing could be seen, and, as it was after-wards discovered, there was not the slightest cause of alarm, yet the vast mass of people were panic-stricken.

Men, women, and children turned towards the

exits, dashing over seats with mad, blind, reckless haste; crushing and pressing against each other, until at every opening they were wedged into solid masses of struggling, fainting human beings. The strongest trampled recklessly over those who were under foot, and then, amidst groans and oaths and prayers, the crash of falling plaster and splintering timber was heard, followed by a momentary dull, awful silence. A staircase had given way, and the whole place quickly resounded with shrieks of living and dying, as this new horror lent itself to death.

One useful characteristic which has often served me well in life is that of perfect coolness and presence of mind in times of great emergency and imminent danger.

When the first rush was made that night, I remained standing for a moment, taking in the situation. The flying crowds, pressing to the front of the theatre : the numerous articles of all kinds left or flung away in attempted escape; the vast stage cleared of performers, and forming an easy exit for many of the audience if they had but retained presence of mind enough to avail themselves of it— all these things passed quickly before my eye and through my brain. Then, quickly scrambling over the front of the gallery, I swung myself into the boxes, and again into the pit. Arrived in the pit, I clambered over the orchestra and across the stage, and in a few moments was in the street.

Later on that night I reached a lodging-house on the city side of the river, with a sense of greater hopelessness than ever. But, instead of realizing the mercy of my deliverance, I grumbled more than ever at my " ill-luck." And yet I had stayed long enough

in the neighbourhood of the theatre to learn that
scores of men, women, and young people had been
either maimed or killed in that awful panic.

Before I went to sleep that night, I determined to
seek out the doctor the next day, and accept his offer
of a place in the Home for lads just being started.

I carried out my purpose the next day, saw the
doctor, and, long before my usual bedtime, I was
lying with a bathed, glowing body, clothed in a clean,
though well-worn shirt, in a little coarse, snug bed, in
that Home for working street boys.

Where was that Home situated? I have tramped
for hours (during recent years), and spent more hours
still in all kinds of enquiries, but have never found
a clue to its whereabouts. It was a thing of mush-
room growth, I know. It came up to-day and was
gone to-morrow, as we say, its final exit being almost
as much of a *fiasco* as that meeting described in
an earlier chapter.

In trying to locate the place it has always seemed
to me that it was in a narrow by-way, somewhere
very close to Flower and Dean Street. But exactly
where it was I have never been able to ascertain, and
it does not really matter now.

The house was very old, very dilapidated, crowded
closely amid a lot of others in the narrow street,
whose houses were not planted with an even front,
like many streets, but where every building had its
own lurch inwards or outwards, like a mouthful of
snaggle teeth.

The establishment was run, for the lady who
had conceived it and paid for its running, by a man
named Nat and his wife.

Two more unsuitable people could not possibly be

found in all London, and to them chiefly, if not wholly, I believe, was due the utter failure of the experiment.

But of this another chapter must treat.

Chapter IX

A REVOLT

THE man was one of those queer specimens met with occasionally. In height about medium, thin and spare, with a freckled face, and small, deep-set, ferret-like eyes. His hair was of a glaring red colour, worn short, except at the ears, where it was trained long, and plastered with some greasy compound against the upper part of the cheek, in the shape of a figure six. His face was clean-shaven, except the chin, where he wore a tuft of long hair, usually known as " a billygoat."

For meanness, trickery, and low cunning, mated with brutality of the sly, aggravating order, surely there never was a more perfect type than Nat.

He, together with his wife, had been installed as superintendent, servant, cook—in fact, they comprised, as I explained in the last chapter, the whole establishment.

The idea of the foundress was to provide a Home for street lads, who, being willing to work, should be taught independence and self-reliance at one and the same time, by paying a certain portion of their earnings in exchange for food and shelter, and for certain instruction in night-classes—when the organization should become sufficiently developed to warrant the starting of these latter privileges.

Twenty-four was proposed to be the limit of the number to be taken. There were but four when I entered the Home, which had increased to seven before I left. The manner of that leaving I wrote years ago, and though it can reflect but little credit upon me, yet, in looking back over the events, after the lapse of many years, I can at least plead the boyish impetuosity of untrained youth in extenuation for the escapade, as well as the maddening influence upon my nature of the low, mean tyranny of the man over us.

It was Sunday, and the dinner-hour.

The scene would have formed a quaint subject for a painter's brush—the square room, cold-looking in its new whitewash on walls and ceiling; its rough unpainted shelves, partly adorned with cheap tin plates and mugs (the others are in use on the table); that same table, with seven plates and seven mugs; a white jam-pot filled with salt; a brown japanned tin pepper-box; with knives and forks of the very commonest quality.

Opposite each plate stood a rough street-waif, some mere children, others big grown lads, though all comparatively young. All felt the grace before meat, though short, yet a mockery from such a man as Nat Nasty, as they had privately dubbed him.

But now Nat is speaking: his voice is thin, with a whining, canting twang about it, as, with hands crossed upon his breast, and the whites of his eyes turned upwards, he slowly repeats the usual grace, " For what we are about to receive," etc.

The grace finished, he said in oily tones, " Now, my good boys, you can get on with your dinners."

The biggest, boldest-looking boy of the party,

whose face seemed full of mischief and good-humour, glancing down at the smallest of the boys, who sat next to him, noticed that his plate contained nothing but a large "hunk" of bread.

The other boys' plates were well filled with vegetables, pickled pork, and pease-pudding, and the sight of little Tumbler's plate with nothing but bread upon it roused the indignation of Wops (as he had long been known upon the streets). On his entrance to this Boys' Refuge, he had been re-christened by the "powers that be" as Walter Wilson, and by the name of Walt he was usually known to his new companions.

The eyes of all the boys were fixed eagerly upon me, as I appealed to our whining bully, saying, " I say, you, mister, where's the little 'un's dinner?"

" He's got it on his plate, young imperence!" came the reply, in aggravating, oily tones.

All my hot, young, passionate blood was fired, as much by the man's manner as with the answer itself. I grasped the situation at once. The boy, a weakly little fellow, the youngest of the party, had been too ill to work that week, and had, somehow, incurred the mean, petty spite of the bully, Nat.

Boiling over with anger I declared war against the the tyrant, crying, " Oh, oh! my dandy! that's yer little game, is it? Because the little 'un has been indoors all the week, too sick to work, and couldn't bring in any rhino, you think he won't have any pork or pease-pudding. Well, your mistaken, I tell you, for we stick by our pals; don't we, cullys?"

My appealing glance and question was immediately responded to by a chorus of voices shouting, " We does!"

Taking my knife, I scraped a portion of my share of the Sunday's luxury from my plate on to that of the little trembling child's at my side. Every boy did the same, until the little fellow's plate was like Benjamin's portion when Joseph dined his brethren.

Nat turned upon me fiercely. In his passion he forgot to use his customary oily tones, his voice now sounding more like a loud-creaking hinge ; he roared, " What blessed bis'ness his hit of yourn, I should like to know, 'bout other people's dinners? an', jist to show yer my mind upon it, I'm a-goin' to take that there plateful away again."

" Take the little 'un's dinner away, after we've given it to him ?" I cried ; " not if I know it, you don't ; we sticks together, too, over this job, and my pals will see that you don't touch the boy's plate ! "

Taking my stand behind the little fellow, and patting him encouragingly on the shoulder, I bade him go on and eat his dinner in peace. The other boys went on with their dinners. I ate mine standing, my plate in my hand, my watchful eye upon the foaming, baffled tyrant, who raved and paced about the room, but always keeping at a safe distance from the table.

The dinner plates were almost cleared, when the bottled-up wrath of Nat Nasty broke out. He began to abuse me, and all boys in general (he did not except the gathered company, as common politeness decrees he should have done, but vigorously, rancorously included them).

Inspired by the sound of his own voice, perhaps, he came close up to me, shook his fist in my face, and hissed out, " Fur two pins I'd give yer a jolly

good hidin', yer imperdent young vagabond, and
then ——"

I leaped to meet his onslaught. He fell back with
a sudden scared look in his face. I told him he
ought to be ashamed of himself; the little boy had
broken no rule of the Home; he was supposed to
have his dinner the same as the others; that if the
doctor's lady friend were told of his (Nat's) meanness
and injustice, she'd take *our* part. Then, coming to
his threat to thrash me, I bade him begin.

I might have said much more but for the fact that
my eye lit upon a big tin dish half filled with pease-
pudding, and, with a sudden sense of the comic,
I grasped a handful of the soft, greasy mess, and
hurled it into the scared, shrinking face of our tyrant.

Not a boy among the party could resist the
temptation to join in such a soft, warm assault as
this, and in a moment the phlut, phlet, phlot of the
pease-pudding shells, as they struck and burst in the
face of the tyrant, sounded above the shrieks of our
delighted laughter.

I knew that my sojourn at the Home was practically cut off by this action on my part, so, wishing
the lads good-bye, and giving Nat Nasty a mocking
farewell, I seized my cap, and with the parting word
to the boys, " I'll be sure an' see some of you to-
morrow," I raced down the stairs, and out into the
street, relieving my uproarious spirits with one of my
favourite yells of " Chuck-urr-err."

The remainder of that Sunday was rather a dreary
time. I found myself, late in the afternoon, on London Bridge (I used to gravitate to this spot in my
times of trouble as if by instinct, or by some irresistible natural law of sequence).

Until it was quite dark, I watched the river and its craft, a longing to try a life on the water coming to me with great power. The sight of the *ocean* rovers that lay *east* of the bridge, with their taut set-up, their bunted sails, snug-looking decks, with their carefully coiled ropes, and the thought of all the unseen, unknown, and therefore (by me) exaggerated delights which the forecastle below would yield, all made me long to try a life on the ocean wave.

As the early night closed in I moved away across the bridge to the Surrey side, mentally deciding to " try my luck " on that side of the river for a time.

This decision, which I duly carried out, cut me off from any further sight of, or acquaintance with, the boys whom I had left at the Home, and also hindered the doctor finding me, when, having heard the story of Sunday's battle, he tried to search me out.

For six weeks, my mind constantly dwelling upon the sea, I worked fairly successfully on the Surrey side of the river. My ideas of a sailor's life had all been derived from the low-type nautical plays I had seen at the " penny gaffs " and low theatres ; and I had no means of knowing that these represented scenes and sailors were as unlike the real thing as is the proverbial " chalk and cheese." I had heard *stage* sailors sing :—

> " Smiling grog is the sailor's best hope—his sheet anchor,
>   His compass, his cable, his log ;
>   That gives him a heart which life's care cannot canker."

The idea of " grog " had no attraction for *me*, for I had vowed never to drink intoxicants, since they had robbed me of a father.

But if the oft-sang grog had no attraction for me,

the prospect of seeing foreign lands, and of returning "with dungaree pockets lined with heaps of golden guineas," had every attraction. My philanthropic merchant had not turned up, and my expectations from that fancied source of a new and better life had grown faint and shadowy.

My mind was full of the heartiest parts of so-called sailors' songs—that is, the songs which, in those days, sailors were credited with singing. I heard them at the low houses of entertainment where I spent so many of my evenings. I would hum these songs as I shouldered a parcel for some one who, glad to save his or her muscles and strength by the expenditure of twopence or threepence, employed me as porter. I hummed or sang Dibden wherever I went, until I began to feel that there could be no life to equal a sailor's. As to the dangers, well, like Barney Bill, I began to "pity those poor folks on shore now," and would throw all my mistaken soul into the sentiments of the verse :—

> "Go patter to lubbers and swabs, do you see,
>   'Bout danger, and fear, and the like ;
>   A tight water-boat and good sea-room give me,
>   And it ain't to a little I'll strike.
>   Though the tempest top-gallant-mast smack smooth
>   should smite,
>   And shiver each splinter of wood,
>   Clear the deck, stow the yards, and house everything
>   tight,
>   And under reef'd foresail we'll scud :
>   Avast ! and don't think me a milksop so soft
>   To be taken for trifles aback ;
>   For they say there's a Providence sits up aloft,
>   To keep watch for the life of poor Jack ! "

I spent many hours on *the* Bridge. I use the

definite article because, though there were many other bridges spanning the Thames over which I sometimes passed, yet it was London Bridge which possessed the chief charm for me, since from there only could I see real *sea-going* ships ; all to the west of the bridge were but river craft.

With my very limited knowledge of things nautical and geographical, I would yet try to picture where those waiting, loading, and unloading ships went and came.

"There go the ships !" says our Authorised Version, and I remember how, years after those days, but long before I was a converted man, Mr. Spurgeon's wonderful sermon on that text (which had fallen into my hands) thrilled me, and awoke everything nautical within me, for it is a wondrous utterance.

Speaking of that text reminds me of a little incident which occurred to me about a year and a half *after* my conversion, and while I was still in the navy. I was serving in a revenue cutter at the time. We were cruising off the southern coast, were anchored off Eastbourne or Hastings, I forget which, and I was spending an hour or two ashore.

On the beach I got into conversation with a fisherman about divine things, when, in some way, he brought round the subject of the inaccuracies and *apparent* contradictions of Scripture. He declared his implicit belief in the Bible, but said that some of our translators must have blundered considerably.

"For instance," he said, "there's a werse in the Psalms as says, ' There go the ships ; there is that leviathan . . . these all wait upon Thee, hat Thou mayest give them their meat in due season.' You knows the werse, I makes no doubt?" he added.

I admitted that I did, but asked, "What's wrong with it?"

"Well, a pretty sight o' wrong," he said, "as fur as I can see. Look here! I suppose we'd best call the leviathan the whales, an' sharks, an' sich-like *big* things in the sea; well, nat'rally enuff, these wait on God fur their meat, an' He have a' pervided fur 'em. But what about ships? They're included in that werse, an' ships an' leviathan are said *all* to wait upon God fur their meat. But as to the ships, why, there ain't a morsel o' sense in that; somebody have made a mistake in translating: I makes no doubt that God have put it all right in the 'riginal."

I saw the good fellow was right, there was no sense in the first part of the verse, if that word "ships" was to be accepted. But I could give him no explanation of the mistake, neither could I afterwards find out, until more than a dozen years had passed, then the explanation came.

Mrs. Helen Spurrel, the compiler of "The Literal Translation from the Hebrew of the Old Testament," sent me a copy of her book. The first place I opened, the first verse my eye lit upon, was the 26th of the 104th Psalm, and I read for "ships," the "nautilus."

How clear, how beautiful that made the verse! "There go the nautili; there is that great leviathan . . . these all wait upon Thee, and Thou givest them their meat in due season." The pretty, fragile, tiny nautilus, and the ponderous monsters of the deeper ocean, small and great, alike the subjects of God's care and providence—the thought is lovely!

That plain, unlettered fisherman's instincts were

right—some one had blundered. I like to remember, in these days of sweeping criticism of the Bible, that if there are inaccuracies in the text, it is the outcome of some human failure in translation, and not that God has made a mistake. If there are *apparent* contradictions in the Word, it is because our spiritual eyes are holden, or because, from warp of judgment, bias of tradition, or some other equally blinding cause, we see contradiction where, actually, harmony exists.

But I am voyaging over the waters of modern criticism, while my readers are doubtless anxious to follow my career, from the London pave to the deck of a ship.

How I got afloat must be kept for another chapter.

Chapter X

AFLOAT

" WANTED ! ! !

" FOR THE ROYAL NAVY

" Strong and healthy boys, from 14½ to 16 years of age "

THIS legend headed a flaring wall advertisement that arrested my attention as I passed through a street in Southwark, and the inducements held out looked so liberal, in print, that it is little wonder that I was caught by the offer. I stood looking at the bill ; there was nothing to show me the dark, bitter side of the life. It said nothing about the petty tyranny of men and officers, whose highest attainment in naval life seemed to be the right to bear the hated nickname of Bully. It said nothing about the birch, and rod, and cat-o'-nine-tails, that often became the portion of poor Jack, not so much because he merited it as because his "Bully" captain was in an ill-humour and must have some safety-valve for his spleen. It said nothing of the training on the lower deck in a school of vice, so awful, so filthy, and so physically and spiritually dangerous that an earthly lifetime of longest duration would not be long enough to obliterate its memory or effects.

No, I saw nothing of this, and I therefore determined to find my way to Woolwich, to H.M.S. *Hebe*, the receiving ship, and try to get taken into the Navy.

As soon as I had determined on my course, I set myself to earn and save every copper I could, with a view to the purchase of a more decent fit-out of clothing than that which I wore at the time, knowing, or at least supposing, that a fairly respectable appearance would help me a little in my application.

When I considered myself quite ready for my purchase of a new outfit, I once more made my way to Petticoat Lane, entering it this time from the Aldgate, instead of the Bishopsgate end, and keeping well clear of the shop where I had been put to such shame before.

I had learned something of the ways of the world since my last visit to the Lane, and was able on this occasion to make a very fair bargain, and to leave the Hebrew colony presenting a very fair appearance.

Next morning, I made my way to Woolwich, and decided to spend a day, or two, or three even, if I thought it necessary, while I took the bearings of things, that I might know how to go about my business in the easiest and most successful manner.

I found one day quite sufficient for my purpose, and after a night's sleep at a lodging-house, I made my way to the jetty, opposite to which the *Hebe* lay, bent on making my application.

I was met with the question :—

"Well, young shaver, what do you want?" The speaker was a short, sturdy man, dressed in a naval uniform, with the black tarpaulin hat, the regulation whisker, worn on a skin the texture of a coarse canvas, and the colour of a port-wine stain on a mahogany table.

"I wants to jine the Navy, sur," I replied.

" I guess you'll wish you'd been born a dawg afore you've been aboard six months, young 'un ; but it ain't no manner o' use a-talking to sich as you, yer never believes it ; so go on there to that office, and see if they'll give yer the papers."

I was questioned, passed on to the doctor, and stripped for medical examination, and finally received a form, to be filled up by my parents, and attested by the clergyman of the parish in which I resided.

" And when you have these all filled up duly, return here with them, and you will be admitted on the books at once ; that's all, now be off with you." These words, uttered in brisk, authoritative tones by the official in charge, made me fully understand that, for the time, I was settled with.

Passing over the gangway, I presently landed on the quay again, deep in thought, and muttering, " They've got to be signed by both the parents—if *both* are living—and to be attested by the clergyman of the parish ! "

" That can't be managed, exactly," I mused ; " but yet, someway, those papers have got to be signed. I must think out some plan."

Presently I found myself in the neighbourhood of the railway station. It occurred to me that I might get a job of porterage, and thus help to combine money-earning with the new business that was occupying my thoughts.

A moment or two later I spied a commercial traveller, carrying a large and a small bag. Racing across to him, I proffered my request : " Carry the big 'un for you, sir? I'll carry it all round for you for a tanner (sixpence), sir. Look at me, sir ; I'm quite respectable, ain't I ? "

The man had a good-humoured face, and glanced at me keenly as he said, " Oh, yes, you're respectable enough ; but are you honest ? "

I assured him I was, he accepted my statement, or perhaps he was a student of faces, and believed that he read honesty in mine, and the *big* bag was transferred from his hand to my shoulder.

For three hours I tramped about with my temporary employer, and all the time there was slowly forming in my mind a scheme for getting those naval papers signed.

My commercial evidently became interested in me, asked me many questions—I am afraid I answered these queries with an ultra-jesuitical amount of " *inward reservation.*"

Finally, when he asked me what I was doing in Woolwich, I told him frankly, and explained that I wanted to get the naval entry papers signed, and made this astonishing proposition to him :—

" I told you I'd carry your bag all day for a tanner, sir, but I won't charge you a farthing, if you will only sign those papers for me, and so help me to get aboard the ship, where I can earn an honest living and get a pension at the end of my term."

" Why, you young monkey," he said, " don't you know that if I were to sign those papers for you, it would be forgery, and I should be transported for life ? "

I assured him that people were never transported for any such things *unless* they were caught, that he could never be caught, even if the discovery was made that the papers were fraudulently signed, for no one would know who wrote the signatures, since even I did not know who he was, and would likely enough never see him again.

He suggested other difficulties, only, however, to try me, I think, and to see what I would say.

I have no doubt that this keen business man got a considerable amount of amusement out of all the by-play which accompanied our negotiations ; but in the end I won my case, and in a quiet little coffee-house he signed the papers, and on my arrival at the railway station, a little later on, when I turned over to him the bag I had carried, he gave me a shilling, and a hearty wish of " Good luck."

The next day I carried my papers on board once more, my stature was taken, I was medically examined, and was received as a second-class boy. The same afternoon I was measured for my clothes, and was then free to wander over the ship, to wonder at all I saw, and to be plagued and hoaxed, after the usual fashion, by the older boys, who supposed themselves to be full-flavoured salts, since some of them had been quite *six weeks* in the Navy.

How distinctly I remember my first night in a hammock ! My old sleeping-place in that Shoreditch slum came up vividly before my mind, and I seemed to see poor little Tickle swinging to and fro in his egg-chest.

When at last I fell asleep, I had a fearful nightmare, in which all the events of that fatal night were reproduced, until, with a yell of horror, I awoke to find myself sprawling upon the deck, and my hanging bed swinging by one lanyard, just as Tickle's egg-chest had swung over his bleeding, prostrate body.

For a moment it all seemed so real to me that I shivered with horror. Then a boy got out of a neighbouring hammock and helped me to re-sling mine, explaining that new-comers generally got "lowered" like that; it was part of a new chum's first experiences.

This explanation helped to calm me, for I saw how the operations of the "skylarker" who had lowered me had entered into the nightmare from which I had suffered.

The days which followed were filled with ever new and very varied experiences; all of them novel, many of them unpleasant, but *none* of them nautical —from my idea of what constituted things nautical.

"Why is this?" I asked myself; then, as the contrast between my own outward appearance and that of most of the other boys struck me, I knew that the lacking nautical flavour was due to my being still clothed in shore clothes, whilst the vast majority of my shipmates wore the uniform.

At last I got my sailor-suits. What a strange experience it was, the first feeling of those strangely cut garments! I put them on as I got up one morning, and went on deck to holy-stone.

Has the reader ever seen—and *heard*—holy-stoning? It is not good for the nerves. I had none in those days, and it did not hurt me from that standpoint, though it would prostrate me physically and mentally to-day.

Imagine, if you can, seventy boys, all bare-footed and bare-legged, the trousers rolled up to the thighs, and each boy kneeling on a narrow strip of board, with the body thrown well forward, and the two hands grasping a square stone about the size of a brick. The deck is wetted and sanded all over with coarse sand, and the boys, throwing all their weight upon the stones, drag them towards them and push them from them, till the sand is reduced to a thick, creamy-like substance, which, when eventually washed off, leaves the deck brilliantly white—at least, when quite dry. That is holy-stoning!

Talking was prohibited while at this work, though, of course, a considerable amount of it went on in undertones.

"How do yer like yer togs?" asked my next neighbour in the kneeling rank.

That was a question I had been asking myself for the last three-quarters of an hour, and I answered, as nearly as possible, as I felt, for it was entirely a matter of *feeling*, I can assure you.

"The togs ain't so bad," I said; "the stuff seems all right, but it's the cut that's so queer. I feel like an empty sack tied up in the middle, and with both ends open and full of wind. As to the trousers, they're so wide in the legs that when the breeze blows up I ain't sure that I've got anything on them at all. The fact is, *I feel tight where I ought to be loose, and loose where I ought to be tight.*"

Some weeks later we were suddenly filled with the wildest excitement, for we were told that next day we were to be drafted to Plymouth. The very name of that western town smacked of salt water, and I am not quite sure that, to some, it did not sound even foreign.

The next afternoon we were mustered for parade on the quarter-deck, our bags packed and piled at the gangway. The chief officer delivered himself of a short address, in some such words as :—

"Boys, you are leaving this receiving ship to-day; it has been more like a home in its working than any other ship you are likely ever to have. You will soon now commence the sterner duties of a naval career. You will arrive at Plymouth some time in the early morning, and be drafted at the Admiral's pleasure to the two training ships, the *Impregnable* and the *Implacable.* You all leave here with 'Very Good' upon your discharges ; keep this record up. The steward will serve out to each boy a parcel of food, and the master-at-arms will give each boy a threepenny-piece to spend on the road. Mind no boy forgets himself and spends this money on drink, and by a drunken freak disgraces himself, the service he has chosen, and the Queen he serves. That will do, boatswain."

With this speech, which was duly mimicked by more than one boy on the journey during the next few hours, the captain smiled complacently and walked away.

The steward served us out some rations, and cheered by the boys who were not included in that draft, we went ashore, and proceeded by train to Paddington, *en route* for Plymouth.

Chapter XI

AN EVENTFUL JOURNEY

THAT same evening, owing to a block on the line, the whole batch of us were detrained at a large station on the way to Plymouth, with the prospect of having to wait until midnight before we could pursue our journey.

It had just become an exceedingly difficult problem how to keep such a large number of lads safely, and amused. They were boiling over with animal spirits, and felt that the accident which blocked their way was so much license for them. While, upon the other hand, those in charge knew that to lose their grip upon them might mean even losing some of the boys themselves in desertion.

Three ladies and a gentleman who, like the lads, were blocked through the stoppage, appeared to be much interested in the boys, and, in course of conversation with the senior officer in charge of the party, found out the difficulty of restraining the lads, and happily suggested a way out of the dilemma.

The gentleman, having sought out one of the railway officials and stated the difficulty, said, "My three lady friends and I are accustomed to hold bright evangelistic services together, and are even now on our way to a distant town for that purpose. We carry a harp and a portable harmonium with us ;

we have it here, and if you would grant us the use of a large waiting-room or shed for the purpose, we would in a few minutes arrange for a meeting, and I believe we could easily gain these lads' attention."

The permission was very readily granted, and with the help of one or two railway-men who were off duty, and half a dozen ladies, who volunteered their help, a meeting was arranged. The boys gladly acquiesced when kindly invited by the ladies, and filed into the room and took their seats most decorously.

The gentleman was tall and fine-looking, with an athletic figure and a distinctly military bearing. His voice was clear as a bell, and rang out in cheery tones, "Now then, lads, we are going in for a jolly time. I believe in joy, and mirth, and brightness, so long as it is not a sinful sort. I like good music and bright singing, and I'm sure I can speak for my other friends here when I say that we are all extremely obliged to you for coming to help us sing, and to have, what I believe you will call, a jolly time. You see we have got some music. Suppose my sister and I now play you something lively on the harp and harmonium to start with, then our lady friend here will, I am sure, sing us a solo."

In another moment the eyes of the boys were dancing with delight, and more than one set of five fingers rattled time on the chair-backs, to the bright strains of a pretty air that was played by the nimble fingers of the brother and sister.

"There now, that's not so bad for a start, is it?" said the gentleman, as he rose from the harmonium and glanced merrily towards the boys.

A moment later a few chords were struck together

on the instruments, then a lady's voice rose clear,
rich, full, singing :—

> "Oh ! tell us who's the builder of your vessel—
>   If she's mighty, if she's safe ?
>   The great Jehovah is the builder of her,
>   She is mighty, she is safe.
>   The Father, Son, and Spirit, three,
>   Built her, and sent her out to sea ;
>   And this assures both you and me
>   She is mighty, she is safe.

>> "We'll stem the storm, it won't last long,
>>   We'll anchor by-and-by
>>   In the haven of eternal love,
>>   With Jesus ever nigh."

The tune was bright, and the chorus had a fine
swing with it, so that when the whole party on the
platform had sung it over twice, the leader of the
party said to his sailor-boy audience, "Now then, my
lads, let us see if you cannot sing that chorus."

It suited the humour of the boys to be thus appealed
to, and after one or two attempts, they sang the
chorus correctly and heartily ; then the soloist went
on :—

> "Oh ! tell us, is your vessel in good order—
>   If she's mighty, if she's safe ?
>   Yes, we can say to all who come on board
>   She is mighty, she is safe.
>   Her keel is Christian unity ;
>   Her masts—Faith, Hope, and Charity ;
>   Her flag—'The Saviour died for me.'
>   She is mighty, she is safe."

The swell of sound, as the chorus was taken up by
all at a given signal from the leader, was most inspiring, and three times over the words rolled forth :—

> "We'll stem the storm, it won't last long,
>   We'll anchor by-and-by
> In the haven of eternal love,
>   With Jesus ever nigh."

Then came the last verse :—

> "Oh ! tell us, whither do you mean to steer her—
>   If she's mighty, if she's safe ?
> To heaven above, and that is where she'll land us,
>   She is mighty, she is safe.
> Thousands in her have gone before,
> Their toils and sufferings all are o'er,
> They've landed safe on Canaan's shore :
>   Come on board her, she is safe."

Working as these friends had doubtless often done among the Cornish Methodists and Bible Christians, they had caught many quaint, happy melodies, such as the one that was now sung ; and, fortunately, they had a large measure of that sanctified common-sense which enabled them to adapt themselves to the style of their congregation, " that they might win some."

Brief, touching, suggestive, was the prayer that followed ; the leader evidently prayed in the Spirit, and a dead stillness reigned as his words arose. Specially was this the case as he said, " O Thou loving Saviour, Christ, we thank Thee that Thou hast made Thyself our Pilot on this stormy sea of life, and when our frail, dismasted, helm-wrecked little ships would drift and drift, and wreck and founder, Thou dost come on board and safely steer us home to heaven, Thy fair haven of eternal rest."

When the prayer was finished and the boys quietly raised their heads, they were subdued and silent, and many of them had tears standing in their eyes.

The third lady of the party was tall and dark, with

jet-black hair, naturally wavy. She now stood up, with a small Bible in her hand, and with sweet, winning voice said, " My dear sailor brothers—for that is just what I feel you are to me. I have a dear brother at sea, a captain of a ship, and I love the sailor boys of our land ; and I am sure I feel a real sister to you ; but I do want you to start this new life of yours on board ship with a good pilot. I want you to know your sins forgiven, and Jesus as your Commander. Suppose I tell you a story of myself, that very few have ever heard, but which I think will help you to understand what I want you to learn and to know. I was born in London——"

I really couldn't help it. I didn't mean to interrupt, but it seemed so natural just to blurt out, " Ah ! I thought you was a cockney ; so's we."

" Yes," continued the lady, with a quiet smile at the nature of the interruption, " I am a cockney, and when I was about fifteen years old I began to try to be very religious. I thought if I did not go to all the services of the church, and attend faithfully to all the fasts and other ordinances, and say many prayers and read many chapters of the Bible—if I did not do all this, God would be angry with me. So, month after month, and year after year, I went on like this, till at last I thought, ' Surely God must be satisfied with all this,' and though I did not feel and know my sins forgiven, I supposed I should when I came to die.

" Then, one Sunday afternoon in May, I was out with a friend, and we came to a piece of waste land near some railway arches, and saw a crowd of people listening to a man-o'-war's man, who was preaching. Of course we did not intend to stop, but just then some heavy raindrops began to fall, so we stood up for shelter under one of the railway arches, and we were obliged to listen.

"Oh, what a voice that man had, and how earnest he was! He had evidently been telling the people his own experience, which I judged, from after-words, was much like my own ; but my attention was soon arrested by his next words, 'I tell you what it is, friends, the more religious I got the more I got dis-satisfied with myself, so I told my wife's mother all about it. She was a tidy sort of body, and I know lived up to what she perfessed ; but she made me regular mad at fust. She regular laughed at me, and says she, " Ain't satisfied with yourself? No, I shouldn't think not, neither ; why, you sailors—and you, Jem, in particular—are awful choice over yer clothes, and ef yer duck trousers and white drill frock ain't like snow itself you get awful riled, and then you goes to God and says, 'I've " dabbed " out myself and made myself as clean as I can, and I hope, merciful Lord, you'll be satisfied with me.' Why, I tell yer what it is, God says, 'All your righteousness is as filthy rags.'"

"'Well, mother,' says I, 'what shall I do?'

"'"Believe on the Lord Jesus Christ," she said. "God was, God is, satisfied with His atonement for your sin. The Blood of Jesus Christ cleanseth us from *all* sin. Accept God's way of salvation, pitch overboard your own, believe His word, trust His grace, and then——"

"'But here, stow it for a minute,' said I ; 'ain't I got to do none of these things I've been doing for my salvation?'

"'Then she sort o' smiled quietly, as she said,

" No, nothing at all *for* your salvation, but many things, *because* you are saved, you will do."

" 'Well, we talked over lots of texts, and presently I see what a fool I was. I took God's Word in perfect trust, believed in the Saviour for me, and was satisfied with Jesus and His salvation instead of myself.' "

The boys had listened to this part of the recital of the sailor's sermon with breathless interest, and seeing their rapt attention, the lady continued,—

" Now, dear lads, that simple sailor's speech showed me my mistake, and I forthwith trusted Christ and mistrusted myself. Perhaps some of you never yet thought anything about these things; perhaps some have, and have thought they would try and be religious. Just look at Jesus on the Cross instead. Remember He was nailed there for *you.* God was satisfied with that Sacrifice, and bids you trust Him."

That meeting lived in my memory through all the after wild years of my life in the most vivid way, and often and again I wished I could forget it, for it had a knack of recurring at all kinds of awkward moments, when I would rather have forgotten such words than remember them.

Ten years ago, when I began to write up my past experiences, I wrote the above description of the meeting, not that I had any verbatim report of it, but the vivid recollection of the whole proceedings, helped by my then knowledge of the Way of Life, enabled me so to reproduce the meeting that, like a literal mental photograph, I saw and heard again even the minutiæ of that impromptu meeting.

There was some quiet, personal dealing with the

boys at the close of the meeting; but I remember that there came a sudden call to us to take our seats in the train, the way being clear for our going on.

We arrived at Plymouth about five in the morning. How clearly all the experiences of that morning stand out in my memory—I ought almost to say *consciousness*, rather than memory, for even the feel of the fresh, sharp, morning air that blew upon my hot head and cheeks, and found its way inside my loose serge frock, and wide, open-necked flannel, remains with me.

Then how strange everything in that old western town, of nearly forty years ago, looked to my London-trained, untravelled eyes. By the time we were well under way, walking through the town to Mutton Cove, it was half-past five, and sailors and marines were turning out of every street and alley, many of them bearing unmistakable marks of overnight's debauch, and all seeming to be bound the same way as we lads were going.

By half-past six we were safely on board our respective ships; half of us were shipped to the *Implacable* and the other half to the *Impregnable*. I found myself on board the former vessel.

Our first experience was a very welcome one, being breakfast, consisting of a rich, thick cocoa, with nearly a quarter-inch of a greeny-coloured fat swimming upon the surface, and as much "hard tack" (biscuit) as we could eat in the time allotted for the meal.

We were still busy over breakfast when a ship's corporal came to the table where I sat, with twelve others of our draft, and with a merry smile on his face said, " Now, you boys, look lively ; we want you all in five minutes' time on the middle deck. We shall have a nice performance there ; seven boys have been *so good* that we are going to reward them, so you'll see what sort of prizes such good conduct wins."

A few moments later we new-comers were hurried up on to the middle deck, where we were ranged in a line against a thick ridge rope, which seemed to run from one end of the deck to the other.

A few loungers were about on the deck, but our attention was concentrated upon the scene *inside* the ridge rope.

Lashed securely round the stern of several of the large guns was a rolled hammock, and at once we knew that some one was to be flogged.

I refrain from describing the degrading scene, but it impressed us new-comers very decidedly. That, in fact, was why we had been marched to this front place, that we might witness the sight.

When all the boys and crew of the ship—over five hundred—were reported present, then, one after another, seven unfortunate boys, who had been sentenced to " two dozen each," were flogged, or birched.

Some bore the punishment doggedly, while the blazing fury of wild beasts flashed from their eyes ; others fainted under the lash, and were released thereupon ; but all were " seized up " and received all they could stand.

" What do you think of that ? " asked one of my *Hebe* chums.

I remembered the advice given me by one of the

corporals on the receiving ship at Woolwich, and contented myself by replying,—

" What I think, I *do* think, but we'd better none of us *think too loud.*"

But if I held my peace as to my thoughts, it certainly did not hinder my thinking deeply, the result of my thoughts being that I decided to desert at the very first opportunity ; for every fibre of my being revolted at the filthy, degrading scene I had just witnessed.

Chapter XII

A CRUSHING FAILURE

IT did not take many days to become familiar with
the routine of the ship, and to see exactly how
to act, so as to keep out of trouble with all who had
any authority over us.

Thursday and Sunday afternoons became the
great delight of my life, for on these two days leave
was given for the shore, from about one o'clock to
six. I forget how I usually spent the *Sunday* afternoons (there was no Miss Agnes Weston then), but
every *Thursday* I made my way to the railway
station, and generally managed to sit half an hour or
so without being disturbed and warned off.

Only to see a train full of people get out at the
station, or another crowd board an outward-bounder
filled me with a kind of melancholy pleasure; for I
told myself that, at the very first possible moment, I
would join a similar party of London-bounders, and
be free of the hated life into which I had so unwit-
tingly sold myself.

I was full of fun and life, and no one ever suspected
that from the moment I saw those boys flogged that
I lived for one purpose only, but it was so.

All I could make and all I could earn I saved, as
well as what I received week by week. I earned
often as much as two shillings or half a crown a

week. I would scrub a hammock for threepence; sell a dozen hand-made clothes-stops for twopence. I bought cheap sweets ashore, brought them on board and doled them out in halfpenny lots, making about six hundred per cent. profit, and in scores of other ways added to my pile of savings.

Not that I loved money for itself, or that I had any miserly spirit, but I had a purpose in view; for as soon as I had enough to buy a suit of shore clothes, I intended to desert. I loathed the life, I was cramped every moment, and longed for the old freedom. I hated the petty tyranny, but my purpose kept me outwardly calm under it. In short, just the things that had not appeared on the bill and which had induced me to join, were the things which fretted my boy's nature.

Where, I asked myself, was the naval life I had seen depicted on the stage of the gaff, or low theatre? Where was the life I had heard described in such thrilling stories as " Tallow and Marlinespike ; or, He would be a Sailor," or " Bobstay Jack, the Jolly Skipper of Georgia " ?

While speaking of these sailor-*boy* days, and having mentioned Miss Agnes Weston's name, I cannot refrain from adding a word of wondering, grateful praise for all that has been accomplished for Plymouth, and Portsmouth, and for naval men and boys, by that God-raised, God-guided, Christian woman, and her bands of devoted workers.

I can remember (shudderingly now) how, in those old days in Plymouth, that touts, male and female, would hover about Mutton Cove and North Corner, like sharks around a ship, like carrion birds that hover over and about a battle-field, ready to waylay the training-ship boys, and by evil suggestion, and surreptitiously-shown immoral pictures, incite them to evil; then lead them off to the vilest houses in the neighbourhood, where they not only instructed them in vice, but would manage to strip them, by cajolery or by confusing their brains with drink, of everything they possessed, short of their uniform.

Many a lad, falling under their wiles, has parted with his stockings, his silk handkerchief, pocket-handkerchief, his knife—everything, in fact, the loss of which would not be noticed on his arrival on board—and, of course, all the little cash he possessed.

Every boy, on coming ashore on Thursday, received a "joey" (threepenny-piece), which was deducted from his magnificent wage of *sixpence per day*. But this threepenny-piece did not represent all that many of the boys carried ashore with them, for the majority had mothers, and other relations, who sent small remittances, in stamps or postal orders, " to their sailor boy at sea."

Over the awful scenes enacted between those human sharks and helpless boy victims, in those long-ago days, I drop the veil. I doubt if it would be possible for such a condition to exist twenty-four hours in these times; for with the miracle-working wand of God's grace in her hand, with a sanctified common-sense way of working, with the power of a smiling, yet bull-dog tenacity of purpose in her service, and in her way of moving Public Opinion, Agnes Weston, and her co-workers, have made it impossible for the open, unblushing trade in boy-life and morals, which once existed, ever to be seen again.

May God bless every worker among our tars, whether they seek to save the merchantman, fisherman, or naval man. Who can estimate the value of the work of Rosetta Child, in Ratcliffe Highway, London, of the various Sailors' Homes in the great English seaports, of the smaller Homes and institutions that, like a thin white girdle of love and mercy, wind in and out around our coast, doing what they can for Jack, against the thousand and one snares and traps set for him?

Who can gauge the value of such a work as the "Seamen's Christian Friend Society," with its many Homes and Institutes all around the coasts of Great Britain and Ireland? The very name is an inspiration, for what do our sailors need more than a "Christian Friend," wherever they land? And, once converted, no man makes a better missionary, at home or abroad, than a saved sailor. As the Rev. Charles Spurgeon (son of the great pastor) once said at a gathering :—

"I am persuaded that Christian seamen possess a religion of heroism. Sailors, I suppose, see a great many molluscs and jelly-fish, but they do not take their pattern from the medusa of the sea. They are men that have got real stamina and backbone in them. Whenever I have talked with them, and I do generally get among the sailors on board ship, I have found in conversing with them that they have distinctive principles. They know what they believe, and believe it right up to the hilt. Christian sailors are men that have real grit in their composition. Have you ever heard a sailor pray? I have. He seems to mean it when he puts his brawny arms round the Angel of the Covenant, holding on with a Jacob's grasp to that mighty hawser of infinite strength which God has given in His blessed Word, and pulling up the sails of hope that the breeze of the Holy Spirit may fill them and carry his craft along. There is another thing about Jack I like. He is a man that has got a lot of uncommon sense. He knows how to do a thing, and when to do it. If he wants to get at one of his mates he goes at him very carefully, works alongside gently, and then with all speed he boards and takes captive the heart that he has longed to win for Jesus Christ."

And who that has ever been in a meeting of the "Christian Lifeboat Crew," in the fo'c'sle of Miss Child's "Welcome Home," London, could ever forget the sterling common-sense, or the fervid utterances of the Christian sailors?

To all and every one who would know, we unhesitatingly say, that *Christian* work among sailors pays an enormous percentage, spiritually; and it is *spiritual* results that are alone worth really caring for in the long run.

As an old Christian sailor, writing about Christian work among sailors, I could well fill a volume about the various Societies that are pulling a many-banked oar, in the Argosy of Grace, on behalf of our Jacks; but though I dare not stay longer on the subject, if any word of mine shall incite "men and wives at ease," to help our sailor *Christian* societies, by whatever name known, then the Christ, "who pressed a sailor's pillow, and consorted with fishermen for three years of His public life, will see to it that no single helper goes unrewarded."

I had been a year nearly on board the *Implacable*, and was shortly expecting to be drafted to a training brig, which, under a new Admiralty order, had been rigged for sea, with the idea of giving the boys a little taste of actual sea routine before their final drafting to some ship bound for a foreign station.

I had several pounds saved, and, in my mind, had arranged all the plan of my desertion.

Once or twice of late I had spent a night ashore, that I might have a turn at the theatre, and, at the same time, make the course clear to complete my plan for desertion—in this way. I needed to be known a little at some lodging-house, that I might have such a place to go to, to change my sailor clothes for my private suit, which I had arranged to purchase when all my plans were complete.

I chose a quiet little eating-house, at which to stay from time to time when I spent a night ashore, and now, when the last week came, I spent two nights following ashore, on the last night but one purchasing my suit of plain clothes, and leaving it locked up (by permission) in the bedroom, ready for use on the next night.

"The best laid schemes of mice an' men/ gang oft agley," the immortal Bobbie Burns has told us, and there are few among the sons of men who have not proved the truth of the line.

That *last* night came, and, never dreaming of failure, I made my way to the railway station, secured my ticket for London, then, keeping out of general sight until the last moment, I stepped across the platform, had my foot upon the step of the carriage, when I felt a heavy hand grip my shoulder, twist me round, and back upon the platform, just as the guard's shout of "Right away!" rang out, and the train moved slowly out of the station.

I did not know how my plan had become known until next morning; I only knew that I was a prisoner in the hands of a plain-clothes officer, who, to all the pretty little fictions to which I treated him, simply smiled and kept an amused silence.

Half an hour later I was locked up in a cell, puzzling over the whole affair, and feeling wretched enough to wish that I was dead.

Suddenly I remembered, that when I had been searched at the bar of the police-station, I had not noticed my lucky halfpenny.

My lucky halfpenny, as I called it, had a hole in it, and possessed certain other marks, supposed (so I had learnt on the London streets) to invest the copper coin with peculiarly lucky attributes. I had carried it with me always, in all my changing experiences, since the day when, under Tickle's tuition, I had imbibed the notions of its value.

In changing my clothes at the eating-house, I had left my lucky copper in my sailor trousers pocket, and now I declaimed loudly against myself for my folly, declaring that I could not have expected any luck in my desperate enterprise of that evening under such *un*lucky conditions.

Next morning I was haled before the magistrate, charged with desertion, and handed over to one of the ship's officials to be dealt with by naval authority.

During the hearing of my case I learned how my plan had failed. The servant girl of the house where I had changed my clothes, had grown suspicious over certain of my movements, and being a native of the place, and knowing that any tracing of a deserter to the house would mean trouble for her master, she had informed him of her suspicions, he had me followed to the railway station, and information given to the police there.

To this day I can remember the horror I felt when, before being marched down to Mutton Cove, on leaving the court-house, I heard the click, and felt the cold chill of the steel of the handcuffs on my wrists.

With a momentary humiliation I hung my head; then remembering how the speciousness of the statements of the bill, that had induced me to join, had deceived me, and feeling *morally* in the right, though it was decreed that I was legally in the wrong, I felt my spirits rise, and lifting my head, I walked as proudly as a conqueror, rather than as the conquered.

A few days later I received my sentence, of three months' imprisonment.

It was nearly the middle of October when I arrived before the great, sullen-looking gates of the prison, and passed in out of the bright autumn world without. The usual formularies were gone through : I was searched, stripped, my description accurately taken, then my hair was sheared close to my head, and the icy-cold bath had to be plunged into.

In the waters of that bath I was supposed to leave every vestige of my identity with my past—for three months, at least.

My very name became lost to me, and all my personality was sunk in the *number* allotted me—it was, *I think*, No. 98.

Chapter XIII

AN INFERNO

"WELL, young fellow, how long have you got?"
"Three months, sir."

"That's right to start with; be civil, and it will help you. But how came you to get three months? What was it for?"

"'Cos my luck's out."

The warder smiled as he looked at me, then said, musingly, "Well, that's a new idea. I've heard of all sorts of reasons for you fellows coming to prison, but I never heard before that luck was like a hawser that ran out so far, and then failed its owner. But what did you do to bring yourself here?"

"Slung my hook from the *'Placable*, sir."

"Oh, I see, desertion!" Now, the warder probably did know all this, or at least he could easily have found out from the prisoner's charge sheet, but he was a decent fellow as warders go, so he talked with me to find out whether I was sulky, or lying; whether I was a character, or just the ordinary type of boys of my class.

Upon the floor of the cell lay a pile of old, well-seasoned tarred rope, which was to be picked into oakum, so fine, that, when held aloft and shaken, it would readily fall almost hair by hair. Addressing me, and glancing at the number on my left breast, he said, " Well, Number 98, have you ever picked oakum before ? "

" No, sir."

" Well, I'll give you a lesson, as the amount of food you get will depend largely upon how much oakum you pick."

Then, sitting down upon the three-legged stool, he took up a bunch of the yarns, first rubbing them together to loosen and soften them, then alternately beating the two ends of the bunch upon the stone floor. Then, taking from the side of the bundle a round ring of rope, into which, securely spliced, was a square-edged hook, he said, " Now see, you slip this ' fiddle ' over your leg, just above your knee, and take one strand of the yarn at a time, drawing it backwards and forwards through the hook so" (suiting the action to the word) ; "then, when it is so far frayed out, you pick it apart—so."

I watched the operation, and soon settled down to do my best, though the four-pound heap looked immense, especially when separated into single yarns.

I was thankful for the help given me, and presently alone plodded on with the strange new work, saying to myself, " Now then, here goes to conquer difficulty number one, for if my meals depend upon my work, —and prison fare is none too bumping at the best,— I must either work or starve."

Altogether, these long, cold, weary days and nights were not the most unprofitable to me, for at the night school I began to develop something like a real taste for reading. When alone in my cell, I began to read the Bible (the only book the chill apartment contained). I read it through from Genesis to Revelation, though, naturally, I failed to understand very much of it.

The New Testament (the Gospels, at least) fascinated me, and many things heard in earlier days recurred to me with more or less power.

Once again I stood in Pegleg Entry, and heard little Tickle's voice singing—

> "With His precious blood He bought us ;
> In the wilderness He sought us ;
> To His fold He safely brought us—
> Oh, how He loves !"

Then I seemed to hear my little friend reciting again the story of that meeting with little Katie, the whole thing jerked out by Tickle as he was carried on my shoulders on that sad, but memorable night.

That hospital death-scene rose up clear and distinct before me, with the rapture of that dying boy, and that strange, semi-divine sense that saw things within the veil.

Then there was that later experience of the meeting in the railway station, and to my dim, untutored, religious perceptions, there appeared an unbroken connection between all these things. And now, as I read again the words of Christ, and the story of His sacrifice for sin, a great longing came surging up in my heart, that the joy of conscious acceptance with God might be mine.

I could not have put it in that way ; I should only have scratched my head, and said, " Well, all I know is, I want something that I haven't got."

One day I felt this desire so strong upon me that I determined to consult the chaplain. Pulling the lever that communicated with a square plate outside my cell, and which then immediately sprang out, remaining fixed till replaced from outside, I was answered by a warder: "Well, Number 98, what do you want?"

"I wants to see the chaplain, please, sir."

"I hope you are not coming the pious dodge, because it don't go down very well here, and specially with such a parson as ours is."

In a weary voice (for this intelligence from the warder had somehow damped my ardour), I replied, "Well, I want to git right inside, for blest if I ain't all somehow now."

When, later on, I had an interview with the chaplain, that official, in a hard, steely voice, and an icy manner, inquired, "What do you want with me?"

Did it never enter the head of this "hireling" that those under his care might want something of the Master—the Saviour he professed to serve? Perhaps not, but that was what I really wanted. I wanted to "see Jesus!"

But the chaplain waits for an answer to his question, "What do you want with me?"

I tried to explain, but cleverer, better-educated persons than I was, have found this a difficulty. To tell out soul needs, in human language, is not always easy. But at last, hurt at the impatient tone and off-hand style of the chaplain, I blurted out, "I wants to git converted, please, and I don't know how."

With real astonishment the cleric looked at me and said, "Converted? What do you mean? Where have you heard about such nonsense?"

I rapidly told what I did know; some of the things I had thought, and, above all, the words I had read again and again, "'Except ye be converted and become as little children, ye shall in no wise enter the kingdom of heaven '; and I'm bound to get there if I can, sir, 'cos I promised a friend I would, and——"

I was interrupted by the chaplain, who said, in his iciest tones, "Well, 98, I shall make a note of your number, and if I find you attempting to give trouble and take up other officials' time as you have mine, I'll report you to the governor, and get you three days' dark cells."

" Report me to the governor ? " My eyes were wide open with astonishment as I repeated this threat of the chaplain's ; then tears stood in my eyes as I said, " Please, sir, I ain't a-gammoning, I'm in dead earnest ; and I can't sleep o' nights fur thinking about it. Won't yer tell me what I ought to do ? "

Was the chaplain ashamed of himself? We cannot say, but his next words were in a little milder key, as he said hastily, evidently wishing to close the interview, " Well, well, be as good as you can, boy ; I will give you a card of prayers for morning and night, which you'd better say. I wouldn't read too much of the Bible, because you will not understand it, and it will only upset your mind. Then, when you have finished your time, behave yourself, get confirmed, and keep to the sacraments, and—and—then—— Warder ! take this boy back to his cell."

Was that to end it? Was my quest worth no more than that? Was there no way for a boy in prison to get what Jesus promised—Rest? Pity me ! I gave way to natural disappointment when I was back in my cell, and laid my head upon the table to think or weep. At least, I would have laid my head on the table, only it came in contact with the thick Bible that lay there.

Somehow it seemed to me that that Book had something to do with my present sorrow and disappointment, and in a momentary fit of rage, I picked up the Bible and hurled it violently across the cell. It struck the door just as one of the warders was passing.

The man was one of a type *sometimes* found among prison officials, who are ever striving to get cases for report. Opening the door rapidly, he stepped inside, and seeing the Book lying where it had fallen, he turned to me, saying,—

"Well, Number 98, what do you mean by such abominable conduct as this, throwing your Bible about, eh? I shall report you to the governor to-morrow."

The door closed with its harsh, loud clang, and the bolts of the heavy lock fell to, with their hideous thud, thud, and I was alone again. I sprang from my seat and cursed my fate, and registered a fresh vow to desert again as soon as I was freed from the prison and back in my ship.

The governor awarded me three days' *dark* cells for my crime.

How easy for the official lip to pronounce the sentence "*Dark* cells"! How easy for the poor prisoner, at this date, to write the words! But who can describe the horror of the experience!

It is not lying on the bare, hard boards with no covering; or the mere morsel of bread, with the jug of icy-cold water; or the solitariness of the confinement; or the rebukes of conscience—no, none of these things make the three days' dark cells like three days of hell upon earth. No! The horror is the *darkness*!

We write and speak of "a darkness that can be

felt," " a palpable darkness " ; but the mere reading of terms of speech will never convey to the soul what the endurance of utter, blank darkness means to the man or woman who has to suffer it.

The shock of the first moment! The deepening horror of the succeeding moments, when minutes are millenniums, when the blackness presses its evil fingers against your starting eye-balls, until they feel like circling currents of liquid flame, and when the brain reels and rocks, the soul sees hideous shapes, the fingers clutch at nameless horrors which you cannot see, but which seem to press upon you from every quarter of the black apartment.

Food you loathe, water you shun, because to reach either you must grope about amid the unseen shapes that press upon you.

Then there comes a time—whether you have been confined an hour, a day, a month, a year, or even a decade, you have no power of gauging—when your silent horror slowly changes. Every nerve in your body twitches like a living thing; every nerve in your brain becomes a writhing, quivering, fiery wire. Your throat grows dry and hard ; your tongue is dried up like leather exposed to a tropical sun ; you sway and reel like a drunken man, you lie down, lest you should fall, but the violent agony increases, until you beat the stone walls and floor with your fists, and you shout and yell with the ever-present, ever-pressing horror. You are mad, temporarily mad, for this is the *delirium tremens* of the punishment of black, hell-like darkness.

By-and-by sleep comes ! Blessed restorer of nerve and brain ! You wake, your whole body aches with the effects of your late violence. Your hands are stiff

with the dried blood from their wounds, and from the
bruises and partial dislocation of the joints, consequent
upon your beating the stone walls with your fists
during the most violent paroxysm of your delirium.

Time's wheels move round, but you hear no sound
of the great machine, no click of wheel, or whirr of
winding up, and see no tell-tale hand to show how
the hours drag on—they never *fly* to a man in dark
cells.

After ages (apparently) have gone by, and sleep
has come more than once, and food—dry bread and
water—has been taken, your door is opened. The
light in the corridor outside is a dim light, but it is
more than your eyes can stand at first, and a large
spasm of pain leaps from two points in your brain.

You close your eyes quickly, but not before you
have seen a huge, shadowy form looming in the up-
right, oblong square of light formed by the open door.
You know it is a man, a warder, but the vision strikes
upon your consciousness with a similar impression to
that received when you see, through a mountain mist,
the highly-magnified, blurred form of some other
tourist whom you are approaching.

Upon your ears the voice of the warder sounds,
saying, "Time's up, Number 98! Come on ; let's have
you out of this !"

You open your eyes again. The throb of pain this
time is not so acute. You make your way towards
the light, the man, the corridor,—towards release from
the stone hell you have lived in for three days and
three nights.

As you move, it strikes you that the human voice
—even a prison warder's—is the sweetest music you
have ever heard. You follow your warder; he leads

you to your cell. There is your oakum, your stool, all as you left it ; but now, in the light of your release from the late horror, how changed it all looks !

The door closes behind you, you are alone in your cell. That cell which seemed an inferno three days ago strikes you as being a nook in an Eden. You lift your eyes to where the barred stone glass window pierces the wall of your cell, and though you hated that impenetrable stone glass three days ago you give thanks for it now.

With a gesture, that is an unconscious act of praise, you stretch your arms upwards, and turn your open palms to the lovely light, while you involuntarily murmur, "Oh, how beautiful ! "

Then tears come—gracious, relieving, healing tears —and with your face buried in your hands, you sob like a whipped child. When the tempest has passed, and you uncover your face, your eye lights upon your copper wash basin in the corner of your cell, and you remember you have had no wash for three days. You fill your basin with water, and though, perhaps, there is a rule somewhere against such a proceeding, you strip yourself, and seizing your little square of coarse washing flannel you proceed to wash and bathe your whole body. Then, before you dress, you shake out the dust of the dark cell from your clothes, and five minutes afterwards, with body all in a glow, you sit down on your stool, slip the rope fiddle over your leg, snatch up a handful of yarns, and begin oakum picking with a zest, and a real pleasure, which is born of the horrors of the utter inactivity of the last three full days and nights.

Somehow, prison life never seemed quite so hard to bear after that awful dark cell experience.

It was a long time though, after that, before I would touch a Bible again; for something akin to hatred of all thought of religion sprang up within my soul, the result of my late experience with the chaplain, leading up, as it had done, to that awful punishment of darkness.

Chapter XIV

OF MANY DAYS

"CLEAR away! stand aside!" cried the rough voice of a seaman, who carried in his hand a large, bright yellow flag, which he waved continually. He walked at a slow, not much more than funeral pace, glancing every now and then over his shoulder at a little party that followed him.

The party consisted of a junior surgeon in charge of a patient who was being conveyed to the Naval Hospital, Plymouth. The bearers were twelve in number, so as to form relays ; the patient was being borne on the shoulders of the men in a swing canvas cot.

The waving of the yellow flag proclaimed that the disease was infectious, and passers-by hurriedly walked down side streets, or slipped into shops, to avoid any risk.

Once only during that journey did the poor patient appear conscious, then he relapsed into unconsciousness once more, but in due time was safely housed in the small-pox ward of Plymouth Naval Hospital. He had the disease very badly, and, as the days rolled round, nurses and doctors looked grave and shook their heads. "The fellow must have had it on him so long before he gave up, and then caught a cold

upon it while in his weak state." This was the
verdict of the senior doctor, and it was true.

I had been out of prison about ten days, but for
the last three or four had felt very ill. I shrank,
however, from seeking the sick-bay and the doctor's
advice and help, and kept about. At last, as I sat on
the end of the mess-stool one evening, in a half-doze,
and feeling that strange sense of life all around, yet
as if I had no life, when every sound had a peculiar
effect, and rushing noises as of many falling waters
rushed through my brain, I suddenly found myself
hurled off the seat, and sprawling on the deck.

Two of the boys had quarrelled and commenced
to fight ; a terrific blow aimed at one of the boys by
his antagonist was only avoided by his cleverly slip-
ping aside ; but the blow was not really lost, for my
poor face caught its full force, and I was felled to
the ground. I lay quite insensible, was carried to
the sick-bay and attended by the surgeon, who
speedily discovered that I had the small-pox.

When the crisis had passed I was blind, and for
nineteen days saw nothing. When I say that I saw
nothing, I mean no object, though a faint sense of
light was present with me. I think my doctors and
nurse thought that the effects of the disease might
mean future total blindness, though they did not tell
me this at the time.

But on the twentieth day my sight returned suddenly, largely, I believe, through the shock of a
terrific explosion that occurred in or near the town,
and which shook the hospital ward, in which I was
lying, as though an earthquake were abroad.

" I can see, nurse ! " I cried, and in a moment she
was at my side bandaging my eyes, fearing, as she

explained, that the sudden strength of full daylight might injure them.

Thank God, no ill-effects followed, and I recovered my sight fully ; in fact, in after days at sea I became noted for keen sight, and I shrink from saying here from how far off I could read a ship's name on her stern, at sea, with the naked eye, or tell the time by a clock ashore, when we have been coasting. One of my officers once tested this power of my sight with the splendid ship's glass we carried, and through which he spied at the face of a church clock at Folkestone (I think it was) when he had overheard me tell a shipmate the time, which, through the clear air, at four o'clock on a summer's morning, I had easily read with my naked eye, as we jogged slowly by that south coast town in a revenue cutter.

After nearly three months' sojourn in the great Naval Hospital (for my convalescence was very slow), I returned to my ship, much to the surprise of all my shipmates, a report having, somehow, got abroad that I had died in the hospital.

I ought, to the honour of my nurse, to say here, that in spite of the virulence of the attack of small-pox from which I had suffered, I came out almost literally unmarked by the fell disease. I was the only patient in that long ward of fully twenty beds, and more unremitting attention it would be impossible to conceive than that which I received from the noble-souled young Welsh nurse who chiefly attended me. By an incessant use of chilled oil, upon my face and neck, during the irritation stage of the disease, I escaped all disfigurement ; the only marks I retained being one or two in the forehead, incurred through a momentary failure of patience upon my part.

The one great purpose of my heart was still to get clear of the navy, and when I returned to my ship I kept that purpose ever before me.

For two or three days after my return to the ship I was supposed to have but the lightest of duty, and, wandering about the ship, still feeling very little like work, I came to that part of the deck where the carpenter's benches were, and where the carpenter's crew worked. As I watched one of the men I put my hand out to steady a piece of work he was engaged upon, and like a flash it came into my mind, "Why don't you try to learn some such trade as this? it would help you in your proposed desertion!"

I hung about those benches all day, and made myself useful. I steadied a plank when it was being sawn, or when its edge was being planed; I heated the glue-pot, straightened copper nails, flattened copper rivets, and a score of other things.

Just before eight bells (four o'clock in the afternoon), when the ship's carpenter-in-charge—who was not a *working* hand but a warrant officer in blue cloth and gilt buttons—came upon the scene to see that the deck was properly cleared, I ventured to address him, and to ask him if he could not get me taken on as a boy at the bench. I explained that I had just come out of hospital, and that I had a desire to learn the trade.

The chief petty officer carpenter, hearing my appeal, backed it up, by saying I had made myself very useful all day, and that he believed I had some *gumption* (fearful and wonderful is that undefinable word).

The result of my appeal was, that in three days'

time I donned a white duck working suit, and began a new bit of experience as " carpenter's boy."

For sixteen months I worked hard to pick up all I could of the trade, then once more I made a dash for my liberty.

I need not detail again all the consequences of this second attempt at desertion. I was caught before I actually had made a fair start, and received sentence of another term of imprisonment—six weeks this time.

I had nearly completed this second term when H.M.S. —— was commissioned to sail for the East India Station, and, two days before the expiration of my six weeks, I was suddenly summoned from my cell, and despatched to the above vessel, which was waiting in Plymouth Sound, ready for her final orders to start.

Under the charge of a marine sentry, I was kept a close prisoner on the lower deck, while the bustle and confusion of taking aboard the last of everything, —letters, telegrams, stores, officers, etc.,—was proceeding on deck.

At length,—unseen by me, of course, because I was on the lower deck,—the " Farewell " bunting flew out from the ship's mizen, and at the same time the ssh, thud, ssh, thud, of the engines hissed and throbbed through every part of the ship, telling that we were under way.

When that first engine throb sounded, my marine warder turned to me, saying, " You are no longer a prisoner ; you can go for'ard now. Your mess, the master-at-arms said, would be number 19."

I was still dressed in the suit of shore clothes I had purchased for my second desertion (my first suit had been confiscated), and wondering how I should fare at sea, I went forward, found no one in the mess, and passed up the fore-ladder to the upper deck, to look my last on England for many a long year.

That same evening a pile of cloth, serge, duck, drill, flannel, dungaree, worsted, thread, buttons, tape, etc., etc., were served out to me, and I was informed that I must make the various stuffs into a certain number of garments, according to the regulation naval pattern.

This was all new to me, as I had hitherto had all my clothing served out to me ready-made, not *given* to me (for *grace* was an unknown word in the economy of the navy in *those* days, whatever it may be in *these*), but charged to me at the most extravagant, outside price, after the fashion of the Service then.

With the help of an old sailor I soon learned to make my clothes; and though my "back-stitching," with which much of the work was finished off, was at first very coarse, and none too regular, yet this defect was quickly remedied as the months went on and I had more practice. By the end of my first eighteen months in a sea-going vessel, my sewing was as neat and finished as that of almost any one aboard.

For a week, nearly, after leaving Plymouth, I suffered intensely from sea-sickness, a malady which I never got over, and which laid the foundation for the years of weakness and prostration which have been my continual lot since the year 1886 or 7.

The question has frequently been asked me, "Are there sailors, then, who never get over that awful *mal de mer?*" to which I reply, I have known quite a dozen who have been martyrs to the sea-scourge, by which I mean that they not only felt bad and ill on every new turn out of port (for hundreds of sailors are affected in *that* way), but that the specially afflicted ones *are never free, while at sea*, from acute nausea, headache, giddiness, etc. I once sailed with a clever ship's joiner, named Peddie, who had been twenty years at sea, and who, like myself, was always in a state of semi-prostration from the cruel sea-grip.

The weather when we left England, early in January, was bitterly cold, and we beat down Channel in the teeth of a snowstorm ; but almost as soon as I had recovered sufficiently from my first bout of sea-sickness, we were dropping anchor off Madeira, and were basking in the delights of semi-tropical weather.

Just as we anchored, an American man-of-war steamed out, with homeward-bound pennant flying forty feet away from her lofty masthead, and her band playing " Home, sweet Home," while a lump was climbing into the throats of nearly three hundred souls on board our vessel.

For whatever manner of man he may be who is leaving home, as we all were, for foreign service for several years, there is a sense of lonely, desolate home-sickness, that creeps over him when he sees a ship *homeward*-bound to that tune that melts all hearts, " Home, sweet Home ! "

What a crew we were, taken all in all ! What a study of character we should have made ! What varied types of face and expression we exhibited ! What dialects, what brogue marked our speech !

There was the irrepressible, " unspeakable " cockney, with his sharp ways, his " nippy " tongue, his everlasting wink, which either exasperated or amused, according to the mood and the character of the witnesses of it. The cockney sailor of that day invariably talked in the strange, uncouth-sounding back slang of London, which was a foreign tongue to his more solid west-country shipmate, who, with an intense love for his native Devon or Cornwall, and strong predilection for " pasty," made so great a contrast to his cockney mate.

Side by side with these two distinct types of men were other two—the sturdy, independent Yorkshire and Lancashire men, with their rugged, burred dialect, their shrewd common-sense, and—more often than not—their clogs, packed away in their bags, and two shapely feet at the end of their legs, that would wag those clogs through bewildering steps, to tunes that made every listening nerve in the hearer's bodies a marionette.

We had a few impulsive, warm-hearted Irishmen, who were always in the black list because of their love of " cook-days " (*i.e.*, extra grog), but who would give away their last dollar, or rupee, to help a chum. A few canny Scots, keen, cautious, sinewy-framed men, were among us, together with a small sprinkling of others from the various counties in England.

If the crew was varied in its composition, so was the staff of officers. Some of the oldest and most aristocratic families of Great Britain were represented, though these were often among the poorest officers as far as finances were concerned. Then there were the sons of rich plebeians ; others whose fathers had been, or were even then, naval officers, and in whose veins ran the brine-flavoured blood of centuries of naval heroes.

But whoever, whatever we were, officer or flatfoot,

we were all glad to look upon the town, Funchal, before which we had anchored.

As we stood looking at the land, with the strains of that American's band just reaching our ears as she steamed gaily away, I caught the sound of a stifled sob, and looking from whence it came, saw a small boy, the smallest in the ship, standing close by me.

He was very fair, almost as a girl, with a smooth skin, a round, childish face, deep blue eyes, and light curly hair. There was a look in those blue, tear-laden eyes such as one sometimes sees in the eyes of a starved, beaten, homeless dog, and it called out all my deepest sympathy.

There was a moment's pause in our work, and guessing something of what the little fellow was feeling (he reminded me very much of Tickle), I began to sympathise with him, and to try to give him some cheer.

In a few brief words, broken by more than one little sob, he told me his story, and my heart ached for him, and I longed to be able to comfort him.

My words of sympathy were suddenly cut short by a stunning blow, as two huge, tar-stained hands banged my head and the head of the little fellow sharply together, while the harsh voice of a bull-necked seaman bid us clap on a rope, the end of which he thrust into our hands.

He had a low, sensual, brutal face, filled, as he looked at us, with a look of mixed scorn, hatred, and contempt.

A moment later, speaking to another sailor, who stood holding on to the stopper of a rope, he said, pointing over his shoulder to us,—

" That's the miserable muck that jines the sarvice

now, a parsel of baby-faced, mother-sick, snivelling
little brutes that ain't fit to fetch a ha'porth o' milk
for a sea-sick cat, let alone run a ratline, or fight
for their Queen and country. Bah, I ain't got
patience with 'em ; an' ef that young 'un comes foul
o' me at all, he'll find my flipper round his lugs,
smart, or my name ain't——"

A pitying smile came over the face of his companion—pity, doubtless, for the poor, mean-spirited
man, as well as for the home-sick boy, as, looking
him straight in the face, he said,—

"Well, Joe, I don't think we must blame the
young 'un too much. I guess I'm about as smart
a seaman as any one aboard this old tub, though I
do say it myself, and yet I remember I was a sight
worse than that blue-eyed little chap there. Yer
see, we ain't all made inside jist alike, and we ain't
all had the same sort o' homes, and friends ; and I
remember how I cried and snivelled for a good
month when I first sailed in the *Gorgon*."

"More fool you," growled the other.

"That's what lots of chaps said," continued Charley's advocate. "And I mind me well how the
captain of my top got hold of me at the end of
that first month, and jawed away at me just about.
Ses he, 'Why, yer stoopid young monkey, does yer
ever want to see yer blessed mammy any more ?
'Cos ef yer does, wot's the good of crying yer eyes
out ; why, ye'll be as blind as a booby, and then yer
wouldn't be able to tell yer own mother from a
cat's-meat man ; there, go along with yer, and let
yer mother see she's got a man for a son.'

"Well, I'll tell yer what it is, Joe, that sort of
put me on my mettle, and I cocked up my chin as

pert as a recruit with his first leather stock; and when I met my old ship again in the *Cossack*, last commission, he was bo'sun then, he sort o' opened his peepers a bit.

"One day he says to me, 'I say, Harry, you've picked up a bit since the day when I hitched on my jawing tackle to you.' And I says, 'Yes, bo'sun; but look here, don't never yer be too hard on a youngster as is home-sick. Just try and think wot yer own feelings would be, if, after yer'd joined the service, thinking all the while it were just the very best and jolliest thing a boy could do, yer sort o' woke up to find yer taken a header out of the warm bed, so to speak, of your home and friends, and plunged right into a cold bath on a winter's day. Instead of yer mother's kind handling, yer was like an organ-grinder's monkey, got more kicks than ha'pence. Lots of people all round yer, yet all strangers, everybody looking after No. 1, and spite of the crowd yer felt *alone*. And sich loneliness is summat awful. Then that ain't all, for a week or more, as the books put it, yer's 'writhing in the bitterest throes of sea-sickness,' till, like a dying dolphin, ye've turned all the colours of the rainbow. Why, ef a fellow only had a little finger ache at home, his mother nursed him as ef he'd a fever; and all the while a youngster is sea-sick, he's kicked and cuffed about like a college football. He feels starved, but he can't go the fat pork and salt horse and bone-dust biscuit.

"I tell yer what it is, I never sees one o' them bills with, 'WANTED, BOYS FOR THE ROYAL NAVY,' without feeling I'd like to tack a little bit of my experience on at the end of it, summat like this,—

"'Oh, yes! oh, yes! oh, yes! This is to give notice, that I've been in the Navy more years than I have fingers, and I knows the truth of wot I'm writing, and the printer as printed this bill don't. I'm writing 'Gospel truth,' and I want to say to you, boys of England, ' Look before you leap,' or you'll make a mistake, and jump out of the frying-pan into the fire. If ye're sea-bewitched, jist remember it ain't all gold lace and prize-money ; there's short commons, and cat-o'-nine tails. If yer don't like having a little discipline at home, how'll yer stand the cast-iron, aggravating, tantalising, tormenting discipline of man-o'-war life ? If yer will take an old sailor's advice about joining the Navy, well, here it is— *DON'T.'*"

I give this little conversation as nearly as I can recall it, as it contains some truths, which, even if I could have *written* them a little more elegantly, they could not have been more clearly stated.

My nearly fifty years' experience of life has taught me that there are three kinds of sickness for which, as a rule, there is little or no pity given—love-sickness, home-sickness, and sea-sickness.

The friendship begun that day with my little blue-eyed shipmate, was destined to be a very close and pleasant one.

But while I have been writing these details, the ropes have been coiled down in the ship, and we, the crew, have freedom to look about us without fear of having our heads banged together, after the fashion that little Charley and I had so recently experienced.

The ship's side (the *port* side) was by this time thronged with bum-boats from the shore, laden with fruit, etc., for sale.

I wished I had some money, but I was penniless. I saw my shipmates stagger up the side-ladder, with arms laden with bananas, oranges, shaddock, etc., and I turned away at last, sick with a longing which I could not fulfil.

As I turned away I heard an old sailor say to a young marine, "Old clothes is the things these fellers likes to get 'old of; an' if yer've got a old suit o' clothes yer can make a big deal."

My heart bounded at this news. I hurried below, routed out the suit of shore clothes I had worn on board, and did indeed make a good deal, for besides returning with a pile of varied fruits, I had some silver in my pocket.

What a striking book of illustrations of Bible truths might be compiled from experiences gathered in a cruise round the world, or after a life-time spent at sea! Should time permit I may some day attempt such a volume, meanwhile what a wonderful illustration of a great Bible truth did my " lucky deal " at Madeira provide.

I gave old clothes for silver, bread, and fruit. And God is ever seeking to make man understand how He will give for man's filthy rags of self-constituted righteousness the silver of His Redemption, the Bread of Life in Christ, the gracious fruit of the Spirit—" love, joy, peace," and all the other attendant graces.

The language of Jesus Himself was, that He had been especially anointed to preach good tidings to the meek ; to bind up the broken-hearted, to proclaim liberty to the captive, and the opening of the prison to them that are bound. To give to the mourner, beauty instead of ashes, oil of joy instead of mourning, a garment of praise instead of a spirit of heaviness—in fact, all God's exchanges are of this character.

I went down that ship's side with my suit of old clothes, I came back rich in silver, bread, and fruit. I went, years after, to God, clothed in the filthy rags of my own miserable efforts, to find peace and pardon ; and He stripped me, bathed me in the pure and precious blood ; clothed me with the garments of salvation ; filled my hands with the coin of the heavenly realm,—coin that is not affected by the currency of the world, and which is international, and cosmopolitan in its character—and loaded my life with benefits, renewed every morning and repeated every evening, *so that they are always fresh* ; taught me that the gold of His land was good, and that its treasures were all open to me, to use, to trade with, for Him. He put a new song into my mouth, even praise to our God, so that come weal or woe, health or sickness, joy or sorrow, I can go on my way, singing :—

> " His goodness stands approved,
> Unchanged from day to day ;
> I'll drop my burdens at His feet,
> And bear a song away."

Blessed exchange, of which my Madeira deal was but a very faint illustration.

Chapter XV

SIERRA LEONE

FROM this point in my story, I cannot bind my-self to follow events chronologically, since to do that would mean that I should have to inflict upon the reader much that could hardly be expected to interest.

Neither will space permit me to include a host of striking situations which came into my life, with adventures in connection with every vessel I served in, all of which might well form the basis (many of them have already served this purpose) of stories of adventure, etc.

Readers of " Wops, the Waif," will necessarily find some things here that they found there, but to attempt anything on arbitrary lines of adherence to the above story, would mean that I should have to include, in this auto-biography, much that was not actually personal, to the swelling of my volumes to an undue size and length. These explanations have now so far become a necessity, that readers of this volume who have also been readers of the " Wops " series, may not misunderstand the present arrange-ment.

*   *   *   *   *

It was, I think, while we lay at Madeira, that I made a startling discovery, viz., that my old friend the doctor, who had befriended me in London, was one of the medical men of this ship.

At first I thought that my eyes must have deceived me, for he was very much altered. The years since I had last seen him had streaked his black hair with grey, and though there was a tender graciousness in his look, his face was much aged.

At the earliest possible opportunity I sought him out. He was as much amazed at seeing me as I had been at seeing him.

Not all at once did I learn the full cup of suffering that had led him to secure an appointment in the navy. Briefly, the story ran thus.

Just after my disappearance from the " Home for Working Lads " he was to have been married. The morning had arrived, the bride was descending the stairs from her dressing-room, when she fell, in some way, inflicting such injuries upon herself that she died in a very short time.

No wonder the doctor's face had aged, his hair become streaked with grey, or that he had, chiefly, spent the past few years away from the land that was so fraught with sad associations.

I did not understand the chastened character of the doctor in those old days, when I met him again in the ship ; but in the light of salvation since received by myself, and in the light of the experience of other souls chastened of God, I can now understand how his sorrows were, at the time I served in that ship, mellowing him, fitting him for his translation to Christ.

I am sure none of his brother officers understood him ; sometimes I have thought, from things which have recurred to me, in a half hazy fashion, that they *barely tolerated* him. Doubtless his witness for his Master was too definite for their toleration, for certainly he did live a Christ-like life—I know it *now*.

There is a verse of that wondrous 53rd Isaiah (the eighth) which for years after my conversion puzzled me exceedingly, and I could find no Christian, or minister, who could give me any light upon the part which puzzled me—"He was taken from prison and from judgment: *and who shall declare His generation ? for He was cut off* out of the land of the living."

Then one day I met with a well-known Jew, who for many years has held a honoured place at the head of a great Christian institution. To him I said, "What does it mean ? Who shall *declare His genera-tion ?* for He was *cut off——*"

My friend's reply was, "In olden days, under the Jewish law, it came to be the custom, that every *con-demned* man should receive *forty* days' grace before his execution, during which period an official, some-what of the character of our old-time 'crier,' passed to and fro through the town, city, or neighbourhood, and 'cried' the offence and sentence of the man, to-gether with his *tribe*, his *family*, *the branch of his family*, etc., and announcing that any of his *generation* (his family or tribe) who could adduce evidence of innocence, could appeal before the forty days for a new trial."

But Jesus had no forty days' grace ; no one de-clared His generation, or gave opportunity for a new trial ; but *He* was taken from judgment straight to death ; *He* was cut off, and now the question, "Who shall declare His generation ?" remains in God's word, unanswered. Unanswered, except where, and when His own redeemed ones live the life of that Christian doctor, and boldly, definitely witness to the *real* generation of our Christ—"that *He* is the Son of the living God; the promised sacrifice for sin; that He was made sin, was made a curse for us; that He redeemed us with His blood; that He hath made us kings and priests unto God; doth keep us by His power; and is coming again, in the air, to receive us unto Himself; and will present us faultless before His Father's throne, with exceeding joy."

This is the *declaration* of Jesus, which is to be in our lips, and in our lives. This surely is to be our answer to the unanswered question in the eighth verse of Isaiah liii.

My doctor, doubtless, declared his Lord's generation in this fashion, and therefore became unpopular.

As I do not propose, for reasons already stated, to follow each event chronologically, it might be well to briefly tell the story of the doctor's exit from our ship while I am writing of him, lest I should forget it.

One morning he did not appear at breakfast, and his absence being noted, some little chaff and banter went on among the officers in the ward-room. Some one suggested that a rap or two upon the "Tabernacle" door (they had nicknamed his cabin the Tabernacle) might be advisable.

The steward was sent to perform the summons; he returned, saying that he could get no response. One of the officers went himself, and getting no reply, he hauled back the door in its slide, and there, upon his knees, he saw the doctor.

A strange feeling of awe came over the officer; he spoke, but, receiving no answer, he bent over the kneeling figure and looked at that drooping face.

He touched his hand; it was cold. Then he knew that he was in the presence of death.

Lying on the bed before the dead man was the open Bible, and the portrait of a beautiful girl. While pleading with God for his fellows, doubtless, "he was not, for the Lord took him."

With a grave face, and a reverent step, the officer left the cabin, closing the door quietly behind him, and once more entered the ward-room. He was immediately greeted by the wit of the party with, "Well, did you find the saint at prayer?"

"No, gentlemen!"

What was it in the tone and manner that struck all present? They could hardly tell! Yet all looked fixedly at the officer as he replied gravely, with a tremor in his voice, "No, gentlemen, the doctor has done with prayer. He is dead!"

"Dead!"

The men who, five minutes before, sneered and jested at "the saint," trembled, shuddered, now. The power of that consecrated life had been felt by them, though ignored, and while shocked and saddened, they were likewise ashamed.

The news soon passed from stem to stern of the ship, and there was but one feeling, one expression— that of loving regret.

As for myself, I was crushed and saddened beyond all expression, and felt reckless enough to do any mad thing, now that I had lost this friend, who had always been so kind, and so eager for my salvation.

*   *   *   *   *

To return to my own personal story. Madeira left behind, our next halting-place was Sierra Leone, a wondrously tropical-looking place in those days.

The moment our anchor was down what a scene ensued!   Scores of canoes surrounded the vessel, laden with bananas, mangoes, plantains, limes, yams, sweet potatoes, joggery, and all sorts of strange things —at least, strange to the eyes of most of the crew. Then there were the native washerwomen, all clamouring for precedence for the washing of the different messes; the boat with the doctor from the shore; and a white face or two from the " mission "; a boat with a messenger, laden with mail bags ; and last, but not least, a long canoe, paddled by twelve semi-naked blacks, with an intelligent-looking Krooman seated in the stern, who, with a paddle, steered the boat.

This man, in accordance with west-coast custom, came to arrange for the shipping of his band of Kroomen, who would be taken on board to do the hot, dirty work of the ship while she was in the tropics.   After a brief interview with the captain, it was decided that his men should be shipped, and come on board next day.

The day following the vessel's arrival at Sierra Leone, Johnson Macauley, as the head Krooman had been christened on his first entrance into Her Majesty's Service, and who was very proud of his name, arrived on board with his twelve hands.   They formed a striking picture ; their suits of naval white duck, bleached in that tropical sun, contrasting so vividly with their almost jet-black faces, which were in most cases horribly disfigured with brandings and tattoo marks, the remnants of heathen or slave days.

As they came over the ship's side, they were told to fall in for inspection on the quarter deck, the crew of the vessel meanwhile gathering in a body just before the main-mast, interested and amused spectators.

After a few words between Macauley and the captain, the former stepped briskly out towards his men, and shouted, " 'Tention, Kroomen!   Answer to you's names.

" Tom Snowflake."

" Yah, sir."

" Jim Banyan."

" Yah, sir."

" Jack Toby, Ike Handy, Noah Snowball, Tom Shark, Joe Chickens, Phil Softly, Charl Flatfoot, Abel Surley, Bill Surprise, Alexander Cooper."

All these, interspersed with the ready " Yah, sir," as each name was called, caused fresh amusement to officers and crew ; the oddness of the names being accounted for only by the humour of those who, years before, had dubbed them so on their first entrance into that service.

Each of the Kroomen had several bundles made up in large, gaudily-coloured handkerchiefs, which are, in themselves, quite a speciality in the African trade.

The one man who possessed a chest was of enormous stature, and had a frame equally well proportioned.   He was a cooper by trade, and had been shipped as such, and was known as Alexander Cooper.

He was a remarkable character, had been a convert to Christianity for many years, had seen some surprising adventures, and was a source of never-ending delight to those privileged to listen to his stories, told in that strange, broken English which always seemed to lend piquancy to the story told.

I remember how, having lost sight of this man for

a year or two, I met him again on another vessel, and, on renewing acquaintance, I heard, among other things relative to the interim, that he had been to England.

Anxious to know his impressions of " the great white land," I got him to talk about it. Suddenly, during his recital, his face grew quite grave, as he said, " Sar, I see him snow in Hinkerlan'!"

" Saw snow, did you, Alec?" I replied. " Well, what did you think of snow, eh?"

" All my peoples axe me dat ar," he said, " an' I try to tell 'em what snow am, what him like. But him no easy to tell, sar, 'cept dat I say, ' You want em know what like snow am? Well, den, look, *snow am rain goned fast asleep.*'"

There was a quaint poetry about this description that has always struck me as being exceedingly pretty, and characteristic of the native African mode of thought and expression.

I may find room for some of the cooper's stories on the horrors of the slave trade, when, later on, I have to deal with my own share in the chasing of the slavers.

One of the most amusing memories I have of my first visit to Sierra Leone, concerns the wonderful black washerwomen who thronged our decks, seeking laundry work. For, though Jack can wash clothes with the best laundry-woman in the world, he is always glad enough to pay for it to be done, when he can find some one to relieve him of his " suds-dabbing."

Many of the Sierra Leone washerwomen were very fine specimens of their sex, and with their gaudy, picturesque attire, and their quaint speech, yielded a considerable amount of pleasure and amusement to us.

There was a middle-aged sailor in my mess, named Dicky Parker, who had been on this coast on his last commission. He searched the faces of the black laundry folk very eagerly, but missed the face of the girl who, little over a year before, had washed for him.

"Where's Meme Johnson?" he asked one of a group of the women, explaining, at the same time, that Meme had washed for him before.

The women laughed, and one of them, acting as spokeswoman, said, "Dere ain't no Meme Johnson now, sar; Meme *Johnson* no lib now."

"Dead!" cried my shipmate, in surprised horror.

"No, sar, she no dead!" came the startling reply, "*but she no lib*, Meme Johnson, now; she married, sar!"

By which the woman meant that as Meme Johnson she was not now known, for, having married, her identity had become merged into that of her new, her husband's name.

It is very bewildering how the African will use that word *live*, or "lib," as they pronounce it. Instead of saying that a certain thing exists, or that it is in a certain place, whether the thing be living or dead, whether it be a button or a banana, a ship or a sheep, a forest or a fowl, they say, "*it* lib" here or there.

I remember a very amusing case of this in one vessel in which I sailed. The cook had a coloured boy, who knew but little regular English, whose duty, among others, it was to feed the fowls in the hen-coops. Two days after leaving port (we had had dirty weather all the time, and the birds in the coops were frightfully overcrowded), he came flying into the galley with looks of horror, and arms akimbo with fright, as he cried, " Mi g'ashus, sar, dere's ten more *dead* fowl *lib* in de hen-coop ! "

Oh, the wonder of some of the scenes of those days of tropical sailing ! Some of them live in my mind to-day with a vividness that is almost startling, so realistically do they present themselves.

One sunset at Sierra Leone I see now as I write. The evening had been excessively still, an awesome silence rested upon all the sea, and upon the rising, tree-clothed shore. The sun was not visible, for the wide expanse of sky was full of cloud-drift. A double line of fleecy white cloud, whose edges were scalloped with gold and pink, stretched across the heavens in a wide semi-circle, that took in three out of the four points of the compass. The sea, below and in the actual wake of this semi-circle of cloud, was a fiery, blood-red on the horizon, shading inwards, towards the spot where we were anchored, with an ever-deepening tone, until in places it was almost a chocolate hue.

Here and there, these red and brown tints were slashed with streaks of quivering gold, that were powerful enough to dazzle the eyes, and which were caused by long rifts in the cloud-banks above.

With the stealthy movement of some forest panther creeping to its lair, a long, snaky-built, three-masted, fore-and-aft schooner crept over the swelling sea, and moved, like some wondrous picture-effect, into the realm of those blood-red, sunlit waters.

Her white cotton canvas sails, and her tall, shining masts, were sharply silhouetted against the fiery background. Then, with a suddenness that in the silence was startling, there was a rattle of ropes, a succession of hoarse cries from the officers, the thunder of thick-booted American sailors, and the clouds of white canvas were swiftly gathered up, like the folding of some mighty sea-bird's wings. Then came the roar of cable as it leaped and rollicked over the iron-shod hawse-holes; the vessel swung to the tide, dipped her bow once or twice, as though she curtsied to our statelier craft, then once more things were comparatively still.

The sea's face had changed by this time. The tones had deepened. The reds were dark brown; the chocolates were purple black; the fleecy clouds were palls of crape, that hung from the galleries of heaven, in mourning for the death of the day; riding lights climbed the ship's masts by way of the halyards, and set themselves to shine down for the night, while the stars above in the violet heavens came out one by one, and greeted each other with twinkling winks or solid planet stare—and men said, " The night hath come ! "

Chapter XVI

MID STORM AND CALM

THE Cape of Good Hope ; Simon's Town, with its dockyard ; Cape Town, with its strange cosmopolitanism ; Wynberg, with its beauty, and a score of other South African items, have been so often exploited in the pages of books, magazines, and even daily papers, of recent years, that I need not waste a moment upon the subject here.

One trifling item I may, however, just mention in passing. I was, in common with most of my shipmates, amazed at a feature of fishing which we saw constantly repeated. Simon's Bay was perfectly alive with fish (it *always* was, I think, in those days), and the blacks, who managed the fishing, would say, when you went down into their boats, " How much pricee fish you want, Jack ? "

"Oh, threepence ! " perhaps the reply would be, and down went a line with a baited hook, only to be hauled up again, almost immediately, with a fine fish squirming at the end of it.

Another man asks for a *sixpenny* fish. Another line, of another *length*, was lowered, and the fish which was hauled up would be double the length and weight of the threepenny fish.

A distinguished member of several of the English scientific societies, who held an officer's commission

on our vessel, investigated the matter, and explained
that the fish of each age kept certain strata (if one
may use such a term in relation to the sea), and that
the blacks had ascertained this, and lowered different
lengths of line to reach different strata of fish.

"According to your faith be it unto you," said
Jesus, and that word remains for us to-day. I have
often thought, as fishers of men, how far do we limit
God, by limiting the length of our spiritual fishing
lines? If there are mightier hauls of souls to be
won from the crowded sea of the world for our Lord
than those we have ever yet taken, by the use of a
longer line of faith, shall we not, before God, hence-
forth seek to be fishermen after God's measure-
ments.

What a wondrous word of cheer our Lord gives us
in that fifth chapter of Luke, fourth verse: "Let down
your nets for a draught." Peter, and his other fisher
brethren, might have said (adopting fisher-lore talk),
"Everything in fishing goes by luck. We let down
our nets *hoping* to take something, but we *never can
be certain of a haul.*"

But Jesus said, "Let down your nets *for a
draught*"; and there are no trials of luck when the
Divine word is given. And now, to-day, when Jesus
sends us forth to fish for Him, and says, "Let down
your nets for a draught," *He* is responsible for the fish
that are to be, that will be taken. We may not
always be *on watch*—it may be our watch below, or
we may be in the sick bay—when the net is hauled
in, and therefore miss the sight of all the fish taken,
but we *shall* see the " catch," when we get home.

Once clear of the Cape, bound northward through
the Mozambique Channel, I saw my first shark at

close quarters, one of the hugest of its species, which was hauled inboard with great glee by half a hundred laughing seamen.

No one, save those who have seen one of the largest of these cruel, filthy creatures opened, would ever believe the strange contents of their stomachs. A book, as surprising as the " Adventures of Baron Munchausen," might easily be compiled upon the odd things found in sharks.

One of the most remarkable stories I ever met with in this connection refers to the recovery of a ship's papers :—

"The English cutter *Sparrow* brought a brig into harbour at Kingston, Jamaica, under the suspicion of being engaged in the slave trade. As the captured vessel had no papers from which the charge could be clearly substantiated, conviction was impossible, and the suspected brig was discharged. A few hours before the time she was to leave the harbour a man-of-war arrived, bringing some documents which proved her guilt beyond the shadow of a doubt.

" These papers had been obtained in a most surprising way. While cruising off St. Domingo, the man-of-war's crew had indulged in shark fishing. One monster was secured, and, on being cut open on deck, a bundle of ship's papers was found in its stomach. They were the very documents flung overboard by the captain of the brig when she was boarded by the *Sparrow*. Curiosity prompted the captain of the man-of-war to examine the papers, and the result was that he brought them before the authorities at the nearest port. The unlucky brig was detained, and eventually condemned on the evidence thus romantically acquired."

It was while in the neighbourhood of Madagascar that I made my first acquaintance with a real cyclone, which was prefaced by one of the most wonderful of all Nature's freaks.

It was the evening before the first actual outward signs of the coming storm, and on all the ocean, and on board the ship, there reigned an almost absolute stillness. Suddenly the silence was filled with a low, weird strain of exquisite music.

There was nothing in view, alow, aloft, or around, yet the music was *everywhere*. If you walked forward it was there, if you walked aft it was there.

Did it come from the port side? You went across to listen, and every beat of the silent air upon your brain was a musical beat.

Perhaps it came from starboard? You recrossed the deck, and the wondrous strains swelled and trembled as fully as ever.

You climb the rigging, and every touch of your bare feet upon the ratlines seems but to strike new notes of weirdest beauty.

You return to the deck, and the music peals all about you. It rolls over the sea on every swell. It clambers up the vessel's side; you look aloft, where the mystic sounds seem to climb more melodious than ever. Then, as you stand in wondering awe, with unseen skilful *clef* fingers, the sounds slide downwards again, and gather about your feet, and beat upon your ears, and fill all your senses, till your heart stands still, lest its beat and throb mar the voluptuous, mysterious strain.

A few ethereal-looking clouds sail sluggishly across the sky; light, white, feathery things they are, suggestive of winged spirits. You wonder, are these spirit voices? is it the music of heaven? And while you wonder the last quivering note dies away.

The spell upon all hands is broken, and a hoarse-voiced sailor, who has sailed this sea before, changes his quid in his cheek, and, with the look of an oracle, announces, "We're in for it, my dandies! We'll have the highest ole game, o' fightin' the *elements, an' takin' care o' number one, as ever wur, afore we're twenty-four hours older. An' if we don't go to Davy Jones's, every man Jack on us, it'll only be 'cause Provi' (Providence) is overhead, an' 'cause our ship's a stiff 'un, fur that ere moosic never comes 'cepts afore a cyclone, an' then only in this 'ere Mozambique lattertood, so I've yeard."

What was that strange, wondrous music which had filled all space? I do not think any one knows. Scientists and travellers have studied the subject, but no one has discovered the secret. There is nothing supernatural in it. It is one of *Nature's* secrets, and she can keep her secrets well.

Similar phenomena are to be met with in other parts of the world, some of which have been satisfactorily explained, while others remain as profound a mystery as ever.

Among the other *un*solved of these mysteries are the famous "Guns of Burrisaul." Burrisaul is a station on the delta of the Ganges, and there, in the rainy season, mysterious sounds are heard resembling the discharge of artillery.

Only in the rainy season, and from the southward, they have been heard for a hundred miles, yet, on the coast itself, they appear further south still. Where it is, what it is, this continual booming of cannon, no one can tell. Nature has held her secret of the

"Guns of Burrisaul," as she has held the secret of the weird cyclone music of the Mozambique.

I have never met anything in *nature* like that mysterious music of Mozambique, though I have met something like it in the realm of grace ; when men and women, beaten and buffetted upon the sea of life, smile, with the peace of God shining in their faces, because their spiritual ears are filled with the music of Divine comfort and communion.

How strange it is, that the vast bulk of people who gather in our churches, chapels, and halls, should become so satisfied with *mere religion* that they should miss Christ, His personal friendship, His communion, His cheer, His comfort, the music of His grace, through all their days.

I remember a grocer who marked up a sugar in his window at *one* penny per pound, and whose shop became crowded with would-be customers for his sugar (upon which he actually lost money at that *selling* price). To one person, who clamoured for a large parcel of the *penny* sugar, but who wanted nothing else, he said, "Where do you get your *tea*, ma'am ? Not here, I know. You must get your sugar where you *buy* your tea."

Oh, the pity of it, that myriads of people who profess to be (or, at least, pass for) Christians, expect Christ to be their strength and stay in the hour of sorrow or death, but who never look to Him to be the sweetness and joy of their general life. Religious services for Sunday (or a part of the day), the Bible, and *saying* prayers, for times of dangerous illness or seasons of bereavement ; but the world, its froth, its effervescence, its shifting drama, for the general life, and when they want to be specially happy and gay.

10

They want to buy their sugar of the world, but they expect to get their strength, in times of need, from the Christ, whom they have slighted in their easier times. To such there is no wondrous music, prefacing, accompanying, succeeding life's storms, because their souls are out of tune and their ears are dulled and gross.

Some one has written :—

> "If I knew the box where the smiles were kept,
>   No matter how large the key,
> Or strong the bolt, I would try so hard ;
>   'Twould open, I know, for me.
> Then over the land and the sea, broadcast
>   I'd scatter the smiles to play,
> That the children's faces might hold them fast
>   For many and many a day.
>
> If I knew a box that was large enough
>   To hold all the frowns I meet,
> I would like to gather them, every one,
>   From nursery, school, and street.
> Then folding and holding, I'd pack them in,
>   And turning the monster key,
> I'd hire a giant to drop the box
>   To the depths of the deep, deep sea."

There *is* a box where smiles are kept and where frowns can be drowned, its name is TRUST. Trust in God, trust that has not one broken link in its chain, and whose every link is divinely metallic, and emits the music of praise, as the tuning-fork of our grandfathers gave forth its keynote for song.

The cyclone came in due course, not perhaps the worst I ever passed safely through, but certainly the one (perhaps because it was the first experienced) which made the deepest impression upon my mind.

We were only on the outer edge of that awful storm circle, and the question has often arisen in one's mind, after many years' experience of the sea, whether, had we been caught in the centre of that ring of tempest, we should ever have come out. The probability is that we should not.

Of its horrors I need not write, but as I dismiss it with a line, the wonder comes to me, as it has often come to me before, how the Psalmist could have been able to describe so graphically a storm at sea. There have been lengthier descriptions written since he wrote his, but none that can compete for wonder of completeness of description of the sailor's state in a storm. What is there in any language to equal the description of the 26th verse of Psalm cvii. : " They mount up to the heaven, they go down again to the depths : their soul is melted. . . . They reel to and fro, and stagger like a drunken man, and are at their wit's end."

* * * * *

Once clear of the cyclone, and sailing or steaming northwards (we were under no press of time), we fell in with more than one ocean adventure; sometimes these were of the farcical order, at others tragedy and drama were their distinguishing characteristics. For all such I have neither room nor time, save as I may mention one here and there, up and down the pages of my book, by way of illustration of some side of sea life, or because it was connected, in some way, with my own career on board.

One scene of this period comes back to me as I write, and I give it for its teaching.

A Despairing Plea.

"The morning was a typical one for that tropical sea. The ship, like a thing of life, swept the sunlit waters, with many a graceful bend and bob, many a curtsey and pirouette. Only a few persons were on deck, for, man-of-war though she was, all hands were below at breakfast. The allotted half-hour was barely over when the shrill whistle of the boatswain's mate's pipe rose above the hum of three hundred voices, of the chink of iron basins, the rattle of mess kettle handles, and the swish, swish of the waters through which the ship was rushing.

"Accompanying the shrill treble pipe was the bass voice of the boatswain's mate, as he bawled that awful cry, 'Hands witness punishment.' With many a 'Hurry up, hurry up,' from ship's corporals and master-at-arms, the crew were quickened in their movements up the various hatchways.

"When all were gathered on the upper deck (a deep silence resting upon them), the officers gathered aft, the captain and doctor standing a little apart from the main group of 'gold-lacers.' With startling suddenness the bugle note of 'Attention' deepens the hush.

"An opening is made through the packed masses of the men, and a prisoner, stripped to the waist, is marched between two marines close up to the gratings that are lashed into the ship's side.

"Amid a painful silence the doctor examines the prisoner, whispers a word to the captain, and the latter reads aloud the charge, and warrant for punishment. Then in firm, full, measured tones, the captain cries, 'Boatswain's mate, do your duty.'

" The hard, toil-stained fingers of the petty officer are drawn through the nine tails of the lash, with the same nonchalance with which an athlete pushes his fingers through his hair, then the strong right arm is raised, the nine tails sweep the morning air with the hiss as of many snakes, and falling upon the bare back of the prisoner they——

" But we refrain from description ; it is too painful, too horrible.

" When only the sixth lash has fallen, the quivering face of the flogged man is turned appealingly over his shoulder towards the place where the chief officer stands ; and in a voice, every note of which is like a separate wail of agony, he cries, ' Oh, captain, captain, for my mother's sake, give me *one more chance, one more chance*!'

" The lash was already sweeping through the air, but at that cry the boatswain's mate let the cat fall harmlessly at his side. He waited for the captain to speak.

" Every syllable of the chief officer's words falls clear out upon the ears of all the gathered crew, as well as upon the ears of the prisoner : ' You know full well I have tried you every way over and over again. I have let you off with light punishments. I warned you the last time, that if you persisted in your evil courses you would come to the gratings. You had your *last* chance ; you flung it recklessly away.'

" Just for one second the voice paused, then with a nod to the boatswain, the captain added, ' Go on with your work,' and the lash fell again and again, until the unconscious, bleeding man was borne away to the sick-bay."

All that was thirty years ago, nearly, but the sight lives in my eye, my brain, my heart still, and to-day I think of the myriad of souls who are flinging away their only, their last chance of mercy.

The Gospel rings in their ears ; is presented before their eyes in book and tract ; sounds all about them in sacred songs. Yet the message of grace is being ever refused. What will the refuser of grace do? What will he say when brought to that Great White Throne, as my old shipmate was brought to the grating and the lash ?

> " Some one will knock when the door is shut —
>   By-and-by, by-and-by :
> Hear a voice saying, ' I know you not ' :
>   Shall you?   Shall I ? "

Chapter XVII

OCEAN INCIDENTS

THE Japanese hang over the prow of a new ship about to be launched a large pasteboard cage full of birds, and the moment the ship is afloat a man pulls a string, when the cage opens and the birds fly away, making the air alive with music and the whirr of wings. The idea is that the birds thus welcome the ship as she begins her career as a thing of life. And there were many times in those days, when to stand for'ard, on our vessel, and look aft and aloft at the same time, was almost to conceive the ship to be a sentient living thing.

Is there anything more beautiful among created things than a noble ship, under full sail, sweeping the deep ocean's breast with her snowy wings outspread? Especially is this the case when the vessel is seen under the blaze of a glowing sun, or the mystic shimmer of broad moonlight.

On one of these sunny days, while sailing northward on the eastern side of the Cape, when our smart corvette was a cloud of white gleaming canvas, and she bowed and curtsied with the grace of a Spanish *danseuse*, and skimmed the blue, sun-kissed waters that heaved and swelled with musical splash and murmur, and when all hands were light-hearted and gay, there came from aloft, hurtling through the air, striking this and that rope or stay, the body of one of our leading seamen.

We gathered up his dead and battered form and bore it amidships, and prepared it for burial. Next morning, early, while the awed and silent men gathered around the gangway, and the chaplain's voice recited the burial service, the still, cold form, sewn in its hammock shroud, and weighted with shot, was slid from beneath the Union Jack into the deep, deep sea.

At midnight, the night before, a sudden calm had taken the place of the brisk sailing breeze we had been enjoying. The calm continued. The awful death of poor Scroggles had affected the men strangely. The horrible monotony of days and days of calm added to their depression, until the officers became concerned.

This sullen, depressed, discontented mood of the crew must be changed, was the feeling of those in command, and the captain summoned the acting manager of our theatrical troupe, and (a-la-Victoria Rex) *commanded* a performance to be arranged at once.

"Let it be farcical; let there be no drama or tragedy," was the order. And, forthwith, every one was busy — some constructing the theatre; the players rehearsing their parts; and that night, on the boards of the Theatre Royal, H.M.S. C——, there was played, "Turn Him Out," and "Good For Nothing."

It seems hard to believe, when I look at my grey-bearded face in the looking-glass, that ever I could successfully impersonate the leading female characters in those sea-stage productions; and yet I did,

and could fill a small volume with the recital of
singular adventures met with in that connection,
especially during those months when, our ship lying
at Port Louis, Mauritius, we engaged the theatre,
and played constantly before the people.

Among the drollest of these adventures, was one
connected with the getting a silk dress made, for the
part of the Marchioness of Villafranca in a certain
comedy.

I had been told that a Madame Etty would be the
best person to go to. To this lady's emporium I
therefore went. Her English was very limited indeed ;
my French was nil ; and a gentlemanly hair-dresser of
the neighbourhood was fetched in to be interpreter.

When Madame Etty had grasped the situation,
that the smiling, white-uniformed young sailor
wanted a stylish lady's dress made to fit *him*, she
fairly screamed with laughter.

Leading out from the shop was a large work-room,
where some twenty or thirty creole girls sat working
at dress-making and millinery. Madame's high-
pitched voice and screams of laughter easily reached
the ears of these dainty, pretty little dusky girls, who
left their work *en masse* to listen and to watch.

I selected the dress-length. Then came the task
of measurement. Madame declared she could not
perform this office upon a gentleman, so the friendly
hair-dresser, coached by her instructions, essayed the
work.

More screams of laughter followed, especially as
the poor male measurer could not, for a long time,
be made to understand the mystery of measuring for
the *train* of the dress.

Of all that followed, with the fitting of the wonderful creation of the dressmaker's art, I pass over. Madame, with a party of friends, was in a box at the theatre on the night when I first appeared wearing the dress.

To this day I remember the amaze, not to say awe, with which I started back on first beholding myself in the glass, when the hired French costumer and maker-up had finished with me. My beautiful hair (artificial), my enamelled face, the earrings in my ears (fixed *upon* the lobes with springs), the wreath of crimson roses twined amid my hair; everything was such a triumph of the maker's-up art, that I was utterly speechless with amaze, scarce able to conceive it was myself at whom I looked.

A heavy wager (as it afterwards transpired) was laid that night between two military officers, who were in the house, as to whether the personified Marchioness was really a man; one of the wagerers declaring it must be a woman.

To decide the matter they found their way to the wings, where I was waiting my next turn on the stage. Just as they arrived, not seeing them, and being very much annoyed by the carelessness of a half-drunken marine who was acting as scene shifter, and who had capsized a tall glass of lemonade over the train of my dress, I was railing out in real nautical swear-word lingo—and in my *natural* voice.

The two officers stared at me, then, with a burst of laughter at the turn of events, they rushed away to the front of the house—and to settle up their wager.

I have digressed. I was speaking of the play on board the ship, given as an antidote for the sadness of soul among the crew consequent upon the awful death of our ill-fated shipmate, Scroggles.

The evening passed off all right, except that the huge musical box, which played fifty tunes, which belonged to one of the officers, and which served us for an orchestra (we had no band on board), went wrong, and would not stop its playing when the check was put upon it. Our captain grew testy over the muddle this caused, and finally shouted, "Smother the thing! Roll it up in a hammock or something, and carry it out!" This was done, and the performance proceeded.

Among the men who played that night, the low comedian, who took the itinerant toy-seller in " Turn Him Out," was a messmate of mine, whose brother was then beginning to make a name upon the London stage as a low comedian, and who has since become one of the most noted actors of his class, and known to all the theatrical world as " Arthur Williams."

I can hear the nasal twang of my shipmate even now, and see the twist in his features, as, with a basket of toys on his back, his hat stuck round with dolls, and a huge windmill held in his left hand, he set the sails of the mill going with a pull of a string held in his right hand, as he, in true street-seller fashion, shouted, " 'Ere's yer toys fur yer, gals an' boys, an' only a 'appenny each! Will no fond parient invest the small sum o' one 'appenny to bless the life o' his or her *h*infant *h*offspring."

Here there came a pull at the string, and while the mill-sails swirled about with a rattle and swish, the nasal voice rang out again, " *H*observe! that the slightest *h*agitation o' the *h*arm sets the whole *h*edifice in motion *h*in-de-pen-dent o' *h*any *h*artificial *h*assistance from the *h*air, or the *h*at-o-mis-fere."

Of course all hands laughed ; the object of the

evening was to make every one laugh, and to cure them of their doleful dumps.

Most intensely do I love a *honest*, hearty laugh ; I believe holiness and mirth—pure, honest, innocent mirth—go well together in the sight of our tender, loving Father, God.

I am not here offering any comment upon the means (under present consideration) by which the laugh of that particular evening was raised ; but I do feel how blind a thing it was, on the part of our chaplain and captain, to devise and permit the moved hearts of their men to be diverted from more solemn considerations (under the circumstances which had so affected all hands) by the substitution of farces for the message of God as to salvation.

"Be astonished, O ye heavens, at this, and be horribly afraid, be ye very desolate, saith the Lord. For My people *have committed two evils*; they have forsaken Me, the Fountain of living waters, and hewed them out cisterns, broken cisterns, that can hold no water." . . . "They have healed also the hurt of My people *slightly, saying, Peace, peace ; when there is no peace.*"

An Artist Sailor.

The writing of those words " Peace, peace," recalls a remarkable young sailor to my mind, a shipmate of mine in one of our ships, and a remarkable scene in connection with him.

I forget his real name ; we used to call him " Middy Marvel." He had shipped on one of the training ships at home as a *first*-class boy, though he must really have been eighteen, instead of sixteen, at the time. When he sailed with me, a few years after, he was a tall, gentlemanly young fellow, bearing the rating of an ordinary seaman only. Every one, officers and men alike, knew that he was a gentleman born, though how, or why he was found where he was, he would never satisfy anybody.

He had a marvellous gift as an artist, and many a sweet little picture of tropical life (painted ashore), or seascape (painted on board), found its way from his brush to the walls of the officers' cabins.

One day, while sailing Southern seas, with the ship becalmed, I stood silently watching the face of " Middy," as his eyes moved slowly around over the face of the waters, and travelled aloft from yard to yard, from sail to sail.

There was an almost painful sense of hush upon all things—sea and ship. The ship lay like a log on the water, only rocking sluggishly from side to side, as she was moved by the long, regular ocean swell ; the creak of the yards grinding against the mast as she lurched over, the dull, hollow flap of the sails as they hung useless, the click and twitter of the reef points against the canvas, and an occasional scream of wild sea-bird, together with the strange, deep purple appearance of the distant horizon, all lent an almost uncanny feeling to this quietest of quiet moments.

Middy, more to himself than to me, said, " What a picture this silent ship, on a silent sea, would make ! If I could have a boat, and lay off on the waters, and paint the old craft now, I'd call my picture ' Peace,' for it would be a perfect emblem of real peace."

Just at this moment the captain came on deck, mounted the bridge, and casting one hurried glance towards the purpling horizon, he shouted,—

" Boatswain's mate ! "

" Ay, ay, sir."

" Call all hands !   Hands shorten sails ! "

" Ay, ay, sir."

And then there penetrated into every distant recess of the ship the shrill whistle, followed by the hoarse cry of the boatswain's mate, " All hands ! hands shorten sail !   Hurry up ! hurry up !   Now then, lads, double up sharp ! "

As my shipmate and I sprang away from the ship's side to answer the pipe of the boatswain's mate, I met the astonished gaze of Middy, who muttered,—

" Furl all sails ?   Why the skipper must be a fool ! there's not a catspaw moving ! "

Our captain had sailed these seas too often to be deceived, and in less than half an hour we were in the throes of a fearful squall ; and but for the timely taking off of sail from our vessel she would probably have been caught aback, and driven down, stern first, into the cruel, merciless ocean.

All night and the next day the storm, prefaced by that sudden, awful squall, raged furiously, and to Middy Marvel there doubtless came the consciousness of how ignorantly he had misjudged the character of the scene and condition which he had called " Peace."

How often, since my conversion, has that incident recurred to me, and recurred with pain, since it is such a true type of one of the saddest sides of life, in the Church and the world.

There are thousands of people whose only peace is a false one.   Instead of being on the Rock, they are being rocked in the cradle of the devil's lie.   Their peace is only a lull that prefaces a storm ; it has in it all the elements that go to make up a storm—the awful storm of God's wrath. Of such, God's word says, " For when they shall say, ' Peace and safety,' then sudden destruction cometh upon them, as travail upon a woman with child, and they shall not escape."

The danger lies in the fact that so many souls are indulging in the rest that rests upon appearances, upon mere Church membership, or outward conformity to religious observance. In short, they have a man-made peace, *a rest without reconciliation*. God's word is clear enough, that the only true rest and peace springs from our reconciliation with Him, by repentance and faith in our Lord Jesus Christ, who hath already made reconciliation *with* God for us, and who waits to see us reconciled *to* God through Him.

DERELICTS.

Who is there among those whose home has been the sea for many years, but has felt the sadness of a great pity steal over them, as they have passed—and sometimes repassed again and even again during one year—some derelict vessel.

It is a piteous sight, and the thoughts engendered thereby are always sad. Sometimes at dawn, or out of a thick mist, or at night in the half-light, such a ship, with her sails spread (*some* of them, at least, while others, that have been hastily furled, and have since broken away from the gaskets that fastened them, flap and fly in the wind), will sweep past you with a suddenness that is startlingly uncanny.

The many superstitions of sailors, as to phantom ships, have doubtless had their origin in such glimpses of derelicts.

The reason of abandonment by the crews of such

ships, cannot always be found or guessed. Sometimes it may be mutiny, in which case an examination of the ship's interior would reveal the signs of a frightful tragedy. Sometimes some fearful epidemic has either slain all hands, or so many of them that the remainder have taken to the boats in sheerest terror.

Twice in three months such a derelict passed one vessel in which I sailed in the Indian Ocean. She was under plain sail the first time, and swept past us out of a deep mist, like some ghostly Flying Dutchman.

Three months later we saw her again. Her sails were split into whip-like lashes of canvas that flapped the air as a child will flick his toy whip. Two of her topmasts were gone, and the wrecked and splintered lower masts were hampered with a raffle of broken ropes and stays.

She swept out of sight amid the thickness of a dirty day. Where would she go? What would become of her?

She might run across the bows of some unsuspecting craft, during the darkness of night or the thick gloom of a fog, and wreck the vessel who, all unsuspectingly, ran into her. Then if she herself escaped (a derelict is like the proverbial cat, with its *nine* lives), she would drift on, a menace to all ships on the sea, a daily increasing wreck in herself, until some day, or some darker night, with every seam of deck and sides gaping to the ocean's wash, she would slowly sink into that great graveyard of ships and men—the *depths* of the sea.

Yet there had been a day when she started fair and true as a new vessel, her bows sprinkled with the christening wine, flags flying gaily from her mast-heads, or her rainbow stay of dressing; when Lloyds classed her as A 1; when her owners counted upon great gains from her voyages. But she ended as a derelict.

Oh, the derelicts one meets upon Life's sea! Rudderless men and women—Christless, therefore hopeless and helpless. And, saddest of all thoughts, the vast majority of these might be brought into the port of God, very early in their derelict days, if God's own people would but go out after them, with Spirit-taught skill, and fling around them the mighty hawsers of a Christly love.

Even as I write I recall what I read a few days since. At a great meeting of ship-owners, it was pro-posed to invest so many thousands of pounds in some new vessels, whose work it should be to scour the Atlantic in the neighbourhood of the great American liners' track, the track, too, of the great Anglo-American trade, and to lay hold of the de-relicts (there are, it is said, sixteen afloat every day in the year in that North-Atlantic track), and if con-sidered worth it, that they should tow them into the nearest port, if not, to destroy them with dynamite, or by some other approved way.

Oh, for a Christlike fleet of godly men and women, who will leave the beaten tracks of mere public wor-ship, and the delights of hearing and receiving beautiful truths, and who will go forth as derelict hunters—hunters, seekers, saviours, of men and women!

Chapter XVIII

WHAT DO SAILORS SING?

I HAVE often been asked, "What do sailors sing? Do they sing those queer compositions of Dibden's, which are supposed, by most landsmen, to depict so truly the life of a sailor?"

After many years' experience at sea, an experience that touched both the naval and mercantile services, I am bound to confess that the most which Dibden ever did by his songs, for the hundreds of sailors whom I have known, was to raise a smile, a discussion, or provoke a growl.

There is one such composition which, in my sea-days, used to be laughed to scorn by every type of sailor, the song entitled, "The Sailor's Consolation." I make no apology for inserting its four verses here, since I have already explained that, while dealing chiefly with the personal elements of my own life, I am also desirous of giving glimpses of what sea-life was thirty to forty years ago.

Fancy sailors, who are always longing for the joys of home and the pleasures of shore life, caring to sing "The Sailor's Consolation":—

> "One night came on a hurricane,
>   The sea was mountains rolling,
> When Barney Buntline turn'd his quid,
>   And said to Billy Bowling:

‘ A strong nor’-wester’s blowing, Bill ;
  Hark ! don’t ye hear it roar now ?
Lord help ’em, how I pities all
  Unhappy folks on shore now !

“ ‘ Fool-hardy chaps who live in towns,
  What danger they are all in,
And now lie quaking in their beds,
  For fear the roof shall fall in :
*Poor creatures, how they envies us,
  And wishes, I’ve a notion,
For our good luck, in such a storm,
  To be upon the ocean !*

“ ‘ And as for them who ’re out all day,
  On business from their houses,
And late at night are coming home,
  To cheer their babes and spouses ;
While you and I, Bill, on the deck
  Are comfortably lying,
My eyes ! what tiles and chimney-pots
  About their heads are flying !

“ ‘ And very often have we heard
  How men are kill’d and undone,
By overturns of carriages,
  By thieves, and fires in London.
We know what risk all landsmen run,
  From noblemen to tailors ;
Then, Bill, let us thank Providence
  That you and I are sailors ! ’ ”

If ever such doctrine was true of English sailors,
it certainly has not been at any time during the past
forty years.

Dibden’s “ All’s Well ” is, or was in my time, a
favourite. “ The Anchor’s Weighed ” was another
favourite song on board every ship.

Then there were certain singing features which
were almost universal to all ships. The *rural*-born

sailor was wont to treat us to " The Farmer's Boy,"
with its chorus—

> " To plow an' to sow,
> To reap an' to mow,
> An' to be a farmer's boy."

The same type of man—his speech might have the
dialect of Hants, Berks, Wilts, Somerset, Suffolk, or
other agricultural county, but the songs were usually
the same—would sing us " The Poacher," when after
telling how he laid his snare or net, and having—

> " Put down five,"

he'd

> " Ta'k 'em up aloive,"

he would wave his hand as a signal for the chorus,
and the two or three hundred voices of his shipmates
would roll forth the refrain—

> " Fur it's my delight,
> On a shiny night,
> In the season ov the ye-e-ar."

If the singer happened to be a town-born lad, the
lugubriously-comic strains of " The Horrible Tale,"
with its senseless inanity, beginning with—

> " It's a horrible tale I have to tell
> Of the sad misfortunes that befell
> A very respectable familee—that once resided
> Just—in the very—same street—that I—did,"

would greet our ears.

This would be varied by the town-bred singer by
some such musical monstrosity as " Kemo Kimo,"
" Champagne Charley," or " Joe in the Copper."

Songs contributed by the marines were usually more martial than naval. But the chief favourites with all classes were songs which were full of sweet and tender sentiment, such as "Maggie's Choice," with its pathetic refrain—

> " I tell them they need not come wooing of me,
>   For my heart, my heart is over the sea."

I have known a grizzled, bearded old salt clear his voice, wait for comparative silence, then apostrophising some fair sweetheart, carol forth—

> " What shall I bring thee, maiden, say?
>   What gift from o'er the sea?
> To prove when I am far away,
>   That I fondly think of thee?"

Then the deep bass voice would take up the maiden's speech, and the reply in song would roll out—

> " I ask no gem, no pearl I crave,
>   No gift from o'er the sea."

The fully developed reply showing that the maiden would be perfectly satisfied with the love of her sailor-sweetheart when he should return again.

"Let me Kiss him for his Mother," "The Daisy I picked from off my Mother's Grave," "The little Green Leaf in the Bible," "Please give me a Penny, sir," and "Father, dear Father, come Home with me now"; these are the type of songs our sailors loved to sing, except when they were three sheets in the wind, then such doleful strains as "Barbara Allan," or " The Sailor's Grave," would be heard, with a hic-coughed out "Tom Bowline," that would have made Sims Reeves shudder.

Very few people, I imagine, have any idea how deep a reverence sailors have for sacred song ; and to every teacher of the young, every Bible-class leader, Sunday-school superintendent, conductor of night classes, and any and all who may have to do with boys and lads, I would say, be careful what doctrines the hymns which you teach your scholars contain, since, very often, the only theology which remains in the heart of the lad who breaks away from shore life, to follow the calling of the sea, is the theology of the hymns sung in early life.

While it is true that Christian workers, since the advent of P. P. Bliss and Ira D. Sankey, have awakened to the possibilities contained in spiritual songs, there is, I find, a danger in some quarters that the jingle of tune should become of more importance than the scriptural truth of the words.

It is good to remember that the gondola of Gospel song will find its way where the lumbering three-deck man-of-war sermon cannot possibly reach, but the gondola must be built of sound timber—Bible doctrine.

One special occasion when sacred song broke out among our sailors recurs to my mind as I write. It was in the harbour of Trincomalee, Ceylon. Oh, the wonder of that harbour ! The size of it ; its spaciousness ; its beauty ; its privacy, when once you are inside ; its lovely hillsides ; its echoes ; its—well, everything that makes such a place wonderful, while at the same time it is too much so to be described.

The East Indian fleet were gathered there. There were to be evolutions on board and ashore, and general inspection by the Admiral.

One evening, when it seemed too sultry for any

one to care to move, when the decks of the three-quarter circle of ships were littered with men tired out with a stiff day's sham-fight, with field-pieces ashore, a little lad on the vessel's forecastle began to sing, "I think, when I read that sweet Story of Old."

Clear and strong, sweet and pure as the blackbird's note in spring, the boy's voice rang out, growing stronger and stronger as he felt the inspiration of old associations with the beautiful old hymn, and doubtless helped by the many voices which joined his as he sang.

By the time the second verse was reached, all our ship's company were singing, in full voice and absolute harmony. Our officers crowded forward into the waist, while above the bulwarks of every ship in the harbour the men of the various vessels showed up, all evidently in a state of intense listening excitement.

When the last note of the last line of the last verse had been sung, there was silence for the briefest second, then the hillsides rolled back their wondrous echo :—

"Shall crowd to His arms and be blest."

There was a thickness in everybody's throat for a moment, then, from every ship, there sounded forth a perfect fusillade of hand-clapping, mingled with a roar of bravo artillery.

As the plaudits died away, a few bars of music, from a well-played concertina on one of the other ships, prefaced the singing of "When mothers of Salem their children brought to Jesus"; and, led by the voice of the instrumentalist, all *his* ship's company, and the ship's company of every other vessel, sang the sweet old hymn of our childhood's days.

So this impromptu concert of, perhaps, fifteen or sixteen hundred voices, went on, until every ship had had its turn except the Admiral's. This was a case of the first shall be last, as far as service precedence was concerned.

The sun was sinking fast, and we were wondering if the Admiral's ship would take a part in the leading off of a song, when suddenly a mighty burst of many voices, evidently carefully started and led, came from the flag-ship, and the still evening air fairly trembled with the opening line of the Te Deum Laudamus :—
" We praise Thee, O God, We acknowledge Thee to be the Lord."

The tune was Jackson's superb setting, and the effect of the many voices, with the background of sound of the echoes among the hills, was too marvellous for any pen description.

The sun set more and more rapidly, and as he set he flung from his prodigal palette a largess of gold and colour all over the wondrous harbour, until there was a symphony of colour as well as of sound.

" O Lord, save Thy people," rang out from a thousand voices, as the light faded and the hill-tops flung a violet shade over their foliage-clothed sides.

" O Lord, let Thy mercy lighten upon us," rolled out upon the evening as the sun disappeared.

The officer in charge of the deck of the Admiral's ship, doubtless delayed the " making of sunset," for a moment or two.

But when the last note of the repeated, " Let me never be confounded," had flung forth its *word-prayer*, then the sharp crack of the rifles upon every ship, followed the fire on the Admiral's vessel, every ensign was lowered, and the bugles of the fleet broke the spell that had rested upon the singing crews ever since that first boyish voice had sung "I think when I read."

Some one who reads this account will say, "But not six men in a thousand of those sailors cared for the God to whom their songs were addressed." Granted ; but it shows the hold which Christian song had upon their memories, and is a proof of the need of teaching true scriptural sentiments when we train our young, as well as proof of the power which spiritual song may become.

While touching upon sailors' songs, a word or two about their usual evening amusements, when at sea, may prove interesting to our readers ; for I am often asked, "How do sailors spend their evenings, when work is done for the day ? "

As a matter of fact, a sailor's work, like that of a working mother's, is never done ; but usually, if the weather be fine, Jack counts upon the two hours from six to eight as tolerably free, when, in response to the permit of the old-fashioned piping, "Hands dance and skylark," all the fantastical singers and dancers muster on the fore deck, most of the crew turn up on deck, prepared to be amused in any way which the event and the man of the hour may provide.

When there is nothing else moving, Jack can always fall back upon the fiddler and a waltz. Sailors, in my sea days, were mostly good waltzers, as they might well be, seeing how much practice they had, even though one's partner was a "lumber-footed tar," the tobacco-smoke from whose pipe had a knack of forming circles about your face, as you danced, like the rings around a planet on the pictured page of an astronomical treatise.

But very often the ship contained one or two naturally comic men, fertile in imagination and resource, who would spring a surprise upon their shipmates, by suddenly appearing in one of the emptied hammock nettings (which are formed in the hollow of the bulwarks), and in some clever disguise, impersonate some itinerant seller of merchandise, or perhaps the character of a quack doctor.

We had two such men as this in one vessel in which I served abroad, who were adepts at such scratch entertainments, and often appeared as rivals for public support, one in the starboard, the other in the port netting, in the fore part of the ship.

One such evening as this ended most tragically.

One of these favourites had climbed into the netting on the starboard side of the deck ; he was a tall, thin fellow, who was capitally disguised, and whose elongated appearance was heightened by wearing an abnormally high white pot-hat, with a broad black band about it.

With a brilliant lantern on either side of him, he began to explain that he had been commissioned by his wealthy master, the Duke of Westminster, to bless mankind—*sea-faring* mankind, he was careful to emphasize—by parting with twenty pounds' worth of jewellery and other articles, for the small sum of one penny.

Then from a bag hung at his side he drew forth a broad gilt wedding ring ; then a chased keeper ; then a jockey-cap-and-whip breast pin ; then a broad belcher ring (as he termed it) ; half a dozen imitation shillings ; a forget-me-not brooch ; and, finally, an imitation five-pound Bank of England note ; " enough, altogether," he assured us, " to set up a shop in a village where nobody lived, and the five-pound note would pay the first quarter's rent."

All these articles could actually be bought in the London streets, thirty years ago, for a penny, and our entertainer had caught the peculiar " patter " of the London itinerant.

He made some considerable show of selling packets of his wares to the assembled sailors, when, suddenly, the hoarse voice of a short, stout man sounded from the port netting, with an, " Hi, hi, here yer are ! I'm all the way from Kamschatki, in New South Wales, and I want to introduce to you my wonderful Californian cement, warranted to cure coughs, colds, chilblains, catarrh, consumption, and bunions, and all the ills to which flesh is heir to while condemned to breathe the hemisphere (atmosphere) all about us.

" Talking of the hemisphere we breathe, ladies and gentlemen, reminds me of a school examination, when the girl was asked what we breathed.

" ' Hemisphere ! ' she replied.

" ' Of what is the hemisphere composed ? ' asked the teacher.

" ' Of four jasses, please ! ' replied the girl.

" ' Gasses, you mean, child,' corrected the teacher. ' Name them, please ! '

" ' Oxygin, hydrogin, nitrogin, and—and——'

" Poor little gal, she had the other gas on the tip of her tongue, at least she had had it there many times before when she could get hold of her mother's bottle.

" ' Well,' said the teacher, ' can't you remember the other ? Does it end with " i-n " like the others ? '

"The child's face brightened, and she repeated her reply,—

"'Oxygin, hydrogin, nitrogin, and (triumphantly) London gin.'"

For a few moments the jewellery-seller's audience left him, charmed by the yarns of his rival. Then the former made a desperate bid for their attention, won it, and the crowd flocked back to the starboard side, leaving the Californian cement dealer without a soul to listen to or watch him.

After a few minutes some turned to see how he was taking his defeat, but he was nowhere to be seen, and every one concluded he had retired from the field for that time.

No one gave him a thought after that. He was in the middle watch that night, but he missed his muster. At breakfast next morning he did not appear. Then for the first time alarm was felt, the hands were turned up, and the ship was searched, but he was not found.

But, with its broken string twisted around one of the wire stays, in the chains, immediately behind where he had stood in the netting the night before, there hung the box which he had worn suspended round his neck, and in which he had a few paper packets of ship's sand wrapped, which were to pass for the famous cement.

We never saw our shipmate again. We were a thousand miles from land, and only one hypothesis was open for us to accept—he must have fallen backwards overboard and been drowned, or devoured by the sharks that infested those seas. Whether he turned giddy, had a fit, whether it was a sudden lurch of the ship that overbalanced him, or whatever might have been the cause, the fact remained, that he had gone to a sudden, awful death.

What a book might be written upon the " Humour and Pathos of the Sea "!—a book of facts which even the wildest imagination of the professional writer could not outwrite.

Chapter XIX

"HOW LONG, O GOD, HOW LONG?"

I HAVE spoken of the Krooman Cooper in an earlier chapter, saying that it was possible I might have to allude to him again; and as this chapter will deal with slaving and slaver-chasing, some of poor Cooper's testimony may well find a place here, as a preface to the subject in hand.

I have described the man personally before, and now need only say that he was an exceedingly quiet man, appeared to mix very little with the others, loved to be alone, and when not at work was generally found reading a large-type version of the Psalms or the New Testament.

Of course, all sorts of fun was made of him by the crew, but his invariable reply, with a broad smile, showing a set of magnificent teeth, was, " Bery well, shentlemen, you laugh, but me best off."

It was soon found that he was exceedingly clever in making little fancy barrels and other curios, and on account of his steady, quiet ways, he became a great favourite among the officers.

I have referred to the interest with which his stories were listened to, when he could be prevailed upon to tell some of them.

Asked, one day, to tell something of his past, how he came to be a "government man"? whether he had ever been a slave? how he came to be made a slave? and how he was freed, he replied :—

"Ah, that bery sad to me to tell all dat, but 'spose you likie to hear. Please God, it help you to tink how good He is, then me tell you."

"Go on, darkey, but don't give us too much religion ; it's the yarn we want," came in reply.

"Well, I dunno for sartin, but tink me 'bout thirty year old now. Me born in place they call Shire Valley; me 'member it quite well. Me big boy, 'bout fourteen year old. Me help fader do him work ; me gader de nuts to make de palm oil ; and do lots work b'sides. Dat such lubly little place, lots ob pretty little house, nice round tops, round as cannon ball, and plenty much bigger than de capstan ; and we all so happy. We worship idol ; we wear ' fetish ' for good luck, we hab plenty feasts, and we tink idol like us, and do us good, because we gib him rice, and nuts, and plantain, and all sort.

"One night, ah ! me 'member it so well, just so it only yesterday. De sun go down behind de big palm-trees, all de shickens go to dere perch ; de piccaninnies go sleep ; and den me mammee and fader, and me too go. But some time in de night, it all bery dark, when, all to once, we wake bery much froughtened, for we hear great noise, and yell, and shout, and guns and pistols go bang, bang, bang, and den we hear poor black peoples cry and groan, and den—and den——"

Here the poor black's face was wet with tears, and as the memory seemed too much for him, one of his listeners said kindly, " Poor old fellow, perhaps he would rather not tell it all, if it cuts him up so."

"Tank you kindly, sar," said Cooper, as he dried

his eyes, and wiped his face with a bright-coloured silk
handkerchief; "Tank you, I better now. We all run
out to see what matter in street; den we find plenty
men, with cutlass, and gun, and pistol. Dey shoot
all de old black peoples what no good to sell for slave,
and some ob de bery strong men in the village, dat
am bery fierce, dey fight like mad mens, but de
others shoot dem dead. We all bery much co'fused,
dunno what to do, and dey soon make all ob us fast.
Dey hab got chain, and big, heavy wood collar, and
bery soon we all made into big gang. We no want
to do eberyting, but dey hab long whip, wid tick
lash, and dey slash poor darkey plenty much, till
great big wale come up on de flesh, and we cry bery
much."

Loud expressions of bitter wrath, against the Arab
traders and dhow owners, broke forth from more than
one lip, and every one seemed filled with an eager
desire to be engaged in a slaver chase at once.

"Go on, Coop," cried his listeners; "we'll fight all
the better for your story, when our chance comes."

"Bery glad, sar, if dat help you ter fight de slaber,"
continued the good fellow; "me do lub to see dhows
caught, and slabe made free. Well, all dis take long
time, and bery soon de sun rise, and de daylight
come, and den we see our mudders and grand-
mudders, some ob dem dead, and some dying. I
look all 'bout for my fader and mudder, and I see my
fader. Him lay dead, shot trough de neck, and my
mudder, oh! she such lubly woman—she tall, and
beauty face, and her skin so smooth, and shine like
a dollar. Well, I see her presently, but she chained
up with lots ob oder women, and she look so sad.
She look to where poor fader lay dead, then bery

slowly she lift her eyes and look round, and she see me, and try to smile, but me see her heart bery sad.

"Den de mens dey drive all dem black peoples, what no good to sell, all up into one place, all in heap, and den the leader him laugh, and shout to him men, 'Now den, pepper away,' and dey shoot, and shoot, till dey shoot dem all.

"Bum-bye, dey set fire to all de houses, and dey burn and blaze, and soon de lubly place all black and bad look ; den dey march us plenty much ebery day. We get tired. Some can't walk, and dey shoot dem on de road. One or two get away in de nights, but dey not missed often, and we wonder what dey do, and however dey get de collar off.

"One day, we bin marching 'bout a week, and me see woman fall down ; she in oder gang, not in mine ; den, when dey turn her round, me see it my mudder, and me hear one man say she fine woman, fetch plenty money, but she done up, she no walk farder. Den de chief man, he swear bery much, and say, no one else shall hab her if she recober on road, so he make 'em hang her up to tree by de neck, and den my mudder die."

Here the poor fellow sobbed aloud for a moment ; then, brushing the tears from his eyes, he drew himself up proudly, while his eye flashed fire, as he continued, in a firm voice :—

"Den I make up my mind, and dat night I get away. I try to fine place where dey hang my mudder, but I no find it. Plenty days pass ; I find it hard to get food, but one day I go sleep near river ; I wake when I hear noise ; I look troo de bushes and see two white mens in boat, and tree black mens wid de paddles ; but boat no move, him stuck on sand lumps in water a little way from de shore, so I go in, and pull, and push, and presently him come clear. Den de white man speak ; him know my speech, and ask me 'bout meself. He speak kind to me, and dey soon get de collar off, and dey take me wid dem."

"Who were these white men, Cooper?" inquired one of the listeners.

"Dey missionaries, and I wid dem after dis fur long time ; den dey tell me idol no use, dat Jesus Christ, *Him only*, help black man same He help de white man. He say dat plenty sin am in me, and den he show me dese words in de Testament."

Suiting the action to the words, Cooper took out his own Testament from his pocket, and read Romans 5th chapter and 12th verse : "Wherefore, as by one man sin entered into the world, and death by sin ; and so death passed upon all men, *for that all have sinned.*"

As he read these words in his broken English, his listeners were very quiet, yet no one said, " Stop ! " no one seemed to care to prevent him, and the man himself seemed deeply moved as he continued :—

"Ah, me soon find out me all wrong. De missionary talk plenty times wid me, but me somehow no see de way. One day, massa missionary, him preach beautiful, he tell 'bout Jesus, how He pity poor men, black and white, and He ask Him Fader, de great King in heaben, to let Him come down to dis earth and die instead ob dem. He come like picca-ninny ; He 'bey Him fader and Him mudder ; He go to school, grow up an' be man ; go 'bout and preach, tell peoples He ' be lifted up like serpent in

de wilderness,' and when peoples bitten wid sin look
to Him, like peoples look to de brass serpent in de
wilderness, den, when dey look, and beliebe He died
for dem, den dey hab eberlasting life. Plenty tear
run down me face, and den, as de missionary tell all
'bout de cross, and de nails, and de crown ob thorns,
and de good Jesus do all Him Fader in heaben want
done for our sin, den He cry right out, ober all de
world, to ebery peoples, 'It am finished! It am
finished!'

"When me hear dis, me jump up in de mission-
room, an' say, 'Oh, Jesus, you hab finished it for me.
I tank you so much, I do belieb it for true'; and den
—den I so happy, because *I hab eberlasting life.* An'
long time after dat I learn beauty verse :—

> "'Long my prisoned spirit lay
> Fast bound in sin and native night ;
> Thine eye d'fused a quick'ning ray :
> I woke, de dungeon flamed wid light.
> My shains fell off, my heart am free,
> I rose, went forth, and followed Thee.'

"And, oh, my shipmates, if you hab no 'surance ob
salvation, if you dunno you've got de eberlasting life,
please make haste to Jesus for it, or else——"

"Thanks, Cooper," interrupted one of his listeners,
who had enjoyed the story but who did not want the
"preaching." "So I suppose you escaped all the
horrors of being packed between decks of a slave
ship, and of the slave market?"

"Yes, sar ; but I hab been in five ob Her Majesty's
ships on the slabing ground, and hab seen all sorts
dre'ful things."

He told us things which, while fully confirmed by

our own after-experience, are too horrible and ghastly
to come in here.

How well I remember my own first experience of
slave chasing! It was on the Sunday following that
awful squall which had opened the eyes of Middy
Marvel as to the treacherousness of the proposed subject for his " Peace " picture.

The usual captain's inspection had been carried out,
the hands, in white duck trousers, white drill frocks,
and white caps, had been duly dismissed. The order
had passed along the decks, " Rig church."

The men passed to and fro rapidly, carrying the
stools on to the upper deck to form that quaint, but
picturesque sight, " Church at sea."

There was no sense of reverence among them, the
merry joke and light jest freely passing round.

The usual conundrum was asked, " What's the difference between me and my mess stool? " and the
answer was given, " The stool has to be *carried* to
church, and I have to be *driven*."

All is arranged on the quarter-deck for the service.
The fold-up pulpit is fixed, and covered with an immense Union Jack ; the books are placed on the
stand ; the bell tolls as it would in some quiet little
English parish. The men muster aft and fill the
seats ; the officers take the chairs arranged in the
rear of the pulpit. The bell ceases, and, escorted by
the ship's schoolmaster, who acts as clerk, the chaplain
takes his place.

Opening his Prayer - Book, he reads, " Let the
wicked forsake his way, and the unrighteous man his
thoughts : and let him return unto the Lord, and He
will have mercy upon him ; and to our God, for He
will abundantly pardon."

And thus, step by step, the service proceeds till they commence presently to sing, "I will arise and go to my Father."

There is something rich in the swell of this body of men's bass voices, and they are just repeating the refrain, "I will arise," when a voice, loud and clear, rings out from aloft, from the masthead, where, seated upon the cross-trees, the look-out man watches,—

"Deck ahoy!"

"Well," cried the officer of the watch, "what is it?"

"Dhow in sight, sir."

"Where away?"

"Just off the starboard bow, but she's a good many miles off, sir."

Then, in the quick, sharp tones so usual to naval officers of these times, the officer, after a whispered word with the captain, shouted,—

"Boatswain's mate! Pipe down church."

In a few moments all vestige of church was gone, and officers and men were full of intensest excitement. Their first dhow in sight! Steam was got up, every stitch of canvas was set, everything done to drive the vessel in swift pursuit.

"A stern chase is a long chase."

The dhow had some miles' start, and, in common with that class of vessel, was built and rigged to sail like a witch, as sailors say. Hour after hour passed before they seemed to gain upon her at all; but at last she can be just seen from the deck, and now a new impulse is given to the excitement. Already there are several sweepstakes started, and fully paid up, and betting runs high as to the hour in which they will overtake her, and the chances whether she is slave dhow or trader.

Then, about the middle of the afternoon, a captain's order is issued that all hands are to have an early tea, so that the coppers may be filled with fresh water, ready to wash the slaves when taken from the dhow.

After this early tea "all hands" are turned up to get out the first and second pinnaces. To clear away and hoist out the first and second pinnaces at sea was an immense labour; it was a very different thing to lowering the cutters from their davits. But here was a call upon the men that spurred them to any labour —a slave dhow, doubtless heavily-laden, packed with slaves, and each slave, whether alive or dead, representing so many pounds of prize money. Then, too, there was the love of adventure, the glorious excitement of the chase, and, above all, the fierce hatred of the British tar to the principle of slavery; all these things combined were enough to make every man excited.

Excited! Well, that is a tame word to describe the condition of these jolly Jacks. They were off the east coast of Africa; the allotted months for the traffic in so-called "domestic" slaves were passed. No slave-laden dhow could now land her vile cargo ashore under the protection of the Sultan of Zanzibar's pass, according to the "*domestic*" system. No; such vessels must now either steer north, running the blockade of the English cruisers, or, with equal risk, taking advantage of the shore haze, creep under the coast and surreptitiously land their living freight. So far as the cruisers were concerned, their opportunities for capture were now freed from the handicapping processes that for months had fettered them.

From the bridge, where the captain and first lieutenant stand (quite as excited as the men), there comes the order,—

"Top away your lift! Steady! Take a turn with your stay! Falls all clear, bo'sun?"

" All clear, sir."

"Man your falls! Steady taut! Run away then!"

And there is no mistake they did run, those men of H.M.S. *C——*. Not a discontented face, not a sulky tone, not a flagging step, but with set teeth and determined, bulldog tenacity, they gripped that rope, and making light of the ponderous weight that swung from the lifts, they raced along the deck with a cheery hurrah that not even discipline or a captain's eye upon them could check.

A little later, and we are within shot range of the slaver. The usual blank is first fired, of which no notice is taken, and it is evident that the Arabs mean fighting. Not that they have any idea that they can beat us, but, knowing that death awaits them when captured, they determine to sell their lives as dearly as may be.

Why need I detail all that followed? The first actual shot fired from our long bowchaser tore away the parrel of the yard on the dhow, which, with its mighty sail, fell crashing across her deck. A few Arabs were killed and wounded by the falling yard, the rest were ballooned in the great sail, from out of which they cut their way by slashing openings in the canvas with their hideous dirks.

Our boats, with bow ordnance and crews fully armed, surround, board, and engage the slaver, and in an incredibly short time the prize is taken, and two to three hundred British throats ring out a three times three.

But oh the piteousness and horror of the unloading of the slaves! The dhow had been nearly a month at sea, as was afterwards ascertained. During the whole of the time this living mass of negroes, men and women, together with a score of children, had been prisoners below. Fastened securely to the slave deck with leg-irons, they had sat, or lain, festering in dirt and vermin, throughout those long weeks.

Over two hundred human beings were packed in this hideous fashion. Men and women alike, packed in rows, were seated with their legs drawn up till their chins touched their knees. Here and there a dead slave still retained his or her position between the living, because there was no possibility of falling either forward, backward, or at either side.

Rice had been served out in small quantities twice a day, but they were awfully lean, and gaunt, and weak; and as the sailors, with rough but tender touch, lifted their nude bodies from the accumulated filth, and saw their terrible flesh-sores, more than one of these rough seamen wept like children. The stench was fearful, and the moans of the weakest, together with the groans of the stronger slaves, would move the coldest and hardest heart.

Two boats had been cleared out and swung inboard upon the deck of our vessel, and every washtub in the ship was requisitioned to serve as baths for the poor black souls. The ship's coppers (after the early tea had been served out that afternoon) had been filled with fresh water, and from this supply of boiling water the impromptu baths were constantly replenished.

Every man was busy bathing the poor creatures,

having torn up his oldest under-flannel to make soft washers for the poor bodies of the blacks.

In almost every case they were utterly helpless, and had to be bathed as you would bathe a sick baby. The children (poor little mites) could be laid in to soak, two or three at a time, while one was being actually cleansed ; but with the poor, helpless women and men the process was a much longer one, for besides the accumulated horrors of dirt, of a month's close confinement, which had to be soaked and washed off, there was the fact that their poor skins were so bruised and broken, that the work was necessarily slow.

Many a sailor's eye shed tears of pity as he pursued his bath-work upon the bodies of those poor women and men.

The remark is often made, " I suppose there is nothing of this kind in these days? " If there was not, I hardly think I should have included this chapter in this book. But even as I write these words, I know, as well as though I was on that East African coast, witnessing the slaver's villainies, that the work is going on still, and that, too, to an extent of which people can scarcely conceive.

Sometimes, in our daily papers, we see a paragraph of a dozen or twenty lines, to the effect that " the boats of H.M.S. —— have just captured a dhow, having on board slaves to the number of ——," etc. People read this without a thought of what it means.

When I write of these things I dare not let all my soul go out through my pen, so I close this chapter with a few words of that grand old slave advocate —John Greenleaf Whittier :—

" Who bids for God's own image?—for His grace,
Which that poor victim of the market-place
    Hath in her suffering won ?

   " My God ! can such things be ?
Hast Thou not said that whatsoe'er is done
Unto Thy weakest and Thy humblest one
    Are even done to Thee ?

   " In that sad victim, then,
Child of Thy pitying love, *I see Thee* stand,—
Once more the jest-word of a mocking band,
    Bound, sold, and scourged again !

     *   *   *   *   *

   " Hoarse, horrible, and strong,
Rises to Heaven that agonising cry,
Filling the arches of the hollow sky,
    HOW LONG, O GOD, HOW LONG ?"

Chapter XX

THE GAMBLING VICE

I HAVE more than once spoken of my constant sea-sickness, and my hatred of the Service—a hatred which led me to attempt desertion *twice*, before I left England for my first sea-going ship, on a foreign station.

On that vessel, in spite of the constant fire of disgust of the Service which burned within me, I so schooled myself as to *appear* satisfied. My character was V. G. (very good) whenever at general muster the characters of all hands were read out.

I had developed considerable nicety of work and finish as a carpenter, and was for a long time, by the captain's order, specially set aside to work for him as his joiner. He was a distinguished member of the Geographical Society, and of several other scientific societies, and it was an open secret that naval matters were, to him, of very little importance, compared with travel, specimens, etc.

Whenever he went on shore I went with him, boxed his specimens, sampled and tested the colour, grain, and markings of fancy woods, and, in short, acted as general factotum.

In this way I saw much that was interesting—places, races, customs, peoples. Thirty to forty years ago scarcely one English intelligent reader in ten thousand even knew the name of Port Blair, that strange island penal settlement to which life-convicts were sent from India. Not a great deal of it is known even to-day, but this remarkable place fell to my lot to see thoroughly while in attendance upon my captain.

Burmah, with its wondrous pagodas, its interesting peoples, its marvellous scenery, its swift, imposing river-way, came in the programme of those days. Rangoon, Akyab, Maulmein, and other interesting places were duly visited.

A piece of special retributive work, upon a noted Chinese pirate, who had been ravaging with fire and sword all the smaller places upon the Penang coast, took us, in search, into that marvellous Eastern Archipelago.

What a wonderful place this was, with its winding, tortuous, intricate water-ways between the myriads of tiny islets, the wondrous tropical overgrowths, so covering the entrances to these water-ways that when, with yards pointed fore and aft, we steamed into them, the lofty, tree-like foliage would spring back again, and completely hide the entrance, and shut us in as effectually as though some curtain had fallen behind us.

The story of the capture of that pirate, like many another story of these days, must be omitted in so brief a record as the present book must necessarily be; it must suffice here to say that the old proverb, " Set a thief to catch a thief," found another proof in our chase.

The government at Rangoon had in its pay an old Chinese pirate. This man was lent to us as pilot, pirate-catcher, and interpreter, with the result that, after three or four of the most thrilling days I ever spent (in the neighbourhood of the above-mentioned islands), we carried our captured pirate back to Rangoon, and handed him over to the authorities, who soon after despatched him for his life-time of villainy.

It was while lying off Rangoon, on the occasion of this second visit, that one of the most awful fires I ever witnessed—certainly the one attended with the most terrible loss of life—occurred. I include it in these autobiographical jottings because it was brought about through gambling, a vice which, in my old days at sea, wrought fearful havoc in my own life.

In the Wake of a Gamble.

In a huge storehouse upon the wharves at Rangoon, British Burmah, sit two Chinamen. The place is packed from floor to roof with merchandise of every description, waiting to be shipped and exported.

The air is redolent of spices, and many an aromatic odour blends with the faint smell of jute and the earthy smell of packed cotton.

The men have made themselves a little clearing among the huge bales. Upon one of these is an oil lamp, which sheds a sickly gleam upon their broad, flat, sallow faces.

A keen observer would have noted the same traces of passion upon these Chinese features to be found on those of English, French, American, or any other nationality, when similarly engaged.

What is it that so absorbs these two Celestials? Gambling? Yes; one does not need to catch the click of the ivory to know that here are two more slaves to that cruel vice.

How closely each watches the other ! How eagerly either seeks an opportunity to cheat ! And, soon, one detects the other in the very act.

Hot, angry words follow. Already every passion is inflamed by the arrack they have drunk, and they speedily come to blows.

With a spring like a wild cat one throws himself upon the other. There is no secure foothold for them as they wrestle and writhe amongst those piled stuffs.

Blinded with a murderous hate, they do not notice the overturning of the lamp. The oil quickly spreads among the jute, the burning wick lies for one moment on the inflammable stuff, then, quick as lightning, there bursts forth a terrific blaze.

Drunk with arrack, play, and passion, they show no presence of mind. They have no thought except to save their own skins. They make no attempt to arrest the progress of the flames, but flee from the burning mass.

Along those mighty wharves are tier upon tier of warehouses, crowded with every description of inflammable stores, and soon those awful flames are racing along from building to building.

The wharves are built on piles—huge wooden piles —that bear thousands of tons of the rich products of the East.

Beneath these piles, moored to each other, are hundreds of boats in which dwell thousands of human souls—Chinese boat-people—a vast floating population.

Above them the flames roar and rage. Down upon

them, through the wide cracks in the planking of the wharves, the blazing oil and tar trickles and flows, carrying death in its fiery streams.

A few cast off their boats, and, half-dazed with fear, push tremblingly out upon the broad waters of the Irawaddy.

The fire has got a mighty hold. Like some giant furnace the whole mass of buildings, wharves, stores, and piles glow with a fiery, scorching heat.

Almost abreast of the burning wharves lies our vessel. The paint on her sides blisters and cracks ; her tarred stays run with slow, hot streams of liquid tar, melted by the fierce heat of the fire. It is evident that the fierce heat will soon fire the vessel, and rapid preparations are made to drop her down the stream.

The ship's cutters return one by one from ineffectual efforts to save the infatuated Chinese who are burning in their boats. Then, slowly, the splendid corvette drops down the stream and reluctantly, but compulsorily, they leave the awful scene.

Among our crew was an able-bodied seaman, a man of forty years or near about. He had seen a great deal of service, but it was not hard service that had seared and scored his face so terribly.

Lining his forehead, face, neck, and hands, were deep channels, which seemed to have eaten their awful way far into the flesh. His nose was almost completely gone, and his ears were split and shrivelled till they had lost all their natural shape.

He was a silent man, caring very little about anything except seamanship, gunnery, and grog. The last was his great bane.

During the fire upon the wharves, and especially as

he watched the falling ruins and traced the darting flames as they licked up the lives of the poor, helpless Chinese, he seemed ubiquitous, and full of an irrepressible excitement.

All this was so unlike him that during the quiet of the last dog-watch, the second night after the fire, some of the more curious questioned him as to his unusual activity and excitement. But very few were expecting the story that followed.

"Most on yer hev heard about the old *Revenge*, and that she wur burnt at sea," he began. "Well, I was in her, an' I guess I am purty well marked through it."

He pointed to his face, and spread his hands out before them as he spoke, a grim smile upon his face the while.

Poor fellow! All his smiles were grim to the eyes of those who saw them. They could not be otherwise with that disfigured face.

"I don't know what the Admiralty put down as the cause of that fire on their books, but I know wot we, who wur on the lower deck, allus said wur the cause. Yer see, shipmates, it wur like this yer. We wur chock-full o' cockroaches—great fellows, three inches long. An' there wur allus a sight o' gamblin' an' bettin' in the old *Revenge*. We used to bet on anythink. I remember when one of our chaps took a header from the foretop—accidental, o' course—that he misfortunately hit hisself on the bits when he purled over off the stay as he struck at first. Well, it wur a long time afore the doctors thought he'd ever git over it. An' there wur more bets laid on his life or death than I've got fingers or toes. Well, that ain't here nor there.

"I wur goin' to tell yer 'bout them cockroaches. We used to get a half a dozen ov the biggest, an' half a dozen short bits o' glim (candle), 'bout quarter-inch long, light 'em, an' drop one drop o' melted fat on they cockroaches' backs, an' stick the lighted candles on 'em; then git 'em in a line, an' race 'em, an' lay some tight odds on 'em, I can assure yer.

"Well, the day as the old packet kotched fire we'd had some of these races on the lower deck, an' some of they cockroaches got off into their holes wi' those candles all alight. The Admiralty kin jist put down wot they likes as the cause o' that fire, but some on .us as knows more than they cocked-hat gintry, allus believed as the *Revenge* wur sot on fire that way."

The sailor paused for a moment, took out a fresh quid, then, with a deep-sea sigh, continued, "I s'pose wot's burnt in don't come out very easily; leastways, I don't guess I'll ever forget that time aboard that burning wessel. There wur a awful lot o' our poor chaps as lost the number o' their mess, an' went to 'Davy Jones's Locker,' an' I don't want to be hard on' em, but they was most of 'em regular 'Mother Carey's chickens.' Not but wot I b'lieves many on em kinder remembered summat o' the things as they wur told an' teached when they wur youngsters. I mind, when things wur 'bout as bad as they could be, a chap started singin',

> ' Jesu, Lover o' my soul,
> Let me to Thy bosom fly,'

an' very soon there wur a lot singin' it. An' though I don't purfess to be 'ligious, I knows this much, as cf a feller gits face to face wi' suddent death like that, an' sort o' feels as he's all wrong, an' right down

from the bottom o' his heart sings out genuine-like,
'God be merciful to me a sinner,' then I takes it God
Almighty 'll be merciful to him. Well, be that as it
may, I wur one o' them as got saved, but not afore I
wur purty nearly done fur.

"I hung on underneath the bow o' the old boat as
long as I could, an' the lead wot wur on top o' the
bowsprit melted, an' *dripped* fust, then run down in
streams, run through the cloth o' my cap, down my
forehead, guttered along my poor old cheeks, an'
kind o' filletted itself through my ears, an' on to my
hands.

"Yer all knows I'm 'bout as ugly as sin; I ain't
much to look at, I knows; I ain't no better an' I
ought to be; but there's one thing as yer can book
agin me—an' that is, I ain't never done a bit o'
gamblin' or bettin' since. An' yer can stake yer
dollars on this fact bein' as true as truth—that is,
that the fool as plays with the gamblin' devil not
only hurts hisself, but brings all sorts o' sorrer on the
innercent as well."

Eight bells struck at that moment; the old sailor
gave a quick, heavy sigh, then added, "There goes
eight on 'em. I must be off. P'raps in future yer
won't be quite so eager to give or take odds on
everythink as is movin', an' p'raps yer'll sort o' fur-
give poor old chop-dollar face fur bein' so ugly, seein'
it ain't all his fault."

I have preferred to give this true story in, as nearly
as possible, the language of the old sailor himself,
since any polish would have robbed it of much of its
pathos and force.

Though kept through all my life from yielding to
the drink-fiend (the effect, doubtless, of the horror

and shock that came to my child-soul at the suicide of my dear father), yet I, very early in my sea career, yielded to the snare of the demon of play.

There was nothing in those days too sacred, or too trifling, upon which we would not bet or gamble in some form. The vice gripped my whole soul, at one time in my experience, until there was nothing that I would not sacrifice to make the wherewithal to stake.

Two notable instances of this infatuation stand out clear and distinct in my memory. The first occurred during the second year of my foreign service. I had played at doubles, with dice, for several nights with varying success, until at last I was cleaned out completely, and did not possess a copper, or, as we used to say in the East Indies, a *markee*.

All day, after my last night's losses, I was moody and dispirited, after the fashion of the *unlucky* gambler. The next evening, in turning over my ditty box, I found a soiled, but unused stamp. My old opponent challenged me to have a "rattle"; I showed him the stamp, saying, "Take this for a penny, and I'm on."

He consented; a pin was stuck through the stamp, and it was fixed up in a prominent place *for luck*. The small square of thick, dirty red baize was spread upon the table; a mess-kettle and a couple of ditty boxes were arranged as a kind of screen, lest some inquisitive or case-hunting ship's corporal should pass the mess, and spy out our game; then the first throw of the dice was made.

In our game of "doubles," as we called it, we doubled the stakes each time. Our first stake was a penny—I won, staked the twopence, and won again; staked the fourpence, and won again. Then on it went—eightpence, one shilling and fourpence, two shillings and eightpence, and so on.

For a long time my "luck" never changed, and £4 5s. 4d. became mine, and my blood rioted through my veins like liquid fire.

An interruption came, the game was suspended for a short time, and when we recommenced to play I lost several successive times.

"Had my luck turned?" I asked myself, for again and again I lost. Then suddenly I won again, lost again, then won several times consecutively, until the £4 5s. 4d. was wholly mine again.

Again and again that solitary stamp had been all I had had to fall back upon, and it had enabled me to start afresh. Now, with everything staked, it came my turn to throw the dotted cubes ; I threw—I lost— I was stripped of everything again.

The consequences of this wild bout of dice-fever were only mental anger and annoyance ; beyond these things, no other *apparent* punishment followed my mad turn. But the second episode at which I have hinted cost me more than this.

We were accustomed to bet upon all the chief English racing events of the year, depending for our tips upon the newspapers we received by mail, and these were sometimes two, and even three, months old.

With the cocksureness of youth and ignorance, I had pinned my faith to a certain horse one year—I am not sure that my trust was not more in the jockey than the horse—and had plunged tremendously.

In feverish, sickening excitement, I waited for the next mail, that should bring us the final news of that devil's carnival, " The Derby."

We were lying at Seychelles at the time, when a

French mail-boat rounded in sight one afternoon, and through our ship there rang the cry, "Liam ni, Liam ni!" (the ordinary back slang meaning "Mail in!")

In half an hour the result of the Derby was known, and I was utterly ruined. To pay those betting debts, I parted with every article of clothing I possessed, except one suit of "whites" and my old night suit, and had surreptitiously to wash out that one white suit every night, ready for next day's wear.

On Sunday I borrowed my sold tunic. My "compo" (monthly half-pay) was mortgaged for three months, and, altogether, I was in as awkward a plight as a man under naval discipline could well be.

However, I comforted myself with the thought that we were not likely to have a Bag and Kit inspection for some time ; and I set myself to work and save, and thus recover my position.

Alas! for human plans. One forenoon a *surprise* inspection of bags and hammocks took place. The hands were mustered, and the captain and first lieutenant, with the usual following of officers, passed down the ranks, the captain indicating, by the word "bag" or the word "hammock," which of these the man spoken to was to fetch at once for inspection.

I shook in my shoes as he drew near to me. He walked past a score of men without speaking, then suddenly paused at a man, and said, "Bag." He skipped one man and said, "Hammock."

I breathed a little freer, for he never picked too many within a short space, and the last man spoken to was only two above me.

On came the autocrat and his following. He looked at me, and—passed me, without speaking. I could have shouted with glad relief.

Suddenly he paused, walked backwards, stood in front of me, and said, " Bag and hammock."

Even as I write, my heart beats like some caged bird trying frantically to secure its freedom—beats as it did that day nearly thirty years ago, when I realised that I was in for some trouble.

I had cut up my blankets, made " lammies " (night sleeping suits) of them ; had sold my bed, and the three ticks, and, as I have already said, sold all my other kit—to pay my gambling debts.

I need not describe the scene that ensued, when I was obliged to confess that I had done away with my bed and clothes, though *why* I had done it, and *how* I had disposed of them, I dared not tell.

At noon, I received seven days' cells punishment, and was marched straight away to the tiny six-foot-by-four cupboard, called, by courtesy, a cell.

It is not pleasant writing all this, but I do want these real life-records to be useful as warnings, and though often at bitter cost to myself, I pen these things, that some, who read (especially lads), and some who will use these stories as illustrations and warnings to others, may be blessed.

From my own personal experience I could fill a volume, twice the size of this, with the stories of lives which have been cursed by the twin demons of drink and play.

One of the greatest evils that can ever befal any person who is tempted for the *first* time by the unholy lust of gaming, *is to win.* Better to have lost, and lost heavily, and thus be warned off the vice, than to win and be seduced to play again ; for there are few *winners* who ever have the strength to do as the lawyer in the following incident did. (I quote the incident from the *Sunday Companion.*)

"ON THE BORDER-LINE.

"A party of five gentlemen had been in the habit of meeting once a week to play poker. They were each of them ordinarily successful in his profession, and were respected in their business and personal relations. The incident given below, which took place at their last meeting for the purpose of an evening's indulgence in their favourite game, dramatic as it may seem, is strictly true.

"That night their stakes were heavier than ever, and one of the five men was a lawyer, who had many important clients depending upon him. He was the most imperturbable of the players, greatly addicted to the game, and, as it happened in this instance, held the highest cards in his hands. He knew that he was a sure winner, for no other combination could possibly beat him.

"The excitement became extreme, and the betting had risen from a few pounds to hundreds. The lawyer for a moment changed colour, then put his hand into his pocket, took out a roll of banknotes, and, counting from it five hundred pounds, laid the notes in the middle of the table, thus covering the last bet. He then said : 'I call you,' which is the technical way of bringing the betting to an end. As he did so he turned pale, and his hand shook as he showed his winning-cards.

"The doctor of the party thought that he was going to faint from the excitement of winning such a large amount, and sprang to assist him ; but the lawyer waved him back and bent his head, trying to control himself. His friends felt that this emotion was due to some unusual cause. In silence they looked on while he did a strange thing.

" First he took five one hundred-pound notes from the heap of money that he had won, and, folding them together, he put them with the roll he had taken from his pocket.

" When this was done he drew a long breath—almost a gasp of relief. Then he carefully separated his own original money from the remainder, and pushed the rest away, looking at it steadily for a second or two without speaking. At length he said, raising his hand and registering a solemn oath—we quote his words exactly :—

" ' I am done with poker. Loving the game as much as I do, I give it up at this moment for ever. I have stepped across the border-line of dishonour to-night. The money I have just put back into my pocket was given to me by a client to be paid out this morning, and if I had lost it I could not immediately have replaced it.

" ' I had it in my possession,' he continued, ' simply because I had not had the opportunity to deposit it in the bank, and in the excitement of the game I forgot that it was not my own. The fascination that would make me do a thing like that is one that I dare not risk again. I cannot touch the money that I won with it, for it was not my own.'

" The lawyer rose and left the room, never to return to it.

" He had unconsciously given a striking illustration of the fact that the essence of character may be lost or saved at the moment when one comes to the border-line between an honest and a dishonest act."

I close this chapter with the words of S. C. Hall :—

> " This is the moral—solemn, awful, true !—
> The gambler never knows what he may do ! "

Chapter XXI

A NEW KIND OF PARADISE

THE effect of that seven days' cells upon me was disastrous. I had nothing to do but think, and my thoughts were not useful or pleasant. I reviewed all my past years of service, and, in the inflamed condition of my mind, every act of tyranny or oppression, every failure on the part of the Government to redeem the pledges made upon that " Wanted " placard, which had helped to decide my joining the Navy, became magnified, until I grew furious, mad.

That my mind in those days took utterly distorted views of many of my supposed grievances, I know now ; but I felt at the time as perfectly justified in thinking and acting as I did, as ever the great apostle did, when he thought he did good service by haling men and women to prison, for their faith's sake.

The inquiry often arises within me ," Are young people *taught* and *trained* sufficiently in the great *principles* which should underlie all the acts of individual life, and by which they should judge things, whether for or against them ? " I am sure that in those early days of my life, my untrained mind and life led me to do, and say, and think things which could never have been possible had I been taught to look more closely at the *principles* that should underlie all acts of life.

Lying in that wretched little box of a cell for seven days, my biassed, untrained mind worked fiercely, feverishly over all my real and fancied wrongs.

I remembered my first acquaintance with ship's cells. I had, in the training-ship, exchanged four pocket-handkerchiefs for four towels with a messmate of mine. I had bought a number of handkerchiefs at various times, and some had been given me by friends, but I was short of towels. My messmate had a surplus of towels but no handkerchiefs—hence the exchange. The exchanged articles were, on both sides, purely *personal* property, and each of us felt that we had a right to do as we pleased with these things.

At the next general bag inspection, an official spied my name upon some of the other lad's handkerchiefs ; this led to an explanation of our " trade " together, with the result that we each received six strokes with the cane, and on my protesting at the injustice of the punishment, I was called " a sea lawyer," and given an additional punishment of three days' *ship's* cells. At the same time I was reminded, that over every port, on the mess-deck, there was a card affixed, stating that it was illegal for any boy to borrow, barter, or sell anything in his possession.

The printed card *was* a fact, but the mischief was, that I and many others failed to see how, because other people made that harsh (so it seemed to us) and stringent law, it could be morally binding upon us, when it concerned our own *personal* property.

Speaking of those printed rules reminds me of a serio-comic incident, that came out of the enforcement of them upon a shipmate of mine.

He was a notorious borrower, a very indifferent

payer-back, and a keen hand at barter. Hauled up at length for some bit of exchange business, he received punishment of seven days' black list, and was told emphatically that if he was caught infringing one of *those* rules again he would not get off so lightly.

There must have been a considerable streak of humour in his composition (he was from Dublin), for he borrowed a boatswain boy's pipe in the dinner hour, and making a tour of the mess deck, while all hands were at dinner, he piped for silence, then, in true boatswain's style, he cried, " D'yer hear there ! I've got seven days' black list fur chopping a lanyard fur some sewing silk, an' this is to give notice that from this time forth, I, Jemmy Carlyon, neither borrows nor lends, exchanges or barters, NOR PAYS WOT I OWES."

I brooded over all the past of my naval experiences while enduring that seven days' cells, until I grew almost literally mad. Once a day I was taken on deck for an hour for fresh air. Here I was handcuffed, and my soul fretted within me to such an extent that, if I could have evaded the marine who guarded me, I verily believe I should have hurled myself overboard—I did try once to elude the guard

Before three out of the seven days' cells had expired, I had determined that, do with me as they would, I would never do another day's work for the Crown—that I would rather commit suicide than live the life I did.

On being released, at the end of the seven days, I was sent to the *benches* to work. This was at once a surprise, and a source of fresh anger to me. I have explained before that I had been made captain's joiner, and it had never once occurred to me during my seven days' incarceration that I should be reduced to the ordinary work of the carpenter's crew.

Of course my late escapade, in the matter of the sold kit, deserved the loss of the captain's favour, but I was in the wrong mood to brook further punishment; and when the chief carpenter, who could be an awful bully when he liked, took advantage of my being out of favour, to be particularly ugly to me, I proceeded to put into operation the course I had planned while in cells.

I refused duty, declaring that I would never do another stroke for the Queen, not if they punished me for life. (I pause here and wonder, as I remember that I am writing of this disloyalty in the great sixtieth year of good Victoria's reign.)

In the briefest time possible I was upon the quarter deck, and being charged with that most awful of naval crimes—" Refusal of duty."

Beside myself with passion, I let my mad speech loose upon those before whom I had been summoned. The captain appeared on deck at the moment, and the first lieutenant stepped aft to speak to him. Half a minute later the captain stood before me, his usual kindly face full of anger and disgust.

Absolutely mad with passion, I hurled my cap down upon the deck, in a savage, defiant fashion, as I shouted, " I mean what I say; you can flog me or hang me, if you like, I don't care, but I won't do another stroke for the Queen, *in* the navy, so there !"

A small crowd of men had gathered in the two waists of the ship, as far aft as they dared to come, listening and watching to all that was said and done. Among them there were many whispered comments, such as "Chippy" (the nickname of a carpenter on board ship), "Chippy's a fool!"

"He's sure to get flaked (flogged)!"

"It 'd be more'n his life was wuth, twenty years ago, to carry on all top-ropes like that."

"I allus thought it was in that chap, only the doctor kept him kind o' square!"

Of course it was a mad thing to do. The officers felt it, and *looked* it, and, for just one moment, even the captain was taken aback.

The next moment, recovering himself, he said, coldly, determinedly, "Master-at-arms, put this man under arrest in irons."

A few minutes later I was lying upon the bare deck below, my legs in irons, and a marine sentry in charge over me.

Quiet and alone, I realized my folly and madness in carrying out my plan in so violent a manner. Then I began to reflect on what the possible consequences of my act would be.

I thought and speculated over many things, and was still thus mentally engaged when a voice hailed my guard.

"Sentry!"

"Sir?" replied the marine.

"Bring the prisoner on deck!"

"Yes, sir!"

In a few minutes I stood again before the captain on the quarter-deck.

His face was full of its old kindliness, there even seemed a touch of pity in it as he said, "During the time you have been below I have thought over your rash conduct, and have come to the conclusion that you were carried away by a sudden passion, and am therefore unwilling to take advantage of your mad act, and expose you to the inevitable consequences should you be tried by court-martial. I do not say I shall be prepared to let you off without some punishment, but if you will promise to return to your duty, and stick to your post as becomes a true man under the Queen, I will be as lenient with you as I dare. If, however, you persist in your mutinous behaviour, I think it is likely I shall flog you without court-martial at once. What is it to be?"

All my passion was dead within me, but my purpose was none the less strong, and I replied, "You are very kind, sir, I am sorry I have hurt your feelings, but I meant what I said, for I hate the navy and will not serve any longer."

The old angry, set, determined look came into the face of my good old captain as he said sternly, "Very well, sir, we shall see. I will give you one hour to reconsider your words; then, if you fail to return to your duty, you may expect immediate punishment."

With a glance at the master-at-arms he said, "Remove the prisoner!"

When I was once more below, and the irons had been shackled upon my ankles, the sentry said, "You're in for a flaking (flogging), my boy, if you don't look out. What are you going to do?"

"I'm going to have a sleep!" I replied, as making a pillow of a folded, unslung hammock that was lying close by, I turned on my side, and in two minutes was fast asleep.

For many years great excitement (when it had passed) had almost the same effect upon me as an opiate, and always drove me to sleep.

What followed I learned afterwards. The sentry was so utterly surprised to see me go soundly asleep, when there was a possible four dozen lashes hanging over me, that he sent for the master-at-arms, told him what had happened, and suggested that I might be ill, to sleep under such circumstances.

The master-at-arms came, looked at me, assured himself that I was really fast asleep, then went to the first lieutenant, who also came to see me.

But I did not wake.

Meanwhile, the first lieutenant had told the captain, who was at first so amazed that he could scarce believe his ears. Then after a consultation with the first lieutenant, the exact nature of which I do not of course know, it was decided that I should be sent on shore to the *civil* prison for three months.

I slept a sound, unbroken sleep, until the hammocks were piped down, the sentry having received orders not to wake me for my tea, but to report when I *did* finally wake.

I awoke hungry and thirsty, ate the food and drank the tea which my mess had sent down for me, inquired the time, and what had happened since I went to sleep.

The next morning I was formally sentenced, and sent on shore to serve my three months.

The civil gaol was used chiefly for the confinement of the natives. Sometimes a European sailor (one of the merchant ship's crews) might be confined here, but so rarely was this the case that the European prisoner was regarded more as a welcome guest than aught else.

I could have screamed with laughter and delight at the life that opened up to me in this place. The governor was a kindly, fat, old Portuguese, who wore.

a semi-official uniform tunic, baggy trousers, a rusty-gold braided official cap, wooden sabots on his feet, and an eternal smile on his greasy, expressionless face.

As soon as the ship's officer who brought me had disappeared, he began to question me in his quaint pigeon-English, and on finding that I was a carpenter, he laughed heartily—such a strange, hollow-sounding, chuckling laugh, that was like the noise of two marbles chasing each other round an empty box, the sharper notes of the laugh being like the click, click, of the marbles when they came together.

He led me into a room quite fourteen feet square, with tiled floor, large rough-made table in the centre, and a wooden charpoy (bedstead) at one side. A few shelves, with an odd lot of books, filled a four-foot hollow in the wall on one side, and two long stools stood against other two sides of wall.

"This vas pe your aparet—ment," he said, adding, "You vill have plenty nicce foot to eat, and——"

He put his hand into his pocket, and drew forth half a dozen roughly-made cigars, as he asked, with an extra broad grin, "You smoke, eh?"

I said, "Yes." He grinned again, pressed the cigars upon me, and gave utterance to a very gratified "Goot, that, very goot!"

He lit a cigar for himself, offered me his match-box, and I followed suit, all the while wondering whether prison, in this place, wasn't spelt P-a-r-a-d-i-s-e.

We were soon both puffing contentedly enough at our cigars, which, if roughly-made, proved to be of very first-class tobacco.

"Come you wi' me?" he said, and I followed him, until we came to a capital workshop, where an open tool-chest, a bench, several half-finished pieces of work, and fresh shavings all about the floor told of recent occupation by a carpenter.

"One man, a preesener, a man of your country," explained the governor, "has peen here, an' work, work, work, efery day for me. He ill now; the doctor say p'raps die. You will work now here; you sall haf cigars each day, curry fish, rice, fowl, coffee, bazaar cake, banana, orange, an' all likee that, so you work well."

I assured him I would work like a Briton, and again could hardly keep from screaming with mirth over the pleasant turn my prison term had taken.

I soon found that I was never to be locked up, that I had the run of the beautiful old garden attached to the governor's house, as well as the courtyard and all the outside buildings. The dozen quiet, inoffensive Singalese prisoners regarded me with almost as much respect as the governor, and salaamed to me to an amazing degree.

After the governor left me, I changed my clothes, putting on a white, coarse canvas working suit, instead of the suit of drill I had worn ashore; then prepared to give my fourteen-foot apartment a good clean out, roof, walls, floor.

I asked the fat, good-tempered peon gaoler for broom, bucket, etc., and he immediately fetched four of the Singalese prisoners to clean the place to my order.

I gave them each a cigar; they grinned, showing their dazzlingly white teeth, then set to work like an army of charwomen and housemaids at a spring cleaning.

And I smoked most contentedly the while, feeling

about as happy as I had ever done in my life, and certainly relishing this prison sentence far more than I should have done the expected flogging, of which I had been agreeably disappointed.

Chapter XXII

A SON OF SCOTIA

WHEN I had seen that the four Singalese thoroughly understood my notion of cleansing my prison apartment, and that they knew how to work when they liked, I went outside to explore the geography of the whole place.

One of the first things I noticed was that on one side of the room allotted me (the apartment formed two sides of an abutting angle) there was another window, but shuttered closely with jalousies. This shuttering I immediately cleared away, flooding the room with light, and, I think, momentarily startling the peon and the prisoners at work inside.

Continuing my outside exploration I came to a garden, which to my eyes, accustomed only to the cramped, unadorned surroundings of a ship, seemed a veritable Eden. Lovely tropical growths, palm-like, fern-like, with flowers of gorgeous hue, roses of every shade, orange, magnolia, lemon, and a hundred other wondrous and beautiful things, grew everywhere.

Humming-birds, with others so beautiful that they looked like marvellous flashing jewels as they flitted from bush to bush, were everywhere; while sharp-eyed, gay-coated, impudent little lizards were scattered as profusely over walls and paths of the garden, and flashed as brilliantly in the sun as the spangles on the "coloured sheet characters" which adorned the toy-shop windows forty years ago.

One or two parsonic-looking crows moved haughtily about upon the paths, screamed at by half a dozen red and green parrots.

There was a sound of falling water somewhere; I followed the sound. A black rope wriggled across one of the paths I took, disappearing in a thick bush of myrtle, and giving a parting hiss as it vanished.

I found the water. In an angle of the wall there had been built in part of an old black and green marble fountain. The small upper basin was dry; the lower and larger basin, the rim of which was not more than a foot from the ground, was always filling from a tiny stream that fell murmuring and splashing into it over the worn metal lip of an old pipe that pierced the wall.

Standing in this wide shallow basin of glittering water, on one red leg, looking like a sleepy sentry, with its half-closed eyes, its head lowered and all atwist, was a lugubrious-looking white stork.

The overflow of water ran into three narrow, artificial runnels that went silently flowing through three different portions of the garden.

Having seen all that there was to be seen here, and noting with satisfaction that through the second window of my prison (?) room I should have this garden for my view, it occurred to me that if there was a countryman of mine sick in the prison, I ought to find him out, and I returned to my room to find the peon gaoler, and to ask him where this sick man was, and whether I could see him.

"Bum-bye, sar, you see him; not now!" was the

answer I received to my inquiry, and contenting myself for the time, I began to arrange my room after my own notions, the Singalese cleaners having finished their work.

It did not take many minutes to arrange the room; then I turned to the shelf of books I had noticed. Some of the titles I have forgotten; some I shall never forget. They were all filthy with much careless handling; foul in odour with stale tobacco and garlic, and thickly coated with accumulated dust.

Among the musty, motley collection there were, "The Babington Peerage," Doddridge's "Rise and Progress of the Soul," "Handy Recipes for a Handy Man," "Metrical Version of the Psalms," "Babblings in Verse for Babes," "The Basket of Flowers," "The Adventures of a Cat through her Nine Lives," "Scotch Paraphrases," "Grimm's Goblins," a volume of "Simeon's Sermons," "Robinson Crusoe," "The Heart of the Holy Mother" (this in some foreign tongue).

Having arranged this queer library according to the size of the books, without any regard to titles or subjects, I was prepared to do anything expected of me as prisoner or guest, or whatever they considered me to be.

It was not until evening that I got a sight of the sick man of whom I had heard, the peon gaoler coming to fetch me to see him. How vividly that evening, and that prison scene stands out in my memory, and lives before my eye!

It was a strange, weird scene! A long, narrow apartment; an old truckle bedstead, with a coarse rough bed; the Portuguese governor standing with a nervous, helpless look upon his expressionless greasy face, and by his side a priest with a small book in one hand, and a crucifix in the other.

One cocoanut-oil lamp with floating wick hung aloft, and cast a dim light over a small radius, and threw quaint, grim shadows distorting every figure and object, and making the whole scene weird and unearthly.

Tossing about upon the rude bed, partly covered with a large tiger skin, was the gaunt form of an old, grey-haired Scotchman.

There could be no doubt about his nationality. If one had failed to read this in the features, his tongue, as he babbled and sang in his dying delirium, would have told the story of his race. He must have had a life of strange vicissitudes, so varied were his ravings.

> "What mind-smith can trace the subtle links
>   That join a man's ideas when he thinks?
>   Given the thought by which he's pleased or vexed,
>   Who can predict what one will strike him next?
>   Given a memory, who can tell us all
>   The other memories that its voice may call?
>   Given a fancy, who betimes can read
>   What other unlike fancies it may breed?
>   Beneath our thoughts, thoughts hidden thickly teem;
>   Each mind is but a stream above a stream."

Thus it was with the sick Scotchman. Suddenly he sat up, and waving his arms about wildly, sang in roystering style a snatch of an old Crimean army song,—

> "Not long shall last the combat,
>   Tho' Russia laugh to scorn;
> The wrongful cause if up to-day
>   Is down to-morrow morn!
> When France unites with England,
>   Beware defeat and shame,

> Ye foes of right who force the fight,
> And fan the needless flame !"

He paused for a moment, and then burst out with the chorus,—

> "Hark ! over Europe sounding,
> The signal——"

Here he broke off as if listening. Did some other signal come to his mind?—a memory of long, long ago ?

Perhaps it was the sound of the "kirk bell," for, lying quietly back upon his pillow, he sang in softer voice to a dreary old dirge-like tune,—

> "The Lord my Shepherd is,
> He does supply my need ;
> 'Mid pastures green and waters fresh,
> He doth my poor soul feed."

Then for awhile oaths and songs, obscene jest and psalm, were awfully mingled, followed by a short season of quiet, and anon by intelligent consciousness.

The priest drew near to his side, and, holding before his eyes the crucifix, said in a persuasive voice : " My son, your end is near ; make confession, that you may receive absolution and the last offices of the Holy Church."

Evidently the mind of the sick man was becoming stronger and clearer, and neglected teaching of past days came with power and force to his heart and mind ; for, looking the priest steadily in the face, he said : " You'll nae doot mean weel, with your co'fession an' your Papist bauble, but grey-haired sinner though I be, I yet mind me weel how my mither tocht me the way to heaven."

" Yes, my son," interrupted the priest ; " but I have power now from the Church to offer you absolution, when you shall have confessed, and——"

" Na ! na ! mon, ye are owre wrang with yer doctrine, yer've no grund to stan' on ; the Scriptures tell plainly, ' There is one God, and one mediator between God and man—the man Christ Jesus, who gave Himself a ransom for all.' An' maybe ye'll be knowin' the scripture which tells how, ' If we confess our sins, *He* is faithful and just to forgive us our sins.' Ye'r wrang, my frien' ; ye'r wrang to come 'tween the sinner an' his Saviour.

> " I want no ither argument,
> I need no ither plea.
> 'Tis quite enou' that Jesus died,
> An' that He died for me."

Again the priest made efforts to win the Scotchman's ears, but the ruling principles of his race came out strong in the hour of his greatest weakness— attachment to the simple Bible truths, hatred of Popery, and love of argument.

The effort of the Scotchman had been too much for his increasing weakness, for he relapsed again into unconsciousness.

Through most of the night I stayed with the dying man, the others having all retired on the return of his unconsciousness.

This midnight vigil with a dying man was the first and only unpleasant feature of my prison life.

Two days longer Geordie McLellan, the Scotchman, lingered between life and death. For a brief interval he once more became conscious. On opening his eyes he glanced round, as if surprised at his surroundings, and murmured in broken utterances, " I thocht me in my mither's cot in Perthshire."

Then presently he spoke again, in the words of an old Scotch ballad,—

> "Then dry that glist'ning e'e, Jean,
> My soul langs to be free, Jean,
> And angels wait on me
> To the land o' the leal."

After a moment or two's pause, his lips slowly parted, and with a quiet, fixed, peaceful look heavenward, he said softly and in broken gasps, " Nae ither name—one mediator—Jesus Christ—He is faith—ful—just—forgive sins."

His mind wandered again for a moment. He had once been a soldier, it was evident, for he tried to raise his hand to his head as he said, short and sharp, with a dying energy, " Password ? Yes ! Blood of Christ—Christ cleanseth from all sin."

A thrill passed through his frame, and the watchers knew that Geordie was dead.

Very little was known of the man, save that he had been left ashore from an American vessel, having been sentenced to three months' imprisonment for violence on the high seas and an attempt to raise a mutiny in the ship. In the prison he had sickened and died, as we have seen, leaving nothing behind him but a bag of clothes and a chest of tools.

*   *   *   *   *

It would but weary my readers, doubtless, if I detailed all my life during this pleasant prison holiday. Let it suffice to say that at the end of my time, my ship having returned to the port, I was fetched on board, but immediately refused duty again, determined, if possible, by constant wilfulness, to get them to discharge me.

But for the fact that the very utmost difficulty was experienced in getting " skilled artisans " for the navy at this time, I feel sure they would have bundled me out of the service as an incorrigible. But my being a carpenter made me more useful to the service than as though I had been an ordinary seaman only.

I think some inkling of the pleasant holiday time my sojourn in the civil gaol had proved, had reached our captain's ears, for on my repeating my offence of refusing duty he sent me to the military prison of Fort George.

Certainly my captain's patience and forbearance were very great, but that of God was infinitely greater.

When in after days I had sought and found the waiting pardon of God, and have stood up as a worshipper in the congregation, tears would flow adown my cheeks, tears that nothing would check, as I tried to sing that wonderful truth of God's forbearance,—

> " Depth of mercy ! can there be
> Mercy still reserved for me ?
> Can my God His wrath forbear ?
> Me the chief of sinners spare ?
> I have long withstood His grace,
> Long provoked Him to His face,
> Would not hearken to His calls,
> Grieved Him by a thousand falls."

But in those far-off careless days, tears of penitence were strangers to my eyes. In this feckless state of soul, I went ashore, a prisoner again, sentenced this time to six *weeks'* imprisonment in the military prison.

Chapter XXIII

THREE MEMORIES

MY new place of confinement was a row of low brick-and-tile buildings, on the summit of a lofty hill, in Fort George. As far as I can remember, there were five or six houses in the row, all with wide open windows that faced the brow of the celebrated Saamee Rock.

The end house, nearest to the military station down below, was occupied by the sergeant in charge of this little free-and-easy military gaol, with its five prisoners. The other four prisoners were soldiers; I was the only sailor.

The discipline here was almost as lax as in the civil prison in the town below; it was even more so, in one respect, inasmuch as when we had given our word not to go beyond a mile from the houses, we were allowed to roam about as we would—*during certain hours*, and in *one* direction.

Of the events of my stay here, three things specially recur to me.

The very first evening of my committal to Fort George, while sitting outside on the wide open verandah, smoking a rough native cigar, the first of these memories occurred.

All the Eastern landscape was hushed and still.

The last rudely-built native cart had creaked its slow, unmusical way to its final stopping-place for the day. The carters and ryots, in their dried leaf-and-mud huts, had eaten their last curried grain of rice. The buffaloes, which had drawn the carts and ploughs all day, were now lying wearily in the quiet darkness of their gloomy little dens of stables, chewing the cud of their evening meal. The cawing crows who had haunted the paddy fields since dawn of day were silent in their rookeries, as I listened to a wonderful story told by the sergeant in charge of us.

Just before sunset the mournful, sobbing, wailing notes of the " Dead March in Saul " had come up in music that was broken by the puffs of the evening breeze. When I heard those pathetic-sounding notes—the wailing, sobbing cornets, the slow, sad rat-tat of the kettles, the deep, hollow boom of the drum—I had asked who was being buried.

The story told to me that night has never left me, and many a time since my mind has gone back to days, farther back still than that evening burial, and, in my soul, that music of the Dead March has had another interpretation.

In the slow patterings of the kettle-drums, I have heard the sounds of a child's hands and feet as they toddled and played in a certain fine old English homestead. I have thought of the beautiful aristocratic mother who watched with delight the play of the little hands and feet, never dreaming of the paths which the feet would tread, or the ruin those fingers would rake.

The sobbing of those cornets has sounded in my soul like the wailing of that poor mother. The deep boom of the drum has been as the Bible echo of the

doom of a lost soul, and across my mind there have
flitted the lines of Rossetti :—

> " Out of the depths of the hollow gloom,
>   On the soul's bare sands he heard it boom :
>   The measured tide of the sea of doom."

And the story that has suggested these reflections?
Well, briefly, here it is. "The Dead March in Saul"
had been played at the funeral of a man who had
died at midnight of the previous day.

"Every one in the station knows the story now,"
said the sergeant, "and it's uncommon enough to be
worth making into a book. The man they have
just buried was known in the regiment as Sergeant
Robinson, but before he died, it was found out that
his real name was George Augustus Rupert Clancy."

[I use fictitious names here for obvious reasons.]

"His home in England," continued the sergeant,
"was one of the loveliest places in the county—
a regular show place. His father still lives in that
grand old mansion ; he is a noble, white-haired old
man, known in society as the Duke of Rhonedale.
Sergeant Robinson was the only son, the only child in
fact, and would, had he lived, have been the Duke in
his turn.

"Rupert, as he was called at home, picked up a
love of play before he was out of velvet suits and lace
collars. He was a handsome, high-spirited youngster,
and his father was so proud of him, especially of his
grace and intelligence, that at seven years old he
treated him more like an equal than a child, and he
would smile when the little fellow gave or took odds
with him on the different events of the year.

"The boy passed much of his time in the atmosphere of the stables, for he had the misfortune to lose his mother when he was only about four and a half.

"Among the stud grooms at Rhonedale, and listening to the horsey talk of trainers and jockeys, he became perfect, not only in the talk of the course but in all the practice.

"One thing went with another. By the time he was twelve, and wore a round jacket, he had learned to drink raw spirits, *and to like them*. At Eton he quickly graduated in other vices, so that by the time he reached college he was a master in all that a fast young fellow is supposed to be capable of.

"Our Captain Melton, here, was at school and college with him (it is through him that poor Robinson's story has got to be known among us), and he, Captain Melton, says that the fastest liver at college never *attempted* to live the pace that he went, and that it is a wonder he didn't come a helpless cropper over and over again in those days.

"He beggared his father. Every stick, stone, and rood upon which the old gentleman could raise a guinea was mortgaged—to the hilt.

"Then there came two ugly things at once. The young fellow was horribly mixed in a Society scandal, and there was a whisper of a forged cheque in another quarter.

"Rupert Rhonedale was missing. A few days later he joined our depôt in Edinburgh, as a private, under the name of George Robinson. He became a smart soldier, but a great blackguard.

"The wonder is that he has held his stripes so long as he has, for he has dared to do things that I never knew any other soldier dare. But he is dead now, poor fellow, and some say that he was a changed man before he died. I hope he was, or he'll come off poorly by-and-by at the Judgment.

"It appears that he knew Captain Melton all the time he was in the regiment, but the Captain never recognised him until he made himself known about a week before he died."

It was quite night before the sergeant had finished his story. The rising moon was shedding her mystic silvery light over all the scene below the hill-top. The palm-fronds looked like gleaming scimitars ; every dome-roof and tower, barrack and house, the heaving Indian Ocean hundreds of feet below, all were silvered with the soft, pure Eastern moonlight.

The five of us who had listened to the story (only fragmentarily given here) were silent enough when it was finished. Each of us went to our own rooms (cells they were called, though they must have been fifteen feet square, and were never locked during all my time there), and each of us doubtless had our own thoughts about the story we had listened to.

"Nothing new in it," some would say, "as far as the principle is concerned; only in detail does it differ from a myriad others."

True! And that is the pity of it, that whether people see it, or believe it, or whether they do not, the fact remains that the *cause* and *effect* of such stories is always with us—drink and gaming the *cause*, dishonour, degradation, death, the *effect*.

These two vices are emptying homes and heaven, and filling hell. They have filled the earth with sorrow and crying, with groans and despair ; they have supplied hell's orchestra with the music the foul fiend loves ; they have broken the tenderest, holiest of earth's ties, and forged the deadliest links in the chains of hell's eternal fetters.

*　　*　　*　　*　　*

Fort George Memory No. 2.

A Wonderful Meeting.

Tum-tum, tumma tum-tum! Tum-tum, tumma tum-tum ! Oh, what a din it was ! The dull thump of the bony Singalese fingers on those " everlasting " tum-tums. The wild, discordant clash of cymbals, the " yah, yah, tula yah mah " of the worshippers, uttered in every possible key, no two voices harmonising ; all this interspersed and varied by blood-curdling shrieks from some of the more frantic dancers (for they danced while they sang and worshipped), made a din that would jar the strongest nerves.

The sight was a strange one, exceedingly novel and picturesque, and withal full of wholesome instruction. The time was about seven in the evening, the place the summit of the Saamee Hill. The background was formed by the long, low range of brick-and-tile buildings, which formed the military prison.

The immediate foreground was broken suddenly by an awful ragged line of black rock, that ran directly down to the little shell-and-shingle cove at the base of the rocks. Stretching away in all its beauty was the Eastern sea. Not a breath of wind stirred the massive tropical foliage ; it was sultry with an Indian sultriness.

Several hundred Singalese—men, women, and children—were gathered in a ring, in the centre of which a yellow-robed priest officiated. The whole service, though unintelligible to the English onlookers, excited the greatest interest, culminating in the wildest astonishment at the unexpected *finale*.

Every one, young and old, among these strange worshippers, bore in their hands a present of fruit or cooked food. Suddenly, amid the wildest dancing and screaming, the whole multitude formed into a wide semicircle, facing the sea, and at a signal from the priest flung their choice gifts into the waters beneath. A few words were chanted by the priest, then the people slowly wended their way down the hill, and once more quiet reigned.

"What did it all mean?" I asked the question of the sergeant, who replied,—

"Years ago, hundreds it may be, for I'm not up in the dates, when the Dutch, or Portuguese, or some other foreign power, took possession of this island, they thought to spite the natives and to make them forget their own religion, so took their chief idol out of the temple down below there, by the great banyan tree, hauled it up this hill, and hurled it over the cliff there into the bay beneath us.

"They thought the natives would not trouble about their worship any more; but there they made a mistake, for these fellows, 'niggers' as people are fond of calling them, don't let go their religion quite as easy as many so-called Christians do."

"That's true, as far as we've seen to-night, sergeant," I was fain to confess, as I remembered that not even the smallest child, carried on the hip of its mother, who had been in that crowd that night, but had had a gift in its hand, and had hurled that gift into the sea to feed the drowned god. Old and young, all alike, brought their gifts.

Then, too, it was particularly noticeable that the

very finest fruits that could be got were brought as gifts. The smartest European trafficker in the bazaar could never have *bought* such fruit, let him offer what price he might for it—*if there was a service on the Saamee Rock at hand.*

Another noticeable feature about this remarkable service was that every one was *up to time.* Not a single straggler in the congregation ; within five minutes of the first arrival all those hundreds of Singalese had assembled—no one was late.

N.B.—Christians and congregations kindly take these three hints towards the solution of the problem, " How to make public worship soul-helpful, profitable, and attractive ? "

1st. Be up to the meeting-house in good time.

2nd. Be sure to bring a gift.

3rd. Let the gift be the very best in your power to offer.

*   *   *   *   *

Fort George Memory No. 3.

A Christian Sepoy.

There was a guard of sepoy sentries at the hill gaol, who were relieved every two hours—one man on sentry at a time.

I had never, until this time, come into personal contact with sepoys, and my only idea of them was coloured by Indian Mutiny associations, by memories of Nana Sahib, of Cawnpore, and other kindred horrors, so that I was not at all inclined to look favourably upon them, until I got to know those who formed the guard of this hill prison.

In all conversations which took place among us,

as we idled away those evenings under the verandah, the sepoy sentry always appeared to take the deepest interest. There was one man, Khady, whom I became intensely interested in, under the following circumstances.

The subject of Religious Profession *v.* Practice came up among us one night, when Khady was on sentry-go, and it was evident that he was especially interested. Very picturesque did he look as he stood there on guard. His drill trousers spotlessly white; his dark tunic, with its bronze buttons, fitting his well-knit figure snugly; his regulation cap, with its white muslin pugaree wound artistically round, and his dark handsome face and glistening oiled black hair. He leaned against one of the pillars that supported the verandah, with his short carbine slung carelessly across his arm, and had evidently followed with deepest interest the discussion of the hour.

"Well!" remarked one of the soldier prisoners, "religion's a thing I don't understand at all. I've only known a few religious people, and them 'as been either out-and-out scamps, or regular long-faced, miserable, doleful, down-in-the-dumps sort of coves, that sort of made you mad to look at, or give you the all-overs to stop with."

"Hold on there!" expostulated one of the others of the group, who wanted to offer a word or two on the matter.

But before he could proceed any farther the other speaker continued, "One gun at a time, old man; let me finish wot I was going to say. Who's supposed to be religious if the parsons ain't, wot preaches religion for others to practise? Well, take the parson as was in the ship as I came in, across from Madras :

he preached a sermon on Sunday agin drunkenness, and on the Tuesday got that drunk hisself that the wardroom servants, or some of the officers, no one knows which, took off his Wellington boots while he was dead drunk on a couch, and then put the right boot on the left foot, and *vice versâ*, as our cook says when he turns a pancake. Then he used to gamble like a gold-digger. Why, I've knowed him stick at cards till the very last minute of a Saturday night, and then hev to git permission of the officer of the watch to have a light in his cabin after hours, to write a sermon to read on Sunday morning. I know that for a fact, for I seed it with my own eyes, and him with a wet towel round his head a-writing away, half boozed.

" Well, then we had a gunner in our company once who was religious. He was one of them miserable, turn-up-your-eyes, glum-like-look-act-and-speak sort, who thought hisself a longsight better than any one else ; who seemed to think religion was made for him special, that he'd took in a special cargo of it, was chock-full from stem to starn, and tried to make every one feel as if they ought to be particular thankful that he condescended to live on the same side of the world as they did."

Then another voice took up the parable and declared that though he did not profess to be religious, he had known some parsons and some ordinary people who were the kindest, brightest, best people the world ever saw.

It was at this point that the sepoy entered the field of discussion. Stepping forth suddenly he said, " Say now, sahibs, me hearee all you say 'bout 'ligion, and me glad to hear you speak, cos it makee me

know you want to know the trufe. Once me like
you, use to see plenty Englishmans, officers, who
have lot of 'ligion, go to garrison church Sundays,
and parade prayers every morning ; but they swore,
and beat poor natives, and did such lots of tings
that poor Hindoos would no do, that I used to say
to meeself, ' Rhady, Rhady, you better stick to idol
and live good, than be Christian and do bad like
them Englishers.' But now I real Christian meeself,
I know which is best, an' where the mistake was."

The dusky eyes of the sepoy closed for a moment
at this period, and his lips moved as if in silent
prayer for help and guidance ; then he spoke again.
" Ah, sahib, it not 'ligion that make de difference.
Mohamet man, 'ligious ; Chinee man, 'ligious ; lots
of different peoples 'ligious, but dese not change like
you tell 'bout. No, de sergeant dat teach me de
way of life 'splain to me, dat it am having Jesus
Christ fur de pardon ob yer sin ; an' den to be like
de garrison inside yer to keep de devil out ; an'
like a friend inside yer, to feast wid yer, an' make
yer full ob peace. All dis is different to peoples
bein' 'ligious : 'ligion, prayers, and bowing down,
and going church and all sorts, cos they think it
some way make more fit to die, or more please to
God, all dis only like poor Hindoo doing penance,
and pilgrimage, and lots of stoopid tings ; we am
sabed by de precious blood ob Jesus, by de sacrifice
ob de Lamb, and none ob dese oder tings any use
till we hab Jesus for our Sabiour." Then, with a
look of pleading in his face at his two eager listeners,
the sepoy said, " Oh, how dat loving Jesus want you
to gib your hearts to Him and ——"

" Guard, turn out !" came sharply, in interruption

at that moment, the swaying lantern of the visiting
officer's orderly having been seen by the sergeant
coming up the hill.

The prisoners passed quickly into their cells, the
doors were closed, and talk for that night was over.

But I could never forget the sepoy Rhady, for a
day or two after this evening he heard me swearing
(that wretched, senseless type of swearing which, in
my sea days, became part and parcel of one's speech).
Waiting a moment, until he could speak to me, un-
heard by any one else, he gently reproved me,
adding, " Why you an' oders talk bad like that, eh?
You mussa never teach you so, eh? "

It was the tenderest, yet most severe, reproof I
ever received, and I liked the man more than ever
for administering it.

Chapter XXIV

A STOWAWAY

I HAVE frequently been asked, of late years, questions more or less in this form : " Did you in your naval days ever find officers, who would so far enter into the study of their men's characters as to *privately* remonstrate with them for unwise conduct, or venture to kindly question or advise them as to how best to use their lives ? "

I have always replied in one way, viz., " I *heard* of such officers—they were few, and very far between—but I never *met* with but one (I leave out the doctor who twice crossed my life-path, and whose earnest character I have fully described earlier in this book). The *one* other officer to whom I allude, was the first lieutenant of the ship on board which I had refused duty, and to which I returned at the end of the six weeks' imprisonment in the hill-top military prison.

It was evening when I reached the ship, and for that night I kept quiet, though I had determined in my mind, that when the time for going to work at the bench should come next day, that I would simply refuse duty again ; still hoping that they would, after some kind of punishment, discharge me.

The kindly action of that first lieutenant, however, forestalled me in my mad purpose.

Next morning, when the pipe went for breakfast and all hands rushed below, I was sent for by the second officer, whom I found standing by the capstan on the quarter-deck.

I gave the salute and waited. "Watson," he began, "I have been thinking a great deal about you of late, and determined to see you and talk to you quietly, and appeal to you, as to whether you could not settle down quietly and serve out the commission."

Perhaps he saw a negative in my face, for he went on, "I cannot understand you. You are evidently not vicious in character; I learn that you never drink, not even your daily grog; the master-at-arms assures me that you are one of the best conducted men on the lower deck; Captain P—— has nothing but commendation to give you; you do not appear to have a lazy bone in your body, yet there remains the one thing ever against you: you have attempted desertion *twice* before you left England; and you have openly refused duty *twice* since during the last six months. What does it all mean?"

He paused. I can see the look of care, of interest in his eyes, even now, as he waited for my answer.

Encouraged by his evident kindly interest (I was even touched by it), I replied frankly, telling him just how I always felt about the navy—my *constant* sea-sickness (not enough to go to the doctor with, yet enough to make my life a misery to me). I told him how an utter hatred had come into my soul for the life of the service within a week of my joining; that I was, even then, only waiting for "turn-to" time to come, after breakfast, to refuse duty again, when I hoped that the captain after punishment would discharge me. I told him, with tears which I could not check rolling down my cheeks, that but for my dear mother I should long since have committed suicide by dropping overboard at sea some night.

He was evidently moved by what I had told him, and took one or two paces up and down, evidently in deep thought.

When, a moment or two later, he stopped in front of me again, he said, in a low voice, "Watson, I am going to trust you very fully, in a way which, perhaps, strictly speaking, I ought not to do, but which I will do, because now that you have trusted me with your motives I pity you."

He had more than once glanced cautiously round to see that no eavesdropper could hear what he was saying, and now, in a still more subdued voice, he went on,—

"We leave here to-morrow, and are bound south for Mauritius. It is a busy place, full of ships trading to all parts of the world. Now, listen to me. If you go to work when the hands are turned up presently, and behave yourself, and stick to your work until we get to Mauritius, then, if you apply to me in the ordinary way, I will give you leave to go ashore at Port Louis with the other hands."

He looked hard at me. There was a suspicion of a smile in his eyes, as he added, "Do you understand?"

I did understand, and I thanked him, saying, "I am very much obliged to you, sir, and I will report myself for duty to the carpenter, as soon as I have had my breakfast."

"Very well," he said, in an undertone, "I will keep my eye upon you, mind!"

Then aloud, so that the officer on the bridge, the helmsman, and the quartermaster could hear quite plainly, he said in stern, official tones : "Don't forget, sir; I will have no skulking on this vessel. Go to your duties at once."

I gave the salute, and dived down the main hatch-way, my heart beating with a great gladness, for I quite saw that the way would be opened for me to desert on our arrival at Port Louis, if I could arrange my plans ashore.

After imprisonment, with the consequent loss of all privileges, I should not, in the ordinary way, be allowed ashore for six or nine months (my memory is not quite clear which term it was in those days) ; but for the first lieutenant to promise what he had, with what I read between the lines as to the suggestion of his offer, was all that I could possibly desire.

Before we arrived at Mauritius I had mentally planned my course of procedure. At the first sound of leave being given, I would get the master-at-arms to take me before the first lieutenant; I would ask and obtain leave—this would probably be for twenty-four hours. During these twenty-four hours I would arrange my plan of escape, then returning to my ship, would make my plans on board, sell as much of my belongings as I could, ask for a second turn of leave, and put into execution the plans I should have made ashore.

All happened pretty much as I had planned. The first lieutenant gave me twenty-four hours' leave with the first batch of first-class liberty men, and while ashore I fell in with the carpenter of a merchant barque, a young fellow about my own age, who knew Shoreditch and Hackney well.

The bond of " TOWNY " between Londoners in the navy in those old days was as strong almost as Freemasonry; and this merchantman carpenter was as pleased to meet me as though I had been a brother.

Within an hour I had confided to him my desire to desert, and he, in response, promised to help me all he could. He had to go on board his craft at eight o'clock, but before we parted he had promised to smuggle me on board hi ship (which was bound for Australia), stow me away until the vessel was well out to sea, keeping me supplied with food and water until it was safe for me to make my presence known.

I went down to the quay and watched my new friend off to his ship; then, restless with excited thought, and full of fierce longing for the hour to come when I should be on board the merchantman, I strolled clear of the town, in what was perhaps a natural desire to be alone.

How still it was outside the town! The odorous tropical night was full of a beauty all its own. The stars stepped out one by one, like spangled dancers upon a violet-hued stage, who, one by one, answered to their cue.

Once I caught a view of the chief street of the town, its few lights in shops and roadway only serving to make the dulness appear more marked.

From a bit of rising ground I looked down upon the waters of the harbour, and noted how the vessels were moored in two straight lines, ready to slip out to sea at the first warning of a typhoon or cyclone, the riding lights at the mastheads, rocked to and fro with the motion of the vessels, reminding one of the swaying, luring lights of old-time Cornish wreckers.

I walked on, until suddenly from out of the thick darkness a silent ghostly procession came towards me. I drew back into the side of the road and watched a burial party, headed by four black-robed priests, pass on towards the town, the coffin borne high upon the shoulders of the silent bearers.

Not a whisper came from the more than a score of people who formed this strange procession. They came out of the black darkness of the moonless night, tramped past me, and were presently swallowed up in the darkness beyond.

What this night funeral meant I was never wholly sure, but as I heard that an epidemic of plague broke out in the island shortly after, I have since thought that this might have been an early victim, who was being buried secretly at night.

When the procession had got well away, I turned and walked slowly back to the town to the Exchange Hotel, where I had secured a bed.

Five nights later, when I was on my second leave ashore, I dropped down in a waterman's boat, alongside the barque on which my new friend was carpenter, and joined him on the deck,—he was on the look-out for me.

I was dressed in a grey tweed suit, and carried a canvas hand-haversack with me. The waterman was dismissed, he thinking that I was one of the crew of the ship returning from leave.

As it happened, I could not have arrived on board at a better time; all the crew who were aboard were in the forecastle, and except for my friend the carpenter not a soul was on deck. He had been engaged in battening down the cargo hatches, ready for sailing in the morning.

There was one small hatch—the foremost one—which he had left, in view of my coming.

Watching his opportunity, he passed me down this tiny square, passed down the lantern, took another swift glance all about, then dropped down himself, drew the hatch over, and showed me the most comfortable spot in what was intended only to be but a *temporary* hiding-place for me.

The cargo was one of sugar and dates; this was covered with old sails to protect the *bags* of cargo from wetting, should there be any leakage in the planking of the deck overhead.

He showed me, by the light of the lantern, how he had arranged a kind of hollow in the cargo, and fitted it with special layers of canvas, to form a bed.

"We might be delayed a day or two, you know," he whispered (we dare not speak except in whispers, lest the hum of our voices should be heard through the bulk-heading which parted the hold from the forecastle).

"It is well to be prepared for emergencies," he continued, as he showed me a store of food that would easily last me four days.

Holding the lantern against the bulk-heading, he pointed to a square, about eighteen inches each way, and whispered, "That opens out of my berth, opens on my side, so whatever happens in the way of delay, I can always look after you in the food line."

Having given me all directions, seen me take up my position in the hollowed-out place he had made for me to lie, we shook hands heartily, he extinguished the candle in his lantern, then passed up the hatchway and disappeared.

Just for one moment my eyes took in the square of slate-coloured haze of light that appeared as he held up the hatch ; one star twinkling in the deep, violet-blue night-heavens looked down upon me like a kindly pitying eye, then all was black, close darkness.

The memory of that star was often a comfort to me in days that were to follow that night.

The darkness of my stowaway state did not affect me as the darkness of the cells had done during my first imprisonment at Plymouth. For here, in the hold of that sugar-ship, I was confined voluntarily, and I was, as I hoped and believed, about to sail into liberty.

My hiding-place was not calculated to yield much comfort, should my stay have to be prolonged, for there was nowhere more than *two clear feet* between the upper crust of the cargo and the beams of the deck above, and many a hideous whack did I receive upon the head before I learned to remember my cramped surroundings.

For awhile I laid awake, full of thought. I heard the carpenter cover and bar the little hatchway down which I had passed. I heard the bump of the jolly boat against the ship's side, as she brought the shore party aboard, and I knew that more than one of the men were three sheets in the wind, by the staggering footsteps over my head.

Things grew quiet ; I had slept but very little for a week past, and now Morpheus held me in tightest grip, so that I never woke until the hands were getting sail on the ship, and hoisting in the jolly boat—*next morning.*

I groped about for my store of food and ate a hearty breakfast, listening to the orders, and to the movements on deck, and mentally following every evolution, until I knew, as well as though I had stood on deck, just what sails were loosed, and ready to sheet home.

I heard the clink of the pawls, as halyard after halyard was taken to the capstan. At last I felt that the ship was moving; we were off, and with a great sigh of relief I laid back in my cradle-like hollow, and thought, " In two days at the outside it will be safe for me to rap on the deck above me, and making my presence known, be hauled up to daylight by the astonished crew, and after a possible bullying from the captain, be allowed to work my way to the great southern continent, where amid its mighty resources I shall doubtless gain an easy independence."

When Youth and Hope go hand in hand, 'tis thus that their possessor ever talks !

Chapter XXV

AN OCEAN BLACK-HOLE

SUDDENLY, as I lay in my dark hiding-place, my heart beating high with hope, I heard a shout —the sound of the voice was muffled to my hearing, of course—evidently hailing the moving vessel I was in.

" Barque ahoy ! " was the sound right enough.

I heard the answer, " Aye, aye ! " from the deck above me. Then followed the noise of a yard being rounded to, the vessel's pace was checked, and almost immediately there was a bump against her side—a boat had sheered alongside her.

I heard the hands called aft, and I lay with palpitating heart, wondering what was happening, half inclined, in my fear, to suppose that by some means or other my absence on leave must have appeared in its true light—desertion—to those on board my vessel.

As a matter of fact, as I afterwards learned, that is just what had happened : my clothes locker had been discovered empty, my *empty* hammock and a rag-bag being the only things in it.

Search for me was to be undertaken as soon as the Port Louis day began; meanwhile, as a ship was seen to be getting under way, it was thought advisable to board and search her.

It was the search boat which I had heard hail the barque, and afterwards come alongside.

After hearing the hands called aft, the sounds of the searching party (their voices as they talked, the bundling about of certain articles in the forecastle) were quite plain in my ears, and I trembled as I wondered if they would demand to have the hatches uncovered, and searching the cargo space would find me.

The time occupied in search and inquiries was not actually more than a quarter of an hour, but to me it was an eternity.

The ship had become as still as a tomb, I could hear the throbbing of my own heart, when at last the voice of the search officer—I recognised it well—broke the silence as he said, " You understand, captain. He's about five foot six in height, with a fresh complexion, light-brown hair, grey eyes. *If* you *do* find him stowed away any time during the voyage, please hand him over to the man-of-war stationed at Sydney. Farewell, captain ; a good voyage to you ! "

I heard the captain's reply, " Mornin', sir, an' I'll do as you say, *if* I find the man ; but as I said afore, sir, it ain't possible that he could be stowed away aboard us, since he ain't in the fo'c's'le, because all my hatches was battened down yesterday early."

I heard the " Shove off " of the coxswain of the boat (how well I knew the voice, he was a messmate of mine), then there was a racing of booted feet along the deck above me, the backed yard was evidently being swung round, the vessel gathered way upon her, and was soon heeling to the wind, on the first lay of her course for Australia.

And I ?   I was a prisoner for possible months, for

it would never do for me to show myself, and be handed over to the naval authorities at Sydney. "I'd rather die where I am," I told myself.

In those days, under the old sailing conditions, sixty days would be ample for the voyage, but there might arise contingencies, which would lengthen the time to a month or even six weeks longer than that.

And all this time I should be in darkness—alone—and never able to sit up fully, or stand up at all, for nowhere was there a full two-foot space between the cargo and the deck.

The history of my incarceration could never be really written, since I suffered too much to be able to remember a thousandth part of my experiences.

The nausea of *mal-de-mer* never left me; in addition to which there were spirituous fumes from the closely packed sugar and dates, which often utterly overcame me—I noticed this more especially when the vessel went suddenly about on a new tack.

The lack of fresh air, the loss of all light, the constant cramp of position, all helped to aggravate my sufferings. I lost appetite, and some days scarcely ate any food, though my thirst was very fierce, for I was always feverish.

This secret supplying of food became such a difficult business to the carpenter, that at last he told the story of my presence to the hands in the forecastle, and asked them to help by keeping the secret. This promise was readily agreed to and religiously kept, the only fear now being whether I should be able to stand the fearful confinement.

One day I woke from a sleep with a sudden start. The hold was full of light, and the voice of a strange man sounded apparently close to my ear.

On deck, the weather was so fine and the sea so calm, that it had been decided to ventilate a little, and the mate was proceeding to examine the condition of the sail-cloths which covered the bags of cargo, by crawling fore and aft on his hands and knees.

I had only time to crawl further down into the cradle-like hollow, where I usually lay, and cautiously cover myself with a wrapping of sail, when the mate passed over the very spot.

His hand with all his weight came down upon one of my shoulders, and his knee was pressed into my side, as he crawled over me.

At last the danger was over, I heard him climb up upon the deck through the open hatch and I began to breathe again.

Before I ventured to uncover myself, two thoughts rushed through my mind. The first, how narrow had been my escape of discovery; the second, of pity for the anxiety which, I rightly supposed, my poor friend the carpenter was suffering.

For four hours that hatchway was left open, and when once I had recovered from my fright, and my eyes had become a little accustomed to the light, the joy of seeing it, and of inhaling the fresh air, was more than I could bear without weeping.

What a red-letter day that was in my strange and awful imprisonment! First the carpenter, watching his opportunity, visited me, and cheered me, by telling me that all the crew were my secret friends, even to the cook.

"I shouldn't wonder," he added, "if one and another of them don't drop down to see you in the dinner hour."

That is just what happened. When they had eaten

their dinners, they lit their pipes, and sat about on the combings of the hatchway, talking and laughing, but always keeping an eye aft, as one after another dropped down upon the cargo, and came over and made my acquaintance.

They were a quiet, respectable lot of men ; nearly all Danes, Swedes, and Norwegians. The cook, who also visited me, was a good fellow, an old Scotchman, who, when I told him that all my forbears on my father's side had been Perth folk, declared that sooner than I should be discovered and delivered up to the naval authorities, he would himself lead a mutiny, and maroon the officers, and—well, it was all very wild talk, but it was honestly, kindly meant.

The closing of the hatch about four o'clock in the afternoon left me once more in the black, close darkness, and days and nights were again alike to me.

Once every twelve hours or so, the tiny square in the bulk-heading would open, and my food would be passed through to me. Sometimes a few whispered words would be exchanged, but this had to be done very cautiously and sparingly, for both the mates had an uncomfortable knack of coming forward and listening.

In talking over this feature of the conduct of these officers in after days, I was not surprised to hear that most of the crew believed that the mates had some faint suspicion that the " wanted navy man " *was* on board, and that they listened and peeped, hoping to get a clue.

A few days after the opening of the hatch furious weather set in, that lasted for nearly a fortnight, during which time, deprived of all fresh air, I suffered fearfully.

Then, as the days went on, the cold became so intense I could scarcely live.

"We're obliged to run before the gale," said the carpenter one day, as he handed my food through the small door, " and now we are down south among the icebergs. Things look very dicky with us sometimes ; but whatever comes, if there's anything like having to leave the ship, I'll not forget you, but will come and open the shutter, so that you shan't die like a rat in a hole."

He was as good as his word, for when about midnight two days later, the driving ship found herself with a huge berg on either side of her drifting fast down as though between them they would crush her, and when it looked as though it was to be every one for himself, he raced below, opened the shutter-way, helped me through, and wrapping a rug round me, led me into the square of the forecastle hatch, that I might be prepared for any sudden emergency.

He stood close by on the deck, and I, with my head just above the combing of the hatch and screened by the foremast, gazed on the most wonderful sight I had ever seen.

The sky was a wondrous steely blue, sea and sky and ship were flooded with brilliant moonlight. Bearing down upon our vessel, as I have stated, were the two icebergs, one on either side of us.

Majesty, rather than beauty, was the thought of the mind on beholding these floating monsters for the first time, though when the wonder at their size had passed, the exquisite beauty held one speechless.

On they came, and on we went, every rag of canvas we dared to carry driving the vessel between these icy Scylla and Charybdis.

Moments were as hours. Not a soul spoke. No sound broke the awful stillness, save the grind of a yard parrel aloft, the flick of a rope's end, and the rush of the waters as the vessel's stem cut them, and flung them splashing to starboard and port. From the bergs there came no sound.

How long the suspense lasted I do not know; I doubt if any one on board thought of time. But at last the danger was passed, we were clear of the threatened squeeze of death. I caught the hurried whisper of the carpenter, " Down with you, here comes the mate ! " and dropping down the hatch, I flung off the rug and made for my lair.

Once more God had saved me from an awful death, and from discovery as a stowaway.

Forty-eight hours later, when the wind had chopped suddenly round, we were able to lay a northerly course, and with a spanking sailing breeze soon run out of the colder latitude, and the danger of the ice monsters of that Arctic region.

Chapter XXVI

"SHARLEY BOY"

IT was exactly three months after leaving Mauritius that the sugar barque moved into her berth alongside the Circular Quay, Sydney, Australia.

Easy enough to write are those two words, "*three months*," but no pen could fill in the gap of my sufferings between the first and the ninetieth day.

It was well that the vessel had been hauled alongside the quay, otherwise my landing would have been a very difficult affair, and might even have led to my discovery and arrest.

How they managed to get me into the cab that waited on the quay I never knew, for in getting me out of the hold into the forecastle I fainted from excessive weakness, and the mental strain and anxiety.

It was a pitch-dark night, heavy rain was falling, there was scarcely a soul about on the quay, and the Customs officer who had come on board was hobnobbing with the captain in the cabin.

When I awoke from the deep faint I had fallen into, I was in bed in a comfortable room ashore, and a dear, motherly old woman was bending over me, tears of pity in her eyes.

After receiving the first-aids, and recovering sufficiently to take some delicious beef-tea, my good friend the carpenter and the old Scotch cook appeared, the one bearing a great washing-tub, the other two pails of water, one boiling and the other cold.

As tenderly as I had once washed rescued slaves from that dhow, did these two good fellows wash me from head to foot, then with a sweet, clean flannel night-gown on, they laid me carefully back in bed, and told me a few of the incidents of my debarkation.

I need not attempt to record the daily events of the next fortnight; it was a case of slow but sure recovery. The day when I was at last able to trust my own legs to carry me round the small but pretty back garden of the house where I lodged, marked an epoch in my life.

The weather was lovely, I soon got out every day, walked a little way, then took the omnibus and rode as far as it went, and after a spell in one of the parks, took a return 'bus, and so home again.

How home-like were some, yet how foreign were others, of the conductors' hails from the footboards of those omnibuses!   "Cornhill" and "Strand" were homely enough, but when your ear was assailed by "Woolloomoolloo," as a possible destination, you wondered how near that place might be to the end of the world.

As I grew stronger, and could take long walks, I loved to get into the Botanical Gardens, round Lady Macquarrie's chair, and to wander amid the beautiful blend of the natural and artificial which made the Gardens so charming to me in those days.

In a month I was quite recovered, and was ready to start work when I should find it ; and this I decided, for reasons of safety, would be better up-country than in the city.

I had decided to begin to seek employment on a certain day, which would be the day after the departure of the sugar barque, which had orders to sail to another Australian port, to load up with copper. All hands came to see me during the last twenty-four hours, and from a safe place I watched the ship in which I had been saved, and in which I had suffered, spread her wings and fly away.

I felt wretchedly lonely when I returned to my lodgings to tea, and told my good old landlady that I felt as though I had lost a whole family of brothers.

She did her best to cheer me, then laying a little parcel by the side of my plate she said, "I was to give you this when I was quite sure that the ship had gone."

Wonderingly I opened the parcel. There was a note first, written by the carpenter, and it ran something like this :—

"DEAR CHUM,—We're off by the time that good old Mother Elliot will give you this. The best of friends must part, and we all wish you good luck. You can't get on much without chips in Australia, any more than anywhere else, so all us chaps have chinked in a bit to give you a start. Please accept the enclosed five pounds *as a loan*, to be paid back by you to somebody else when you come across 'em, who wants a lift over a rough road. With a 'good luck' once more to you, we all says 'So long!'"

["So long!" I should explain, for the sake of the unnautical, is a sailor's fashion of saying "Good bye, and God bless you!"]

The man in my position who could read a note like that from a little crowd of sailors, who had already risked much to serve a stranger, and not find tears of gratitude fill his eyes, must be made of different stuff to what I was.

I remember that two or three great tears dropped upon the slice of bread and butter I had on my plate, as I handed the letter over to my good landlady, and opening the little packet I spread the five pounds out before her.

She cried with joy over the gift; then taking the affair as a text, she tried to preach God's goodness to me, as she had already done often before.

I have often wondered why, when so many people at various times in those old days yearned over my soul, I should yet have remained so obdurate. I could have given no *reason* for my forgetfulness of God, even if I could have found any *excuses*.

※   ※   ※   ※   ※

On Hire.

"Say, now, what's yer booming round for, stranger?" The voice had a strong nasal twang, generally attributed to our Yankee cousins. The owner of the voice twirled round on the tiniest top of the tallest office stool that surely had ever been built. It was in a queer little box of an office, the walls of which were garnished with sundry dirty-looking maps of colonial interest.

This abrupt speech was addressed to myself, as adopting the style of the first speaker I said, in strongest nasal tone, "I guess I'm after a job, and they do tell you are an agent."

"That's so. Where do you hail from?"

"Old England, boss."

"Scissors you do? Yer don't glib like a Britisher. Where did yer pick up yer style?"

“From you, boss, I guess. I ginrally cottons to
the ways of the crowd I git among. I'm good for
anything that's square, either with red rag or flipper.
So, what about a hire?”

The “Inquiry and Advance” agent laughed heartily
at this rapid adaptation, saying, “Well, I guess you're
the sort we want this side of the pond. Can you
rough things a bit?”

“Rough things, eh? Well, try me,” replied I, “an'
ef I don't turn out real grit an' glass paper, then I'll
eat my hat. There, wot d'yer think of that?”

“Think of it, stranger? Why, that you'll do; and
if you're ready to start up country to-night, on a
rough run among rough people, I guess I'll engage
you slick off, ef we agree on the dollars.”

I venture to give the above interview in as nearly
as possible the terms in which it took place, because
it will show something of the merry mood in which,
the day after the sailing of my friends, I started out
in search of work.

The morning was very bright, with that exhilarating brightness that always struck me as being
part and parcel of the normal weather of Australia.
As I trod the streets from my lodging-house to the
“Inquiry Agent's” office—I had noted it some days
before—I had felt the power of the morning's ex-
hilaration, and moved along as on air.

Entering the office, I had been greeted as recorded
above, and catching the cue from the agent had
replied in the same style.

Of course I learned afterwards that this particular
agent's style of speech was not colonial, but some
type of mongrel American, the man being an impor-
tation.

We speedily came to terms, and at six o'clock that evening I found myself one of a number of other passengers crowding a steamer, that was bound round the coast to several ports of call.

A strangely, beautiful incident marked our departure from the quay.

I was taking a deep interest in the final loading efforts, when my attention was suddenly arrested by a burst of song. It was an old hymn being sung heartily by a large crowd of people upon the quay and a band of about a dozen on the ship. .

How sweetly the words came upon the evening air, amid heart-breaking farewells and the many-tongued voice of clamorous commerce,—

> "Come ye that love the Lord,
>   And let your joys be known ;
> Join in a song with sweet accord,
>   While ye surround His throne.
> Let those refuse to sing
>   Who never knew our God,
> But children of the heavenly King
>   Must speak their joys abroad."

There was something evidently very generally familiar in both words and tune, for voices gradually joined in from all quarters. Again the swell arose,—

> " The God that rules on high,
>   That all the earth surveys,
> That rides upon the stormy sky,
>   And calms the roaring seas ;
> This awful God is ours——"

Shouts from ashore of " Bless the Lord ! " " Amen!" and " Glory ! " burst out as that last word " ours " was sung, though it did not interrupt the song, for

it went swinging along in ever-increasing melody
and strength,—

> " Our Father and our love ;
> He will send down His heavenly powers
> To carry us above."

" Haul in your big fore-and-aft hawsers, my men,"
the stentorian tones of the captain gave order. The
chorus of the hymn was being sung ; the sailors
caught the infection, they sang with the people, as
hand by hand they hauled in the thick, heavy rope,
to the joyous rattle of,—

> " We're marching to Zion,
> Beautiful, beautiful Zion,
> We're marching upward to Zion,
> The beautiful city of God."

The song goes on, the vessel has got clear of
the quay, handkerchiefs wave, tears fall, yet from
the shore the inspiring words still float out, and,
sweetened by distance and the charm that the water
gives to musical sounds, the words follow the ship,
growing fainter, yet each distinctly heard,—

> " The men of grace have found
>   Glory begun below ;
> Celestial fruit on earthly ground
>   From faith and hope may grow.
> Then let our songs abound,
>   And every tear be dry ;
> We're marching through Immanuel's ground,
>   To fairer worlds on high."

When at last the quay was out of sight, and the
last sound of song had died away, the little band of
Christian emigrants aboard fell on their knees upon
the deck, while a grey-haired old man led in prayer,

committing themselves, their friends, the ship, the sailors and passengers to the care of God.

There was a little smiling among some of the crew and passengers at this unusual devotion, but most present felt the safer in the ship for that earnest prayer.

By midnight that night the vessel was struggling in the throes of a three-quarter gale of wind, and scarcely a soul in the ship among the passengers but was *hors-de-combat* with the direst sea-sickness.

For myself, it was the old story, and for a little while I wished I had turned crossing-sweeper again on the Sydney streets, rather than put myself in the way of my old enemy.

Sometime in the night I was roused by the piteous wail of a child, crying in low, broken sobbings, " Muver, mu-uv-er ! me wants—wants my—my muver."

The sounds came from just beneath my bunk, and leaning over I saw a dear little fellow of three, or three and a half years, standing forlornly on the rolling deck, just in the dim light of the cabin lamp.

He was a pretty little chap, with fair curly hair, the brightest of blue eyes, and was as plump of form as a full season's partridge.

Leaping from my bunk, I stooped down on the lurching deck, and putting my arms round the little fellow, I kissed him comfortingly, and told him he should come into bed with me, and to-morrow, when he'd had a nice sleep, we would find his mother.

I easily surmised that, amid the horrors of sickness that the female cabin must have held, this little baby waif must have strayed away, and having suddenly realised his position as lost, he had broken out into the wail which had attracted me.

I had no difficulty in persuading him to come into my bunk, and with his chubby little arms about my neck, his hot, moist tear-stained cheek resting against mine, the pair of us covered by the same rug, we were soon fast asleep.

I was awakened next morning by sundry tweakings of my eyebrows, poundings on the chest, and other juvenile demonstrations of impatience, while the little voice cried, " P'ese, misser man, o'os dot to wake up."

I did as I was told—I woke up. The little fellow was perched astride of me, looking the very picture of roguish health and beauty—save for his need of a morning wash.

I hugged him to myself with a loving kiss and said, " What's your name, little man ? "

" Sharley," he replied, adding, " Who's 'oour name, p'ese ? "

It was on the tip of my tongue to reply with my own name, then a sudden thought struck me that my old street name would amuse the child, so I said, " Call me, ' Wops,' Charley ! "

The little fellow fairly screamed with laughter, as he cried, " Oh, oh, 'oo is funny, 'oo is, Wops."

Then with a sudden eagerness of look and voice, he asked, " Has 'oo dot a No's Ark ? me is. Aunty Titty div it to me ! "

Then came a perfect torrent of questions of all kinds from his fertile little brain and rosy lips, until his tiny personality resolved itself into a three-foot note of interrogation, and I laughed until I cried, with the comicality of the whole affair.

The gale continued furious, and every one was ill.
I climbed out of my bunk, lifted down my little waif,
found the washing berth, and as well as the awful
motion of the vessel would let me, I had a good wash
myself, washed the boy, and combed and curled his
pretty hair ; then, as his little pinafore was much too
dirty to harmonize with his lovely fair skin, I washed
the little garment, dried it at the galley fire (a process
which only occupied a few minutes). But as no man-
of-war's man can bear to see a garment *rough-dried*,
I laid hold of a pint-and-a-half beer-bottle that was
rolling about on the big cabin floor, and after the
fashion of the sea, *I mangled the pinafore.*

This is easily done, by folding the garment the
width of your roller, taking care to smooth each fold
out carefully as you go, then roll the folded thing
round your bottle-roller, straining it tightly as you
roll. Then take a board (I used a long notice-board
which hung on the bulk-heading on this occasion),
and laying the rolled garment upon a table, and the
board on top of it, throw all your weight on the two
ends of the board, and roll backwards and forwards.

The pinafore was as smooth after this rolling as
though it had been ironed, and when I had picked
out the crochet edging that adorned the sleeves and
neck, and carefully rolled out the tape strings, and
put the little newly-laundried thing on my *protégé*, I
was egotistical enough to say, " There, Charley boy !
your own mother could not have done it better."

One or two of the hands who had come across me
had a laugh at my efforts, supposing, I expect, that I
was the child's father.

Breakfast was laid for a few, but only two, besides

Charley, came to the table, and the dispatching of the food by the solitary pair (of whom I was one) was little short of a work of art, so fearfully did the vessel plunge and roll.

Charley ate well, and seemed happy enough to be with me, only repeating, at all sorts of odd moments, "Muver, come back bum-bye, an' bring Charley a bun."

I got hold of the steward and, explaining how I came with the boy, asked him about the child. Did he know of a woman who was ill, who had lost a little one, etc.

Poor fellow, he was awfully worried, and at his wit's end, and replied, " If you don't mind having the child, sir, and he don't mind staying with you, it would be a godsend to the mother if you would keep the little chap, until we get out of the teeth of this gale. I tell you, sir, I've been thirty years stewarding, but I never saw anything more awful than our women's cabin as it is now ; and it's going to be worse before the day's out. Poor souls, they lie in their bunks like dead things most part of the time, and how it will be before we get through into the quieter waters of the river's mouth, I don't know. Keep the child, sir, and you'll be doing somebody a deed of charity."

The steward was right about the weather. That day was *one* of, if not actually, the worst I ever experienced at sea, and how we lived through it I cannot conceive.

I kept the boy with me, and grew as fond of him as if he had been my own, while he certainly lavished more love and kisses upon me in the brief period of our acquaintance than any other human being had ever done in a hundredfold greater period of time.

The day passed, and the night. At dawn we

began to get into smoother water.   The vessel had to make a run up the river, and by breakfast time she was over the bar at the mouth of the wide stream and moving through water as smooth as a mill-pond.

The passengers were soon on their feet, and washing and smartening up became the order of the day. The women, poor things, crawled up into the brightness and warmth of the sunlit upper deck, and here the steward and sailors served them with tea and other refreshments.

I took my pretty boy-waif round among them all, to find his mother, but no one owned him.

" Steward," I said, getting hold of the poor, tired-out, overworked fellow, " there must be some women below in their bunks still, for this boy's mother is not here.   Can I take the little chap in the cabin and try and find her ? "

" Certainly," he replied, and in a couple of minutes I was carrying the little fellow in my arms through the women's cabin.

" Now, Charley boy," I whispered, " you call for mother as loud as you can."

" Muver ! Muver ! " rung out his little voice, his blue eyes roving swiftly along the line of middle bunks.

A woman's face appeared over the edge of one of the bunks. " Dere she is, dere she is ! " yelled the little fellow delightedly, as he almost leaped from my arms.

The woman was too ill to speak, but she clasped the child passionately to her breast, while tears of grateful gladness coursed down her cheeks.

When the boy had half smothered her with kisses, he looked roguishly over his shoulder at me, waved his fat, dimpled little hand, and cried, " Dood-bye, Wops ! dood-bye ; me'es dot muver now ! "

The mother, a pretty little, fragile-looking thing, not much more than a girl, tried to thank me for my evident care of her child, and with a sudden passion of sobbing, talked about dying, but I assured her that when once she was on deck, and had had some food, she would soon recover.

Securing the services of two of the women who were willing to help, we presently got her on deck, and after some refreshment she quickly picked up. She heard all the story of my care of her child, with the details of the pinafore washing, from one of the sailors, and seemed too much moved to speak.

There was a sequel to this incident which I may as well mention here. A year later, while in Sydney, and spending the evening at the Prince of Wales's Theatre (Opera House, I think it was called)—theatres being the only form of amusement I ever cared for in my unconverted days—I stood up to stretch my limbs between two of the acts, when I heard a voice call my name, and, looking round, I saw Charley's mother, with a big, black-whiskered, handsome man.

Her excitement at seeing me seemed beyond all control. Only two seats parted us; many people had gone out during the fall of the curtain, so I easily made my way to the pair.

Her eyes filled with tears as I draw near her, and, with the abandon of her own little Charley, she put her arms about my neck and kissed me, as with a flushed, excited face, she turned to her husband, saying, "This is the dear man who kept our Charley in the storm that time."

It was a strange meeting, and led to my receiving much kindness and hospitality at that time.

Chapter XXVII

"AS A MOTHER"

WRITING of little Charley and his mother recalls to my mind another scene which I witnessed in London, many years after, in the first year of my converted life, and which has ever seemed so full of spiritual teaching, that I venture to give it here, since I desire to make this book as useful to the unsaved as entertaining and useful to the saved reader.

I was walking through the Borough one spring morning, when just in front of me a little child, a girl about four, looked round with a startled face, and wailed out for her mother. A crowd quickly gathered, and every one seemed bent upon either questioning or comforting the little waif.

Elbowing her way through the crowd, a big, red-faced fishwoman, with her sleeves rolled up, and her bare arm sprinkled with fish scales, stooped down before the child, and asked,—

"Where's yer live, my precious little pet?"

"With muver!" sobbed the child.

"What's yer muver's name, dearie?"

"Muver!"

"Poor little lamb of her, if that 'ere ain't a sight to melt a hiceberg, then I don't know what is," said the woman, as she thrust a penny into the child's hand.

Then a brewer's drayman tried to comfort the child, and gave her an apple.

"I say, little 'un, don't cry," said a small ragged street arab, as he wiped her eyes with his ragged shirt sleeve. "Look here! here's a glass marble fur yer; ain't got no more, or else I'd giv it yer."

A little girl coaxed her mother to give the sobbing child an orange from her market basket; a picture card was added by some one else, but still they were unheeded, and the same pitiful wail rang out, "Oh, mu-v-ver, muv-v-er!"

A policeman now arrived on the scene, and while he was stooping over the weeping child, and had just decided to take her in his arms to the station, the crowd opened to let a lady-like young woman pass through. She appeared to be well known to some of the women, and evidently recognised the child, for she spoke to it soothingly, as she wiped the tears from the little stained face, saying, "Why, Nellie dear, have you lost mother, my pet? She's only round the corner; we'll soon take you to her. Don't cry, darling."

It was a very sweet face that suddenly came into full view as she rose from the stooping posture with the child in her arms; in the other hand she carried a small open basket with a few tracts and a small Bible, and one or two tiny posies of flowers. She soon explained everything satisfactorily to the policeman, and was about to walk away with the child in her arms when the little one shouted in gleeful tones, as she stretched her arms out eagerly, "Muver! muver! here I is!" And in a moment a flying, bonnetless woman had caught the child from the fair girl's arms, and was passionately kissing it and pressing the little creature to her bosom.

Wondrous picture of a soul's need, and of the only thing which will ever satisfy that need !

"As one whom his mother comforteth, so will *I* comfort you, and ye shall be comforted in Jerusalem," God has said in His Word ; and though the primary meaning of that passage is prophetical, and refers, doubtless, to the future of God's chosen earthly people, yet still we may safely accept a distinct spiritual teaching of the passage for the present dispensation, and for all peoples who hunger for *soul* rest.

He can, He will, He does comfort (or satisfy) like a mother, because, like that tender parent, *He knows us from the beginning.* "He knoweth our frame," knows every varying characteristic of each life, every peculiar idiosyncrasy, every shade of reticence that would and does keep the hungry, yearning, unsatisfied soul from speaking of its need to even the dearest earthly friend. He knows all these things, and everything else that prevents the soul from trusting Him, and has known the difficulties *from the beginning—* whatever, or however great they may be. And His word to us *each* is, "As one whom his *mother* comforteth, *so* will *I* comfort *you*."

Like a mother He comforts with the *present kiss and the promised reward.*

Like a mother He comforts in the *deepest of life's sorrows.* When we seem instinctively to turn from every human comfort, if we will but turn to Him, oh ! how great will be the satisfaction, the comfort to our souls. That blue-eyed drummer-boy, in the American battle-field hospital, dying in agony, turned snappishly from all who sought to comfort him, as with tears in his eyes, and sobs in his throat, he cried brokenly, " Mother could comfort me, if *she* were here."

He comforts like a mother, with *the fullest satisfaction* of desire. That child I saw lost in that crowded street in London was as fond as any child, of pence, oranges, pictures, apples, toys, etc., all of which were thrust into her little hands to comfort her little heart ; but these things did *not* comfort the little one, *while it was lost.* And a lost soul, a soul unsaved, an unconverted, unregenerate soul, can never be satisfied with earth's gifts—wealth, pleasure, friends, fame; none of these things can satisfy, can comfort the soul, out of Christ. Religion even cannot satisfy—I mean religion in the mere abstract; the soul must rest upon *Christ* in His atoning work, must be filled with the life *of* Christ, then life *for* Christ, before it can know real, solid, undisturbed rest. And here comes in God's promise, " As one whom his mother comforteth, so will I comfort you, and *you shall* be comforted," as only the mother could comfort that lost London child, though its little arms were full of gifts ; so only can God comfort and satisfy the hungry, yearning soul of man.

He comforts the penitent sinner, the returning backslider, *as a mother will pardon and receive her prodigal, when all other friends have turned their backs upon him.* For, in the language of Whitfield, " God will receive the devil's castaways."

" *In Jerusalem*," He says He will comfort them. For there is only *one* place where He can meet with souls to comfort, to pardon, to satisfy them, viz.—*The Cross of Atonement.*

> " O safe and happy shelter !
> O refuge tried and sweet !

O trysting-place where Heaven's love
   And Heaven's justice meet!
As to the holy patriarch
   That wondrous dream was given,
So seems my Saviour's Cross to me
   A ladder up to heaven.

" There lies beneath its shadow,
   But on the farther side,
The darkness of an awful grave
   That gapes both deep and wide ;
And there between us stands the Cross,
   Two arms outstretched to save,
Like a watchman set to guard the way
   From that eternal grave.

" Upon the Cross of Jesus,
   Mine eye at times can see
The very dying form of One
   Who suffered there for me ;
And from my smitten heart with tears,
   Two wonders I confess,—
The wonders of His glorious love,
   And my own worthlessness."

Yes, there at the Cross, the place of blood-shedding for sin, there *only* can God meet the sinner, and there only can He give pardon.

A Midnight Landing.

To resume the thread of my story : at midnight of the same day as that on which the steamer crossed the bar of the river and got into the smooth water, enabling little Charley's mother, with the others, to " pick up their feathers," as the sailors put it, I had to disembark.

The night was inky-black, and how the captain of the steamer knew (for *see* he could *not*) where to pull up, and how he managed to range alongside the rude quay, and yet carry nothing away, has always been a mystery to me ; but he did it, and did it well.

I had kissed little Charley's hot, red cheek as he lay asleep, and bade his poor fragile-looking little mother good-bye, and was passed over the side of the steamer by the light of a lantern held by a seaman, then heard, rather than saw, the black steamer move off into the blacker night.

With a strange, uncanny sense of loneliness, I stood amid the darkness, my bundle in my hand, wondering how I was to find my way to—anywhere.

Before approaching the landing-place, the steamer had hooted once or twice with its steam whistle, but as yet no one had appeared.

Suddenly I was startled by a "cooey" not far away. I was too much of a "new chum" to essay a "cooey" in return, but calculating that a real good cockney "Tal-lal-lal-litee, litee, lie-lie-tie," would reach as far as a colonial cooey, I gave vent to a regular blood-curdler.

A hearty laugh followed my reply hail, while a cheery voice shouted, "All serene, chum ! I'll be with you in a crack ! "

A moment or two later the form of a man emerged from the darkness, saying, as he greeted me with a hearty hand-shake, "We'd a'most giv yer up fur ter-night, fur we've bin' spectin' yer fur the last eight hours. We heard the hooter whistlin' off, so I hurried along. But come along, we're only about five minutes off home, an' all hands is a-sittin' up to gie yer welcome like."

He said a "welcome," but even his words had not quite prepared me for the reception I got.

The roomy kitchen was ablaze with light from wood fire and lamp ; the table piled with food, and every member of the family greeted me with hand-shaking and smiles, as though I was one of their own kin who had suddenly returned into their midst.

All night through we sat and talked, and it was only when the day had fully broke that I was sent to bed, the others, as I afterwards found, commencing their daily work.

When I woke it was in the forenoon, and I sat puzzling for a moment as to where I could be ; then, suddenly remembering, I said to myself, " Well, if this is what that Yankee agent calls roughing it with a rough lot, I guess he must have been brought up with a silver spoon in his mouth."

I found the same heartiness of welcome awaiting me when I got up, and presented myself to the women of the house—the men-folk were all at work.

By the time I had had a good refreshing wash in an outhouse, dinner was ready, and the men, in response to the cooey of one of the grown-up daughters of the house, trooped into the mid-day meal, each one greeting me heartily.

Over the dinner (which of course was my break-fast) I apologised for sleeping so late, declaring that I was ready to begin work as soon as the meal was over.

The family looked at one another, and exchanged smiles, then the head of the house, a fine old man over sixty years of age, laughed outright, as he ex-plained that I was to go to a settler nearly twenty miles across country, but that he had promised my employer to have me met, and to put me well on the road to my station.

An hour after dinner, under the convoy of one of the men, I started for my real destination, which I reached safely just before sunset.

Next morning I began my bush life, which for freedom, go, and a dash of occasional adventure, was as heaven to me. Timber felling was my first experience, followed by, and interspersed with, wild ridings (I had to learn to ride, without lessons, while pursuing my daily work), cattle-tracking, ploughing, burning of land, sowing maize, etc.

The adventures which befel me during the first ten months in the bush would easily fill a good-sized volume, but the crowning adventure which terminated my stay in these parts, and almost terminated my life, is the only one I can stay to dwell upon, and this must have a chapter to itself.

Chapter XXVIII

LOST IN THE BUSH

THERE was a small township some twenty miles away ; and as I wanted to make some purchases (for I had decided to remain the year with my settler-employer), and as I felt the need of a few days' change, I got a holiday, proposing to visit the township mentioned above.

" You'd better take the little mare," my boss had said. But the animal had been lame for a week, and I shrank from using her, so I declined the well-meant offer, and started to foot it.

There was no beaten round, but I felt so confident of finding my way that I started merrily enough.

The bush was brilliant with sunshine and flowers. Long trailing vines had festooned themselves from tree to tree, and these made holiday ground by day for cockatoos and other beautiful feathered things, of gayest and of soberest plumage, and by night for the lively opossum. Now and again, the sharp hiss of a snake would cause me to look well to my footings ; but, on the whole, it was a time of intensest enjoyment, and I tramped along bravely.

I was so engrossed by all the enjoyment I was having, that I took no thought of time, the hours passing like minutes.

I was recalled to a sense of Time's flight with a

shock of surprise, as I realized that the sun was drooping fast, and I knew that, two hours before sunset, I ought to have arrived at the river's bank, just across which the little township, to which I was making my way, was pitched.

I paused to consider matters; then noting an unusually strong growth of vine all up one of the loftiest gums, I climbed it, as I had climbed a ship's stay many a time, and reaching the topmost branch, I looked out across the other tree-tops, looked all around—then shivered, as if from chill.

I had expected to see a clearing, the river, the town close by, friendly roofs of log huts and farm buildings, perhaps, even, the high chimney-stack of some works, saw-mill, or factory. Instead of that, I saw nothing but bush everywhere.

Again that shiver passed over me. I had been long enough in the colony to know that my position was full of danger.

I was lost in the bush.

Descending again from the tree, I stood still, with my hands pressed across my eyes, and tried to think what I must do.

I could think of nothing else but to press on while the daylight lasted. I did, and, when darkness finally overtook me, I sank down, jaded and worn out, hungry and thirsty—*but not hopeless.*

Gathering together a heap of dried leaves for a bed, and assuring myself that, when daylight came, I should find some way out, I settled down to sleep.

I did sleep—a long, deep, refreshing sleep, that nerved me, when I awoke, for renewed effort.

I tightened my belt to ease the gnawing hunger I felt, and started to walk again.

With only brief intervals of rest, I walked until
noon, then feeling spent and used-up, I felt I must
have a real rest, and walked on a few paces, looking
for a comfortable place to drop down.

Suddenly my eye lighted on a sight that made my
heart stand still with fear, my spine thrilled with
horror, for there before me was the bed of leaves
from which I had started in the morning.

Huge drops of perspiration burst from every pore
of my skin—perspiration that stung as it oozed, then
left me chilled and clammy. The whole meaning of
all I had heard about lost men in the bush burst
upon me; for I had heard, and read, that such unfortu-
nates " described circle after circle in their wanderings,
ever returning to their starting-point, till they went
mad with terror, took their own life in despair, or
relapsed into helpless idiocy, and died of starvation."

Would this be my fate? " God help me!" I
moaned.

I rested for a while on the bed of leaves, and tried
to think what I must do now, my thoughts ever
returning to the same point—Try again.

I was sick and faint for want of food, but most for
want of water. It was now nearly thirty hours since
I had tasted anything. I rested, even dozed a little,
then rose again, wearily, and plunged forward.

On, on I moved, wearily, yet never without hope.
There were berries growing everywhere, but I did not
know their character and feared to eat them, lest
there might be death in their tiny globes. Once I
ventured to chew the young tendrils of a vine, but the
fierce agony that filled my throat and tongue (I did
not actually swallow the matter) was so terrible that
I did not venture upon another experiment of the

kind, though I suffered untold agonies from my thirst.

All the afternoon I moved forward. The sunlight filled the bush with a great glare at times, at others, the closeness of the leafy lattice above made the way shady and cool.

Suddenly, right before me there appeared a wide vista of sunlit open space, that seemed to lead to a clearing beyond. New strength came into my limbs, my heart beat high with hope, I laughed aloud—that is to say, as loud as my leather throat would let me —I felt that my troubles were at an end.

I kept moving, but my feelings were beyond my control ; I took off my broad-brimmed, grey felt hat and waved it high above my head as I lipped—(there was hardly a solid hallo left in my baked throat and tongue)—a " Hip, hip, hip, hurrah ! "

I skipped like a child as I drove my hopeful way towards the sunlit opening before me. The sun was getting lower each moment, but the clearing toward which I moved seemed more assured than ever.

Then, presently, it dawned upon me that the light towards which I was moving with such passionate hope, began to fade, to grow deeper, darker. My hope wavered, but I pushed on, until I stumbled over something that turned every drop of blood in my veins to icicle—*I had stumbled over my old bed of leaves.*

I had circled the old route once more, I had performed the mad, insane circuit of the lost man in the bush; and in spite of my twenty years, I sank down upon the bed of leaves, buried my face in my hands, and sobbed and wept like a child.

When I looked up again, the stars gleamed in the

young night sky. Once a star had given me cheer,
when I had seen it looking down like a pitying eye
upon me, before the hatch of that sugar barque had
been drawn over; but now it seemed as though the
stars above me looked coldly down. The fact was,
hope was momentarily dead within me, and all
things, the stars included, took the colour of my
hopelessness.

Often of late years, and now again as I write these
lines, the thought has come over me : " Oh, the utter
loss to the man and woman in times of great emergency, to whom God is but a name, an abstract
being ! When prayer, if even remembered and exer-
cised, becomes only like the cast of dice, the turn of
a roulette-wheel, that may be lucky or not, according
to grim Fate's dictum of chance; when *words* of
prayer, even if uttered, become only the cries of the
animal voicing the law of self-preservation, because
the soul of the crier is dead towards God, has no
basis of appeal other than that of the unregenerate
creature, which, like a lost sheep, bleats for rescue,
for food, for the waterbrook."

Does God hear the prayers of the unregenerate
man in times of horror such as that with which I am
dealing ?

Yes, He surely hears, and often answers in unexpected ways, even though the man has no claim upon
Him, other than that of the creature.

But the difficulty for the *man* is, that he is not
conscious of any living union with God, upon which
to base his prayer; so that, to go back to my former
simile, if he prays, he prays as the lost sheep bleats,
from the animal instinct of self-preservation, and not
from the spiritual intelligence and apprehension of

the regenerated soul, that knows that *if it is best for him*, and most to the glory of God, to be saved from the death that stares him in the face, God will save him, but that if otherwise, to depart and to be with Christ, *is far better.*

I did not attempt to pray amid the hopelessness of that time. I did not think of such a thing. I remember looking up at those cold-looking stars; then suddenly I lost consciousness, as a dead faintness overcame me.

Faintness must have merged into sleep, for I awoke at dawn, cold, stiff, strained, and filled with a dozen new agonies of pain.

I staggered to my feet, and stumbled on, and on. Sometimes my limbs gave way beneath me, and I would sink down or fall sprawling upon the ground.

Some time in the day I determined to lie down, bear the last sufferings as well as I could, and, if it might be—die.

The heat was awful. My eyes saw everything blood-red. My thirst beat down the gnawing wolf of hunger, and maddened me. I tore at the vines, I snatched leaves, chewed them, spat them out, and ravenned at others with my teeth, only to desist with the shuddering fear of being poisoned—for I still clung to life.

Now and again I made effort to rise, gave a little spurt, then sank down again. How long I lay, writhing in agony, hysterically sobbing, welcoming the touch on my tongue of an occasional tear, I cannot tell.

At last I got upon my feet again, staggered along, swaying to and fro like an overloaded porter, deliriously muttering inarticulately. Then I fell, my head striking the trunk of a gum-tree.

When I roused again it was night. The night before I had noticed no moon, but now I watched, in a dreamy, half-conscious way, the moon make its slow way up between two huge tree-trunks.

Suddenly a sight filled my eyes that quickened my deadened faculties. Across the face of the slow-moving moon there seemed to be drawn two fine lines, like the lines on a copy-book page. What could this appearance be?

For a few moments the wheels of my poor weakened brain moved so sluggishly, that I could not grasp the half-formed thought that was struggling to come to birth. Then, slowly, the dawn of the wondrous hope which was written between those two lines broke, and I wept like a child, as, staring up through my tears at the narrow silver bands, I tried to say, "They're telegraph wires."

My brain formed the words, the hard, dry leather thing in my mouth, which passed for a tongue, moved to the thought of my brain, but there was no sound save a dead, hollow rattle.

But with the thought, hope leaped strong within me. "Where there are wires they must lead somewhere!" said thought to me.

"But which way must I follow those lines? One way they must lead into wilder, uninhabited country, the other way must lead me *quickly* to the town I seek. Now which way ought I to go?"

I had no thought of God, or of prayer, but I had a "lucky" button in my pocket.

I knelt up on my knees, I filliped the button off my thumb nail, thinking, "*Shank*, I go right; *blank*, I go left."

Up in the moonlight whirled the button. It did

not soar very high, for I had no strength to toss it. My weakened frame swayed to and fro as I watched it. It fell, and I fell face down upon it, when I had assured myself that the shank was uppermost.

"I steer to the right!" I tried to murmur the words my brain dictated. My tongue moved dumbly to obey its nerve master's bidding, but no sound came.

I rose in the light of that still rising moon, and, with one long, grateful look at the gleaming telegraph wires, I found strength to stumble along into something like a trot.

Of one of his heroes, in one of his inimitable homely poems, Will Carleton has written :—

> "He is worn and worried, hot and panting ;
> He staggers at every footstep's planting ;
> The hot blood races through his brain ;
> His every breath is a twinge of pain ;
> Black shadows dance before his eyes ;
> The echoes mock his agony cries.
> But still he rushes on—yet on—
> Until at last some distance won,
> He mounts a fence with a madman's ease,
> And this is something of what he sees."

Almost might these lines have been written of my race that night, but I have none too clear a memory of the details. How long I ran, I do not know. I only remember that at the first sight of a light gleaming in a distant window I raced until my head felt like bursting ; the veins stood out full and tight, like strained cords ; my brain was a furnace ; my chest was a blazing volcano, burning to belch forth its fiery stream of blood ; my every breath was like the air of a smelting furnace.

I did not feel the ground I trod ; my soul became all eye, and the eye was filled with the sight of that beacon light ahead.

Nearer and nearer it came towards me,—for it was the light that seemed to move to me, and not me to it.

At last it seemed that I could touch it ; I laughed aloud in the dry, cackling fashion left to me, I stretched out my hand to reach the light, my sight became blurred, I reeled, and fell against the closed door of that colonial homestead. Then all was a blank.

Chapter XXIX

A MINISTERING ANGEL

"'AH, sure! The holy mother and all the saints be praised, he's coming round, the darlint. An' it's a sweet-faced broth of a boy he is fur sure; his ould mither's darlint, an' she nearly losin' the same by bein' lost in that bush, with its millions ov trees, an' them same nothin' but botheration an' vexation to chop down, sure, and to gobble up all the lives ov the beautifullest boys under the sun, as mischances to lose their way, like this darlint has! Oh, whist, whist! it's himself as is openin' them blessed peepers of his own, an' me, that's been a-watchin' him the last hour, niver got a sight of the colour of them same!"

I had actually *come* round, it was not a matter of *coming*. I had been conscious, in fact, for some time, only that my watcher had been busy preparing some food for me, and had not noticed my awakening. I had had water, several drinks of the blessed life-giving fluid, and the memory of the delight of those drinks came to me as I once more returned to consciousness with the same kind of ecstasy that remains after awaking from some delicious dream.

In some such terms as those recorded above my watcher apostrophised me, as she noted the signs of my final awaking.

When I opened my eyes fully, I found the speaker to be a most remarkable specimen of her sex. Tall —she would have been tall for a man—with a large, angular, raw-boned frame, real Hibernian cast of features, coarse red, freckled face, with a frowsy mop of hair, rudely bunched up on the top of her head, of the most vivid type of the hue vulgarly known as "carroty." Her huge arms were coarse-grained and the colour of an old tanned sail, which her rolled-up sleeves fully displayed. Her short, thick linsey skirt was looped up, displaying a pair of immense feet, encased in a pair of men's half-wellington boots.

This was the angel of the house who was ministering to me, and I hold her memory in grateful admiration to this day.

"Bide still, me honey!" she said, as she took a basin of soup she had prepared, and with which she proceeded to feed me slowly.

I grew ravenous, and great tears streamed down my cheeks, and mingled with the beads of my perspiration, as I begged for more.

With her eyes full of pity, but her voice full of firmness, my nurse said,—

"Oh, my darlint, it's yerself that 'ud jist roll over and die outright ef we let yer have yer fill out at onct. Then what good wid it be fur yer to have spint yer breath an' the life of ye's, a-racin' an' a-runnin' in that same style ye's did, and follerred the light ahint the window, I doubt me ye did, like a moth at a rush-light. But by the same token ye wer better than the moth, fur yer jist thumped yersel' up agin the door, an' so made yersel known, sure, an' was saved by myself an' the blissed Virgin."

She was right, good soul, and she knew just how to

handle a case like mine, and under her care, and with the kindness of the whole family, I was soon fairly well, though it was many months before I *felt* quite right. I am not quite sure that I have ever wholly recovered from the effects of the strain on my nerve, and of that long, hideous abstinence from water.

My escape was a narrow one, and though in those days I fear I really never thanked God, I am sure my whole being has been a praise-pulse ever since my conversion for that and every other wondrous deliverance from death.

I cannot find room in this book for a tithe of the experiences that crowd upon me as I write; but, without entering into details, lest my soul forgets *all* His deliverances from death, I will here mention four special cases.

Twice I fell from aloft—once, striking the pad-like arch of the covered hammock netting, and falling *in-*board upon a sail that was partly unrolled on the deck for repair; and once striking several ropes in my downward career, thus breaking my fall, and mini-mizing the results of it, so that only a couple of broken ribs and a few other trifles fell to my lot by way of *after* effects.

The third narrow escape from death was when, while at work in a boat that hung at the davits, while the ship I was then serving in was running through the Portland Race, a sudden lurch of the vessel threw me overboard.

I had hold of the becket of a large empty water-breaker as I fell, and, by some instinct, I retained my hold of the breaker, so that when I struck the sea I managed to secure a hold of the other becket (rope handle) and to draw my body partly over the breaker, which acted as a lifebuoy, and kept me up until my rescue by one of the ship's boats a full quarter of an hour later.

My fourth narrow escape was in one of the Eastern dockyards. They had set up in one of the houses a new machine in which I was greatly interested, and I went to watch its working. I was wearing a loose drill jumper at the time, and I must have got too close to the great wheel, for I suddenly found myself caught in its flying gyrations, and was being hurled round with it.

There came one awful moment of time when I was in the very centre of its orbit, and, with every faculty fully alive, and with the awful swiftness of thought given at such times, I realised that to go round *with* it meant death, and I wondered how I could be saved.

"*His* arm is not shortened that it cannot save." *He* wanted my unworthy life ; *He* had a miracle of grace which He longed to work, through His Son Jesus, and this is all I can give as explanation of the fact that, instead of being carried round on that wheel, I was hurled forward from its centre of revolution, and carried clear of the machinery beneath.

I went flying through space, over a wide, rushing, driving belt, and fell into a large open chest in a corner of the great shed.

The sides and ends of the chest were lined with spanners and wrenches, the centre being empty. I must have gone into that chest in a more or less doubled-up fashion, and have opened out when inside.

The only persons present were Hindoo and Cingalese workmen, who, after staring wonderingly at me in my boxed-up predicament, must needs stand

and jabber away indefinitely over the situation before coming to look at me.

The sudden arrival of a European changed the aspect of affairs, and with British promptness he began the work of relief.

They could not seem to lift me out of the chest, I was so jammed in ; but fortunately it was but a rotten, crazy old thing, and to force an end and the front out was the work of a moment only.

Insensible, breathless, and bleeding, I was borne away to the hospital, where it was more than twenty weeks before I could breathe a long breath naturally, and without pain.

Oh, the deadly, aggravating inertness and apathy of the ordinary Hindoo in those days ! Have they improved, I wonder, since then ?

To God, who is rich in mercy and grace, belongs the praise for these four and every other deliverance from death vouchsafed to me.

To return to that colonial homestead, under whose roof I found shelter and tender ministry when my awful bush experience had so nearly cost me my life.

In three days I was able to crawl about again. My first visit was to the post-office, where to my delight I found a letter from my dear mother awaiting me ; it had only arrived that morning.

I had written a letter before leaving Sydney acquainting her with the *fact* of my desertion, but not, of course, with the horrors attending it. Then when I had engaged, through the Yankee agent, to go up country, and had got from him the postal address of the station to which I was booked, I added this to my letter, and posted it to mother before leaving the city.

I forgot that a government that will forget to right a sailor or a soldier's wrongs, *for a lifetime*, would not forget to stop my half-pay to my mother, *immediately* it was known that I had deserted.

This information of my latest escapade had therefore reached my mother three months before *my* letter arrived.

If I felt delighted at the sight of my mother's handwriting on the envelope of the letter I received at the post office, the letter itself saddened me very much. She was far from strong, had a presentiment that she would hardly live out another year, and she yearned to see me.

At the end of my first three months in the bush, I had sent her home every penny I could spare of my wages, with a cheering letter. But this letter of hers decided me to dare all risks of recapture by the Navy, and make my way home at once.

As soon as I was well enough to get back to my settler-master, I arranged with him to leave at once. This was easily managed, for he had a cousin and a nephew, two sturdy young fellows, who wanted to get an insight into a settler's life, suddenly turn up on a surprise visit to him.

Two days after my return I started again, to make my way to Sydney.

*   *   *   *   *

The First Lap of My Journey Home.

" Mornin', skipper !   Hev yer got all yer hands ? "

" Why ?   Do you want a berth ? "

" Ay, I do."

" Well, I want a fellow as can take the ship's cook's

place till we get round to Sydney. He's had a bit of an accident, 'cut more than he can eat,' as the saying is, and can't use his right hand. So if you think you can manage you can come aboard, and I'll promise you you shan't be disappointed with yer wages when I settle with yer at Sydney. What d'yer say?"

This conversation occurred between the captain of a coasting steamer and myself a couple of days after leaving my place on the station.

There was no other immediate means of reaching Sydney, and I preferred to work my passage, and thus save my scanty cash, to paying for the luxury of passenger idleness.

In twenty minutes I was fully installed in the tiny deck-galley, as cook of the craft—the actual, but disabled, cook acting the part of *chef*, and directing all my operations.

On our way down the river we picked up half a dozen male passengers, all of whom had been more or less successful in the colony, some of them as diggers.

I have never been to Monte Carlo, to Homburg, or inside any of the great gambling hells of the world, but that voyage home to Sydney with those men gave me a deeper insight into the ways of gamblers than any of my own man-of-war experiences had given me.

I have known three meals lie on the deck all about them, each practically untouched, so utterly absorbed did they become with the passion of play.

Nugget and gold dust changed hands rapidly, and in sums of alarming amount, as it seemed to the more steady-going watchers of the play.

This band of gambling diggers, though all wild

and rough-looking, were very diverse in character, and drawn from many stations in life.

There was a shepherd, who had found caring for wool too tame an employment when he heard the stories of rapid fortunes made in a day with pick and shovel.

A man who had once been a thriving tradesman in Cape Town, but who, stricken by the consuming thirst of gold, had left all for the new quest, was now one of the maddest of the band.

A heavy-bearded, villainous-looking man of forty years, or about, would hardly have been recognised by his old congregation to whom he once preached in London, when, as a popular minister, his church was filled to overflowing with eager listeners to his marvellous eloquence. But all this was before the drink had captured and robbed him of all that he once held true and sacred. Now he is the biggest blackguard, the greatest swearer of the group.

But of all the party there was one who most of all interested me. A tall young fellow of about twenty-five years of age, fair, with light wavy hair, and hands slender and delicate in spite of his recent work with pick and shovel. He had been an officer in the army. What had severed the link that united him to the upper classes, perhaps no one there knew, but that it was now most effectively severed was very evident. There was a vein of sadness, almost of melancholy, about him, and this deepened every day he was on board, in proportion as he grew more reckless and lost larger amounts. At length one evening, as by the fading light he played his hand, he flung the last card down with a muttered curse, rose, and walked suddenly away.

By the dim light of the "fo'c's'le" lantern he sat and wrote something on the back of an old envelope, enclosing it in another and sealing it. Then walking out upon the deck, he climbed out upon the stump end of the bowsprit, and was seen sitting as if to catch the evening breeze, which was blowing up faintly, making the otherwise sultry air endurable.

Suddenly the report of a revolver was heard, and amid the little cloud of blue curling smoke he was seen to drop into the sea.

For one brief moment the players stopped and glanced forward, then settled down again as apathetically as though it had been the scream of a sea-gull instead of the death of a fellow-man with a soul !

The little note he had written was found afterwards upon the lid of a locker close by, and on its being opened later, contained these few emphatic words : "I shall die by my own hand in a few moments. I am wrecked, ruined, damned by cards. Once my fingers turned the leaves of the Word of God, and my eyes drank in its blessings ; now they have watched the cards as my fingers shuffled them, and having staked all I have or can ever hope to have, even my soul, I have cast the die and lost. No one will miss me. I am better out of the way. If there is such a thing as Divine mercy for such as me—may God have mercy upon my soul !"

Who he was, or what his history, none knew, and his late companions, with the gambler's callousness, did not seem to care. Within an hour that band of men had apparently utterly forgotten the awful suicide of the victim of their vice.

For myself, I was glad when I arrived in Sydney, and was clear of the ship, the scene of this tragedy.

Chapter XXX

HOMEWARD BOUND

MY intention, on arriving in Sydney, was to make my way to the quays where the shipping lay, to ascertain what vessels were bound for England, then endeavour to ship on one of them that I might have a little nest-egg of cash on reaching England.

I went straight to the good old woman who had nursed me back to health, when I was carried helpless from that sugar barque. She received me gladly, and her room being empty, she accepted me again as her lodger.

The next morning I made my way to Circular Quay to make inquiries as to English-bound ships.

While there, to my amazement, I suddenly saw two sailors in the naval uniform approach the place where I was standing. I knew them well, they belonged to the ship I had deserted from at Mauritius, they were even now wearing the gold-lettered name of the ship upon their cap-ribbons.

They were "yarning" away very earnestly as they walked, and I saw that they had no eyes for me or for any one else. I had no time to evade them without calling down attention upon myself; but, as the hot blood of a great and sudden nervousness swept through me, there came the memory of how altered I was.

I had been absolutely smooth-faced when on board the old ship, shaving every day. Now I had a full beard and a moustache, a twelve months' growth, begun in the stifling hold of that sugar ship, and continued under the semi-tropical sun of Australia's bush. My own mother would not know me—as a matter of fact, six months later when I saw her, she did not recognise me at all easily.

Then, too, every one knows how dress will alter appearance. My shipmates had never seen me in any other dress than the tight-where-you-ought-to-be-loose and loose-where-you-ought-to-be-tight costume of a man-of-war's man, and now I was in an up-country dress, my hair was long, and I was wearing a very wide-brimmed felt hat.

Still, for all my thought of the disguise, I felt exceedingly nervous at this proximity to the pair, and managed to turn my head, and pretended to look across the harbour.

When they were quite close to me, one of them said, "Which do they call number four, I wonder?"

He spoke to his mate, and the allusion was, I think, to the number of the landing-stage.

Suddenly they turned to me, and asked which was number four, and whether I had seen a man-o'-war's cutter anywhere about.

I met their glances fully, and, affecting the nasal drawl I had once amused myself with in dealing with the shipping agent, I replied that I had not seen the cutter.

A Chinese waiter-boy slipped over the bow of the vessel by which we were standing at that moment. He had heard the sailor's question, and, pointing further down the quay, he volunteered the information in his strange pigeon-English,—

" Mlan-ee-wlar bloat dlown alongee lere."

Following the direction of his finger, we could just see the white side and varnished gunwale of the boat.

The sailors were in no very violent hurry, and having recovered my nerve, and being curious to know how the vessel, which I left on the East Indian station, came to be here on the Australian station, I put a few carelessly uttered questions to them, which elicited the facts that the ship (as was not uncommon, it appears, in those days) had been transferred to the new station, that they had been lying in the bay some weeks, but that so many men had deserted for the goldfields and an up-country life, that they were going out on cruise the very next day.

With a " So long, chum," the two sailors passed on to their boat, and I was left musing on one of the strangest turns in the wheel of circumstances I had ever met with. I could not get the encounter out of my mind, and for half an hour, at least, I sat upon a quay bollard-head thinking over a hundred things, but finally decided that I had nothing to fear from any chance recognition on the part of any of my old shipmates whom I might meet.

Later on I began to make further inquiries as to English-bound ships, and just before noon I found a vessel that was loaded in ballast, that wanted to ship a hand who would be willing to come on board at once, and do painting and other odd jobs before the regular crew was shipped for the passage home.

In ten minutes it was all settled, and I had agreed to come on board that *night*, and begin work the next morning at twenty-five shillings a week and my rations, with a home on the ship (not bad wages, but then men could not be got easily, every one was flying, or had flown, off to a new goldfield).

Having arranged matters in this way, I went ashore again, had my dinner, acquainted my landlady with my proposed change, then went out for a stroll. Some fascination seemed to draw me to the farthest end of the quay. I wanted to see my old ship.

There she lay, a picture such as the modern navy could not show us. How long I sat looking at her I do not know. I was aroused by people's voices, as they talked of "boats," "get back before tea," " such a lovely day," etc.

Then the thick voice of a waterman took up the strain, " Lovely day fur a spin out on the bay. Have a trip to the man-o'-war ; she goes off to-morrow, an' the Lord knows when she'll be back agin."

A sudden desire filled me to go off and see my old ship. After the adventure of the morning I felt tolerably safe, and if I moved round the decks of the ship in company with a party, I should stand less risk of recognition.

The wildness of such an adventure appealed to something within me, and I stepped forward and told the waterman I would make one to go.

Five minutes later he pushed off, with eight of us on board, two of us, myself and another male, taking an oar to help pull the boat.

At the gangway of the man-of-war we were received by one of the petty officers of the day in the ordinary way, and were conducted round the ship, in which, *as shore-folk, we were all very much interested, myself especially.*

What wondrous fables our guide told us! His tongue had a very decided *nautical twist*.

As we moved along the lower deck my heart throbbed violently, for my brain was crowded with exciting thoughts and memories. As I passed my old mess I looked keenly round it, and in that one long look, besides recognising four or five of my old messmates, my eye lighted upon my dear old ditty box, with my initials "S.T.W." inlaid in the front of the satin-wood box, the letters being in black ebony.

I remembered how I made that box, during one of my spells of convalescence, after one of my accidents.

But I dared not stay, and as my party was slowly moving, I moved on with them. We spent half an hour altogether on board, then tipping our guide, we went over the side into our boat, and pulled back to Circular Quay.

Next morning I began my new life on the great merchantman. She belonged to the "White Stars," and was going back to England loaded with wool, and would take twelve passengers.

Two days later, a strike, which had been threatening for some time among the lumpers (ship loaders and unloaders), became an actual fact, and the difficulties attending the work of unloading and loading vessels became tremendous.

There were several hundred tons of ballast on board our ship that must be got out before she could load up, and our skipper was in a fever of haste and anxiety. He could get no man to come on board to work, so he proposed to the four of us who were on board that we should help him out of his difficulty by getting out that ballast. We could use the donkey

·engine, and he would give us so much per ton for the job, or thirty shillings per day each.

We held a consultation, and decided on the tonnage payment, drew up a brief agreement, and got him to sign it as well as ourselves. He held one copy, and each of us held a copy.

That job put many pounds into my pocket, and by the time the lumpers came to their senses, or won their demands (I forget the circumstances), we had finished one of the stiffest bits of work I ever did, for, besides the heaviness of the work, we worked sixteen hours out of every twenty-four.

I have no space to record my voyage to England, one of the most exciting events of which was the discovery that the wool cargo had fired. The discovery was made sufficiently early to save any absolutely untoward circumstances, though no one felt really safe until we were in the English Channel.

We were some weeks beyond our expected time, having had fearful weather south of the Horn, and had consequently run short of some foods. A huge Scotch steamer, whom we signalled, helped us out of our provision difficulty.

Oh, the excitement among all hands when we sighted old England! "The Start" was the first land we saw, and my heart was full of the wildest delight at the thought that in a comparatively few hours I should see England, by which, in those days, I meant London. For many years I, *mentally* at least, spelt England with the six letters L-o-n-d-o-n.

I still share all Richard Le Gallienne's admiration for the great metropolis, and now, as I write, my brain recalls his lines :—

> "London, as beautiful at set of sun
> As though her beauty had but just begun ;
> London, that mighty sob, that splendid tear,
> That jewel hanging in the great world's ear.
> Strange queen of all this grim, romantic stone,
> Paris, say some, shall push you from your throne,
> And all the tumbled beauty of your dreams
> Submit to map and measure, straight cold schemes
> Which for the loveliness that comes by chance
> Shall substitute the conscious streets of France.
> A beauty made, for beauty that has grown,
> An alien beauty, London, for your own.
>
> O wistful eyes, so full of mist and tears,
> Long be it ere your haunted vision clears,
> Long ere the blood of your great heart shall flow
> Through inexpressive avenue and row ;
> Straight-stepping, prim, the once adventurous stream,
> Its spirit gone, it loiters not to dream,
> All straight and pretty, trees on either side,
> For London's beauty, London beautified.
>
> Ah ! of your beauty change no single grace,
> My London, with your sad, mysterious face."

Ever since I left the Navy, twenty years ago, I have lived in the provinces, for ten years in an island home, much of the other ten in remote villages, but my heart is in London. And, though many people will fail to understand it, yet the fact remains, that nothing refreshes me when I am brain-fagged, jaded, and altogether run down, like a day, a week in London. Only to move through its streets, to catch the cockney accent, to feel the mighty pulse of its mightier movement, to catch, from some quieter spot, the hum of its myriad peoples, the rush of its thronging traffic, the roar of its powerful lungs, is for me to get a physical and mental fillip, such as I get nowhere else in the world. And nothing ever impresses me more *spiritually* than a sight of London's teeming population, so that, not content to sigh,—

> " Oh that the world might taste and see
> The riches of His grace !
> The arms of love that compass me
> Did all mankind embrace,"—

I feel quickened for service, quickened to do what little I can to bring Christ, Salvation, Hope near to those who, as yet, have no hope beyond the present.

More and more the thought presses upon me, as my years go on, that there is no responsibility resting upon me as to *how* my message for Christ will be received ; but the responsibility upon me *is the delivery* of it.

When my health allowed me to voice the message of Hope, of Salvation *through* Christ our Atonement, to scores and hundreds every night, it was a glad, a gracious service to me. But now that my voice is stilled, and the pen has been put into my hand by God, I can rejoice equally, especially when I remember that, at the lowest computation, my reading congregation numbers a million a week.

A wondrous privilege? True, but a great, a solemn responsibility! And whoever thinks of praying for Christian authors? A few quiet, unknown Christians *may* in their private devotions, but when do we hear Christian authors and publishers prayed for in our public services? Yet who, in these days of uncertain sounds, need it more ?

In the earth there are many voices : I thank God for them all. I thank Him for Nature's voice, with her wondrous song and story, her parable and her pictures ; but Nature cannot tell me of lost man's need, or speak to me of the privilege of spiritual service, or incite and inspire me to that service; so I thank God for that other, that Higher, that Highest of all voices—the Spirit's.

And as I have looked upon London's teeming population, I have heard His voice, again and again, saying to me,—

> " Go ; labour on, while it is day,
>   The world's dark night is hastening on ;
> Speed, speed the work, cast sloth away ;
>   It is not thus that souls are won.
>
> " Men die in darkness at your side
>   Without a hope to cheer the tomb ;
> Take up the torch, and wave it wide,
>   The torch that lights Time's thickest gloom."

I wonder if this digression, through cockney enthusiasm, needs apology? If it does, reader, please accord it, even though you smile while you give it. But believe me, in the days when I was afloat and in other lands, the London instinct in those of us who were Metropolitan-born, was as strong as anything ever recorded of the sons of the land of my forbears, for their

> " Land of brown heath and shaggy wood,
>   Land of the mountain and the flood."

I remember an interesting little incident concerning the love of the Londoner for all that reminded him of " the dear little village on the Thames."

Half a dozen of us (all in white man-of-war uniform) were in one of the bazaars at Madras. One of us had just remarked upon the familiarity to the sight of a word branded on a packing-case outside a fancy stall—the word was " Houndsditch."

This set our tongues running on that part of London, and we were soon tramping, in speech, over the various thoroughfares in that neighbourhood. A discussion arose, we drew away to a spot where the bare ground was smooth and polished by the constant traffic of naked native feet.

A piece of chalk was produced, and we began to illustrate our argument by sundry map lines on the brown ground. Quite a little crowd of natives stood about, puzzling over our movements, and over our heated talk.

The chalk line was run from a supposed Aldgate Church to Cornhill, with Houndsditch off to the right, the Minories off to the left, Fenchurch Street forked from a point, Leadenhall Street starting from the same point, and giving the line to Cornhill.

There's this, there's that, there's the other, became the order of the moment, as point after point along Leadenhall Street was ticked off with the chalk, by one of the most vehement of the naval geographers "An' then comes the Heast Hindy 'ouse," he rattled on; "I oughter know, seein' as 'ow I uster work right opposite."

There was a momentary lull in the argument, while we studied the chalk map, when the silence was suddenly broken by a woman's voice, strong with the cockney accent, saying, "Well, what have you done with St. Mary's Axe?"

Every face was turned up, every eye fixed upon a stout, comely-faced, elderly woman, who, smiling down upon our astonished faces, said, "Lend me the chalk."

The chalk was passed over to her, and with one or two strokes she put in St. Mary's Axe, Surrey Court, and one other opening which every one else had forgotten.

A few words passed between us, and we learned that she was a soldier's wife, had been in India nearly twenty years, was soon going home, and, as we realized, had never forgotten her London, or lost her cockney accent.

Not one of us had exchanged speech with an English woman, I expect, since we had left the Cape of Good Hope, even if we did there ; and our delight was unbounded, and we insisted upon making her a present, in honour of our " towny-ship."

She laughed, and did her best to refuse, but finally permitted herself to be won over ; and, accompanied by us all, she led the way to a shop in the bazaar, selected a shawl, and after shaking hands with us each bade us good-bye, and wished us " good luck to get home again to Cornhill, Houndsditch, Aldgate, or wherever we dwelt—when at home."

Three days after the arrival of the wool ship in the Thames on which I had shipped in Sydney, the crew being paid off, I started to find my mother, who had moved twice since I left England.

Chapter XXXI

A RUDE AWAKENING

ON arriving in London, and after a day or two
spent in seeing friends, I began to cast about
for some profitable employment. My dear mother
had quite recovered from the weakness which had
alarmed me so, and which had induced me to leave
Australia so hurriedly. She was now very comfortably situated, though she felt she would like to
have me remain in London, that I might be near her.

I had managed to save nearly fifty pounds, the
result of my work on the vessel in Sydney harbour,
and my wages as a seaman on the homeward voyage,
and was easily induced to speculate with this, under
the following circumstances :—

I was introduced to an eating-house keeper, who
had a business in the eastern part of the city, who
needed a little more capital to extend his business.
He was an out-and-out good business man in his own
line, and we came to an arrangement in this way.

I was to invest my money in the business, take
a small fixed weekly wage, and a small share in the
final profits, while, at the same time, I was to give up
all my time to the business.

I had been with him about two years, our trade
had wonderfully increased, and I had taken sole

charge of the select dining-room used by our regular customers, and had won many friends among them.

One day, just before our first diners began to turn up, there came a peculiar clasp-like tap on my shoulder from behind, while a voice said meaningly in my ear, " I want you ! "

" Me—e—e ? " I gasped, as I turned to face the speaker ; " what for ? "

I was told afterwards that my face, as I turned, was deathly pale, and my eyes were filled with alarm.

This was in my first momentary surprise ; then— but too late—I managed to say coolly, and in an off-hand, ordinary tone, " Oh, certainly, sir ! It's a little early, but some of the joints are ready, sir. There's boiled mutton, caper sauce, and——"

My customer smiled, as he said, " All right, young fellow ! You've cut enough capers, and I can't stand sauce."

He spoke in low, meaning tones, adding, " You know very well what I want of you. I saw it in your face that first moment, when you were off your guard—I want you, Sydney T. Watson, for desertion from H.M.S. ——, East Indies."

Of course, I looked blankly astonished, and I believe any one but a professional detective would have been deceived. But this man was not deceived.

" Now, look here," he went on, " I don't want to make things unpleasant. I know my man, and I am sure of him, so you had better not give me any trouble."

I was fighting for my liberty, a liberty bought at a great cost, and I could not give in without an effort.

I protested that I was no sailor. " Look at my hands, sir," I said, spreading out my well-kept fingers before him ; "did you ever know a sailor with hands like these ? "

But it was no use, the plain-clothes man would not be cajoled.

My partner appeared on the scene, a little knot of business men, our regular early diners, crowded round, and each expressed incredulity as to my being the man wanted ; but the detective, with his " eternal calm and everlasting smile," was inexorable, and a few minutes later I was being driven sharply away, in custody, in a cab (which *I* paid for).

During that drive, I decided upon the *rôle* I would play, namely, utter ignorance of ships, the sea, or sea-life, and, if no untoward event occurred to upset my plans, I felt sure I should be enabled to carry out my part.

Before the magistrate, at the London court, where I was first conveyed, I *began* to play my *rôle*, and so far convinced him that I was the victim of mistaken identity, that he said to the detective, " I must, of course, give you the opportunity you seek, of bringing this man under the notice of the Admiralty officials ; but, you may depend upon it, that you have made a mistake ; *that man was never a sailor—look at him !*"

Every one in the court looked at the prisoner ! A murmur of sympathy passed round, for in truth he looked very little like a sailor as he stood with his brown melton overcoat, with deep velvet collar, over the black coat and trousers, with open vest, and wide expanse of white shirt front and the white tie of the professional waiter.

Three hours later, still in charge of the detective, I was rowed alongside H.M.S. *Hebe*, the receiving ship stationed in the Thames.

The detective stated his mission to the quarter-master on the gangway, who, in sharp, peremptory tones, addressing me, said :—

" Go aft ! "

Still bent upon carrying out my *rôle* of ignorance of the sea, I looked aloft, around, everywhere, in a puzzled, bewildered way.

" *Aft*, I said," repeated the quarter-master ; "go *aft* ; do you hear ? "

I began immediately to walk *forward*.

With a grip on my coat-collar, the quarter-master swung me round, and bawled, " Now then, booby, hev yer forgot which end o' the ship aft is ? "

With the lie of the *rôle* I was playing upon my lip, I said, " I beg your pardon, friend, but I do not understand sea-phrases, having been a landsman all my life."

If a man have no fear of God before his eyes, and is playing for such a stake as I was, a lie is considered (wrongly, of course) one of the rights of self-preservation.

Obedient to the twist upon my shoulder, I turned and walked aft ; then, as I went, receiving the further command, " Stand on the quarter-deck," I mounted upon the hatch of the main ladder, and was met with a storm of abuse.

" Why, you blessed idiot, don't you know what is meant by the quarter-deck ! " bawled the irate petty officer.

" No, sir ! " meekly.

At this moment, the captain, who, unnoticed, had been pacing the other side of the deck, but further aft, crossed the deck.

Just as I stepped off the hatchway, a young seaman

came up from below, and we met face to face. He did not see the captain, and he was too excited by the encounter to be cautious ; so after one wondering look into my face, he held out his hand, and roared out, " What cheer, Syd ? So they've nabbed you at last ! "

" Oh, oh ! " said the quarter-master, laughing, " that's how the land lays, is it ? Where did you know this young fellow, Jack Summers ? "

" On board the old —— ! " replied the seaman. " We was messmates there ! "

It was true, we had been messmates during the first half of that last commission, from which I had run. As a waiter, I was beardless, as when he first knew me, and he easily recognised me.

My assumed part had failed, and once again I found myself a prisoner, in irons, on board ship.

Of the weary weeks which followed, I have no heart to write, even if I had the space to spare, or thought it would interest my readers.

I was transferred to Sheerness, to the admiral's ship, and by a strange coincidence, was just in time to see the ship from which I ran, paid off. I heard the gay strains of the band that played my old crew to the railway station, as they started for their eight weeks' leave :—

> " With their pockets lined
> With dungaree and guineas.'

And I ? Well, I went to L—— Naval gaol for three months—an exceedingly light sentence.

The full horrors of the separate and *silent* system were in force in this new place of my confinement, and though I had been conversant with both systems,

in the Plymouth prisons, yet there there were many
qualifying sides to the discipline.

At L——, the *separateness* did not press upon me
quite so much as the silence, because, after a time, I
was given work in the carpenter's shop, which was a
large, roomy place, with a *comparatively* pleasant
outlook.

Yet, in spite of this favour, the long evenings, from
four o'clock, spent alone in my cell, and the weari-
some Sundays, were separate and solitary enough to
make my cell a stone purgatory, after the delights of
three years' shore life; so that the language of my
soul became the language of " The Prisoner's Song,"
written by a *separate* man on the wall of his cell :—

> The roses bloom in the garden,
>   The bee comes wooing the flowers ;
> The song-bird pipes to his nest-mate,
>   Through all the golden hours.
> The breeze is freighted with fragrance,
>   From forest, and field, and lea ;
> But youth has fled, and hope lies dead,
>   So what are they all to me ?
>
> The blue bird rocks in the tree-tops,
>   Free as the summer air,
> Swings and sways, and warbles,
>   With never a flutter of care.
> Memories never haunt him,
>   No thought of the morrow has he,
> But the guarded wall like a sombre pall
>   O'ershadows it all for me.
>
> I sit in the glowing twilight,
>   And gaze on the evening sky,
> On the glorious sunset banners
>   That athwart the hill-tops fly,
> Till the diamond eyes of heaven
>   Look down on the bond and the free ;

But I see the stars through the prison bars,
  So what are they all to me?

Ah ! the flowers have lost the perfume,
  The summer breeze is still ;
The bees are naught but gluttons,
  And harsh the song-bird's trill.
For the mighty voices of nature,
  Of heaven, of earth, of sea,
Have nought of cheer for the prisoner's ear,
  What ! what are they all to me?

Of the work given to me to do, while employed alone in the carpenter's shop, I could tell some very amusing things—there were several dozen Oxford picture frames, made to given sizes, which afterwards appeared for sale in a window of a house, with which the warder who had chiefly to do with me, and my work, was intimately connected. There were—but, lest I should be tempted to tell tales out of school, perhaps I had better sum up the matter by saying, that the memory of many of my P.P. jobs of work makes me smile to this day.

Of the other special side of punishment which pressed hardly upon me, after my long spell of freedom—*the silent system*—I must leave for another chapter, since a remarkable incident occurred, years after, as a result of that silent system.

Chapter XXXII

LIP-READING

ONE result of the silent system was, that its victims learned, more or less, to speak with one another by one of two systems—the finger language of the deaf and dumb, and the language of the lip, when the words were formed without utterance.

I set myself to learn the first, and all unconsciously to myself I learned the second. I am not at all sure that I should have said I *had* learned the lip-language, but I more than once discovered that I could read perfectly the unuttered speech of the man near me, as he silently talked with his mouth.

Long, long after that prison experience, and when I had been converted many years, and had long been working as an evangelist, I had a singular proof of how the memory unconsciously treasures things, and will bring them to the surface when a need arises.

I had gone to W——, to take the place of a very successful evangelist, during his absence on sad domestic business. My friend had been in the thick of a mission when this sudden summons came to him, and I felt how difficult it was to go in and take hold of another man's work. But remembering that it was the *Lord's* work, that we were both His servants, and that I had not sought the service, but that it came in the order of God's call, I went.

I arrived on the Saturday, in time to have half an hour's talk with my friend, saw him off by train, then began to prepare for my Sunday.

The services on the Sunday were to be held in the largest hall in the town, those of the week in a somewhat smaller hall. Among the workers whom I was asked to use in the meetings, as opportunity served, was a young man whose life had been recently given up entirely to God's service.

He had been a great athlete, and if my memory serves me rightly, he had also been a stage acrobat. He was a handsome fellow, with a strong, intellectual face, a splendid head, crowned with hair that was jet black, glossy, and a mass of natural curls. His figure, and every movement of it, was full of a rare grace ; I don't think he could have been awkward, if he had tried.

The first meeting was on the Sunday afternoon. It was August—one of the hottest I ever remember in this country—the huge hall was packed, and one was glad to wear the very lightest of clothing. My young athlete wore a garb which, in its lightness, served, unintentionally on his part, to show his figure to the best advantage.

I gave him the hymn-book, and asked him to open the meeting. As he stood up and waited for perfect silence, my eyes travelled over the great congregation, surprised at the large proportion of really superior people who helped to fill the seats.

As my eye searched the faces, and my heart was lifted in prayer that blessing might come to some in the meeting, my glance was arrested by two ladies who sat about a dozen seats from the platform.

It was not their faces, their costumes, nothing of

this, but their *lips*, which had arrested my glance. They were sisters or cousins perhaps, I thought, for they were much alike. They sat side by side at the aisle end of their seat, and one had bent her head towards the other, and was whispering : " That man with the hymn-book has been an actor ! "

" Do you think so ? " asked the other.

" I am sure of it ; just watch his movements, and look at his face."

My young friend gave out the first verse of the hymn at that moment, and with a swift exchanged glance of meaning, the two ladies rose with the congregation and began to sing.

For myself, I was intensely startled. I had never practised reading lips since those old, sad, weary days in L—— prison, and here had I, all unconsciously to myself, read the lips of these two whisperers, quite forty feet, I should think, away from me ; and that I had read them correctly, I was as fully assured as though the words had been *spoken* in my hearing.

The service proceeded—I engaged in prayer, other hymns were sung, I read a scripture portion for lesson, and in due time I rose to give the address.

I had purposed to speak from the words, " *Until He find it*," but now that the time had come, I could not, I dare not ; for that inward voice of the Spirit, which all who leave themselves free for His guidance know so well, bade me give another message—the message of the read lips.

" A strange thing has happened to me," I began, ' since this meeting commenced." Then I told the story of the lip-reading, adding, " No one can know of whom I speak, save God, and the two persons who spoke together. Whether they are male or female, whether they sit on this side or on that, whether they are close to me or at the distant end of the hall, no one knows, but God, themselves, and myself; so it would be utterly impossible for any one who listens to me, to discover of whom I speak, save the two friends themselves, and they know that I speak the truth."

I stated here exactly what had passed between the two ladies, and in one swift, sweeping glance over the sea of silent faces before me, I caught the pale-ness of one of the late whisperers' faces, and the flush on the other face.

A solemn hush came over my soul, and over that great meeting, as I said, " Now, friends, the thought in my heart is this : If I, a weak, finite, sinful man, have been able, almost unconsciously, to read the lips of these friends, how much more solemn is the thought that God is reading all our hearts at this moment, and He knows who of us are saved, are His children, born again, or who are still unsaved, still under condemnation ! "

A text was given me of God, and I preached from it. What the text was I cannot remember ; I only remember that the service was one of the most solemn I was ever in, and that through all the time, like some silent, interwoven strain, there seemed ever present behind my *expressed* thoughts, the music of Tersteegen's thought :—

> "Lo ! God is here ! let us adore,
>   And own how dreadful is this place !
> Let all within us feel His power,
>   And silent bow before His face ;
> Who know His power, His grace who prove,
> Serve Him with awe, with reverence love."

When I had finally pronounced the benediction, I made my way quickly, as was my custom, to the door, that I might watch for distressed souls.

The crowd poured out in unusual silence. I shook hands and spoke to a few whom I could reach, and presently the two ladies came up abreast of me. Both were flushed; one tried to pass me without taking my offered hand; in the eyes of the other, as she searched my face, there were tears.

In a whisper that none could hear but herself, as I shook her hand, I said, "I read rightly, did I not?"

She inclined her head in assent.

"What, then, of God's heart-searching?" was all that I had time to add, as she passed out.

When the last of the congregation had left, my host joined me, and we walked home. I felt as though I would have preferred utter solitude and communion with God, but my kind host was so full of the solemnity of the meeting, and the strangeness of my platform statement, that he began at once to talk about it.

An hour later, as we sat at tea, my host was summoned to speak to a visitor. On his return to the tea-table he was very excited, for his visitor was a leading gentleman of the neighbourhood, the guardian of the two ladies whose lips I had read. They had told him all the story, assuring him that I had told every word they had whispered exactly, and he felt that he must come to see my host, to inquire whether I was a true man of God, *or whether I was a Thought-Reader?* He added that there was the greatest excitement in the town, and that the doors of the hall, when he passed, were thronged with people, who were talking of the "Thought-Reader" who was to preach.

This was all very strange and wonderful, but I felt, and my host felt, that God was in this matter.

The hall was packed to suffocation that night, hundreds were turned away who could not get in, and God came mightily in our midst in the meeting, and souls were melted under the power of the Holy Ghost, as *He* convinced of sin.

The two ladies were there again. They came night after night until the Thursday night, after which I had to leave for meetings at Oxford. I keep no record of numbers—God does that, and He makes no mistake, while we are very apt to make wholesale blunders—but many received the blessing of Life in Christ, and others were spiritually blessed, during those five days' services. Among those who could rejoice were the two ladies, who spoke gratefully kind and encouraging words to me on more than one occasion, they having quite forgiven me for using them as a text.

Have I ever had a similar experience in a meeting? No! neither have I ever *tried* to repeat it. It was an unpremeditated, spontaneous act, that reading of the lips, and was altogether too solemn a thing to be imitated in fleshly power, or programmed mentally before a meeting.

I have been conscious of the same power of lip-reading at other times, in other places—in the railway carriage when travelling, in other public vehicles, in private homes, etc.—but I do not remember having it since at any time when ministering in public worship or services.

If I am asked, "How do you account for the incident at W——?" I can only say, with the deepest reverence, "HE *shall bring all things to your remembrance.*"

✳   ✳   ✳   ✳   ✳

To return to my life-story. During my three months' incarceration in L—— prison, I once more began, towards the end of my term, to read the Bible in my cell, and my mind began to revolve spiritual things.

On my last Sunday in the place, I was powerfully impressed during the service in the chapel.

How strange are those prison chapel services, where every man sits in a separate wooden, sentry-box-like compartment, unable to see a single fellow-prisoner, or to be seen by a single one of his fellows !

Scarce a face shows the faintest shadow of real interest in any of the proceedings, except in the singing, and this exercise becomes, at times, quite a delight to the men. A strong, well-trained male choir is always impressive, but when the choir consists of several hundreds, and the singing is in harmony, the effect is really very fine.

The singing of the Psalms, of the Jubilate, the Te Deum, and the Magnificat in L—— prison was very impressive, though the effect upon the heart of any truly consecrated Christian visitor and listener would not have been the merely musical, but that deeper thought,—a thought of sadness,—how sorrowful a fact, that scarcely one, if there *was* even one, of the singers, who was in a spiritual condition to say, " My soul doth magnify the Lord : my spirit rejoiceth in God *my Saviour.*"

If the congregation was a spiritually unsympathetic

one, what could be said of the ministry? The wondrous beauty of those Church prayers was all utterly lost in the break-neck gabble with which they were rendered. The seven, ten, or twelve minute homily that was read, was the veriest husk and chaff. The benediction, that closed the service, was uttered at railway speed.

Always the same—always lifeless, heartless, dead— it is little wonder that these services affected the prisoners no more than the prayer-wheel devotions of the Eastern heathen affects the worshipper who turns his wheel.

But on this last Sunday of my term, a new voice broke the chapel silence, and, from the first, the voice which spoke to us won its way to our interest and attention.

All through the service the interest deepened, and many a forgotten sacred memory must have been aroused that morning. My own heart was deeply stirred, and the day was one never to be forgotten by me; for it was, doubtless, the beginning of a series of heart experiences that eventually led to my actual conversion.

On the Tuesday following, an escort from H.M.S. *A——*, Portsmouth, came to the prison for me; my time was up, and I went out into the streets of L—— with a glad, yet sad heart. I was glad to be so far free, but my heart was heavy with its first real sense of dissatisfaction with self, while I was ignorant of *how* to find satisfaction in Christ.

Chapter XXXIII

ALONE ON THE SHORE

ALMOST immediately after my release from
L——— prison, and my *re*-entry into the service
(for, by my desertion, I had lost all the time I had
ever served before), the South African war broke out,
and I volunteered for one of the newly-commissioned
ships, hoping to be able to redeem some of my past
in stirring war services.

I was accepted, and went on board H.M.S. ———,
full of highest spirits, and noblest resolves for the
future.   All was hurry on board, for British lives
were in danger, and our vessel had to do everything
in the greatest haste.   Only forty-eight hours' leave
was granted, to say good-bye to loved ones, *and this
only to those whose leave was good* (men who, like
myself, had only just *finished* punishment, were not
eligible).

This seeming injustice to those of us who *had
completed* terms of punishment once more roused my
hottest feelings (it had always been a sore point with
me, in the Navy, this special injustice), and I rebelled
against it.   I would not leave the country to go on
a perilous service, from which I might never return,
without saying " Good-bye " to my dear mother, and
I tried strategy to win what was otherwise denied
to me.

The early, wintry evening was quite dark when the liberty-men assembled on the quay of the dock-yard, from the ship, to be inspected before starting for the railway station. The inspection took place by lantern light. The men were in two lines. I had passed over the side with them, dressed in my best, and took up a position about the middle of the *rear* rank.

When the first rank had been examined, the order came, "*Front* rank, two paces to the front, quick, march ! " As the front rank moved, I moved quickly from the *rear* rank, and managed to squeeze my way between two of the already inspected front-rankers. They guessed what it meant, and made the way easy for me.

The rear rank was inspected, I remained undiscovered, and marched gaily enough with the others out of the dockyard, and in an hour was *en route* for Waterloo. I spent a few brief hours with my mother, then with a sad good-bye on both sides, I started to go back.

At Bishopstoke, where I had to change for Portsmouth, there was some hitch, through a block on the line ; and an hour before I eventually arrived at my ship, my absence had been discovered, and on my arrival I was placed under arrest.

Next morning I received sentence of six weeks' imprisonment in the same prison I had just left.

For a time I felt utterly crushed, and declared to myself that I would not try again. But during that second term better thoughts prevailed, and I grew deeply anxious for a change of heart, feeling assured that a change of heart would mean a change of life.

At the end of the six weeks I was once more

escorted to the *Asia*, from whence I was almost immediately drafted to H.M.S. *Z*——, stationed at Cowes, Isle of Wight, as guard-ship to the Queen, when Her Majesty was at Osborne, while at other times she was stationed at Netley, in Southampton Water.

On arrival on board my new ship, I was made carpenter's yeoman (store-keeper), and was at once placed in charge of the store-room, a large, roomy place in the fore part of the vessel, *below the lower deck*, where no daylight ever came, but which was lighted by candles almost as thick as my wrist, held in huge lanterns with powerful reflectors.

My concern in spiritual things deepened every day, for I had comparatively little to do, and my life, except at meal times, was utterly private, since often a whole day would pass without a soul ever coming down my store-room ladder, except the inspecting officer in the morning.

In the mess to which I had been told off on my arrival on the ship, was a short, thick-set, merry-faced lad about my own age, whose tongue was rich with the raciest of Irish brogues.

Some time before he had found Christ, while he was studying the Scriptures. " He saw no man, save Jesus only," the Word of God and the Spirit of God being his only teachers.

Just how he and I began to talk together, neither he nor I can remember ; but we did begin to be chums, and he soon found out where I was, spiritually.

I wanted salvation, but I wanted to *feel* saved, and, as he reminded me the other day when we met, he kept insisting that I could only be saved by *faith*, and live by *faith*, and that *feeling*, or consciousness of salvation, came from the knowledge that the soul had *believed God,* and trusted in His Son, and was therefore safe for time and eternity.

Of this dear fellow, the most precious earthly male friend I ever had, and of his wonderful life-work, I could write a large volume. In fact, God willing, I hope to do so before this year has expired, for his story is one of the untold marvels of this century.

The eyes of the whole civilized world this past twelve months have been directed to the Arctic, to the North Pole, and to such heroes as Nansen and Jackson, while the words " Fram," and " Jackson-Harmsworth Expedition," have become household words with us of late.

But all the Arctic exploits (and I give place to no man in my admiration for all that is true and heroic in the careers of our latest Northern explorers) sink into nothing, when compared with the eternal and spiritual results of my whilom shipmate, the loving-hearted Irish lad, known now, the wide world over, as the Rev. E. J. Peck, who for twenty years has been God's Nansen to the Eskimo.[1]

The days and weeks passed, and I got no light to my soul. I longed to be allowed to go ashore, for it seemed to me, that if I could only go and hear some good minister preach, that I should surely see and grasp the truth. But there could be no shore-going for me ; the rule of the service being, that, after a man has come out of prison, he must serve six months on board, without a flaw in his conduct, to qualify for a

---

[1] "The Eskimo : Voices from the Far North." A story of that interesting people for the last 150 years, with some account of workers among them, with life story of Rev. E. J. Peck, and his twenty years' work in the Arctic, will (D.V.) shortly appear.

certain grade of character that would entitle him to
the privilege of leave.

But God had His purposes to fulfil, and " He Himself knew what He would do." The vessel was lying
in Southampton Water, opposite the coastguard
flagstaff that stands at the head of that bit of shingly
beach by Netley Hospital. I used to look at the
shore, watch the liberty men land every afternoon,
and ardently long to be allowed *only an hour's* run.
But all my longing brought me no nearer my desire.

Then one of our gigs got stove in ; we were
short-handed in the carpenter's crew, and the chief
carpenter sent for me one evening to say that the
store-room must be left for a day, and I must take
some tools ashore next morning, and repair the
damaged gig, which was hauled up alongside the
flagstaff on the beach.

God had made the way for me to spend a day
ashore !

It was one of the earliest, brightest days of a
glorious May, and my heart was in a perfect tumult
of delight as I landed next morning at half-past
seven. Sunshine was all about me, above me. Before
me, as I faced the river, when the landing-boat had
left me, the waters, paved with ripples and engilt
with sunlight, looked utterly different to what they
did from the deck of the ship—because there I had
felt a prisoner, but now on the beach I felt a free
man once more.

Behind me, beyond the road which ran into the
hospital grounds, was a copse, full of golden sunshine and sweet spring life. Wild violet and prim-
rose springing from greenest, tenderest moss, lifted
purple and yellow faces to the searcher for them, as

though they would say, " See how God hath set us ; mind you re-set us thus, when you have plucked us, and borne us hence."

> " And at my feet
>   In this retreat
> White daisies' pouting purple buds !
>   Ye, too, sing Benedicite ! "

Thus has that gracious poet, Charles A. Fox, sung ; and these same daisies dotted the copse, like milled-edged silver coins flung abroad in prodigal largess by the hand of Heaven's Philanthropist. The daisy, lovely in its sweet simplicity,

> " From thy little snowy frill
>   Taking heaps of coinèd gold,
> With a hearty right good will,
>   In thine innocency bold,
> Thou dost offer back to God,
> All unasked, thy precious load ;—
> Opening wide in heaven's blue face,
> Fingers dews had clasped in grace."

Oh, how wondrous it all seemed to me that morning ! The four hours and a half between the time of my landing and the time for my dinner passed like a dream, and work never went easier with me ; for I have no hesitation in saying that I did an ordinary day's work in this *half* of the day.

I had brought my dinner ashore, wrapped in a clean towel, and sat in the boat and ate it. Seven or eight minutes sufficed for this, then I felt I must have a run in that copse. I spent a quarter of an hour there, my soul growing dumb before the power of all the beauty, my heart going out after the Unknown, the Unseen, as a man, stricken with blindness, gropes with his clutching fingers.

With a strange, unusual sense of hush upon me, I returned to the half-repaired boat, climbed into the stern sheets, and began to think.

Words often heard unheeded in the prison services came over my soul with a new power, and freighted with questioning, as I murmured them : " We bless Thee for our *creation, preservation*, and all the blessings of this life ; but above all, for Thine inestimable love in the redemption of the world by our Lord Jesus Christ ; for the means of grace, and for the hope of glory."

" I have been thinking of *creation*," I mused, " as I walked through that copse, but I have thought nothing of God's *preservation* of me. Yet, if ever a man has been mercifully preserved through life, then I am that man."

I thought of my salvation from fire and flood ; from shot and shell ; from fever and small-pox ; from drowning at sea ; from falls from aloft ; from that ninety days' confinement in the hold of that sugar ship ; from starvation in the bush.

Preservation ! Why, all God's dealings with me had been one long catalogue of merciful preservations. But I had never really blessed God for them.

" But above all, for Thine inestimable love in the gift of our Lord and Saviour Jesus Christ ; for the means of grace, and for the hope of glory ! " As I repeated the words, some sense of the meaning of the " *above all* " of that wondrous sentence came to me ; and in view of all the heart-searching that had been my experience during past weeks, and with all the influence of dear Eddie Peck's words upon me, I began to bow in heart before God.

At two bells (one o'clock) I re-commenced work,

but conscience, the Spirit of God, remembered words of Truth, all these kept hammering away at my heart, harder than I hammered at the copper rivets in the planking of the boat I was repairing.

I remember once thinking that, just as that boat was shattered here and there, and I was repairing it, so was I shattered in soul, and that God would find some way to *repair* me. I had yet to learn that no repairing of a soul could avail to fit it for eternal life, but that it must be re-*created*, re-generated.

By the time I went on board the ship that night, the weight of the sense of sin had made me more wretched than ever I had been in my life before.

The days, as they passed, grew more weary, more miserable than ever to me. My friend Eddie did all he could to help me, but I do not think that I *fully* confided my state to him. The one thought which pressed continually upon me was, that my sins kept me from knowing and loving God. If only I could have realized the truth, that *God loved me*, and gave His Son to be the propitiation for my sins, how much of misery I might have been saved.

Every hour, every day, would I plan and work to improve my life, and make it fit for God to bless with His salvation, just as shipowners will sometimes seek to fit a rotten, condemned ship for sea again, only to ——. But let me insert my thought here, as I once wrote it for Drummond's Depôt, Stirling. The actual facts and scene belong to an experience in a small harbour on the South coast.

*   *   *   *   *

A Painted Wreck.

The setting sun flashed his rosy, golden rays upon the waters of the narrow harbour, making everything momentarily beautiful. Slowly, laboriously, the little steam tug towed a miserable-looking, barque-rigged vessel up the sunlit waters. The towed vessel looked an absolute wreck.

A knot of fishermen, sailors, and others, watched the tug and her tow, passing many laughing comments on her wrecked appearance. "Where's they goin' to tow her, I wonders?" said one of the men.

"Over to Campbell's shipyard," replied a by-stander.

"Best place for an old tub like that," remarked a third watcher; "going to be broke up, o' course!"

Amid the general chorus of "O' course" that greeted this last remark, the old man, who had first spoken, and who had been carefully watching the passing vessel, suddenly exclaimed, "Well, that's werry strange, that is! But that 'ere old tub is the *Georgia* of London, as I wur in fur about ten year. She wur condemned altogether arter I left her. Well! only to think she should ha' reached here to be broke up."

Reminiscences of former days on shipboard now became the order of the hour, and while the old *Georgia* was being got into position up the creek that ranged down one side of Campbell's yard, the men talked, and the sun set.

Weeks and months passed, and the sailor who had recognised his old ship found his way one Sunday afternoon to the shipyard, curious to see what was being done with the old boat. To his amazement he found her newly painted! Her spars and masts were bright with scraping and with varnish. Her figurehead was gilded, and altogether she looked quite smart.

Meeting the yard-watchman, he inquired what all this meant.

"Oh! she's been done up, patched an' painted, an' all that," replied the yardsman, "an' a crew is a-comin' round in about a fortnight's time to man her and take her to H——, where she'll be loaded, an' make a new start."

"But, man," cried the old sailor, "she's rotten from stem to stern, an' was condemned by the authorities long ago!"

A long argument ensued over the matter, then, at last, muttering that the repaired ship would never live in half a gale of wind, if even she would stand loading, the old sailor walked sadly homewards.

"What a shame!" he said, "to deceive poor men to their death like the owner o' that painted wreck's a-doing, by shipping a crew for her."

A fortnight later the *Georgia*, under a new name, sailed away gay with flying flags and bright with paint and varnish. In due course she was loaded at H——, and left that port for a voyage. But she never returned. She was lost the third day out, one of her boats being found floating bottom up in the Channel. Awful fate for those poor sailors who trusted themselves to paint and polish!

More awful will be the fate of those souls— there are thousands and thousands of them—who, instead of being in the strong, unsinkable ship of God's salvation in Jesus, trust themselves to the paint,

the varnish, the polish of profession, of morality, of
outward form.

*   *   *   *   *

Oh, the polishing and repairing I sought to do
during the days of my seeking after God! And
there are myriads of people to-day trying to *manu-
facture* a salvation for themselves, in the same way.

In my evangelistic work, over a space of many
years, I have met thousands of such people ; they are
always the most difficult souls to deal with personally.

Men and women must wake up to the fact that, by
nature, we are condemned utterly. That we are like
that ship, rotten and ruined from stem to stern, or, as
God's word puts it, "from the crown of the head to
the sole of the foot, there is no soundness," there is
no health in us. *Nothing can save but regeneration ;*
the new Birth in Christ Jesus is the only way of
life from natural death.

How strange it is that awakened souls forget all
the teaching they may ever have received on the
subject of salvation ; and forgetting to look away from
self, and their own futile efforts, shut their eyes to
Christ's finished work, and go about seeking to
establish a righteousness of their own.

It was so with myself at this time. The language
of my prayers, and of my heart, was, "Give me, O
God, the blessing I crave ; *for*, see, Lord, I have turned
over a new leaf. I do not swear now, I do not lie,
but I read my Bible, I pray, I weep ; what more
canst Thou expect? then give me peace ! "

Still I blundered on dejectedly. I could neither
eat nor sleep, and there came a moment when I cried,

"It's no use, I can't do anything more; I have done all I can think of."

In an old poem, dated 1300, there occurs this couplet :—

> "God is a tower without a stair,
> And His perfection loves despair."

How true this is! How often have souls proved this principle of God's ; for it is only when we come to an utter end of *ourselves* that God can undertake for us. Then we realize what Charles Fox has so beautifully written :—

> "And how oft, after anxious provisions of man,
> Flashes in with a silence God's unforeseen plan ! "

God's unforeseen plan was being prepared to be flashed upon the gloom of my sin-weary state.

Chapter XXXIV

THE NEW SAILMAKER

IT was the day after I had come to such an utter
end of myself, when I had practically decided
that there was no spiritual hope for me. It was the
ninth day of my real soul distress, and about half-
past two in the afternoon. I was perched on a high
office stool, at the desk in the upper midship corner
of my store-room, when a voice startled me, saying :
" Give us a light, chum ! "

Even as I raised my eyes to meet the face of the
applicant, there flashed through my mind the thought,
" A light ! Ah, that's just what I want ; for it is all
dark with me."

Between my store-room and the sail-room there
ran, fore and aft, a low bulk-heading, with a fence-
work of perpendicular bars of iron, running the rest
of the way up to the low deck-roof.

The face that looked at me through these bars was
that of a stranger. He was a middle-aged man, in
the blue serge uniform of the Navy, and wearing
three stripes and the badge of a petty officer upon
the arm of his serge frock. His hand was outstretched, holding an unlighted candle, and he repeated his request, " Give us a light, chum ! "

As I passed the lighted candle back to him, he
said : " I s'pose we'll be near chummies, as our store-

rooms are so close. I am the new sailmaker. And you——?"

"I'm the carpenter's yeoman!" I replied.

"What's your tally, chum?" he asked.

"Syd Watson," I replied; "and yours—eh?"

"John Martin!" he answered, and as he spoke he held his lighted candle high up above his head, that he might better search my face with his eyes.

"But, I say," he continued, "you don't look very happy!"

"Don't I?" I said. "Well, to tell you the truth, I am not happy, but just about as miserable as I can well be!"

"Not happy?" said the good fellow. "Well, then, I can tell you what is the matter,—you don't love Jesus; because a man who loves Jesus, knows his sins forgiven, feels how much he owes his Lord, and lives in God's smile, can't help being happy."

With a burst of ready confidence, I cried: "Ah! that's just what I *do* want to know, my sins pardoned! I've been that miserable this last nine days that I've scarce known how to live."

I had no chance to say more, for my new neighbour began to dance about his store-room, as well as the space between the stowed sails and the low deck would let him, crying as he did so, like a veritable Billy Bray, "The Good Lord bless the fellow! Come on round here at once. I've got my bag to unpack, and the first lieutenant and boatswain to see, but your soul is of the most consequence; why—why—why you might die to-night, and then what would become of you? God help the fellow; come round to me at once!"

It took but a moment or two for me to pass on to

the lower deck and over into the sail-room. We clasped hands, and there, in that position, with hands still clasped, the old sailmaker bent his head and prayed: "O Lord, help us both. Help this dear fellow to see the truth as it is in Jesus! Give me wisdom to deal with him, and give us both the Holy Spirit to reveal Jesus; we ask it for the Redeemer's sake. Amen."

In a few moments, in his rough-and-ready fashion, John Martin was probing my soul. "Yes, that's all right as far as it goes! You say you want salvation, and you've done all you can think of to get it. What have you done? Just tell me, then I shall better know how to deal with you."

Then came my almost tearful recital, of prayers, Bible reading, tears, and the giving up swearing, etc.

I was interrupted by a glance of deepest pity from John, who said, "Well! well! Is it possible you can so far have misunderstood God, our loving Father-God, as to think He would condescend to trade with you, for something that cost Him the Blood, the precious Blood of Jesus? You go to Him, and say, 'Look here, Lord, if I don't have salvation before I die, I can't get into Heaven; it's risky to put it off, and if you are willing to give it to me, I don't mind leaving off swearing; I'll read my Bible, I'll say my prayers, and stand a bit of chaff from my shipmates; only please sell me this salvation for these things I offer.'"

My eyes were wide open with astonishment; I gazed at the sailmaker, bewildered to hear my last nine days' efforts summed up thus. And yet the Spirit convinced me how true was the summary.

The old man laid his hand upon my shoulder and looked me straight in the face, as, in a grave, pitying tone—his own eyes full of tears the while—he said, " Jesus Himself bare our sins, and as many as receive *Him* receive salvation. This is, indeed, peace, to know and believe that your iniquity is pardoned, your sin is covered, that Jesus suffered in your stead, that God looked down upon Christ's sacrifice for your sins, and said, ' I am satisfied.' So Jesus, as He hung upon the cross, suffered and bore in agony and shame all that Justice laid upon Him, feeling the whole weight of the world's sin pressed upon Him—all—all—all— sin ; not the least of it being yours, Sydney Watson."

I could contain myself no longer ; for all the while he had been preaching Jesus to me, the Spirit of God had been bearing in upon my soul memory upon memory of long-forgotten truths. Truths which my dead friend the doctor had uttered in my hearing, stood suddenly before my quickened spiritual sense, clothed in living power.

Like a strain of wondrous music from the land whither the doctor had gone, his voice came back to me, breathing words that had often been upon his lips :—

> " Jesus, Thy Blood and righteousness
> My beauty are, my glorious dress,
> 'Mid flaming worlds in these arrayed,
> With joy I shall lift up my head."

" That's it, that's it ! " I cried ; " I believe it, I believe it ! It is Jesus who has done all the work, and upon Him my sins have been laid ! "

We looked into each other's eyes, we clasped hands and there was silence for a few moments.

"Shall we praise, chummie?" asked good old John presently.

Together we knelt, and all my soul broke out in sobbing speech, as I cried :—

> "Just as I am, without one plea,
> But that Thy blood was shed for me,
> And that Thou bidst me come to Thee,
> O Lamb of God, I come!

> "Just as I am, thou wilt receive,
> Wilt welcome, pardon, cleanse, relieve!
> Because Thy promise I believe,
> O Lamb of God, I come!"

In that hour God gave me Eternal life, and never for one moment since have I ever doubted my acceptance with God. I have had, during the twenty-two and a half years of my Christian life, "fightings without and fears within," sorrows and difficulties, bereavements and disappointments; I have had years of sickness and prostration, but have never for one moment doubted God, *as to my salvation.*

The Spirit has ever borne witness with my spirit, that I was an accepted child of God, for the Witness of the Spirit *is to the Word*, and the Word has not changed, for "the Word of the Lord endureth for ever." And the Word is Christ, and "Jesus Christ is the same yesterday, to-day, and for ever."

I know some dear children of God have made the mistake of supposing that *the Witness of the Spirit* is a certain joyous feeling within them, but this is surely an error. If that were so, then when I have been unconscious of all feeling, when heart and brain and all my poor prostrate frame have been incapable of any feeling, other than that of the overwhelming physical suffering which held me low, then I should have ceased to be a child of God, because I had no witness of the Spirit—*if* the Witness of the Spirit was really only a joyous sense within.

No, no, no! Thank God, the Witness of the Spirit is no fleeting thing of this kind. A witness in a court of law testifies *of a person*, and not of a state of feeling. And, as Dr. Pentecost (I think it is) has said, "Suppose a person is called up in a court of law to give witness in a case, and he began to cry out rapturously, 'Oh, how happy, how joyous *I feel!* I'm sure this case is all right, because *I feel* so happy this morning!' The judge would say, 'Please remember you are here as a *witness*, and the court wants to know what you have to say about *the person* whom you have come to speak for.'"

And it is thus, God's Word teaches us, that the Spirit witnesses that we are born of God. *He witnesses of Jesus;* witnesses to the Saviour's death and resurrection for us; witnesses that God is satisfied with Christ's atonement; witnesses that with Him (Jesus) God hath also freely given us all things; witnesses that we are not only born of God but that we are kept by the power of God, and this witness is always in the Word of God. And the knowledge that comes to the heart of the believer, *in believing*, that God cannot lie, that Christ cannot change, that the Word endureth for ever,—this knowledge of the perfectness of all God's provision for him, fills the believer with joy. But the joy is not the witness, the joy is the *effect* of believing God's Witness—the Spirit.

When I left dear old John Martin's sail-room, that he might change his clothes and report himself to the boatswain, I left with the witness of the Spirit that

I was born of God. As I write all this, nearly twenty-three years afterwards, I pause, open God's Word at the fifth chapter of John's first Epistle, and reading from the sixth to the thirteenth verse, I rejoice that the Witness of the Spirit is still mine—by grace.

Oh, how my dear friend, Eddie Peck, rejoiced when I bore the good news to him !

That night I told the sailmaker all the story of my eventful life, and how I could now see how the hand of God had been striving to lead me all those years. "Yes," I said, in conclusion, "just as that detective tracked me and ' run me down ' at last, so has God's Spirit run me down spiritually. Justice has ' run me *down*,' but Mercy has ' run me *in* '—into the fold of Christ! on to the deck of the Gospel ship ! into the city of Refuge ! into the army of Christ ! Yes, I have known *about* these things for years ; but now I know *Him*, whom to know is life eternal."

Chapter XXXV

SCHOOL OF THE PROPHETS

FROM that first day of my conversion, there began a daily, spiritual fellowship between John Martin, Eddie Peck, and myself. Once a day, usually in the evening, we met together to praise for God's great gift of life to us, and to pray for blessing upon our shipmates.

Just how we came to know of the presence in the ship of another Christian sailor I cannot remember, but certainly, from the first, Tom Yeadle was associated with us.

What a solid, burly fellow he was! How true, how real! I heard nothing of him for many years, and often wondered whether he was living or dead, when, about six years ago, in the strangest manner possible, I heard of him again.

Mr. and Mrs. John St. Barbe Baker, of West End, near Southampton, two of the most devoted, self-denying servants of God I ever met, happened to say one to the other in their home, " I wonder where this friend, Sydney Watson, lives? It would be nice to write to him, if we could get his address, and tell him how God has blessed his books to souls in this neighbourhood."

One of their serving maids overheard the remark, and replied, " There is a Mr. Sydney Watson who lives in Basingstoke, who often preaches in the chapel where my father and mother attend, at Worthing."

With this clue, Mr. and Mrs. Baker wrote me a letter,—like themselves—full of kindness, spirituality, devotion to God. In this way a very blessed, hallowed friendship began between us, first by correspondence, later by personal meeting, when, at their invitation, I went to stay with them, sharing with them the privilege of ministry in their beautiful hall at West End.

In one of their letters to me they said, " We have, close to us here, a Convalescent Home, in which we are much interested, built by a lady in Bournemouth. Rarely a day passes without one of us calling at the Home, and we thus get very interested in the various people who stay there from time to time.

" Among those staying there at present is a very devoted Christian man, who has for years been in the London City Mission, but who is now utterly broken down in health, too ill even to read, though he enjoys being read to.

" Miss S—— (the lady superintendent) has been reading to him the story, ' Wops, the Waif.' The dear man grew more and more interested and excited as the series went on, until, during the reading of the latter half of the third chapter of the fifth book, he cried, ' Why, that's all just as it happened! It was in H.M.S. Z——. I was there, and knew all those men, and those books you are reading to me were written by —— ? '

" ' By Sydney Watson,' replied Miss S——."

This dear fellow, the broken-down City Missionary was my old shipmate, Tom Yeadle.

In those old days on board H.M.S. Z——, when I was first converted, Tom made up the quartette that gathered night after night for praise and prayer.

Very soon we had interested one or two more seamen to join us, men for whose conversion we never ceased to pray. Then, as the days went on, and our little nightly gathering grew more and more precious, we divided the hour we spent, making the study of the Bible a part of the exercises, for we each felt we needed the feeding in the green pastures.

We were hunted about so constantly, from one meeting-place to another, that we eventually summoned up courage enough to make an official application for a spot where we *might* meet, " none daring to make us afraid."

We were granted the use of one of the bath-rooms! What precious times we spent there; how sweet their memory still! One of these evenings stands out vividly before me to this day. Let me recall it here.

An iron room, about twelve feet by nine. Along three sides are massive metal baths, surmounted by huge pipes, and glittering brass taps. The deck is covered with wooden gratings, soddened with water. There is a general impression of cold and damp pervading the place, but it does not seem to affect the ardour of the half-dozen sailors who are gathered there. They are in all sorts of odd positions; some seated on their low " ditty " boxes placed on the damp deck gratings; some perched upon the edges of the long baths; some standing leaning against the side of the bulk-heading. Nearly all have Bibles in their hands, and there is a look of eager interestedness upon their faces.

The subject of the Bible-reading is, " Heart re-

ligion " ; the passages chosen, Deuteronomy, chapters
v. and vi. " Listen to these words again, chums,"
says the old sailmaker : " ' I have heard the voice of
the words of this people, which they have spoken
. . . they have well said all that they have spoken.
O that there was such an heart in them, that they
would fear Me, and keep My commandments always.'
Ah ! it makes all the difference whether a man has a
head or a heart religion. Head religion is like moonlight ! That is, pretty cold, and romantic like, good
for courting couples and pictures, for poets and book-
writing fellows, when they want to make a pretty
scene, but it has no notion of melting ice, or warming
the earth. It's just like that with head religion, there
is no warmth, no life in it. There ain't ne'er a one of
us here as would be so green as to hold out our hands
to the moon to warm them ; *but there are folks green
enough to try and heal broken hearts, and warm their
cold souls with head religion.* Then, when they find it
is a failure, they blame God and the Bible. They say
there's nothing in any religion ; it's all a farce, and
they will have nothing to do with it. Bah ! they're
moon-blind, or they would see the truth as God tries
to teach it all through the Bible, that ' it is with the
heart man believeth unto righteousness.' "

Here the good man tucked his book under his arm,
rubbed his hands together with an almost boyish
glee, as he continued, " Hallelujah for the sunshine—
God's sunshine—the joy of the Lord ! Why, look
here, the other night, when that little chap was singing
his ditty on the upper deck—

' I love the merry sunshine ' - -

you remember how everybody clapped him, and

encored. I could not help wishing that a few of them would learn to love God's heart sunshine. Thank God, He has made it so easy to have heart religion! Every one has the power to trust, to believe."

A few more words from John Martin, and on they read, "And thou shalt bind them for a sign upon thine hand."

"What does that mean?" asked a young sailor. "How can we carry religion on our hands?"

"Well, the idea comes to me like this," interposed one of the others. "If a gent has a regular tip-top ring, a diamond, or something like that, he's not only not ashamed of it, but he takes care that every one shall see it. You see, he'll stick out his finger when he lifts up his glass of wine to his lips; and if he's twisting his moustache, somehow you don't see the twist of the hair, but you do the twirl of that diamond. And it strikes me, that God means to say to us, if our religion is worth anything, people will see it as readily as though it was a diamond ring bound upon our finger."

Then, with a smile at the young sailor who had made the inquiry, the expounder continued, "Don't you remember when you and me were shipmates in the C——, and we went ashore together that time in Madras, how we saw the different sects of Hindoos with their caste-marks in their foreheads, and how proud they were of them, and how plain to be seen by every one?"

"Right yer are, I remember! But what's that got to do with the religion on the hand?" said the young seaman.

"Nothing with the hand," replied the other. "But

that same verse has something about the foreheads too;" and, lifting his Bible, the seaman expositor read, by the light of the lantern which swung from the ceiling, "'And they shall be as frontlets between thine eyes.' That is plainer still, chums; a man might lose his hands, or hide them in his pockets; but with God stamped upon his brow, I guess every one will know he is 'born again.'"

It will be seen by this brief, but faithful, description of that one out of many of our little Bible readings, that, though we knew nothing of the Jewish *phylac-teries* to which Moses doubtless referred in that passage in Deuteronomy, God yet allowed us to grasp *one* of the principles of the teaching contained in the text.

Some people would have considered that our theology in those days was not a very great quantity, but *if we knew little of theology, we lived a great deal of doxology* ; we felt that we were loved by God " with a love

> Of depth so great—of height so far above
> All human ken,"

that we could do no other than love back, and give constant praise for the wonder of His grace, who had made us new creations in Christ Jesus.

The damp discomforts of our meeting-place could never damp our desire or ardour for God, for we grew in love and knowledge, as we spake often one to another, " and a book of remembrance was written before *Him*, for them that feared the Lord, and *that thought* upon His name."

Before leaving the matter of these nightly gatherings, I ought surely to mention a fact which had slipped my memory (how much of interest of these days has become fugitive for want of notes), but of which I was reminded, a few days since, by Rev. E. J. Peck.

Among our bitterest enemies, and one who had an almost unlimited power to hunt us about like partridges (until we officially secured the use of the bath-room before mentioned), was a ship's corporal, named P——. The ship's corporals' mess was cleaned and cared for by a smart, but devil-may-care lad, who held the rating in the ship of First-Class boy.

This lad came down to one of our meetings (they were held in the carpenter's store-room then, of which place I was yeoman). From the very first visit the lad was impressed. He came many times, and whether truly converted or not, certainly his whole life was transformed.

We, Eddie Peck and I, were coming up from the store-room one night, when our old enemy, Corporal P——, signed us to go to him. As we ranged up close to his table he said,—

"What, in the name of fortune, do you do down there with the fellows? They go down devils, and they come up saints."

I give the words literally, as I took them down from my friend Peck's lips, and as I distinctly remembered them myself when reminded of them. They speak for themselves, and prove that God was manifested in the midst of those humble, but happy gatherings.

*   *   *   *   *

A Sailors' College.

From the first, Eddie Peck and I became "inseparables." The fact that we were in the same mess, that we had talked over Divine things together before we knew the others, as well as from a certain natural affinity towards each other, doubtless helped to make us the closest of friends.

One result of our friendship was, that we decided to try to improve ourselves (educationally), and to this end we spent much time alone together in our two-horse mutual improvement society.

Most mornings, soon after four, during that first summer, we were up and dressed and at our studies. The first half-hour or three-quarters we spent alone with God, in prayer and Bible-reading. After that we read and wrote, and wrote and read, simply to improve our minds, knowing no other way to educate ourselves.

Three *apparently* trifling incidents occurred about this time, which were destined to affect my own mind considerably, so that the effects live in my life to this day.

A few weeks after my conversion, I had pleaded hard to be allowed leave, to go to London to see my dear mother.

Five days' leave were granted me, and, light as a bird, I went to Hampstead to my mother, and told her all the story of my conversion to God. She herself had been brought to the Saviour about three years before.

The day after my arrival in London, I went to see a gentleman, W. Cheshire, of Sutton, in Surrey, and Holborn Viaduct, London, an art engraver, who had

been interested in me for years, and always desired
me to visit him whenever I could.

I called at his office, and finding him alone (his
partner being away), I told him all the story of God's
grace to me. His delight was unbounded, for he had
prayed for me for years. "You must come down to
Sutton with me, spend the night with my boys, and
tell my dear wife all your gracious story," he said.

I *had* been to his home before, and had learned to
love the life I saw there, as many an one, out of Christ,
learns to yearn for and love the life he sees in a truly
Christian home, long, long before he shares in its
source.

That night, at family prayer, Mr. Cheshire read No.
227 in Wesley's Hymn Book, beginning—

> "How do Thy mercies close me round !
> For ever be Thy Name adored !
> I blush in all things to abound ;
> The servant is above his Lord !"

They sang the hymn, his daughter accompanying on
the organ. Reading of scriptures and prayer followed, then the younger folk trooped off to bed.

I remained for further chat, my mind full of the
hymn which my friend had read; but though I was
scarcely conscious of it *then*, I know now that that
which had rivetted my mind so was the manner of
the reading, and not so much the beautiful hymn
itself.

When we were alone together (the dear mother had
gone to see her pets safely nested), I remarked on the
effect the hymn had had upon me, and Mr. Cheshire
opened the book again, and went over its many
beauties, pointing them out, and reciting them, as, I

often think, no other man whom I ever met could do.

Evidently he saw that I could be interested in poetry, for, after touching upon one or two more of Wesley's choicest hymns, he got George Herbert's poems, and opening on *Sunday*, read the verses as a whole, then went back over the lines, to show me where the gems of thought and pretty and fanciful conceits were hidden.

That night my soul awoke to the wonders that lay wrapped in poetry ; and when my friend showed me that the Bible was steeped in poetry, he unlocked doors, and flung wide portals, that were destined to be, to my untaught soul, as some wondrous Eastern palace of wealth and delights. My wonder to-day is greater than it was then.

This is not the only blessing I owe to this friend, for he, consciously or unconsciously, taught me many things during the many visits I made to his offices and his home during the years of my man-of-war life.

Certain little daily habits of care of unconsidered trifles,—untying, instead of cutting the string of a parcel ; smoothing out the paper ; skeining the string ; and a hundred other useful time- and trouble-saving items—I learnt of him.

Friends, who have noticed these habits of mine, have said, "Any one could tell you were an old sailor," and have specified their reason for making the remark ; but I always reply to this, "No; the Navy taught me method and discipline, but my friend William Cheshire taught me habits of care and tidiness."

(Perhaps my *wife* would deny my right to the latter qualification.)

But to return to the matter I had in my mind. My friend Mr. Cheshire gave me my first impulse to *sacred* poetry, and taught me how to see poetry in my Bible.

LONGFELLOW.

During that same visit to London, I went with my mother to see a lady friend of hers, a lawyer's wife, who had expressed a wish to see " the sailor son." I enjoyed the two hours there exceedingly, and came away the proud possessor of an exquisite copy of " Longfellow's Poems."

Mrs. —— was a very beautiful woman, very cultured, and read me parts of *Evangeline,* by way of a taste of delights to follow ; and for the next month I fairly revelled in the pages of that book.

I had it with me when I went on shore at Netley for an afternoon's leave, soon after my return from London, and sauntering slowly along to Southampton, I read *Hiawatha* for the first time. I should doubtless have found a seat in the town later on in the afternoon, to have further read the book, but that I was destined to find a treasure that was to prove the last of the three strong influences in my efforts at self-education.

I had wandered up Southampton High Street until I found myself above Bar, and was arrested in my walk by the sight of the second-hand books outside Gilbert's " Ye Olde Boke Shop." Here, among a lot of books, I found one marked 4*d.* It was a " Butter's Spelling Book."

I opened it, wondered what it all meant ; then, as

my eye lit upon the word, "manufactory," and I slowly grasped the meaning of the italicised words, and that our English word was made up of these two Latin words, meaning "a hand" and "work," I fairly gasped.

"What a key to the understanding of words!" I mused, as, turning over a leaf or two, I came upon "Porto—I carry," saw that a "porter" who carried goods, and a "porch" that carried off rain and sun, etc., with other words of a similar derivation, were all members of one family.   My wonder grew.

No human tongue could describe what a marvellous realm that discovery opened up to me, or how it quickened my thought on many things. To the average man or woman, who has had years of grounding in school and college, my discovery may seem but a trifling thing, but to some who read, there will come, I believe, some appreciation of what that "Butter's Spelling Book" did for me.

I ought to say here, before closing this chapter, that my conversion meant not only a *spiritual*, but a *mental* awakening.

Only the other day, since I began to write this record, I came across these words, in the "Life of Henry Martyn."   He says :—

"Since I have known God in a saving manner, painting, poetry, and music have had charms unknown to me before—I have received what I suppose is a taste for them ; for religion has refined my mind, and made it susceptible of impressions from the sublime and beautiful. O how religion secures the heightened enjoyment of those pleasures which keep so many from God, by their becoming a source of pride."

This statement of Henry Martyn exactly expresses my own condition ; for, all I am, or ever shall be, all the delight I have in the fine arts—a study of which are a second life to me—springs from my knowledge of God, in Christ Jesus.

With my newly-gotten treasures, the " Butter's Spelling Book," the " Longfellow," and my quickened sense of the beautiful in poetry, there came into my life many new progressive elements ; and both Eddie Peck and myself set ourselves to work harder than ever. Not that either of us, in those days, had any definite object in this work of education, other than that of self-improvement, and the desire to be sufficiently intelligent not to disgrace our profession of Christianity.

Chapter XXXVI

RED TAPE

OUR new delight in books, and our ever-increasing desire to help our shipmates, led us to think out what we could do for those around us, in the matter of literature.

The story of our effort to help our fellows would find no place here, but for the lesson we learned, how God over-rules for good, for His children, even when the stoutest, longest, government red tape is brought to fetter their spiritual impulses.

After much thought and prayer as to *what* we should do, we decided to send a few pounds to London, to my friend Mr. Cheshire, and ask him to lay the money out in suitable books for lending to our shipmates in the various messes.

There *was* a ship's library, of course, on board our vessel, but it was a very small affair, and *very dry*, and *very stale*, so that no one ever thought of asking for a book. (Things in the Navy, in this respect, have somewhat improved, *I hear*, but in those days a ship's library was an Ezekiel's valley, "*full of dry bones.*")

On receipt of our letter and postal order (I cannot be sure whether it was three or five pounds we sent), Mr. Cheshire was so delighted with our notion, that he started off to see Samuel Partridge, of the well-known Paternoster Row firm.

Showing that good man the letter, and saying, " If two man-of-war's men can do this much, out of love to Christ, for their shipmates, I feel that some of us, who are Christians, and in the book trade, ought to help them a little. What will you do, Mr. Partridge?"

" Do?" said that gentleman ; "I'll do this—for every pound's worth of books you can get in the Row, *gratis*, I'll add a pound's worth, *at the same rate*."

Mr. Cheshire called upon other publishers, and two others specially helped him, Messrs. Shaw, of 48, and Mr. Haughton, author of " Heaven, and How to Get There," and other kindred books.

The price of books twenty-three years ago, and the price to-day, was a very different thing. I think we had supposed that a parcel, in size about two feet by one, would have been about the kind of thing we should receive ; our surprise, when the parcel actually came, was beyond all expression.

The vessel was lying at Cowes at the time, and I was summoned on the quarter-deck one afternoon, and asked what that huge case contained which was alongside, and addressed to me ; and who gave me permission to order goods to be forwarded, to that amount, to be sent to me, since I was not entitled, by rank, to have any box, other than my tool chest, on board ?

I was obliged to reply that, as yet, I had not seen the parcel, but that my chum and I certainly had *sent* for a few pounds' worth of books, to distribute, on loan, to our shipmates in their messes.

I was bullied fearfully by the officer, was told that the government found all stores needed for her men, and that I could order the case to be sent ashore again, as it certainly should not come on board.

Dismissed from the presence of the irate officer, I went to the gangway to see the parcel. It was in Pickford's barge, and measured quite *three feet each way*—a stout, wooden case, iron-banded.

I went down the side to the lighter, explained my difficulty briefly to the man in charge, gave him a tip for his own trouble, and asked him to request his manager to let the case stay in his warehouse until I could get ashore, which would probably be the next day.

After a consultation with Eddie Peck and our other friends, it was decided that I should go ashore that night and see, if possible, Pickford's manager, and come to some arrangement with him as to temporary storage, until we could arrange some way of receiving the books on board.

I saw that manager (he became, in after years, one of my closest spiritual friends), and I found him the best and kindest of men. He was in fullest sympathy with us in our difficulty, as well he might be, for he was secretary of the largest Sunday School in the town (the Wesleyan), and one of the happiest-hearted, most loving of Christians the world ever knew.

Good, kind, brave old Robert Dycer! You have been with the Lord for many years now, but my heart warms as I remember you, and I put your kindness to two young sailors on record here, in honour of your memory!

The commanding officer who had refused to permit the case of books to come on board was taken seriously ill, with gout and other complications, while ashore some days later ; and seizing the opportunity of his absence, I applied, formally, to the next in command, to have the case on board, and received a ready permission.

They had to put a stout whip on the mainyard to hoist the box (any nautical reader will understand this), and, after some considerable excitement, the thing was housed in my store-room, though it only just passed through the square of the hatch.

The unpacking and sorting of that box was a wondrous time, for the contents were altogether beyond our conception of book wealth; and when, two days later, on the Sunday afternoon, immediately after dinner, Eddie Peck and I carried a number of the books, on loan, to each mess, our shipmates were as delighted as they were amazed.

Only one thing was wanted to complete the joy of that first distribution of *loan* literature, namely, the presence of Messrs. Cheshire, Partridge, Shaw, Haughton & Co., that they might have seen how the sailors appreciated their kindness and generosity.

That case of books proved an untold blessing to our ship's messes!

Cheered by the success of this effort to bless our shipmates, yet longing that some more direct spiritual effort might be brought to bear upon them, as a whole, we conceived the idea of getting some godly minister to come on board and give them a real *Gospel* address. Though *how* this was to be managed, we did not know.

I heard a great deal about the work and loving spiritual zeal of Canon Barker, Vicar of St. Mary's, West Cowes, so I determined to go ashore and see him, tell him our desires, and ask his advice.

I went. Was there ever a more genial, loving-hearted man for a sailor to deal with? He boasts, rightly, of his love for sailors; declares how, by his marriage with the daughter of Sir John Ross, the great Arctic explorer, he is allied to sailors and the sea. For real sailor-like hearty kindness he might almost claim the actual description I once heard given of a Bethel parson : " He's a sailor, every inch of him," said the seaman who spoke; " every muscle of his body is spun yarn, every drop of blood in his body is pure Stockholm."

Canon Barker received me loyally, put me at my ease, listened to my story, asked me how I was converted, and was evidently very interested in the whole story.

But he explained that he could no more come on board the ship and speak to the sailors without a special invitation, and special permission from the proper ecclesiastical authority, than he could go into the parish of the next vicar and usurp his place. " But," said he, " I can tell you how you may influence your shipmates for good. In about a fortnight's time I am going to have the first anniversary meeting of the Church Temperance Society in the Foresters' Hall in this town. My friends, Canon Wilberforce, of Southampton, and Canon Connor, of Newport, are to be present with us, with other friends, to speak. Now if you will let me put your name on the bill, as a life-abstaining man-of-war's man, who will be present *in uniform* to speak, you'll draw numbers of your shipmates to hear you, who may be influenced by something in the meeting."

Astonished beyond measure at the Canon's startling proposition, I replied : " Me speak, sir ? I don't know how ! "

" Oh, yes, you do," he replied. " Stand up, and tell

the people what you have told me to-day, why you
are a teetotaler, and how you were converted to God,
and there will be no more useful speech in the evening."

I went to that meeting; what a wonderful time it
was! Up to that time I had not heard half a dozen
speeches in my whole life, and certainly none that
could be named in the same breath as Canon Barker's and Canon Wilberforce's utterances.

It was at that memorable meeting that Canon
Connor, Vicar of Newport, being called upon to
speak, rose, and with voice trembling with evident
deep emotion, said,—

"I have been asked to speak on this great question,
but I am not a *total* abstainer; how, then, can I do what
I am asked? But I am convinced that I ought to become an abstainer, so if Canon Barker will give me a
pledge-card and pen, I will sign at once, and will
then tell you what, God helping me, I will do in the
cause in my own parish during the coming year."

This brought the house down; and when, amid the
wildest excitement, the dear old man had signed the
pledge, with his speech inspired, his face ablaze with
holy enthusiasm, he poured forth a torrent of burning
words of determination to strain every nerve to make
his parish sober.

Did I speak at the meeting, after all? you ask.
Yes; in the simple, natural style of a Jack Tar telling
a yarn, I told my story.

"Where ignorance is bliss, it's folly to be wise," is
sometimes said. Certainly that saying was true of
my presence on the first public platform on which I
ever appeared; for though my little speech was sand-
wiched between those of two of the most gifted

orators of that day, I was so ignorant of public speaking, that *I did not know that I ought to be nervous* among such big guns. Blessed ignorance! How much suffering I should have been saved in later years if I could have preserved it!

There was a strange and far-reaching sequel to that meeting, and to my first attempt at public speaking.

A gentleman was present who had recently returned from a sitting of one of the Church Missionary Society's committees, where the need of a man as a missionary to the Eskimo had been discussed.

The wish had been expressed that a Christian *sailor* might be found, who, being strong and healthy, would, from the fact of his being accustomed to hardships and exposure in his sea life, be the more likely to stand the rigours of an Arctic life than a man more delicately brought up.

This gentleman (how I wish I could recall his name, or I had preserved the correspondence of that time) came off to the ship to see me, a day or two after the meeting; and explaining the needs of the C.M.S., said that he had already written to the Society, telling them that he had heard me give the story of my conversion at the meeting, and that he thought that I might be the very man for whom the Society was looking.

I was amazed at the suggestion. "I to be a missionary? an untutored, illiterate man-of-war's man!" The bare idea took away my breath.

My kindly visitor reminded me that God could, and did, make use of the things which are despised, and the things which are not, to bring to nought the things which are, and to accomplish His own purposes in His own way.

He showed me the Society's letter to himself, gave me one addressed to myself under cover of his, and after much loving, wise advice, he left me to pray over the matter; and, on my receiving light on the path, I was to write—*I think*—to the Rev. Romaine Govett, of Newmarket.

Of course I talked the whole case over with my dear chum, Eddie Peck, and we both prayed over the matter for days. But the oftener I went alone with God, to speak with Him, the more definitely I was assured, in my soul, that it was not God's mind for me to offer myself.

I told Eddie this, at last, and suggested that he should offer instead of me. He, dear fellow, was as amazed at my suggestion as I had been at that of the Society's friend who had visited me and proposed my going.

One of the most remarkable characteristics of my whilom sailor chum, ever since I first learned to know him, up till now, when his name stands for all that is heroic, self-denying, and noble, has been his *humility*.

Strong as steel, resourceful to the degree of genius, unswerving in all that is true and great, he is yet, as he ever was, humble as the humblest child. No wonder, then, that he shrank from the idea of my proposing him for the great career of a missionary.

However, he was willing that the matter should be referred to God, and that if HE showed the open door, he, my godly sailor chum, would go forward in the strength of the Divine might.

I wrote my letter to Romaine Govett, explained the reasons of my grateful refusal of the offer, and suggested the name of my chum as candidate for the training and the post.

God's aftermath, in this matter, had in it all the elements of a wondrous romance (and there is no romance in books to equal God's dealings with the lives of His special workers).

But I cannot tell that story here; it belongs, by right, to another book, to the book already mentioned in a footnote on an earlier page, which, God willing, I hope to write before the end of this year.

*   *   *   *   *

The year (I use the definite article because it was the year of my conversion, and that "year was the beginning of years" to *me*)—the year then, as I said, moved swiftly on, and in pursuing my plan of self-education, and in seeking to serve God among my shipmates, time passed very rapidly.

When the vessel lay in Southampton Water, I frequently went ashore for the afternoon; but when she lay at Cowes (except for the two occasions mentioned—once when I landed to see Pickford's agent, and once to see Canon Barker) I never troubled the shore.

But during the Christmas week, which followed my conversion in May, I was deputed to go ashore at Cowes, on mess business, all unconscious that that visit would indirectly bring about the greatest event in my life—next to my conversion.

But the fullest space of this volume has already been taken up. I have not been able to put in *one fourth* of the events and incidents which found place in my actual life *up* to this period. But I have done what I could, to the best of my power, in the selection of matter, using those portions which I have conceived most likely to interest and help my readers, be their sex, age, or class what it would.

In the case of many persons, whose unconverted lives may have been full of romance and incident, conversion has meant the beginning of a comparatively plain, colourless, uneventful career. Had this been so in my case, there could have been no reason for my writing a *second* volume. But the case with me was different, and I venture, humbly, to believe, that the romance of life and service of the next volume will appeal with greater force to the reader than this could possibly have done.

Truth *is* stranger than fiction !

Butler & Tanner, The Selwood Printing Works, Frome, and London.